White Knights Inc.

A Novel

Copyright © 2008 Robert L. Barrow JD, MD

Hardcover ISBN 978-1-60145-687-8
Paperback ISBN 978-1-60145-686-1

All rights reserved. No part of this publication may be reproduced, stored in a retrieval system, or transmitted in any form or by any means, electronic, mechanical, recording or otherwise, without the prior written permission of the author.

Printed in the United States of America.

The characters and events in this book are fictitious. Any similarity to real persons, living or dead, is coincidental and not intended by the author.

Booklocker.com, Inc.
2008

White Knights Inc.

A Novel

By

Robert L. Barrow JD, MD

*For Lisa Carver,
Thanks so much!
[signature]
6/11/09*

Dedication

I dedicate this to the wonderful Women in my Life.

My wife, my daughter and not least My Mom.

Table of Contents

Chapter One: An Evening in Almaty 1
Chapter Two: Midnight on the Firing Line 14
Chapter Three: A Typical Day at School 24
Chapter Four: A Meeting of Cosmic Insignificance 31
Chapter Five: The Best Laid Plans of Mice and Missiles 52
Chapter Six: Coffee, Eggs Benedict and Particle Beam Weapons 71
Chapter Seven: A Brief Stop at The Hardware Store 92
Chapter Eight: The Bowels of Texas 99
Chapter Nine: The View From Baikonur 109
Chapter Ten: Blasting Out Of Texas 116
Chapter Eleven: A Long Cold Ride In The Dark 124
Chapter Twelve: A Little Light Housekeeping 136
Chapter Thirteen: A Crazy Time To Be In Space 150
Chapter Fourteen: Like Ducks in a Shooting Gallery 168
Chapter Fifteen: There Is A Reason Why They Call It Space .. 181
Chapter Sixteen: We Have Twenty Cubic Miles of What? 189
Chapter Seventeen: Yes, It Is A Very Big Rock 199
Chapter Eighteen: It's a Blast Really 207
Chapter Nineteen: First Steps on a New World 218
Chapter Twenty: Old Gray Belial, Ain't What She Used To Be 226
Chapter Twenty-One: You Can't Just Toss Nuclear Weapons 233

Chapter Twenty-Two: Lost on Belial 243

Chapter Twenty-Three: Sometimes the Big Stuff Doesn't Matter 252

Chapter Twenty-Four: Usually it is the Little Things that Matter Most 259

Chapter Twenty-five: A Little Bit of Miscalculation Goes a Long Way 273

Chapter Twenty-six: Things That Go Around 282

Chapter Twenty-seven: The Great Eye Opens 292

Chapter Twenty-eight: A Few Light Housekeeping Details... 305

Chapter Twenty-nine: News From The Old Country 316

Chapter Thirty: Heavy Weather 325

Chapter Thirty-one: Any Port in a Storm 336

Chapter Thirty-two: On a Clear Day We can See Everything 346

Chapter Thirty-three: B Day 354

Chapter Thirty-four: Welcome to Belial 368

Epilogue 379

Chapter One
An Evening in Almaty

T - minus 00:00:18:00

Katerina took cover in the ugly brick doorway when she heard the first shots ring out like firecrackers. The scant cover provided by the facade of the tenement was preferable to being on the open sidewalk three steps away. A few seconds later she heard the sharp report of another weapon and recognized that she was not the target this time. This was likely just an adjustment rendered by one of the street gangs upon another. She waited a full five minutes until she had heard the tired engine of an ancient truck drive away and no further gunplay before she continued toward her meeting. After a block or two of her brisk walk the entire incident receded into unimportance. Someone in Kazakhstan was buying nuclear bombs and she needed to know why.

Her career with the KGB had mutated into a part time job since the demise of the Soviet Union and her rank now meant very little. Now, the majority of her income came from commissions generated by the sale of the scrap remaining of the Soviet space program. Week by week she sold the shiny wreckage of her space faring dreams. Most of it could, if properly treated, still be used. In fact, some well-heeled western corporation had bought the last two of the Energiya boosters and had sent a load of water into low Earth orbit yesterday. They intended to actually launch a manned Soyuz capsule after it tomorrow along with some additional water. Some sort of private research into a missile defense system was what she had been told. Interesting, but not in the same league with her other business. She was also responsible for technological exports in general. What raised her concern was who was buying tactical nuclear warheads? This was a well-known ingredient for disaster on a global scale. The other thing that worried her was the fact that this man left so few recollections of his actions.

The first shots struck the cheap bricks of the alcove leaving the whine of ricochet and the unmistakable ratcheting of an AK-47 in the stinking air of Almaty. Katerina Yerisivloskaya was already on the way down to the ground behind the decrepit Russian made sedan parked at the curb with her machine pistol clenched in her diminutive grip before the chips struck the pavement. The first round from her weapon caught one of the assassins in the neck and he fell from the roof into the street. His accomplice ducked behind the parapet dodging her second round. Katerina rolled over in time to see the head of her third assailant clear the parapet. A heartbeat later, her third round entered his face just adjacent to the bridge of his nose and he ceased to be threat.

The living gunman on the other side of the street broke the sudden silence with a few automatic bursts through the windshield and windows of the sedan showering Katerina with glass. Another thrifty burst flattened the bald front tires of the sedan and sent a few metallic fragments whining through the air around Katerina.

"Merde!" Katerina said beneath her breath. "There is only so inept these assholes can be. Given enough opportunities, they could get lucky and I could get dead." Her enemy shredded the rear tires of the sedan and one of the obligatory fragments of shrapnel tore a ragged hole in the lining of her long coat. A thin line of blood appeared along the smooth skin of her right calf about nine inches below the knee. Then came the welcome sound of an AK-47 hammer falling on an empty chamber.

Katerina leapt forward and a couple of shots from her pistol taught her assailant to duck behind parapets. Unfortunately, for Katerina, he had another clip for his weapon. In a period best measured in heartbeats, a prolonged burst of automatic fire brought down some of the masonry blocks of the alcove adjacent to the narrow sidewalk. One of these interrupted its fall to earth glancing off the side of Katerina's head just behind her right ear and after stars came blackness.

Gunfire awoke him from idle speculation as he tailed the tall attractive woman agent as discretely as he could manage. He crouched in a doorway instinctively as the first shots rang out. He watched her take out the first two gunmen and the other people in the street fade from view. He was not in a good position to see the masonry hit the woman, but given the sounds and the sudden hush in the gunfire, he could tell that if he intended to have any impact on the outcome, it was time to act. He watched as the surviving gunman descended to the street and crossed to make sure of his victim. A single shot from his revolver lifted the assassin and flung him like a rag doll between two cars on the other side of the street. He rushed down the street to where the woman lay crumpled on the sidewalk.

He looked her over carefully before deciding whether she ought to be moved. She had a small laceration on one leg and had a bloody wound behind the right ear. Tall, at least five foot eight or nine, which was very unusual for someone from this region of the world. She also had dark red hair, marking her as a foreigner like himself. She was breathing evenly and as he watched, she began to stir. He knelt down next to her and was helping her to sit up when he heard the snick of a safety being taken off overhead. He turned and fired at the sound and managed to catch the man with the carbine in the neck with a single round from his revolver. As he was shooting a .357 magnum, the man's head almost left his shoulders.

Suddenly there was a hard object pressed into his right armpit.

"It is an interesting night in Almaty yes? It would be a good idea to place your firearm down at your feet." The words in French with a rich alto voice were in sharp contrast to the machine pistol aimed at his heart. "Perhaps you will be telling me who you are and why you have been following me."

" I am Jack Knight. You are Katerina Yerisivloskaya. I know who you are because we are engaged in some common business. We were supposed to meet about five minutes ago in a restaurant about a block and a half down the street to discuss an export permit. I think we just happened to be on the same street when I saw that you were being set upon by gunmen. Perhaps I should not have interfered?" The man's French was every bit as good as hers. She slowly removed her weapon from his armpit and gestured with it to the pistol lying on the ground.

"No, Thank you for your assistance. I am just becoming more careful with weapons since people began shooting at me. That is, other people's weapons. You are American." This last was spoken in delightfully accented English.

" Yes, I am. Is my French that bad?" Jack replied in English also and slowly retrieved his pistol from the ground and holstered it.

"No, your French is very good and until this moment I had thought from our telephone conversations that you were French."

"Is it my clothes? I am not wearing a sign on my back or anything like that am I?" He assisted the lady to her feet.

"No, I can only tell you that from my experience that no Frenchman would carry a cowboy cannon like that. I have never seen any Frenchman that shot so well under pressure. If you had tried to convince me you were French in the face of this contrary evidence, I would have shot you."

"It is good that I am a fundamentally honest person."

"Yes, and also handy on the scene with large firearms. Shall we attempt to complete our appointment?"

"You know, you are still bleeding."

"Not as much as some."

" We should see to your wounds. Perhaps we should try to avoid destroying this most becoming dress more than it is already. By the way, I don't recommend the local hospital."

"Luckily, that will not be necessary. I was only stunned and you know how it is with scalp wounds. They look much worse than they really are. The leg wound is only a scratch."

"The fact that you're still bleeding might interfere with some of the other patrons enjoying their meal."

"Possibly."

"And your preference would be?"

"Let's go see my Nina."

Ekaterina Terescova Yerisivloskaya was the grandchild of a Russian soldier sent to Kazakhstan to assist in the purge of 1933. He had taken his pick among the Kazakh women dislocated by the purge and gotten her pregnant without benefit of marriage or for that matter her consent. He was young and impetuous and ruthless and the object of his "affections" was but fourteen. In Kazakhstan - of course, it was not called that then - this was a familiar pattern. The invaders moved through, leaving their bastard seed to sink or swim in the dry spaces of central Asia. When he also became a victim of the purge, he was not missed. Even Stalin did not kill everyone. He left the "camp followers" as Katerina's grandmother became upon his "unfortunate" demise. She could not go back to her own people, as her rape by the invader made her an outcast in the Kazakh patriarchal society of near nomads. Katerina's mother was born into a new world that the invaders brought seeking the few fertile areas to grow grain, mines for metals and coal and a new population to add to the burgeoning rough weave that made up the Soviet Union. Natasha, as her mother called her, grew up with the benefits of the new schools including indoctrination into the political correctness of Stalinist communism. When she was eighteen she went to one of the new cities to work in a factory where she caught the eye of a young German technician imported to run the factory and a match was made. Katerina was the fourth of their six children and came along in time to reap the benefits of his joining the party. She was sent to a special school reserved for party members and was allowed secondary education, as she was bright, ambitious and quick to take advantage of opportunities. She was trained in aerospace engineering. Because of her father's position as a loyal party member, the KGB recruited her. She rose rapidly through the ranks and, after her training in the Cosmonaut corp., was a Major when perestroika became an international word. This led to freedoms, which resulted in the dissolution of the Soviet Union. At that time, she was back in the land of her Grandmother's people stationed at the Baikonur Cosmodrome. Her grandmother was still alive and working in a menial capacity in one of the large government buildings in downtown Alma-Ata. It seems that Nina's (Not her "real" name) pension was not sufficiently funded to survive the changes in the state. Her location did however make her an ideal contact and operative for her granddaughter. Their relationship was one of Katerina's secrets and one of the things that her grandmother loved best. They were able to meet at her "Nina's" apartment on a regular basis.

Earlier in the day, she and her grandmother had discussed her coming meeting with Jack. She recalled that her Nina had asked her about who "this man" was.

"If I knew that, it might not be necessary for me to meet him! It is enough for me to know that he might be an enemy of the people."

" Which people is it that he may be the enemy of? If he intended on using these devices here, he would not be so stupid as to meet with the secret police. Why must you meet with him in the city at night - especially in this place where infidels drink?" Whatever else could be said of my Nina, she is not foolish and in her seventies is not so old. Although she had long since lost much of her faith in the Prophet, she referred to anyone who used alcohol as infidels. I did not enlighten her to the fact that I occasionally had wine or vodka when it suited me. Her aversion probably resulted from her short acquaintance with my grandfather.

"It goes without saying that owners of nuclear weapons are the enemies of the people as thermonuclear devices are of no use in hunting. This man is very intelligent and educated, which does not fit a religious or nationalist fanatic profile, so I have no insight into what he intends to do with theses bombs. He could not have gotten the bombs elsewhere. I am most interested to meet this man because his motives are so difficult to understand and predict. Would you rather I brought this stranger home to know where I live!" I must occasionally present my grandmother with an opportunity to push her nose against reality.

"No. " Nina said slyly. "I would rather that he be taken far into the desert, questioned with hot iron, and left for the carrion birds." She was not fond of having her nose rubbed into it.

"Old-fashioned and unnecessarily messy, Nina. I will use more efficient and convenient means should they be required. He may be so egotistical that in the proper situation and with the proper inducements he will tell me without me having to ask questions."

"I won't have my granddaughter play the whore!"

"Nina, I will do what is necessary as I always have but I appreciate your concern and will not compromise my own security."

T minus – 00:00:16:45:30

So much for my attempts to not compromise my own security. Here I was bringing the man I was most concerned about into my secret place - my grandmother's apartment. There were a number of things on my mind. Why this man, who had saved my life, was also trying to acquire tactical nukes was at the top of the list, of course. Also of interest was who was trying to kill me and why. It was possible that my injuries were more severe than I thought. I really had no clear idea why I was bringing this stranger into this concealed part of my life. I pride myself that I am a good judge of character, but to walk into my grandmother's house, bleeding about the face and head with a stranger might not have demonstrated my best judgment. The bleeding had almost stopped and I was beginning to second-guess myself, when we arrived at my grandmother's apartment. It was one of many in the six-story block of dirty grey-brown concrete pseudo stone on the northeastern edge of the questionable district. Nina lived in the middle of the third floor on a corridor, which ran around the circumference of the building. Her apartment was reached via a dark stairwell at the corner of the ugly block. I was still a little light headed from the concrete hitting my head and the cut was oozing fitfully yet. The cut on my leg was clotted. Two of the four fluorescent fixtures set into the ceiling were pulsing ineffectually as we walked past the first four apartments. Three of the peepholes set into the metal doors gazed balefully into the dingy passage. The fourth was dark. I knocked on the door.

It was not immediately clear whether anyone was at home but I heard a rustling that usually meant that Nina was getting out of bed and preparing herself to come to the door. All the small subliminal clues seemed to be present and accounted for. Eventually, the door opened and Nina was standing in the doorway and what appeared to be a small cannon was trained on my rescuer's forehead. " You will be taking off your overcoat now. You will be doing it very slowly and in most obvious manner but without delay of needful time." My grandmother's Russian was, after almost sixty years of nearly daily use, still on a rudimentary level. Her meaning however, was clear enough and without turning, I heard my companion reach for his lapels and begin to pull them back from where they met in the middle of his chest. I walked into the apartment. It would not hurt to have my companion of the last few minutes disarmed. As it was not my idea, I had no reason to apologize. I really did not think Nina would kill him after she had rendered him harmless. I walked into the bathroom and began to clean my wounds. As I had suspected the still bleeding head wound was only a scrape. I cleansed it and applied a stinging styptic. It took somewhat longer to get the dried blood from my hair. It left my hair wet and whatever style it had had washed down the sink - so much for glamour. The wound on my leg was not, however, as superficial as I had originally supposed. There was in fact a small chunk of metal just visible at the rearmost edge of the wound. I took as good a grip on it as I could manage with a pair of Nina's tweezers and managed to jerk it out. It hurt worse than the wound when I received it. I said a few irreligious words and made a few impossible suggestions in the process. The wound, which had stopped bleeding before my ministrations, began making up for lost time. I thoroughly cleaned it out and was careful to be as sure as I could be that there were no other obvious foreign bodies. I may have made other obvious use of my military vocabulary. The sounds present during the other more prominent sensory input were not sufficiently memorable. It was after I finally finished with the peroxide and antiseptic and gotten the ugly thing to stop bleeding again that I noticed that my good satin shoes were ruined. After removing my ruined shoes, I then noted I had also ruined my dress and other accessories. Someone was going to have to pay. Oh, I had already decided to kill whoever had attacked me; I now intended to kill them slowly. It was going to have to be the whole job any way now. I got a tepid shower. I wondered how Nina stood it on a cold morning. I grabbed one of Nina's robes and made my way into the living room.

My American rescuer was down to his underwear, socks, and a gag and was hog-tied with an extension cord in the middle of the living room floor. Nina had removed an arsenal from his person and was going through his wallet and other effects, which she had placed, on the coffee table. Her shotgun was leaned against the wall. She seemed to be in an abnormally good humor as she counted his money and eyed the shiny credit cards. She looked up and smiled as I opened the door. " I have a large old trunk. Shall we strangle him, or bleed him into the sink?"

I laughed and tried to remove his gag. She had secured it to his ankles behind his head. "Nina! I thought it would be alright for you to get his weapons while we talked, but this is too much!"

"You don't intend to waste a bullet on this man who has injured you, do you?"

"I don't think this man has done anything but good for me at this point, Nina. The ones who attacked me no longer breathe." I began to untie his ankles and succeeded in getting his gag out. I did not think that he could speak Kazakh, as he might have been a little more agitated with all this talk of strangling and bleeding.

"If this is the way you treat the people who save your life, I never want to see how you deal with the ones on the other side!" The American was somewhat out of breath. I do not think he could breath too well in his previous position. I finished untying his hands. He sat in the floor rubbing his wrists and ankles glaring at my grandmother who had retrieved her shotgun and again, had it aimed at his face.

"Calm yourself my friend. No lasting harm has been done and I am sure my grandmother was only trying to protect herself and me." I gave my grandmother a hard look over my shoulder. " I will return your clothes, and after you dress, we will have our delayed discussion." I handed him his clothes and gestured toward the small bathroom that I had just vacated.

I personally went to Nina's bedroom and dressed myself from some of the older outfits I kept there for emergencies. I tied my wet hair back with a brown leather clasp, provided myself with some sensible shoes, and returned to the living room.

Jack Knight was just coming out of the bathroom. He was dressed in an expensive if nondescript manner and had an angry look that seemed to reach only his eyes. He was relatively tall for this part of the world - about six feet. He had short dark brown hair with gray-blue eyes. Looking closer, there were a few single gray hairs mixed in with the brown which, given his unlined features, must have been premature. Having seen him with a lot fewer clothes, I knew that he was built like a martial artist. "Would you like some tea?" I continued in English.

"Please, that would be nice. May I sit down?" I gestured toward the ancient stuffed chair beside the floor lamp and set some water to boil. I noticed that Nina still had a gun on him.

"Nina! It is all right! It will no longer be necessary for you to point that ancient shotgun at him. I don't think you have any ammunition in it anyway!"

"And that is another thing that he didn't have to know! How do you know he does not speak Kazakh? He has a very tricky look to him!"

"Nina, make tea! I will handle the negotiations from this point." She gave me a hard look but walked into the kitchen area to finish the preparations for tea.

"I apologize for my grandmother. She has had a very interesting life and occasionally it shows in how she treats strangers. Having been around her for so long, I forget how little she trusts people from outside."

Finally getting the circulation back into his hands and feet, he appeared to relax slightly. "I, on the other hand, am still a little too trusting it seems." His eyes flickered to his weapons still on the coffee table - out of reach.

"I think it best that we keep things as they are for the present - now that we are more comfortable. I am still concerned that I might have to disagree with your business ventures here in Almaty." I brought my own machine pistol from at my side where he could see it. He looked uncomfortable again.

"I understood that the main reason we had to meet was to get my exportation permit signed so that I could take delivery of my goods and leave your country." He appeared as if he were asking for more sugar.

"Some concerned persons don't consider tactical nuclear weapons "goods" in any since of that word. The fact that some of the breakaway republics of the former Soviet Union appear to think so, is just some individual's greed for hard currency. I must personally decide whether the users of these "goods" fall within my definition of enemies of the people. I take this responsibility most seriously. You have been released from your bindings as a courtesy due to the fact that you saved my life earlier this evening. For all I know you set that up to get into my good graces. You may not be a decent person at all, just ruthless enough to sever all loose ends. If I decide that you are such a one, you will not leave this apartment alive."

Chapter Two

Midnight on the Firing Line

T-Minus 00:00:15:45:30

Jack Knight had been in worst places. He was in a tiny apartment in Almaty fully dressed and untied. The old woman that had hijacked him was in the kitchen area making tea and giving him suspicious looks over her shoulder. The woman agent that he had rescued in the wild street battle was now also dressed and no longer bleeding. She was lightly holding a Kalashnikov machine pistol pointed in his general direction. He had reason to know just how good she was with this particular tool. Now that he had a chance to get a good look at her face without a trace of makeup, he could see that she was very beautiful without being pretty. She had a strong nose and dark green intelligent eyes. Her hair was a dark red. Her last statement hung in the air like the smell of smoke. He blamed himself for being in this position. He usually considered himself an excellent judge of character but he had not seen this coming at all. He dared not tell this Commissar what he intended to do with these tactical nukes. He also could see that she might well alert to any well-crafted lie. His purposes could not withstand his loss. It was essential to get these weapons and get away with them. The Soyuz was already in place on top of the Energiya and the huge tank of water tucked underneath. Bob was already at Baikonur overseeing the final preparations. Fueling was supposed to begin late tomorrow morning. He decided to tell her as much of the truth as he could manage without revealing his true intent.

"I guarantee that these devices will not to be used in any terrorist or political act. They will not be used in any way against human beings or in the course of warfare. They will not be fired in anger."

"Mr. Knight, what other possible use can these devices have?" There was not a glimmer of relaxation in those dark eyes. If anything, her grip had tightened on her pistol.

"They are basically big time explosives in small easily moved packages. I and my associates intend to use them in furtherance of mining." There, he had told her the most that he could tell her. Anything else he had to say would be in the form of a negative or denial. The old woman had finished making the tea and brought the service back to the sitting area. She handed Jack a chipped cup filled with the dark strong tea of the region. He accepted the cup and thanked her in Russian, which seemed to be their common language.

"Your lifeless body would be locked in a box on the way to the landfill if I had my way, Infidel! If you are in the least way responsible for my granddaughter's injuries, I will risk her displeasure and send you that way before the Sun rises. Would you like milk or sugar?"

Jack took a little milk to dilute the stiff brew and watched warily while Katerina also fixed her tea, her hand never leaving her pistol. There was a quiet moment while the three occupants of the small room situated themselves and sipped experimentally at their tea. It was much like this land – dark and bitter with a dry after-taste.

Katerina lifted her eyes from her cup and fixed him with a sharp look. "I may be inclined to consider that this is not one of the uses of these "explosives" that I would conclude to be impermissible". That this is not their designed purpose leads me to doubt that they can be safely used so. I take it that there would be no release of radioactive materials into the atmosphere?"

"There will no release into the atmosphere in even the smallest degree. The explosions will also take place at a very remote location – many miles from even the most isolated communities or individuals." Jack took another sip of his awful tea.

There was another pause while these perfectly true statements were being considered. Katerina looked over at her grandmother. "What did you find in his things aside from the money that so pleased you?"

"I found three weapons - Two guns, and a longish knife. The knife has a very fine edge. I have thought of something I would like to use it for later. Additionally, I found a French Diplomatic passport, an American driver's license and another ID card, which identifies this infidel as working for some obscure department of the United States Government. Can we tie him up again? It will be much easier to kill him whether we strangle him or cut his throat." Nina sipped her tea and looked at Jack like a nice piece of fish.

"You work for the Government of the United States? Is this not some sort of test to determine whether to "send in the Marines?"

Jack's tea tasted even worse than his first and second sips. He set his cup down on the saucer and considered his next move. "I do work for a department of the United States Government. It is primarily concerned with international business and finance. I learned of the resources that I wish to acquire through entirely independent means. I fear that my Government not only has no knowledge of my intentions but also would likely strongly object to my means. In this matter, other than my associates, none of who are in your city, I am on my own. If you and this bloodthirsty old woman decide to dispose of me, The US government will not punish you or your country in any way. By the way, I can't speak Kazakh, but I can understand it to some extent."

"Why would you not wish your Government to know about what you are doing? Are you acting against the interest of the United States?"

"Do you want your government to know everything about what you are doing? I did not think so. The truth is that I despise my government. The only thing that I can think of that is worse is perhaps yours. The United States does have the best government that money can buy but at least it is hypocritical about it. If the truth came out people would be embarrassed. Here and elsewhere, the bribery is institutionalized. But no – I am not acting against the interest of the United States."

"I obviously pulled a string." Jack's rage was apparent from his blush.

"You asked. I answered."

There was something about this man. He clearly was not revealing the specifics of his plan but he actually seemed to be telling the truth. Katerina found herself being convinced against her will. He was well trained in weaponry but was also not a spy or secret agent. No secret agent would have allowed himself to be captured in this way. At least, not an intelligent agent. Jack was clearly intelligent as evidenced by his command of at least three languages and working knowledge of a fourth. Yet, his knowledge had obvious gaps. "Where did you learn to shoot like that?"

"Well, I was in the Navy for a time. I would say it did little to improve my skills. My father insisted that all his children be proficient with firearms. Truthfully, I never actually killed anyone until tonight. I really thought that I would feel worse about it than I do. Maybe it will catch up with me later, but those two guys I shot were so clearly the bad guys."

"Bad guys, indeed. What do you know about them?"

"I know that there were six of them and one of you. I know that they were using fully automatic weapons. Other than that and the fact that they are all dead, I knew nothing about them. I know that they attacked you from ambush, which is not my idea of a fair fight. Not that I would always fight fair myself. If the stakes are life and death, I would accept any advantage that life offered me."

"So, they did not work for you?" Katerina already knew the answer she would get.

"I would never hire someone else to do my dirty work."

Actually, not the exact answer that she expected. He had leaned forward in his chair as if to emphasize his point. Katerina had obviously let her guard down as he suddenly reached out, grabbed his huge pistol, and had it pointing at her before she had time to point her pistol at him. Her grandmother started leaning toward her shotgun when an explosion deafened them and the receiver of the ancient weapon came apart as the larger fragments flew into the corner, far from her reach. His smoking pistol was centered on Katerina's chest. "It would now be a good idea to put your pistol on the floor." Jack said this without even a hint of a smile.

"Do you think that I will sign your export permit at gunpoint?" Katerina was infuriated at herself for letting this obvious amateur get the drop on her.

"Whether you will sign some worthless piece of paper or not is now not so an important an issue. The big deal is that I will be leaving this dismal little apartment alive whether you wish it or not. It has now become quite clear that your government is even more dysfunctional than I thought. A decent forgery will probably be more than adequate for my purposes. By the way, " He directed his comments to Nina." You make terrible tea. Tea that bad can't be an accident and to serve it to a guest is positively uncultured."

"What you don't know is that there are no export permits for tactical nuclear weapons. Every other person or group that has tried to get one has been killed. You did not seem to be the typical terrorist so I did not kill you out of hand. I actually thought that you might represent some covert arm of France. As far as I know, there are no good reasons to allow any individual to possess these weapons and many good reasons why the people that want to should not be allowed to live."

"And this entire meeting to get this nonexistent permit was all a farce?"

"It all depends on your perspective. It was important for my business of seeing to it that these weapons of mass destruction did not fall into the wrong hands."

"From your stated position, no one's are the "right " hands."

"I did allow some reputable governments to import the arms."

"And those were the "right" hands?"

"In the generally accepted meaning of the word."

"And this definition was set by those same governments."

"Governments usually last longer than any individual and as they are made up of representatives of the people they can be expected to handle these awful things more responsibly than some individual or group."

"In a few very select cases that may be correct. However, I feel that most governments are immoral. By this, I mean they are corrupt, for sale to the highest bidder, and more interested in maintaining their own phony baloney jobs than in the benefit of the people. What little good done by governments or in the name of the government is done by good hearted individuals of character and principle."

This sounded too much like her grandmother to be totally discounted. Katerina had always been the government or worked for it and it had never occurred to her that governments might not be the best way to do most things. Nina had never been too fond of Katerina's erstwhile employer. Although she agreed for the most part, with the things that she did, she did not altogether agree with why Katerina did them. Katerina had always surmised that Nina's hatred for the Soviets had stemmed from their conquering her little country and ruining her life. However, she hated the new republic's government even more. As far as Katerina knew, they had never done anything to Nina but give her a job that she did not much care for.

"So you feel that there should be no governments?"

"I feel that the governments that currently exist are too large, too intrusive, too ruthless and controlled by too few of the wrong people. If my own or other governments were working properly, I would not be in the middle of some third world country trying to obtain tactical nuclear weapons." Jack was still mad at how he had been treated.

"In what way are they not working properly?"

"That is the issue isn't it? What do you feel that a properly working government should do?" Jack seemed to have worked himself up to some unknown decision and Katerina was interested enough to want to know what that was. The fact that this man was holding a gun on her and her grandmother was no small inducement. Katerina carefully considered her answer. She thought about Afghanistan, Mir and Chernobyl. She thought back through the years since the breakup of the Soviet Union. The first thing was to produce a stable currency helping to maintain, or at least not interfere with, a decent economy. Another was to prevent or assist with illnesses caused by plagues and environmental and industrial disasters. What it all boiled down to was to do for people whatever was too big a job for them to do for themselves.

"A stable currency, a safe environment and public education are pretty basic. I think that a properly working government would protect its people from things they could not protect themselves against. Other services would seem to be optional. I can think of a few things that I would support. A good space program comes to mind as something too big for individuals or even multinational corporations because there is no chance of profit." Jack listened to her answer very thoughtfully and quietly. He seemed to have made his decision whatever it was.

"Commissar Yerisivloskaya, we seem to agree about a great many things. If I can convince you that there is in fact a good reason for me to obtain these weapons, will you help me to do it? I will not pretend that I am able to kill you or your grandmother other than in self-defense. Regardless of your decision, I will leave you both alive although you have expressly threatened my life. Will you listen with an open mind and reserve your judgment until I have put forth my case?"

"I will listen and reserve judgment but I must ask you if you will not put your weapon aside. I find it difficult to think properly staring down the barrel of that huge gun."

"I don't mind putting it away, but I won't give it back to you. I will also reclaim my other effects before I do so, as I do not appreciate being robbed. Jack took back his other pistol, his knife and his wallet along with his other pocket items. He replaced them in their respective places, still holding his pistol. As he was doing this, he nonchalantly kicked Katerina's gun into the same corner as the shattered pieces of her grandmother's shotgun. As he finished with his preparations, he put his gun back into his shoulder holster and sat down in the same chair as before. "Are we more comfortable now?" he asked. "I know that I am, as I began this discussion naked and hog-tied in the middle of the floor with the two of you arguing how best to kill me."

"I will not apologize again for what I consider to be very reasonable precautions under the circumstances."

"And I will never again be so trusting. I am still not certain that I did the right thing in saving your life."

"This, like so many things, remains to be seen."

"It does however, raise a interesting issue. Assuming for argument's sake that I did not hire those goons to do away with you earlier this evening, I am very curious about who did."

"I have several ideas. The most likely suspect is another former agent of the KGB. He and I have a fundamental disagreement about these exports that you and I have been discussing. I see these transactions to be an opportunity to serve my own and other peoples of the world. He however conceives of them as an entrepreneurial exercise. He, of my likely enemies, would have the motive, the informational network and the financial wherewithal to hire that quantity of thugs and arm them. The fact that he spent so much on so little has his finger marks all over it."

"Would his name be Major Kostolinkavitch?"

"You know something of this man?" There was an edge of suspicion in Katerina's voice.

"Yes, I do. Although I have not met him." He added, with a direct look at Katerina. "I was told that I might be able to do business with him if I couldn't conclude my acquisitions with you. It also came to my attention that on several occasions in the past the same serial numbered weapons had changed hands with his assistance and that the receiving parties disappeared. I heard that you were more honest and at least the weapons disappeared as well. I decided to take my chances with you. I was following you to make sure that I was not being set up. Clearly, that did me a lot of good." He smiled thinly and looked at Katerina's grandmother who smiled back.

"Once again, that remains to be seen. Now, perhaps you will tell me why I should help you."

"It all started with my kid sister in graduate school. A little over nine months ago, she was doing some work for her faculty advisor in the Astronomy department while working toward her Ph.D. in Astrophysics. He was ostensibly part of a project to detect asteroids and comets but like all "great" men left the work to graduate assistants. She was working with a blink comparator on some deep sky CCD data when she noticed a tiny little dot…"

Chapter Three
A Typical Day at School

T-Minus 00:09:06:17:45:00

Margaret Knight was not really all that interested in what she was doing. For the most part, it did not require interest, reflection or much of a brain. She was trawling through thousands of consecutive astrophotos of the same areas of deep space looking for tiny little differences from one shot to the next. The pictures had been taken six months apart. There was some degree of skill in using a blink comparator but it was not something an assembly line quality inspector could not have picked up. You look at the first picture and then you switch to the second rapidly. Every thing moved a little as there was a limit to how precise aiming of a big Earth based telescope could be. The computer did quite a bit by lining up known stars. Every now and then, one tiny faint dot moved more than that could explain. As the pictures were taken as little as six months apart, the proper motion of a star could be ruled out. Bang! A new asteroid or comet was discovered.

Margaret was better at this than most as she delighted in finding small differences and figuring out what they meant. Over the last three years, she had discovered or rediscovered four different objects. One of these - a long period comet - had been identified previously but its orbit had been poorly characterized. The other three were very minor asteroids that later were determined to be in what were now stable orbits between Mars and Jupiter.

Today, she could hardly be bothered. She was looking at data from last year that no one had gotten around to looking over. She had not heard from her fiancé since yesterday and she was beginning to lose what little remained of her patience with him. That he was in his lab working the whole time, and not out painting the town with some other woman, did nothing to assuage her ire. The man worked in the same room with a telephone, didn't he? Who did he think he was? She was not some little brainless bimbo to come running whenever he called! She had thought that she would go home to her parents this afternoon after closing out this block of data and try to get Tom back into her father's good graces but Tom was rapidly losing ground with her! Her Mom had suggested this was probably the only way to make this happen. She had invited her brothers home as well so they could talk a little sense into her dad. It was all very distracting. Wait! What was that?

She had caught what appeared to be a tiny little jump by a very dim object or star. She reversed the order of the last two images with a touch of the mouse on a button of the comparator program. There it was again! She checked the NGC with another button and this tiny little object was not there! She had found something new in last year's batch of data. Had this area been surveyed in the first run four years ago? She called up that block and checked out these coordinates. There it was! It had moved even more from the first pictures taken four years ago to the two taken just last year. If it were still in the field in the latest batch of data that had ended the project, she would have six data points and should be able to calculate its orbit. All thoughts of Tom fled as she pursued the new object. The angles were very tiny fractions of a second of arc but she was able to define the curve! She called up her orbital calculator and plugged in her new object. If it was all right with Mr. Newton, she was going to see where this puppy was going.

Orbital mechanics are a straightforward, if complex bit of calculation. What would have been weeks of laborious calculations on paper were accomplished in just minutes with her computer. Within a few minutes from its discovery, the new object had a defined orbit. The bright red line in the three dimensional plot showed the most likely predicted path the object would take over the next nine years. On either side, and above and below, were blue hash-marked lines and green hash-marked lines showing the standard deviation from the mean based on the accuracy of the data entered. All five lines intersected the Earth.

"Oh crap!" Margaret spoke aloud. She re-measured her data points and checked them again. She ran some calibration checks on the orbital calculator and compared them to all total eclipses of the Sun for the last seventy-five years. They all checked out to the limits of the timing devices and geographic measurements available at the time of the eclipse. Everything checked out. Margaret carefully recorded all the original data for the area of space from the computer and placed it on a disk. She also downloaded her measurements and calculations onto the disk. She then wrote a script that reformatted all the disk drives four times after initiation. She took one last look at the tiny little dot on the screen as the image cycled through the six images she had used. "I found you, you insensible demon rock. I'm going to call you Belial." She started the script and left the lab with her disk, leaving no evidence of her discovery.

Margaret headed back to her dorm room and began to pack. She intended to go home this weekend and talk to her Dad as her Mom had suggested. The fact that the world was about to end made this an even better idea. Margaret did not always agree with her father but she always respected his opinion. She respected it not because he was her Dad but rather because she respected how he arrived at his opinion.

He was not given to unreasoning insistence upon his own view and was willing to modify his own if new information came to light. He was generally considered a very impressive scientist, although he insisted that he was not a scientist but rather an engineer. He had little respect for those of his colleagues that operated in the realm of pure theory and referred to them as scientists. He considered himself a more practical man. While he was willing to use theoretical ideas in his work, he did not waste his belief upon such things until they bore fruit in the material world.

This made him more a friend of Newton than of Einstein. More at home with Steinmetz and Tesla than Maxwell and Compton. Thinkers were fine as long as they were precise. His preference was for doers. Well, something would have to be done about Belial and her dad was the best place to start.

T-Minus 00:09:05:05:22:08

Tom White was even a little more excited than usual. He and his fiancé were getting along great, his work was going very well indeed, and it was Friday afternoon in sweater season. He smiled thinking about how great Maggie looked in a sweater. They had a long heart-to-heart night before last and it truly did seem that they had gotten some things settled. Finally, it appeared that she was going to confront her father about she and Tom's relationship. Things just had not been right since her father had kicked him out of the house last December. All they had been doing was kissing fully clothed on the living room couch, and Jake Knight had acted as if he had caught them in flagrante delicto!

The problem was that the phone in his hand kept ringing and ringing and Maggie was not answering it. OK, so he should have called earlier, even last night. He had been so enveloped in his work with the assemblers that he had worked through the night and morning. Only now that all the programming was done and the little machines being constructed, had he noted that it was Saturday morning. It was sweater season and he had not set up a time to meet his fiancé. That, it appeared, was a problem. This was not the first time he had called since daylight.

His work was very exciting right now. Tom had developed nanotechnology to the point of practicality. He had abandoned the straightforward approach of trying to actually build the little machines himself and had fallen back on the existing nanotechnology – living organisms. He had created a tailor made yeast like organism that readily assembled the machines that he designed as long as he used materials that they could metabolize. The big breakthrough had occurred when he was able to manufacture a gene set that added the ability of the organism to metabolize diamond. It made an ideal material to build small machines with. When his experiments had advanced to the point that he felt that he could protect animals from the dangers in their environment, he ran into some major problems. He used some genes from fungi to teach his little organisms to make hyphae like structures on a molecular basis to create a protective network between cells of complex organisms. He felt that he had finally worked out the cellular interface problem that he had noted with his first diamontoids. The trick was to let them sample the proposed HLA type prior to interface. Any tissue would do except for dead skin. Then they had a model of the basic work environment and the milieu in which they needed to maintain relative homeostasis. Previously, the diamontoids had been glommed with antibodies and ingested by macrophages. Because they were totally indigestible, they caused an inflammatory condition similar to gout in the lab animals in which he had tested them. The next batch had not caused this problem and the animals looked healthier than before they had ingested the nanomachines. Furthermore, the shut down sequence he sent to the animals via another ingested batch of diamontoids had worked perfectly with all functioning diamontoids excreted within four hours of the second dose of nanomachines. After he stopped killing his experimental subjects with his tampering, his work had gone much more rapidly with the thirty-second generation now in beta testing. The current crop of diamontoids would protect the animals from viruses and bacteria within twelve hours of ingestion. They reproduced themselves from waste products and circulating nutrients, and the next to last generation had extended themselves from the gastrointestinal tract to the central nervous system and out onto the animals external surfaces. This had been somewhat unanticipated and had been discovered when he took a hair sample from one of the rats and almost broke the scissors! The analysis had revealed diamontoids covering the hair, and interspersed within it, just maintaining homeostasis. This had expanded his thinking about the nanomachines and, as they formed an interlocking surface of diamontoids, his last generation had incorporated protection from extraneous electrical currents.

Why didn't Maggie answer the damn phone! Tom really needed to talk about this next generation of diamontoids and he really wanted to see Maggie for other more personal reasons. He needed a shave, a shower, and he needed some time away from this lab. He had a strong preference to spend that time with Maggie. The problem was that he could not seem to get it all arranged. He waited for the assembler to finish its work. He took the product in its ten small bottles and put them in his coat pocket. He gave up on Maggie's phone and called the general information for her dorm. "Delingrath Hall," a pretty contralto answered almost immediately.

"Hi. This is Dr. Tom White. I am trying to get in touch with Margaret Knight and I have had no luck with her room phone."

"Well, Dr. White, Here in the dorm log it says that she checked out yesterday afternoon."

"Doesn't it also say where she was going?" Tom knew that they would not give him this information if it were too specific.

"It says that she was going home. Would you like to leave a message?

"Please leave my name in case she calls in to check, but I think I'll try to catch her there. Thank you."

As he hung up the phone, he felt a little zing of doubt. He left the lab and went home, showered and packed a small bag. He really did not want to drive three hours after so little, if any, sleep. It looked like the showdown with Jake White was going to happen quicker than he had thought. "I just hope I don't have to drive back here tonight." His voice echoed in the empty stairwell on the way to the parking lot and his waiting car.

Chapter Four
A Meeting of Cosmic Insignificance

T-Minus 00:09:06:11:07:00

It was a great time to be alive. I guess this all depends on who you ask and what is happening to them at the time, but for me and mine, things couldn't be better. Who am I kidding? Things can always be better but then we are not the kind of folks who like to waste time complaining.

People were not building as much as they had in the early 21st but I had managed to sock away most of my income from those years and now made a tidy sum as a consultant. My wife's medical practice still provided a bit more than we really needed to live on. Even though two of the kids were still in school, they had obtained full academic scholarships and worked in the summer and so had ceased to be any kind of burden. Then again, they never had been. There had been the usual power struggles before they learned to be reasonable. Once we had established communications, we never lost them. Consequently, the terrible twos were the last of the terrible times. I am not saying that there were never any arguments. On the contrary, our offspring were as opinionated as their mother and me. That is fine with me. I did not intend to raise a bunch of pushovers. From time to time, my children have convinced me to change my point of view but that goes both ways.

Yeah, things were going well. Madelyne and I were getting along as well as ever and that was well indeed. We had agreed about most things from the time when we met and then agreed to disagree about everything else. We talk about politics and religion, but we do not discuss the great pumpkin - whatever that might be at the time. I am the only person on the planet who can get away with calling her Mad. When she uses my name, she calls me Jake or JK with a cheesy French accent, which always sounds wonderful to me. Hey you! Has always been specific enough from Mad. Twenty-five years can really whip by if you are having fun. And when you have someone that you care about and kids you're proud of - along with the spiritual ease that comes with enough and good health, it's generally pretty much fun. It just keeps getting better.

    October is also my favorite time of the year. Not hot enough for short sleeves or cold enough for a jacket - except perhaps on one of those cool clear nights when the extra pockets can come in handy. October, the month when the mosquitoes die. It is probably a little thing but I hate mosquitoes with the same intensity that they seem to love me - to three significant figures. As I stepped out on my deck and surveyed the purplish western sky, it occurred to me that I had not seen a mosquito since the first real frost of fall last Wednesday morning. Yeah, I love October. Add to this a crystal clear Friday night, a nice fat consulting fee freshly deposited into the bank, a pair of thick filets on the grill, a glass of a good Cabernet in my hand and you may begin to get the big picture. Consider as well that neither Madelyne nor I were working the weekend and you can catch a glimpse of my mental state. Madelyne was in the kitchen cutting up a salad and baking some spuds to go with the fresh asparagus she had put on the stove top with some slivered almonds. I was thinking of building the first fire of the season after dinner. A bright planet had been visible low on the western horizon for some time while I was heating up the grill and now overhead I could see a few of the brighter stars. It looked like Jupiter coming up in the northeast. Madelyne and I had chosen this hilltop in the middle of nowhere just so I could have this magnificent view of the sky. I never got tired of it but sometimes the tiny vampires drove me indoors. I love October.

    I checked the steaks. On a fire this slow, it would take a bit more before a thick filet would need to be turned but you have to check them anyway. It is part of the fun. About that time, I noticed a car coming up the hill. We were not recluses but we but also were not expecting anyone and we built the only house on this hill. I guessed that we would be having company. Damn. As the car got closer to the house, I recognized that my favorite daughter Margaret had come home from school. It could have been worse. It might have been one of our sons and neither of them were vegetarians.

    I turned the steaks over and went to help her with her bag. My beautiful daughter was doing her second postgraduate year in a good physics program at a small but well endowed university about three and a half hours drive away. At least, it took me three and a half hours to drive the distance. The two women in my life have been frequently known to cut that figure down a bit - especially if I, or one of the boys was in the car. I think they just do it to see if they can make us squirm. I had not let it get to me in years. The girls have a bit of an advantage as long as the State Police remained predominately male. I figure that it will catch up with them eventually. I used to drive fast too but then there were many things that I used to do. Car Insurance was already expensive enough. I returned to the grill as soon as the bag and offspring were safely in the house with Madelyne. Yeah, the steaks were done. Hot through and still pink in the middle. I took one last look at the velvety dark sky. Saturn was up at the trailing edge of the constellation of Pisces and I could now tell that Jupiter was at the trailing edge of Aquarius. I already knew from the look on my daughter's face that this steak would not taste as wonderful as I had anticipated. My daughter looked scared.

    I had designed our house to fit where it was. It nestled into the hill like an acorn in its cap although if you will forgive me for saying so, a bit more subtly. It was not even visible from the road as a substantial portion of it was built underground. In spite of my rather major delving, we had managed to save most of the large trees at the lower level of the house. Their tops screened what appeared to be a grassy mound with a deck on one side and a number of rather expensive multi-paned rounded and arched windows of various sizes sticking out at odd intervals and heights. The house itself was built of reinforced concrete but it was impossible to tell this from either the inside or the outside of the house. I have always had a fondness for wainscoting, hardwood floors and solid but somewhat ornate woodwork. I had designed those windows to provide light and selected views of the nice valleys that surrounded our hill. Just for fun, I had designed the family room at the center of the house to function as a solar calendar and in its floor were brass markers where the late afternoon or early morning sunlight would fall on the solstices - morning for the winter solstice and afternoon for the summer solstice. Of course, they only worked if the sky was clear but in the fifteen years we had lived here, it had occurred often enough that it was always fun to wait and see if the chancy weather would come through. The circular fireplace near the center of the room supplied most of the heating required as it had it own heat exchanger in the flue. All five bedrooms had their own windows looking out on a different part of the world. There were small connecting bathrooms between four of the bedrooms a monster with a two-person tub and separate shower enclosure off our bedroom. The lower level consisted of the garage, utility room, shop, storerooms, and pantry. It was such an unusual design that the bankers would have none of it. Because of that, it had always been paid for. The mortgage interest rates were so high when I built it that it would have been nuts to finance it anyway. I was especially proud of the kitchen/ dining room located across the fireplace from my study off the family room. Large with a central island cook top/counter, two of the three entrances to the house entered here. Large high semicircular window facing south acted almost like a skylight and made this the brightest room in the house in any season. This window was very dark when I entered from the deck with the steaks and joined my wife and daughter at the counter. They were finishing the preparation of our dinner and talking quietly. I noticed that they had zapped another potato and had found some zucchini to augment the asparagus and salad upon which, my daughter would insist. I got another glass from the cabinet and filled it with wine for my daughter. After refreshing my wife's and my own glass, I pulled another bottle from the rack and opened it. I left it on the counter to breathe. We helped ourselves to food, grabbed the necessary utensils and sat down to dinner. My suspicions notwithstanding, the steak turned out great along with everything else. We made small talk about the cold snap a couple of days before and what we had or had not heard from my absent sons. By the time that the conversation took on any significance, it was necessary to clear the table for dessert and coffee. We settled into some of Madelyne's chocolate pie and I asked the obvious question. "OK Maggie, What's his name and why have you let him get to you like this?"

My daughter's face, much like my wife's is quite expressive and it instantaneously appeared as if she were attempting to avoid projectile vomiting. "Daddy! What in the world are you talking about?"

"Well, Let's analyze this together. It is Friday night. Fall is your favorite time of the year and don't think that I don't know that one of the reasons is that you get to wear those fuzzy sweaters that emphasize your petite but quite well proportioned figure. Never in your life have you had trouble maintaining your excellent GPA or arranging for one of your admirers to ask you out and spend all his money showing you the best time he could manage. You are not ill and considering the portions of asparagus and zucchini that you put away, it does not appear that you have been recently. We have not heard much from you lately and that is generally the case when things are going even better than usual and you do not really want to fill us in on the details. In addition to the stated observations, let me add the expression on your face when I met you at your car. I do not read minds but I do know when something has you upset. Considering my previous observations regarding your expertise in dealing with your world, I can only conclude that you are up against something that you cannot control. In the light of these facts, I can only conclude that you have met someone that does not love you as much as you think he should. Now tell me his name so I can go beat the crap out of him."

After the thunderous end to my little speech I waited calmly, to hear her refutation and was aghast to see my little girl burst into tears. "Oh, Daddy! It is not a boy or anything like that. I have found out that the world is coming to an end!"

I carefully looked at the bottle of wine that I had opened before dinner and noted that it was still about half full. I immediately poured myself another glass. Margaret had collapsed in tears following her solemn announcement. Madelyne put her arms around the girl and said soothingly, "Of course it is dear. Why don't you tell us all about it." Having determined that my daughter could not be drunk, I began to be concerned. My daughter was not a fool and not given to hysterical or premature conclusions. In the past, her predictions had been very accurate especially when the issue did not depend on the actions of strangers. I sipped my wine, coffee forgotten and waited for Margaret to calm herself.

"As you both know, with a program as small as the one at school, some responsibilities are dumped on the postgraduates. There are some ongoing projects and faculty research, which provide experience for those of us doomed to academia of PhD programs. In addition to my regular course work this year, it fell upon me to continue the deep sky survey they began back in the early nineties. Until the day before yesterday, it had been one of the most boring jobs that I had ever undertaken. The objective is to find and classify long period comets and uncharted asteroids. My job consisted of calling up one screen of CCD data from our automated scope and others around the country and comparing it to earlier screens of the same area of the sky to look for differences. The project was much bigger at one time as they intended to find all the Apollo and Amor class asteroids and map their orbits. My little school is the only one still doing this research. Most of the instruments dedicated for this purpose have now been allocated to variable star observations. Our program is still doing the survey because none of our tenured faculty is into Astronomy and the money they get to continue the study can be diverted into other research. It does not cost them too much to maintain and the labor pays to do it. Our department is best known for work in high temperature semiconductors. As Dr. Taylor told me when he gave me the access codes for the project, "That's where the money is." The old fart has not had an original idea in his career. This morning, I was doing the work thinking about this weekend when I found it. I thought at first that it might be a long period comet but it was so dim at the 26th magnitude that I soon decided that it must be an asteroid. A check of the ephemeris demonstrated it to be uncharted. Apparently, its orbital axis is almost perpendicular to the ecliptic and as things happen, it had a near encounter with Jupiter on its last pass about forty years ago and its orbit has changed. When I calculated its orbit from the previous CCD data, it has become an Apollo. As nearly as I can determine it will hit the Earth about 2:00 PM on July 23 - a little over five and a half years from now. Life as we know it will end."

"Do we have any Scotch left Mad?"

"How should I know, Jake? You are the only one around here who drinks it when Jack is not home. Why don't you go look? While you are there, bring some brandy back with you and a couple of glasses"

I returned shortly with a glass of Scotch, the brandy decanter and two snifters. Margaret was explaining Apollo asteroids to Mad. "You see Mom, an asteroid isn't generally that big a deal. Most of them orbit between mars and Jupiter and do not cause a bit of trouble. There are some however, which have caused a great deal of trouble from time to time. These Apollo asteroids have eccentric orbits and get closer than an astronomical unit to the sun. Even these usually do not cause much trouble. When they pass through the orbit of Earth, the

Earth isn't here."

"Of course the Earth is here, where else could it be?" Mad was getting a little tired and Astronomy was something in which her husband and daughter were interested. She occasionally liked to look at Saturn through the telescope but that was about the extent of it.

"Right Mom, I spoke imprecisely. When the Apollo asteroids pass through the orbit of Earth, generally the Earth is in another part of its orbit. Every hour the Earth travels about sixty-seven thousand miles around the sun. It is extremely unlikely that an Apollo asteroid would happen to pass through the orbit of earth at the same time the earth is also present but given enough time a chimp can strictly at random type the Declaration of Independence. The last time this happened there were dinosaurs living around here. It is a bull's-eye of cosmic proportions. This time the monkey has got our number."

"Did you happen to bring any of this stuff home with you?"

"Still don't trust my arithmetic, do you Daddy? I counted on that so I brought the disks with the CCD data and the one with my calculations."

"Your math has been as good as mine for years Margie, I've just always wanted to look the devil in the eye".

"Well, lets set it up in your study and have a peek at the old boy."

My study is as you might guess my favorite room in the house. It is my professional library, home to my hobbies and a great place to read. I also keep the fastest computer in the house there. There is a small sofa in front of the window, which faces the northeast, and the morning light is good much of the year. I keep a couple of office type chairs at the computer and a venerable leather chair in the corner with a good light and side table. The rest of the room is shelves for books, musical instruments and other things, which change over time. Madelyne got to the couch first and curled up on it so that she had a good view of her daughter and me. I woke up the computer and Maggie appeared with a short stack of DVD's. I got out of the way and let her call up the observational data. "This is the first observation that I could find. It was not actually from our instrument but from one whose funding died before it was reallocated to variable star observations. The CCD imager is actually a high-speed video sampler, which is sensitive enough to detect single photons. This data is great because I can print out composite images but I can also address any point in time during the observation although the image quality suffers and the smaller magnitude stars drop out." She addressed a gadget with the mouse and a small area of the image was enlarged to fill the screen. "You wanted to see the devil, here it is."

Madelyne spoke from the couch to no one in particular, "The dark adapted human eye can detect a single photon." True enough perhaps, but all human eyes in that study were focused on the video display of my computer.

Centered in the screen was a small line. It was not nearly as bright as the stars that surrounded it. "From this you calculated its orbit?"

"Of course not Daddy, I had to use other observations as well."

"Let's see some of the others."

What followed was a series of similar images that demonstrated the motion of the asteroid, as it appeared a small line on the CCD composite images. "Wait, go back one! Can you adjust the interval of the composite?"

She addressed a drop down menu with the mouse and a slider bar allowed her to adjust the length of the time interval of the composite image. The little trace disappeared and some of the dimmer stars disappeared. "I can adjust the sample length like this."

She returned to the previous image and by addressing a gadget with the mouse enlarged the tiny line against a field of stars. "I see what you mean Dad, let's see if we can get a time off this!" She again enlarged the image.

Madelyne came off the couch like a striking snake. "What are you two up to here? That little streak looks like all the others!" She peered into the video screen as if she could require the tiny blip to answer.

"Not quite, Mom. What Dad noticed was that in this image the asteroid appears to pass in front of a star from the perspective of the CCD camera. By analyzing the time the star was covered up we can get a fair idea of how large that rock is!" She enlarged the image once again and now it was clear that a sixteenth magnitude star was behind the trace for a short period of its track. She plotted the entire length of the trace and then adjusted the image once again and measured the tiny spot when the asteroid covered up the star. She then used the numeric entry pad to do some calculations. "Based on the length of the observation, the sampling frequency of the CCD, the length of the track when the star was covered and what I know of the asteroid's orbital velocity, the thing's at least ten kilometers across!"

"Show me your orbital calculations."

Margaret placed another disk in the drive and brought up a graphic program. "This is an ephemeris program. I hook up to the old NASA database every month or so and the positions of the minor planets, comets and artificial satellites are updated. The program itself is close enough for the major planets and their moons." She called up a graphic that showed the solar system from above the plane of the ecliptic and about seven astronomical units out. It denoted the planets with their alchemical symbols and the bright stars and galactic features with numbers and Greek letters. The planetary orbits were pictured as colored ellipses. "This is the system as it appears tonight. I will add the new asteroid as a red five pointed star." She used the mouse to open a menu and the asteroid was visible as a small red star just in front of the imaginary point of view. "Now, I'll project its orbit back as far as I have been able to extrapolate and add the observation points as blue dots. The earliest is five years ago." A dozen or more blue dots appeared above the plane of the ecliptic and were joined by a red line originating with the red star. The red line sloped sharply upward away from the plane of the ecliptic. "Now, I'll extrapolate its path into the future." She pulled down another menu with the mouse and the red line extended down beneath the plane of the ecliptic at a point near the orbit of Jupiter. It came back toward the ecliptic and intersected the green line that represented the orbit of Earth. "Now, I'll show the position of the planets when the asteroid passes through the orbit of the Earth." She addressed another menu and the lines disappeared. The system was then displayed as seemingly unrelated colored points. She then used the mouse to change the perspective and we were treated to views from all sides. It was apparent that the red star and the green dot were superimposed. "Checkmate."

"How accurate is this program Maggie?" This was not my first rodeo and I had seen a few very pretty programs in the past.

"It's as accurate as there is, Dad. I used this program to guide a laser satellite communications project I worked on last semester and at terrestrial distances, it was accurate to within a small fraction of a meter. Over the distances, we are talking about here maybe hundred and fifty kilometers one way or another. The Earth is almost thirteen thousand kilometers across. Even if it is three hundred miles of a six to ten mile chunk of stony iron asteroid will not miss." She altered the display to enlarge the earth and showed the likely area of impact at the South Pole with a ring around it for the expected error.

Madelyne had been quiet during this last bit of explanation but now she spoke up. "OK, so we have a big hole punched in Antarctica. So what! It is going to make a whole lot of crushed ice and might kill a few penguins. It does not look like it gets within thousands of miles of any inhabited areas. Why are you so concerned?"

Margaret got that look on her face that told me that I had

the ball. Madelyne was very intelligent and an excellent physician but her training had not left time for a truly broad exposure. Her main hobbies besides raising our children, keeping me alive and the little bit of cooking that we did together were gardening and reading the occasional romance or mystery. The problem was to give her the necessary information without talking over her head or sounding condescending. It was a familiar high wire act for me and I only fell off from time to time.

"Madelyne, do you remember when Margaret was talking earlier about how the last time this sort of thing happened there were dinosaurs living around here?"

"Of course I remember. It cannot have been more than an hour and a half ago. Do you think I have Alzheimer's or something?" This was not going well.
"No, No, of course not Sweetie, I just thought it might have slipped by in the heat of the discussion."

"I am not stupid, nor am I inattentive! Jake Knight!" This was not going well at all.

"Let me explain, Daddy." There are many reasons why she is my favorite daughter.

"Mom, around sixty-five million years ago this area was very different from the way it is now. Most of the dominant creatures of that era were lizard-like animals that we lump together and call the dinosaurs. One of the big mysteries that puzzled scientist for many years is why after being dominant for hundreds of millions of years did they suddenly disappear. Many ideas were proposed from a change in climate like an ice age, diseases in the dinosaurs or the creatures or plants that they fed upon - the works. Then a scientist discovered that the cretaceous-tertiary boundary - the thin layer of clay above which no dinosaur remains are found - was richer in Iridium than the surrounding soils. He traveled all around the world and found that this was true everywhere. The most likely explanation for this even distribution of a rare element is an even layer of dust containing Iridium over the entire Earth coinciding with the demise of the dinosaurs is that an asteroid several miles across slammed into the Earth about where the Yucatan peninsula is now. There were of course local problems where the impact occurred because these things are traveling about twenty-three thousand miles an hour with respect to the Earth and the kinetic energy released was greater than all the nukes in all the worlds arsenal being detonated at the same time and place. The asteroid and the area where it struck were vaporized and a huge molten hole was opened in the Earth's crust leading to increased volcanic activity over the entire planet. Additionally the dust kicked up high into the atmosphere obscured the sun for years. This killed most of the plant life and the food chains it supported. Because not as much sun reached the Earth's, surface it cooled off quite a bit with glaciers reaching as far south as Louisiana. At least seventy-five percent of all species alive at the time of this disaster became extinct. This included the dinosaurs." Margaret poured herself a sizable glass of brandy and sat down.

Madelyne took her glasses off and cleaned then with a clean white handkerchief she kept for this purpose. "I see." She poured herself some more brandy and faced me from the couch to which she had returned. "Well Jake, How do you intend to deal with this?"

This question from anyone else would have seemed mocking or ridiculous but my wife honestly felt that I could do something to avert the end of the world. My quiet evening at home with my wife had turned into something else altogether. I was saved from making an immediate reply by lights in the drive. I went to the door and greeted my oldest son Jack.

I have never understood my son Jack. I have been told that he and I are just alike but I feel that the similarity people see is like that between a thorn bush and a cactus. We arrive at much the same external expression but we get there by very different routes. Like all my children, he is very comfortable with computers but unlike my daughter and I, he used them for things like spreadsheets, statistics and foreign languages. He used them for other things that he could not discuss with me. We have a strong mutual respect and defer to each other in the areas of our expertise that are comfortably as different as daylight and dark. He had finished school several years ago and had been recruited to work for some obscure branch of the government service that required him to travel a lot - usually at night. His comings and goings were always without notice and I do not know when I had been this glad to see him. "Jack! What a wonderful surprise."

For a young man, my son has very serious eyes and he looked me over as he came in the door and shook my hand. "What's going on? I notice Sis is home."

"Oh, there are a few things that we have to discuss. Can I fix you a stiff Scotch?"

"Thanks, Dad. I will just throw my bag in my room and splash my face. I'll be a minute."

"Join us in my study when you're ready."

I rejoined the girls after I fixed him a drink. When he arrived, he had changed out of his suit into a sweatshirt and khaki pants. He hugged and kissed his mother and sister and then sat on the couch with his mother. "What are you doing here on a Friday night Sis? What's his name and why have you let him get to you like this?"

Rather than a tearful outburst, this question now generated wild hoots and snorts as three somewhat over wrought people allowed their nervous energy to dissipate in laughter. My son first looked confused but then caught the bug and laughed himself. "OK, OK. So what brings you home on a Friday night in sweater season?"

The laughter at this point took on a hysterical quality especially when Madelyne told him, "We are discussing the eminent destruction of life on Earth."

At his outraged expression, the laughter died and the discussion took on its earlier somber quality. "Maggie has discovered an asteroid which it appears will collide with the Earth in a few years. She came home to discuss it with her

Father and I." It was just like Mad to cut to the chase especially when it appeared that our time was so limited.

"Show me what you've got."

Margaret resumed her place at the computer and went back through the evening's revelations. It did not take as long as there were no more discoveries. "We figured out this thing is between six and ten miles across a little earlier. That could be a minimum as we don't have other occultations to determine the axis or orientation as it crossed in front of the star." She then demonstrated the ephemeris program and its prediction of a collision.

"Who else knows about this?" My son's question had occurred to me only minutes before during my daughter's demonstration. He had known about the asteroid a half an hour. Cactus and Thorn bush.

The question took my daughter by surprise. "I don't know, maybe the only people who know are in this room. I am the only student who has access to this data and none of the professors cares enough to look. This data is available only to programs working on the sky survey. I think that we are the last institution with funding.

My son visibly relaxed. "Good, I don't want this information to leave this room."

"What information?" said my youngest son as he entered the room with a glass of milk.

There is that short moment of silence that occurs after the flashbulb goes off. Everybody blinks and their cardiac rhythm resumes. "Where did you come from Bob?" I love my youngest son but I can never predict his actions. Robert and I had the toughest time arriving at an understanding of any of my children. He had left high school early and had taken an equivalency test to enter college. He was only nineteen but already in his junior year at the local university where he was wasting his time in studies of art, history, philosophy and music. He lived with some friends in town and they generally spent their weekends traveling around playing as a band. On top of all of this, his sudden appearance had almost caused me to lose control of my bladder.

"The guys dropped me off at the bottom of the hill when I told them I felt like a little walk in the dark. I love it out here especially when the moon is not up. I came in through the garage door and stopped in the kitchen for a glass of milk. I did not think anyone else was up but with all the cars, when I saw your study light on I just came on in from the kitchen. I did not mean to scare anyone. What is going on?"

"Sorry I snapped at you son. You just scared the pants off me."

Even though Jack wanted to restrict further dissemination of the news, there was never a question of not telling Bob the news. So the CCD data, the asteroid images and ephemeris program were all brought into play for the third time. My youngest son, though not much of a technical whiz, quickly caught on to the significance of the upcoming collision. By this time, it was past midnight and it had been a long time since dinner. For that matter, Bob and Jack had not had any dinner so we all pitched in, made a snack, and sat down at the table to eat. As we sat together and ate, each of us considered the news in silence.

I had my mouth around another piece of Madelyne's chocolate pie and thought about where the water hits the wheel. I was practically certain that I would not be willing to just sit back and let this disaster happen. None of us are the kind of people who would tie one on or take sleeping pills to avoid the issue. For that matter if it could not be avoided, I wanted to be here to spit into the devil's eye. Of course, what I really wanted was something a bit more effective and not some symbolic gesture. "Maybe the government could send a missile and blow it up." It sounded lame to me. I was not alone in this opinion.

"Come on Daddy, If you could get a missile to it in time to do any good and had a nuke big enough to do anything, the best you could expect from a deal like that is to break it into pieces which would still be on a collision course with Earth. The results would be the same." My daughter is so practical sometimes it makes me crazy.

"I don't know Sis, Dad may have something there. If you got the bomb to go off on the right side of the asteroid at the right time, maybe you could change its course - Like a cosmic game of pool!" My youngest son had some familiarity with the game at least - and the optimism and enthusiasm of youth.

"I don't know of a government on Earth that has the type of precision firepower that little trick would require. On top of that is the problem of delivering the payload in time to do any good. From what I understand about orbital mechanics and I am not the guy to ask about that, in order to be effective, it would have to occur with the asteroid at the greatest possible distance from Earth." Jack, as usual had some insight into the virtually insurmountable problems involved.

Madelyne was fingering the edge of the knife she had used to cut the pie, her unfocused gaze on the clock said to no one in particular. "If it were done, when 'tis done, then 'twere well it were done quickly."

"One bomb probably won't be enough. To be most effective the blasts would have to be perfectly placed and be separated in time. Lets get back to the computer." Margaret had been doing some calculations on a scratch pad from a drug company. We went back into the study and she brought up the ephemeris program again.

"I didn't know you knew any Shakespeare Mom!" Robert's focus was fuzzy indeed if he thought that was important right now.

"As I see it the mechanics are moot. No government has the necessary will to accomplish this rescue. Since the collapse of the American Space program after the second shuttle disaster and the splintering of the USSR, the deep space capability of the Earth has been abandoned in the name of deficit reduction. The hardware is out there, but the ground support required to do the job is beyond contemporary budgetary restraints." Although Jack was right, he was occasionally too practical.

"Just because you work for the government Jack, it doesn't mean that it is the source from which all good things flow. Dad is right. A proposal like this would not get out of the steering committee in time to be shot down by the budget nerds. This looks like a job for private enterprise." Robert was obviously getting tired as his associations were becoming more tangential as the evening progressed.

" I think that a manned mission would be necessary to properly place the charges and then double check the results and blast again and again after that if necessary." Margaret was now doing her calculations with the numeric keypad in the ephemeris program.

"I guess with enough money in the right hands, no provision for a ground crew and a whole lot of luck, it might be possible for a private company to do this. The problem then becomes finding an economic incentive to risk capital and lives in what will likely be a one way trip."

"That's not a big problem. Asteroids are made of valuable stuff. The thinking is that there are probably three distinct types - Stony, stony-iron and carbonaceous. This is based on the types of meteorites found on earth. A typical one-kilometer stony iron asteroid contains billions of tons of high-grade steel as the iron contains about five percent nickel. There are also hundreds of tons of platinum, iridium and gold. Separating the materials out would require a few hundred dollars worth of aluminized Mylar to make a parabolic mirror to focus the sun and a good strong magnet. Just vaporize the sample of ore and let the magnet pull all the nickel and iron to one side. I guess you could use a centrifuge to separate the other metals. I haven't thought much about it." Margaret tended to sound like a college professor even when she mentioned things like hundreds of tons of platinum, iridium and gold.

"Hundreds of tons?" Jack was now apparently doing some calculations on his napkin.

"Sure." Margaret had already started to think about something else.

"And you say that this asteroid that you discovered is at least six miles across?"

"Yeah, ten kilometers give or take a kilometer or two."

"Can any of you geniuses think of a way to keep this thing in the neighborhood without it being a menace?" Jack had that glazed look in his eye that he got when he was about to double his stake in the commodities market.

"If we could delay the asteroid by as much as four and a half minutes, it would miss the Earth by a good thousand miles and if we could delay it by five and a half minutes it looks like it would also just miss the moon which would be going away from it in its orbit around the Earth. This would rob it of much of its angular momentum. I don't have a good feel for the mathematics yet but it could be captured by the Earth moon system."

"Maggie, aren't you ignoring the angle of approach? Your first extrapolation of the thing's trajectory has it approaching from the South. To get that lunar braking effect your angle will have to be a lot closer to the plane of the ecliptic."

"No Daddy, that is part of my solution for the five and a half minute delay. If I change the orbit here, "(She indicated a portion of the red curve at about the orbit of Jupiter with the cursor.) "I cannot really do much about the thing's orbital velocity, so I have to make it travel a longer path. Another blast here (She indicated a spot just below the plane of the ecliptic just inside the orbit of Jupiter.) will also change the orbit to be more into the plane of the ecliptic although not quite. It will still come in from the South but now from the South west and it encounters the moon on the way out. As you know the moon's inclination, is about five degrees and the near encounter with Earth will cause it to lose orbital velocity as well as flatten the angle of attack. If we work it right it will be captured into a resonant orbit in the Earth - Moon system."

"So how do you propose to change the orbit of this thing?" By now all sense of reality had begun to recede. Some of the things the kids were saying almost sounded like they could work.

"It is possible that I might be able to obtain the required special explosives from former members of the Eastern Bloc and at a reasonable price-they're still sucking for hard currency." Jack could always surprise me but this is ridiculous.

"What about the problem of getting there Jack?" He still had not realized how impossible this thing was and I needed to bring him back down to Earth.

"Since the collapse of the American and Soviet space adventures there are a number of large rockets available on the market by the pound for scrap. Most of this equipment could be brought back into operating condition by a competent engineer." Once he settled onto something, he was like a pit bull.

"OK, bombs and rockets. What about like support equipment? Living space! The orbit of Jupiter is not just down the street you know. For goodness sake, we would have to survive to get there to do this!" I was beginning to loose my composure in the face of this idiocy.

"Right! So, let me get this straight. We buy a bunch of second-hand nuclear weapons from the ex-Communists, use obsolete and also second hand scrap American and Russian rockets to hightail it out to the orbit of Jupiter where we land on a previously unknown asteroid, dig in and use the nukes to change its orbit and thereby save the Earth and make ourselves ridiculously wealthy in the process!"

"Yep, that about sums it up." Jack had clearly lost his mind. It must have been the shock of learning about the end of the world.

"What do you think the likelihood of success of this stunt is Margie?" All this time she had been doodling with her calculations.

"Dad, if what Jack says is true about the hardware

requirements, I feel that with the right people on the job that there is at least a twenty percent chance of changing the orbit of the asteroid, but we need to get there in the next year and a half or so if the plan is going to work." Margaret had always been inordinately fond of science fiction.

"Bob, would you be crazy enough to go on a stunt like this?" Bob had been taking it all in and in spite of the facts seemed to be taking this lunacy seriously.

"Dad, if you were the design engineer of the project and Sis was doing the numbers to drive the gizmo and Jack handled the acquisition and economics, I would come along if only to wash the dishes and dig ditches." Bob was obviously too gullible. I appealed to the final authority for reason.

" Well, Mad - what do you think?"

"Oh Jake! I knew that you would come up with something! And Robert, I'll wash the dishes, you'll have to hand your father his wrenches."

The room seemed to spin and my eyes started to unfocus - and I really had not had that much scotch. The clear light of reason was revealed as a suicidal trap. All my skepticism had done was force my children into the type of hard precise thinking the situation required. "Well, Madelyne, I guess we better put the house on the market. I think we are moving away." And that was that.

Chapter Five
The Best Laid Plans of Mice and Missiles

T-Minus 00:09:05:07:15

Well, the night was pretty much burned through by the time that discussion ended. It was somewhere on the far side of the wee hours of the morning when the kids finally went to their rooms with the earlier doom and gloom totally dissipated. I was almost totally exhausted, as Mad and I got ready to get into bed. It was all I could do to floss, brush my teeth and splash my face. The evening had turned out so differently than I had planned. It was like a new day in spite of all that. I had gone from despair to a keen edge of excitement all in the space of a few short hours. How odd that all of our children had picked tonight of all nights to come home for their various reasons. As in everything else, there was probably more here than met the eye. I mentioned it to Madelyne but she said nothing - she was brushing her teeth at the time. She was acting as excited as the kids and I had not seen her like this in years. She was not getting old but she was getting set in her ways and this news had busted the rust off the threads. As I reflected on it, my threads must have gotten rusty as well. I have always loved a new project and I was as excited as the kids myself. Too soon in the job to have made any mistakes and always the challenge of avoiding them. I had a few little tricks left up my sleeve and wanted to get up early for some "me time" to work out the jams. I loved my house but it was clearly time to be moving on.

"What in the world are you thinking about Jake?"

Madelyne was as usual curled up against my back.

"The end of the world, and the beginning of the new one. You know, there are many things about this world I would change but wiping out as much as seventy five percent of all life would not be how I started. I guess I would be more selective."

"Yeah, me too. I can think of a few people I would wipe out but I guess I would rather have the option of them never being born."

"You're not talking about abortion are you?"

"Now Jake you know that I don't agree with abortion being used as birth control but you know I also don't think that the choice a woman makes regarding it is any of the government's business. What I was really talking about was a little button that I could aim at someone and they never would have been conceived. That being the case, I of course would forget that I had pushed the button. Murder without personal guilt."

"Wait Mad. If the button caused them never to have been born then you would not have forgotten pushing the button, you never would have pushed it. The reason for pushing the button would never have existed so you would never have to push it. No guilt because no murder."

"That's better than I thought Jake. Why don't you figure out how to make me one of those?"

"Don't be silly Mad. You are forgetting I know how unreasonable you are when you are angry; furthermore, I am not the least bit suicidal. Now go to sleep. We have lots to think about in the morning."

"Now Jake, you know I never get that angry with you." Things suddenly got very friendly and sleep was further delayed.

Saturday morning was one of those beautiful fall days that happen after the middle of October. There was a light frost in the early morning hours, which burned off by, nine-thirty or so. I confess this is only hearsay from my testimony as I slept right through it. Madelyne had already gotten up and around. I was finally awakened by the smell of a coffee pot left on after most of the coffee is gone. It was unfortunate that instead of awakening to the wonderful smell of fresh coffee it was to the stench of that thick black sludge that I began my day. I got up, pulled on some sweat pants and a shirt, and went into the kitchen to keep my house from burning down. I managed to rinse the pot before it needed to be scrubbed and made a fresh pot. I ate a bowl of cereal and took my coffee into my study where I found my family freely associating around my computer. Displayed on the screen was what appeared to be a technical drawing of the Space Shuttle External Tank. "Where did this come from?"

Jack looked as fresh as if he had had a full night's sleep. "I accessed a secure database that I knew about." Secure database and Jack knew about it - big surprise.

"So how recent is this information?"

"This is from the last manufacturing run about four years ago."

"Are these specifications accurate?" A good stiff dose of doubt helps keep you alive longer.

"As far as my sources indicate, only the fact that there is probably even less thickness of aluminum - an artifact of the design." Jack seemed to have his feet on the ground this morning. I began to wonder if this idea might actually work.

"What about thrusters?" This was the aspect of the plan that worried me the most.

"I think that I can get the two remaining Energiya boosters for a few million Rubles and I think that I can get a few Solid Rocket Boosters for a few hundred thousand dollars each." Jack related these numbers with an absolutely straight face.

"A few million Rubles. A few hundred thousand dollars. Right! What are you thinking of Jack! I can't get that kind of money together in a lifetime much less a few months!" I also had to consider that those boosters would only get us the first couple of hundred miles certainly not all the way out to the orbit of Jupiter.

"Well, that's where I come in. In my capacity working for the department of the government that I do, I come across information that if generally known would change the face of international business. I have access to information that if powered by a relatively small chunk of hard capital could rapidly snowball into the kind of money that we need. How much do you think you could get your hands on in the next forty five days?"

"I had to think about that. I had a couple of hundred thousand stashed away in mutual funds. Additionally, I had about sixteen patents that I had licensed but which were still marketable to the right concerns. Then there was this house, a few good stocks and Madelyne's parent's farm which was currently leased. When Madelyne's parents died a few months apart a few years back, we did not have the heart to sell the farm. That did not mean that we could not. For that matter, the man leasing it had been hinting around that he might be interested. " I guess that if I could sell everything for the right price and soon, I might be able to get near two million dollars."

"That's just about what I figured. I feel that I can turn that into six million in the next four months - if I do not get caught. I feel like we can get most of the stuff we will have to have for about four and a half million which would leave a million and a half for bribes and emergencies. Now all you have to do is figure out how to get us there alive and keep us that way until we can set up housekeeping." I guess the biggest thing about my son Jack is that having said this, I actually believed that he could turn a quarter into a dollar if given a little time and half a chance. The real issue to me at this point was whether we as a family had the true desire to take on this responsibility. It would mean many months of hardship and scarcity. Add to this incredible danger with death lurking behind every door and window - if we could have a window.

"Have you kids really given this whole idea enough thought?"

At this, my youngest son jumped off the couch. "What do you mean Dad? Didn't we settle all this last night?"

"Sure, we said some things last night, but in the clear light of day do you still want to try to do this? Last night, it was two in the morning and everyone had been traumatized by the news. Now everyone has had a chance to sleep on it and I wonder if we are all thinking the same way."

There was silence and everyone seemed to settle into their seats. Thoughtful expressions appeared on every face. After a moment, Jack was the first one to speak. "You're right Dad. Let's reexamine the issues and then decide if this is the best course."

"As I see it, if we do nothing, the world will end in about five and a half years. Is there any discussion or differing opinions?" I did not want to get lost in extraneous details right now. If I had to save the world, I would steal the money or anything else I needed to do what must be done. I really needed to know how deep we were willing to dig.

"We pretty much decided that there was no government on the planet with the will or means to accomplish the deed. I think this is the primary reason we decided to take on the job ourselves." Bob could hit the nail on the head from time to time.

"The Congress has been in gridlock for the better part of two decades. Even if the Executive branch and the ruling Legislative bodies are of the same political party they can't seem to do anything except travel first class and eat well. From an analytical standpoint, this seems to be a result of the corruptibility of our elected officials in the face of unchecked lobbying by the myriad of special interests. From a rational standpoint, even the constituencies that those guys represent constitute special interest of a regional nature. They are so busy trying to maintain their own pork barrels that the overall needs of the nation go largely unaddressed. They are so intent on their reelection that none of them has the guts to make an unpopular decision even if that is what the country needs most. Most of

the electorate is thoroughly convinced that their politicians are corrupt but they just hope the old crooks are senior enough to keep the local Federal money dump working. The result of this unenlightened self-interest is uncontrolled deficit spending without any major initiatives and most revenue absorbed by the entitlement programs. Although a superpower by default, the United States has become almost a third world country by the continued deterioration of the educational system, the decay of moral values and the oppression of the productive part of society by a tax structure which punishes initiative and rewards inaction. Of course this is just one man's opinion."
"Well, Jack, I think that most of us can agree with you in principle, the point being that Congress can't seem to decide whether to tie its own shoes much less arrive at a plan during a crisis!" Madelyne had her own feelings about the state of the government having more to do with emotional distaste rather than analysis.
"I think we would be foolish to count on the United States doing anything not so much because of the continued gridlock, but rather because of the lack of national will. During the development of jet aircraft, test pilots were killed left and right. I'm not saying that is anything to be proud of, it's just that after the moon missions and maybe this had something to do with losing the war in Vietnam, let something happen or someone get killed in space and the national reaction is to shut the whole thing down as if we can live in a risk free society. It got to the point that they would delay a shuttle launch for any reason whatsoever and those incredibly complicated machines had so many fail-safes that they would shut themselves down as often as not. After the second one blew up, the whole thing, shuttle, and space station - the works were just canceled. The USA just can't do the job." Margaret had wanted to be like Sally Ride when she was a little kid and she was still a bit bitter about not being able to.
"What do you think Bob?"
"Well, I agree with Jack and Sis, but I think some of

these things are symptoms rather than causes in themselves."

"What do you mean?" I never knew where Bob was coming from - our educations and interests were so different.

"I think that the problem is much simpler than Jack and Sis say. Jack called it deterioration in the educational system and moral decay augmented by individual corruption in the congress. I think that the Senators and Representatives are in fact good representatives of the people that elected them. The problem is that they are just like them in terms of their strengths and weaknesses. They are so poorly educated for the most part as to be unable to understand that this danger exists much less arrive at a workable plan for averting it. They are so busy looking out for themselves in terms of getting reelected and staying out of jail that they do not have time to deal with other people's problems anyway. They are just like the average person on the street. The difference is that the average person on the street would not be elected because his shortsightedness, venality and lack of care for his fellow man have not been carefully covered up by the political publicity machines that a true politician grows around him or herself. We would not vote for someone like us so we elect a fantasy image without the political problems that a genuine character would generate. People with real character do not want to be put through the scrutiny of which election campaign consists. This is where I think that Sis's notion of a national will comes in. When all those test pilots were dying, it was classified. Therefore, not in the national news. When an Astronaut dies, it is instantaneously seen all over the world. It is a difficult thing to see men and women to die and the average person cannot do it even if it needs to be done. The fact remains that because of our obsession with publicity the United States is now paralyzed in the public arena. The only people in the government who can get things done are people like Jack and they do not talk about it. The Brits have some good stuff but no manned capability. This is also true of the Japanese and Indians. The French are as bad off as the United States and were not as well set up in the first place. The Chinese will do it when they have the technology. They have the more casual regard for human life required for difficult choices as demonstrated by their draconian birth control program. They do not currently have the technology - thank goodness. This leaves the former members of the Soviet Union. They pretty much have the technology, casual regard for human life and a strong national will. The problem is of course that they have been killing each other for years and they no longer have the organization. For Gosh sakes, they let their space station burn up in the atmosphere just as the Americans did Skylab. I think we are pretty much on our own." I am going to have to stop underestimating my youngest son. That was the analysis that Jack had thought of but not spoken.

"OK, if we don't do it, it won't get done. Does everyone agree? Lets see a show of hands." I put my own hand up but there were already four hands in the air. "OK, I guess that settles that. Now what about the issue of secrecy?"

Jack was off the couch in an instant. I do not think that keeping this a secret is an issue! We decided last night not to let this information go any further!"

"We did not discuss it. You suggested that it remain our secret and no one said anything. I think that we should be more careful than that and I think that we need to talk about why. Why don't you share your reasons with us." Jack was accustomed to working in an environment where decisions about secrecy were automatic and I wondered if he had actually considered why it should be so in this instance.

"For one thing, if this information became public knowledge or even a state secret my name would be bound inextricably to it. If this happened, I would not have the freedom to use my classified information sources to make the money necessary to finance the project. The other thing that occurs to me is that if this were more generally known, the people who know the most about it would be silenced or discredited. The government has a big stake in maintaining order. I think if people knew the world was about to end that civilization as we know it would end first."

"Does anyone have anything else to add?" A cold silence filled the room as the reality of the need for absolute secrecy became almost palpable.

"OK, I think that Jack is right on the need for secrecy. We are going to be breaking all manner of international laws and until we are out of reach of the admittedly hamstrung governments of Earth, we could be stopped at any time. I felt that we should have this discussion now before we got into the design phase in order to insure that the need for secrecy was clearly understood by everyone involved. We will all have to make some sacrifices. For example, I would really like to discuss this with my brother Charles but that is clearly out of the question. In order to maintain the security of my design files I will now take my computer off line. Maggie, did you bring all the information regarding this with you from school?"

"I believe that I did. I also took steps to make sure that this is the only copy."

"And you didn't discuss this with anyone before you told us?"

"No. Not specifically."

"Not specifically? What do you mean not specifically?"

"I discuss my work with Tom and he would figure out that something was up because I didn't talk to him before I left yesterday. "

"Tom White?" Unfortunately, the name was too familiar.

"Yeah, Tom. He and I have been seeing one another again. I am sure he would know that I was upset. I was supposed to call him last night. With all the discussion, it slipped my mind." There was something that my daughter was not telling me.

"Of all the people that you could have involved, Tom White! The man may be a pretty good chemist but anyone who leaves my daughter hasn't got sense enough to know when to get on the bus!"

"I don't think we would have broken up if you hadn't thrown him out of the house last Christmas!" Was I never going to hear the end of that?

"I think that you overreacted then and I told you so at the time Jake. Margaret and Tom were just lying on the couch in front of the fire watching *Miracle on thirty-fourth Street* when you burst in as if you were insane, grabbed him by the scruff of his collar, and threw him out! You would think that you could trust your own daughter!" Madelyne had never objected to Tom and actually seemed to approve of the scumbag.

"It wasn't my daughter I didn't trust. Besides, I apologized to him."

"Yeah, right, you apologized to him four months later when you saw him at his paper presentation!"

"He seemed to take it fine."

"As a member of the associate faculty, you had just presented him with a fellowship grant to continue his work in colloidal dynamics of nanosystems. What was he going to do, punch you out?"

"Well, he would have had a tough time with that!"

"Lighten up Jake! He is not nearly as bad as you make him out to be. In many ways he reminds me of you at that age and my Dad couldn't trust you either!"

"Must you also twist the knife, Madelyne?" At this, she giggled as I hoped she would. "It's possible that I may have misjudged the boy but he let himself in for it. It may be he is the best guy in the world but Tom White is one of the last people I would like to have involved in this venture!"

"Did someone mention my name?" At this, Tom White strolled into my study as if he owned it. "I pulled into the drive a minute or two ago and when there was no answer to my knock, I came on in."

"There is a doorbell you know!"

"Knock it off Jake! Tom, it is good to see you. I am glad that you could come. We were expecting you earlier this morning."

"We were?" You could have blown me over with a Japanese fan.

"You're not still mad at me are you, Mr. Knight? Say, Isn't that the Space Shuttle External Tank?" Of course, the top-secret display of the American Space hardware was still on the screen. Tom walked over and studied it more closely.

"Why Tom, of course he's not. That is just the shape of his face. Bob, help Tom with his bags. I will get lunch ready. There are some things that we need to discuss." Madelyne had a way of putting people at ease and taking charge in social situations. We had another houseguest and no one seemed to be surprised but me. Maybe there was more than the one program than the one that I knew about here at conspiracy central. Jack came over as everyone else left my study.

"Dad, I think that Tom would make a good addition to the crew."

"Is everyone snowed by this guy but me?"

"Dad, you are the only one that can't see the problem here. Margaret has been in love with that guy as you call him since her freshman year. Probably, the only reason why they have not married is that you seem so dead set against him and your daughter respects your opinion. In this matter, your opinion is a waste because no one is ever going to be good enough for your little girl. You have therefore never given the guy a chance. All that aside, Tom is a world-class industrial biotechnologist that even I know about professionally. I am not sure Sis would come along on this little trip without him. I have spent some real time with the guy, he checks out, and he is not afraid of a fight. That is why he is here today."

"My little girl is in love?" Was it getting hot in here?

"Wake up Dad, and smell the roses or you're going to end up with a snoot full of thorns. And Dad, I think he's wise to the fact that something is going on."

"OK, I'll try to give him the benefit of the doubt."

"He'll meet you at least halfway. I like the guy and I

wouldn't settle for anyone not first rate for my little sister." Knowing as little as I did about what Jack did, if he did not like him, he might not be here.

"Well, let's go and get some lunch and I'll try not to count the spoons."

All things considered, it would have been difficult to keep our business a secret from Tom. While we were having lunch, Steve Griffin, the realtor that Madelyne had called before I got up as I remembered while in my sleeping stupor, came in to get our signatures on the listing contract for our house. Steve was a real go-getter.

"You're putting your house up for sale?" Tom had an instinctive grasp of the obvious.

"Yep." A difficult thing to deny when the man asking the question has just seen you sign the listing contract.

"Well, the world must be coming to an end!" When nobody laughed, I knew the jig was up. He looked uncomfortable and I could almost hear the wheels turning.

"Tom, after lunch, there are some things that we need to talk about." There was no sense in ruining the enjoyment of a perfectly good sandwich.

"Sure." He still looked uncomfortable and the normal mealtime conversation just was not happening. I washed down the last of my sandwich and stood up.

"Want to go for a walk Tom?"

"A walk sounds great."

"We will be back after a while." Tom and I walked out into the October sun.

There are few things as wonderful as a fall afternoon in the hills. The fall colors were at peak and the sun was warm with a cool breeze. A few white clouds scudded across an otherwise perfect sky. We headed down the path into the valley behind the house.

"Tom, I don't recall hearing much about your family."

"That's because there is not much to say. My parents were both only children who married late in life and so I never had close relatives. When I was fifteen, they were both killed in a car accident. I finished high school the following year while the state was still arguing about who should have custody. When I went to college on scholarship after graduation, I was able to argue that I was an emancipated minor. The probate judge who heard the case took a liking to me and agreed that the only restriction was that I would not receive my full inheritance until I turned twenty-one. He personally held the estate in trust for me until I came of age. He would not take a fee and he made that money work hard. If you have heard me say anything about anyone, it was probably about the Judge. He turned everything over to me year before last when I couldn't get him to manage it anymore, but I still call him from time to time to talk and see how he is getting along. I still don't like to talk about my parents."

"I'm sorry, Tom, I didn't know any of that. What are your intentions regarding my daughter?" We were making our way toward the little creek. He stopped and looked me right in the eye.

"There is no point in beating around the bush is there Mr. Knight. Maggie and I want to get married. The biggest reason that we have not already is that you have always been so negative. I do not know what the problem that you seem to have with me but frankly; I am getting real tired of maintaining a fiction that Maggie and I are just dating. Everyone else knows that she and I have been engaged for over two years. Your wife asked me here this weekend and got Bob and Jack to try to be here because she wanted to get this settled. I have wanted to talk this over with you and kept hoping your attitude would soften up - looking for a good time to do so. The last time Maggie invited me to your house, you threw me out!"

"Well, Tom, why haven't you gotten married as you both wished. Margaret is of age and you did not need my permission."

"Would you have wanted to start out a marriage like that? Knowing that your wife's father who she is crazy about cannot stand you? I have tried to be patient but I was determined to talk to you soon. I appreciate your saving me the trouble. So, what's it going to be? Are you going to be a horse's ass or are you going to let your daughter know that it is all right to do what she wants to do?" He was a little overcome and I think a little surprised by his own outburst. He turned and we both continued toward the creek. We walked without speaking, only the rustling of the leaves breaking the peace of the little valley. It is always easy to see where the mistakes that you make are when you look at them through the rear view mirror. Tom was smart, direct and obviously in love with my daughter.

"Tom, I haven't been as intelligent about you and Margaret as I should have been. As you may someday know, there is not a man born that is good enough for your daughter. I hope that you can forgive me for the foolish way I have treated you in the past."

"Of Course, Dr. Knight. I think I can guess how you felt. I have always admired you and your work and thought that we could work this out sometime. So, It's OK with you if Maggie and I got married?" He stuck out his hand and I took it.

"I guess that you better call me Jake, Tom. As far as you and Margaret getting married is concerned - you need to discuss that with her." I looked at the red and gold maple leaves floating downstream in the creek. I turned away and we started back toward the house.

"What's all this about you selling your house? This is one of the neatest places that I have ever seen. You can't have found something better."

I looked around at the green valley gleaming in the fall sun and the colors of autumn afire on the hills around us. "After you talk to Maggie and that gets settled, we have a few more things that we need to discuss." We walked back up the hill to the house.

Soon there was cause for celebration. Even though it was before the usual cocktail hour, we broke out the Champaign that Madelyne had been saving for this occasion and when that was gone, the boys started on beer. My soon to be son-in-law looked a whole lot better with a smile on this face. I shook his hand again. "Have you discussed when this wedding is going to take place?"

"Why don't we finish our discussion?"

He was right. "Let's go into the study." The party then moved into the study. The seating was beginning to get a little tight in there but Tom and Maggie insisted that one seat would do. "Margaret, why don't you start?"

My daughter told the whole story up to our late night meeting with her data disks and the ephemeris program. At that point, Jack began with our plan and reasoning about how we were going to save the world. He left off with his plan to boost our money supply with his secret sources of information and our decision that absolute secrecy would be required. "Of course, that doesn't apply to you Tom." It was my turn.

"As you all know, the biggest of the logistical problems we face is being at the right place at the right time. It is a long way out to the orbit of Jupiter and we do not have as much time as we might like to get there. The Voyager space probes required a minimum of two years to arrive at Jupiter's orbit and they did not have to slow down. They just flew past. We on the other hand have to rendezvous and dock with an asteroid. That means that we have to match its orbital velocity exactly as well as being there at the same time that it is. We could of course wait for it to match its velocity to ours but avoiding that is the point of this discussion. As we speak, the Earth and Jupiter are on the same side of the sun. This is totally beside the point as Jupiter will be nowhere near the asteroid when we get to it. The chemical rockets that we have talked about acquiring will only get us the first couple of hundred miles. They won't do much at all toward getting us out where we need to be."

"What do you mean Dad? I thought that the boosters we were talking about were the most powerful that currently exist." This was well beyond Jack's areas of expertise.

"Right you are Jack but they also burn enough fuel in

arriving at low Earth orbit they become only so much scrap metal when they arrive there. There is simply no way of getting enough fuel into orbit to fly one of those rockets to the orbit of Jupiter. What we need is a more subtle approach. Do any of you remember when you were kids when I worked for the government before I became an independent design consultant?"

"Sure Dad, we lived out west in the middle of the desert and you never talked about what you did for a living." Jack of course would remember the most.

"I was working on particle beam weapons for a big group of projects known as the Strategic Defense Initiative."

"Wow, you worked on Star Wars?" Bob of all people was the only one who seemed excited.

"It was a major waste of money for what I know about it which is more than most. But one of the things I worked on may be of some use here."

"Wait a minute Dad, I thought we were going to grab this thing, not blow it up!" Jack was clearly not pleased.

"Son, the things that I worked on wouldn't have blown your nose, much less an asteroid. At the most, it would have made it a little radioactive. It may have a bearing on our most serious problem - how to get there."

"Perhaps you had better explain what you're talking about Jake." Madelyne was becoming a little impatient.

"OK, what is a rocket?"

"It's a reaction engine. It pushes by expelling the mass of burning fuel out one side. The faster the fuel burns, the harder the rocket pushes." Jack had to prove that he knew something about it.

"Right, but your definition is a little too sharply limited. You can get the same effect by using compressed gas, firing a bullet or any number of ways. If we were ice skating together and I pushed you away, it would be much the same effect as a rocket."

"All right Jake, cut to the chase. What's all this about

rockets and particle beam weapons?" Madelyne was becoming more impatient.

"OK, the essence of rockets is reaction mass. In order to push something away you must first have it with you. You increase the efficiency of your reaction mass by pushing it away faster. Chemical rockets are good for short powerful bursts like those that you need to get into orbit. However, they are too inefficient to use in a long haul like that we are discussing. What I am thinking about is something brought home to me while I was working on particle beam weapons. If you accelerate a subatomic particle to some appreciable fraction of the speed of light, it acquires relativistic mass. Depending on how close to the speed of light that you push it, that can be quite a bit of mass. One of the things that we developed in the project was an assemblage of particle accelerators that could be put into a fairly small space that could accelerate protons to a good percentage of the speed of light." I walked over to the computer and put one of my own disks in the drive. I then called up a graphic. The device looked like a pile of pancakes arranged in a doughnut shape. "Each of these sets of Ds is a separate proton accelerator. These are the injection ports on this side and on the opposite side are the ejection ports for all seven hundred accelerators. Over the years, I have been tinkering with this design. The original idea was separate pulses to be used as a weapon. With all the recent advances in high temperature super conductors, I think that I have worked out the bugs for making it capable of operating continuously."

"You want to use a failed particle beam weapon as a rocket?" Jack was going to have to get the idea of not letting his mouth hang open. It was so unbecoming.

"It's just a much more efficient ion rocket. These guys wanted to use the thing to punch hole in missiles or scramble their guidance systems with the secondary radiation it would cause when it hit the casing. In addition, they wanted to do it from the ground. All the protons tended to collide with air molecules going through the atmosphere and the kinetic energy was lost like the cue ball hitting the racked balls in a game of pool. It was a dumb idea for a weapon but it would make a fine rocket if it operated continuously. Depending on how much stuff we can take with us, we might be able to accelerate a decent fraction of a gravity for months at a time. There are no moving parts!" I always wondered if this little doodle would be of any use.

"You can't get something for nothing Dad. This gizmo is going to use a lot of power." Margaret's practicality had its basis firmly in the laws of thermodynamics.

"Of course it will, Maggie, That is why we will need this nuclear reactor to make it go." At this point, I called up a small nuclear plant modeled on those used on submarines and aircraft carriers. "I'll have to make some changes so it could operate in micro gravity and I may have to change to liquid sodium for coolant - but it makes for a more efficient heat exchange."

Maggie was once again looking like she was just managing to avoid throwing up. "Dad! This thing is going to put out enough radiation to cook us all. I might want to keep my hair or intestinal lining or even have kids someday! We would have to take enough shielding to sink an aircraft carrier!"

"Maggie, you are not thinking three dimensionally. We only have to shield it on one side."

"A foot of lead is going to be mighty hard to get off the Earth even if you only have to shield one wall."

"That's the beauty of the whole plan! The rocket uses protons that we get from water which we will use for part of our shielding and which will also supply our oxygen and will be useful for other things."

She thought it over for a minute. "Dad, this might work!" At least I had won my daughter over.

Bob laughed. "OK, let's lay it out. We buy boosters for scrap and second hand nuclear weapons from the ex commies, outfit a space shuttle external tank and strap on a particle beam weapon to get to an asteroid so we can save the world and become very wealthy!"

""Where do I sign up?" For a man about to be married and just learned about the impending end of the world Tom seemed to have things together.

"You just did." He might work out after all.

"I do have a few things to contribute." He said as he dumped Maggie into the chair and stood up. " One is Financial. My parent's insurance policies were each a million dollars. The Judge was a financial wizard and while he had charge of it and I have not done too badly since. I can get my hands on about four million in the next forty-five days."

"With that kind of money I could have thirty million in four months! We can go first class if Dad's toys do not cost too much! Jack was clearly pleased with the news.

"I had no idea that my future son-in-law was so well heeled! You are going to be a major shareholder!"

"Well when we start this business we'll have to put my name first." He was laughing while he said this.

"Great idea!" Bob was suddenly enthusiastic. "We'll call it White Knights Inc." Which of course, is what we did.

Chapter Six

Coffee, Eggs Benedict and Particle Beam Weapons

T-Minus 00:09:04:22:17:13

I have generally liked Sunday Mornings. There are of course the exceptions. Let's review the facts. I had been told by my favorite daughter that the world was coming to an end in the not too distant future and found out that this same favorite daughter was in love and soon to be married to a young man that I had thrown out in the not so distant past. On the good side, there seemed to be a way that we could forestall the end of the world and possibly profit thereby. My daughter's fiancé had seemed to take my apology to heart but this was shortly after he called me a horse's ass. I have in the past borne a passing resemblance to that portion of equine anatomy but like most people am distressed to have this fact pointed out. On top of these concerns, I found myself almost liking the guy. I guess on reflection that he didn't actually refer to me as a horse's ass but questioned me on whether I would continue acting like one. I suppose that a true semanticist would be interested in drawing a clear distinction between those expressions of distaste but I have never cared for those dweebs myself. On the downside, we had stayed up much too late again and I had continued to drink beer as if I were twenty three. Such behavior has its cost and I was paying it this beautiful sunny morning. When the kids are in the house it is one thing. With my daughter's fiancé in the house, I had house guests. I know persons of average intelligence easily recognize the difference. Personally, I was having trouble opening my eyes wide enough to recognize where I might have left my pajamas and housecoat. Madelyne was in at least as bad shape as I was but even less adept at rising in the morning. This is because she(despite her great beauty) required more repair in the morning. I having less with which to work (not referring to sheer bulk of course) had less to lose in the way of face. So it was I, the man of the house who turned his aching frame from his warm bed and his attention to the preparation of the "House Guest Breakfast". I cranked my eyes open and stumbled into the kitchen attempting howsoever clumsily to preserve the peace of my home in the process. I generally like Sunday Mornings.

Few things cut the guff one finds in one's mouth on a morning such as this as a big glass of ice-cold grapefruit juice. Not for me the hair of the dog. I was going to beat this thing with hydration, a big dose of caffeine and a hot nutritious breakfast. I loaded the larger of the two coffee pots with a stout charge of high ethyl Sumatra Manheling. I then began to prepare Hollandaise sauce. I am not a cook. A cook is someone with training and experience in the preparation of food. Consider the game of pool. A good player can consistently make the shots from where ever on the table he finds the cue ball. Then there are those who can line up the balls precisely in a certain way to be able to sink them all in one shot. It is a neat trick that has very little to do with the game of pool. I can make some of the best eggs Benedict in the civilized world. I am not a cook. My daughter, who determined to be a vegetarian while in her teens, cannot resist my eggs Benedict - although she insists that I make hers without the Canadian bacon. She usually will not eat eggs.

It was with musings of this sort occupying my thoughts and the preparation of English muffins, eggs and sauce and Canadian bacon occupying my hands. Suddenly, a shout rang out shattering the morning calm and what was left of my composure. "Is there anything that I can help you with?" My future son-in-law had awakened.

My nerves, somewhat soothed by the small routines offered by the performance of my single culinary trick once again tightened to just a half a squeak below design tolerance. I realized as the echoes decayed that Tom had spoken at a normal volume. Tom, not being a regular member of the household, had chosen to sleep on the large couch in the family room just off the kitchen. The guest bedroom, the only one not occupied by one of my children adjoined my daughter's bedroom through the bathroom. He continued to demonstrate good sense. "Sure, Tom." I croaked in the voice of abused disuse. "Why don't you set the table?"

"Sure." Tom set about putting plates and glasses on the table along with silverware. When he finished, he came back around the island and watched me. "You know, Jake, I think that I see a problem with your ion rocket idea."

He had thought of a problem. As if there were not at least a hundred and fifty problems that I couldn't help but see if I wasn't trying to look on the bright side. It was actually still a little too bright in here. The main trouble with Eggs Benedict is getting everything ready at the same time. I had worked out a neat trick using the microwave that allowed me to serve it all hot but my daughter's future husband sounded so sincere that I determined to get a little old fashioned for the purpose of hearing him out. "How do you like your coffee?" First things first.

"I like the first cup white and sweet if it is real coffee. Any later ones, I like black. I always doctor instant coffee."

"I guess I would too if I ever drank instant coffee. You know, that is false advertising. It is not instantaneous. Besides, anything worth having is worth waiting a bit for, don't you think?" I made the required number of cups as indicated and carried them around to the counter and sat down. "What's on your mind Tom?"

He took a long sip after blowing across the top of the cup and smiled appreciatively. He paused and appeared to carefully consider his words, as I am sure he did. "I foresee a problem with your ion rocket and I am not sure how you are going to get around it. As I understand your concept, you intend to use particle accelerators arranged in parallel to expel protons at near relativistic velocities. From what I recall of the process, you ionize the hydrogen and use a strong magnetic field and alternating currents to push and pull the protons around a spiral path until they reach a critical velocity and escape at your exit port."

"That's pretty much the story, Tom. With the arrangement I showed you last night, there are certain economies in the number of superconducting magnets required and as opposed to the terrestrial situation, a good vacuum is not a problem. What is the problem that you see?" My journeyman project as an engineer had been the design of machines of this type and it would be interesting to hear what type of problem this young pup thought he saw.

"The problem is the electrons that you striped off those protons. On Earth, you could always just let them go into the big electron sink that the planet provides. This thing that you are talking about is going to build up a hell of a charge with no way to ground it. I don't like to think about the arc that would form at the nearest approach to anything larger than a grain of sand."

As he was speaking, I realized that I had been a planetary chauvinist. I had not given a thought to balancing the charges induced by my little device. Getting rid of the excess electrons would be as easy as Tom had noted. It would be all too easy to zap a lightning bolt of electrons at the site of nearest approach of any nearby body. On top of that, we would be carrying around an excess of Oxygen that I had intended to store pressurized in containers around the ship to use for propellant. In my mind formed an image of my little family charred beyond recognition floating next to a giant asteroid as it slammed into the Earth. "I see what you mean Tom. Thanks for bringing this to my attention." Maybe it was not too late to reconsider the hair of the dog.

"Jake, I thought of this right after you mentioned using an ion rocket and it worried me all night. I may have a suggestion of what to do about it. If you located a metal object at some distance from the ship and put some sharp points on it, you could bleed off the charge gradually - like a lightning rod." There was something to what the boy was saying but I had a good idea that it could be improved upon.

"Tom, my boy you are absolutely right but I think that we should do more than just bleed that charge away with this addition you are suggesting!" I had begun to get excited. We stepped into my study and I powered up my computer. I called up the design specifications for the ion rocket/particle beam and began to make some modifications. I drew three insulated cables extending from the accelerator housing back along the ion beam where at a point four kilometers distant they supported a metal ring with tapering metal points extending into the beam. "This thing does build up a hell of a charge. These three connectors led back to ground in the military design. I had forgotten all about them. But look, with this arrangement because we are using protons as our reaction mass, if we pump our excess electrons down to this ring structure, we have added a linear accelerator! I know that this looks long but to a proton traveling at near the speed of light, it is less than an inch. These long pointed rods actually enter the beam and some electrons will be pulled along with the positively charged beam. Otherwise, it will act just like the lightning rod that you suggested. The higher the charge this ring has the bigger the kick the linear accelerator will add to our acceleration!"

"Do these cables weigh very much?"

"They are insulated superconductors, the insulation weighs more than the cable. A kilometer weighs or I should say masses in at around ten kilograms. Why do you ask?"

"Your original idea has given me another idea. Do you mind?" He slipped into my chair at the computer and began some more modifications. He tripled the number of cables and added cable rings at intervals along the length, shortened them, and then curved them out away from the previous axis of the beam. Then back around to previous axis where they joined in another ring structure. Then he placed a thin tube in the axis that extended from the ring structure back to the ship. "Of course, putting these curves in the beams paths will decrease the efficiency of your accelerator. I have more than tripled the weight because the outside of these cables must now be positively charged. It occurred to me that if your protons are going at relativistic velocities, you could divide them and make them collide and with a squeeze from this super-conducting coil at the juncture, you might fuse some of those protons into helium nuclei. I added this carbon fiber tube to keep the resulting release of kinetic energy from collapsing our cable arrangement. Otherwise, the like charge repulsion should keep it taut"

    I made a sincere effort to close my mouth. Luckily, his attention was on the monitor and he did not see my gaping expression. He had turned my simple little linear accelerator idea into an ion rocket supplemented by fusion. Then another light bulb came on.

    "That gives me another idea, do you mind?" I eased myself into the chair that he vacated and once again modified the wire frame drawing. I added another cable to each of the three sets that he had pictured and then a fourth set so that they were all diametrically opposed and then made them taper toward the ring juncture, to which I added small flanges at each cable set entry. I then added an additional ring sleeve to his design and additional cable rings where the taper was greatest. "This synchrotron bank uses alternating current. The walls of these tubes will be positively charged compared with the proton beams. The charge front, which is negatively charged, will propagate along the entire length of the tapered tubes at a frequency of millions of cycles per second. The entire device will operate like the world's largest vacuum tube. If we taper the beams, we can increase the particle density without the need to increase particle flux. I added these flanges to focus the collision of the beams more accurately. This should increase the number and quality of the collisions. I feel like as long as we are going to have an electromagnetic pulse for every actual fusion event, why not harness it to possibly power the device? The higher the number of effective collisions, the stronger the squeeze applied by this additional superconducting coil, the more increase in the number of effective collisions. It doesn't matter about the plasma density as we are not trying to contain it."

"What is the limiting factor to increasing the proton flux? I think that Tom was beginning to think a lot like me.

"The efficiency of the ionization and the proton separation at the injection ports."

"What would stop you from bleeding some of the power generated in this torus back to the ionizer and the initial particle accelerators?

"Nothing can stop me from doing that. It is just that that end of the rig never produced power before. It occurs to me that by losing the straight tube in the center and varying the length of these cables, we can change the angle of incidence of these collisions from no collision when it will be operating as a simple ion rocket to where the collisions are almost dead on. Then we will be counting on fusion for most of our thrust."

Tom still looked troubled even though it looked like we had just invented a fusion rocket. "What about the eggs?"

"What eggs Tom?" I looked carefully at the drawing.

"The ones I saw you put on to cook before we came in here."

Time has a way of slipping by when you are having fun. When we returned to the kitchen, not only had the eggs cooked until the yokes were green, but all the water had boiled out of the poacher and the small amount of egg white that invariably finds its way into it had burnt to a disgusting mess that had to be scraped out. There was a strong odor of failure in the air. I returned to my tried and true methods and resorted to the microwave. By the time that I had loaded the oven and removed the evidence of my earlier efforts into the sink and garbage, the rest of the family were making their way into the kitchen for juice, coffee and conversation. After a short period, we were all sitting down to breakfast. Madelyne had as usual, cleaned up and looked wonderful. My sons looked like they had slept in one position all night and had their hair sticking up on one side. My daughter looked even better than usual. Personally, I make it a point to not look into a mirror in the morning until I have had my shower. I do not spend too much time looking into mirrors even after that. I like to think that I have hidden charm.

"Daddy, you look terrible this morning. Is your face always this puffy when you get up?" I can always count on my daughter to pull my threads.

"No dear. Your mother beat me up last night after you kids went to bed. Tom, as you can see, you have a wonderful life ahead of you. Speaking of that, when are you going to tie the old knot?" Always take the war to your opponent or for that matter any convenient ally.

"Tom looked up with his mouth full and tried to swallow half chewed English muffin. When he had cleared his airway enough to regain the power of speech, he said lamely. "I haven't given it much thought." As I had anticipated, he said exactly the wrong thing. My daughter elbowed him mercilessly.

"We couldn't set a date until we squared things up with you Daddy. I had been thinking that a June wedding would be nice."

"Margaret, if you consider that the sky is falling, do you really want to wait that long to marry? You have been waiting for two years. Besides, if you want your father to give you away, I have been beating him so much lately that I am not sure that he will survive that long." As she said this, giving no warning and moving not a twitch, her delicate little heel made contact with my shin at a surprising velocity. Her assault was completely silent. She never lets me aggravate the children for fun.

"I hesitate to mention this but our schedule is going to be pretty full in the next few months what with our preparing to save the Earth and all. Perhaps you will consider a less formal alternative. Big church weddings, while stylish are expensive and time consuming. We are short on both money and time. It was clear where my son Jack placed importance.

"Gosh Jack, don't you think that you should let Tom and Margaret decide this for themselves? It's not like they are signing up for tennis lessons." Bob, it appeared had some inkling of the dynamic forces involved in this casual little exchange.

"I'm not a big one for ceremonies myself." Tom was about to start learning things about his wife to be.

"Mother, Let's clear the table!" Madelyne leaped to her feet at once and with a sharp meaningful glance at me assisted Maggie in clearing the not quite empty dishes from the table while Tom and my sons looked on in quiet terror. I stood up.

"Well, boys, lets go outside." At this, because the customary quiet time around the breakfast table had been canceled, the male members of the gathering filed out.

It was much warmer than I would have expected for the last half of October and the clear blue skies indicated that it would be warmer yet. The breeze that had been so pleasant yesterday had died down. I stepped out onto the deck with my coffee cup. The boys were not as quick and so appeared empty handed. Tom looked bewildered.

"Tom, have a seat here and let me explain a few things to you. Perhaps you were too young when your father died or I am sure he would have let you in on this. Jack has heard most of this before but Bob, you ought to listen." I sat down on the bench looking off into the south. The moon was visible in its pale daytime apparition almost overhead. Tom sat next to me on the bench and Bob and Jack dragged up some deck chairs and sat down.

"Are you going to explain the fairy tale theory, Dad?" Jack clearly had a clue.

"There are a few simple rules that must be followed at all times with wives, although equally applicable to girlfriends.

Wives are different from girlfriends. If you wish to remain married or in your case ever get married, you must follow the rules. The first and most important rule from which all the others are derived is MAINTAIN THE FAIRY TALE. The fairy tale is a script by which all good marriages are played. I am not saying that this is something that you can rehearse but rather that the basic plot is always the same. You as the husband are responsible for defeating dragons, killing spiders, dealing with salesmen, defective toasters etc. Another of your jobs is to be attentive to the needs of the Princess. She is the one who sets the dramatic pace. If you do not appear on stage at the proper time or if you appear too soon, the princess will find another prince - and there is always another prince. If you should appear on cue, you must adapt to the princesses pace. Do not race ahead or get left behind. The second rule is that YOU DON'T KNOW THE SCRIPT. This results in some interesting results like the fact that your wife is always right in her arena. If she is right, well, this is obvious. What is not obvious is that when she is wrong she is right if it is in her arena. Practice apologizing and make it sound sincere. It would be better if you really mean it because they have no difficulty-recognizing fakers. The third rule is no matter how trivial a matter you perceive something to be, if it is in her arena, YOU DO NOT HAVE AN OPINION UNTIL SHE TELLS YOU WHAT IT IS. Items on this list that come to mind on this occasion are things like weddings, babies, kitchens, decorating, bathroom etiquette and the exact color of a wall. Arguments are permissible when they cross the line into your prerogatives. Just remember, things are more difficult now that women are doctors, lawyers and let me stress this - all the other traditional men's jobs. It is not so easy to figure out when they cross the line. For me, the best way was to stake out my own territory and defend it. This will work if they respect you. If they do not respect you, you do not want to be married to them anyway. Tom, the bottom line that I need to impart to you is this. You do not have an opinion about when you are getting married.

Margaret has not told you when that is yet. Nor do you hold an opinion about what the wedding will be like. She may ask you about what you want but if you tell her, it will almost certainly be incorrect. She will tell you when and where it is and then it will be your job to show up in the proper uniform. Do you have any questions?" There was a moment of shocked silence.

"Then you think that I should apologize to Maggie?" Tom still seemed a little confused.

"Immediately."

"Can I try to explain?" Tom was proving to be one of the stupidest smart people I had ever known. I was beginning to lose patience.

"Explain what? You don't even know what you did wrong, how can you possibly explain it to her?"

"So, I just go say I'm sorry and ask her to forgive me?"

"Exactly."

"OK." Tom stood up and went into the house. Bob, Jack and I sat quietly. After a few minutes without the sounds of breaking china, Jack finally broke the silence.

"Dad, did I hear you and Tom talking about the ion Rocket this morning?"

"Yeah, he pointed out a flaw in my reasoning that we may have managed to parlay into a fusion drive for about a thousand pounds of extra superconducting buckeyball fabric and cable." I was still astounded the implications of our little chat before breakfast. Tom might turn out to be a real addition to the expedition.

"Exactly what was the problem that you guys ran into using that weapon for a rocket?" Jack always liked guns and knives. He was also attracted to shiny objects.

"Particle beams simply do not work in atmospheres as weapons. Additionally, they intended to use pulses instead of operating it continuously."

"So what you are saying is that this device would work well as a weapon where we intend to use it. It occurs to me that you have left the atmosphere problem behind and your device is designed to operate continuously."

"It still wouldn't work the way they intended to use it. It generates an intense beam of ionizing radiation. I would not want to be on the receiving end of it but I would not want to stand under a chemical rocket either. I guess that for an unprotected human it would be a death ray in the nineteen-fifties/science fiction sense of the term. For that matter, it would take a very sophisticated shield to deflect it. It would punch through a fair amount of solid material and in the process generate a fair amount of secondary radiation. However, even if I could triple the maximum proton flux that I expect it would never make a hole in anything much less a missile casing."

"OK, I get it. It would kill people but it wouldn't be that bad for equipment."

"Well, when you put it that way, I guess it would be pretty bad for most electronic equipment. A proton beam with the occasional helium nucleus at the velocities that I anticipate would generate electrical currents in any conductor it encountered. Eddy currents like that would destroy most semiconductors."

"Ok, Let's sum up. You have a device which would kill people at astronomical distances and at the same time screw up the electronic equipment on which their former lives depended."

Right If you aimed it at someone or they happened to wander into the beam by accident, it would kill them or hurt them real bad." Jack was wearing me down.

"Just like a real weapon." Jack did seem to have made his point.

"Just what is your point Jack?"

"My point is this Dad. As soon as you try to move this thing into orbit, you are going to have every intelligence agency in the world trying to stop you. By definition, they won't have a clue what you intend to use it for and they will immediately assume that you are up to no good."

"That's a good point Jack but you see, I don't intend to tell anyone I'm taking it into orbit. Because we will be working in the best vacuum one can obtain locally, it will not look like a sophisticated device until it is turned on. Most of the difficulty of these devices on Earth is getting a good enough vacuum. I intend to have individual accelerators use standard wave-guides for the purpose of having them manufactured. For all anyone will know, I am building a strange microwave antenna."

"OK, Dad, that might work and I hope it does. However, remember this. The intelligence community knows not only who you are but everything that you have ever worked on over the years and this includes particle beam weapons." Jack got to his feet as he said this and took one last look at the clear, soon to be hot morning sky and went back indoors. I was going to have to give some thought to smuggling the parts for the ion rocket into orbit beyond what I had planned initially. I was pondering this and beginning to notice that my robe was getting too warm in the sun when Bob stood up. I had forgotten that he was there.

"You'll figure it out Dad. It is getting too hot out here for me. I think that I'll go back in and get cleaned up."

"You're right son, let's both go back in. Perhaps Tom and your sister have made up by now and we won't be killed by stray shots." I gave one last look around. It was very warm for the later half of October. As I looked to the northwest, I noticed a few cloud on the horizon. I guess there was still time to wear those short sleeves one last time this year. Bob and I went in.

Madelyne met me at the bedroom door. "Jake, how long do we have to plan this thing?"

"The wedding or the trip to the asteroid?" There are some weekends that go this way but very few.

"Oh, the wedding is all planned. I called Drew Stewart, the Justice of the Peace a few minutes ago and we are going over late this afternoon for him to perform the ceremony. I was talking about the asteroid trip." Madelyne's ability to surprise me does not seem to wane with the years.

"This afternoon?" I think that I was able to close my mouth after this but I and not sure.

"Sure, when have we had everyone here at the same time? Besides that, when are we likely to have them here all again? Oh, Steve Griffin called. He is going to show the house this afternoon."

"This afternoon?" I step out onto the deck for a few minutes and all this happens.

"Steve said that he had talked to Dr. Irving and his wife and they wanted to see the place. You remember that they were over here for dinner last spring after they moved into the area and John just went on and on about the design and the room. Margaret and Tom have called the University and Margaret has withdrawn from school and Tom from his assistantship. They are planning to head out to California this afternoon."

"This afternoon?"

"Tom wants to see the Judge and get his fortune together. Jack told Tom that the sooner that he got the money, l the more money we would have to finance this thing. Now are you going to answer my question?"

"What question?" All sense of purpose and direction had dissolved beneath this torrent of information.

"Have you been listening to me? How long to plan this thing - this trip to the asteroid?" The rising inflection in the voice of my wife left no question that the question was not rhetorical in nature. I gathered my thoughts. From a hardware standpoint, the central questions remaining concerned not only configuration but also assembly and launch location. I was going to need months to examine and test the old chemical rockets needed for our escape from Earth. The Ion rocket with the exceptions of the nuclear reactor and the superconducting magnets and cable could be constructed from readily available parts.

"We have at least a month and maybe two to plan the essentials of the mission. We still have at least four months after that to deal with the details and put the thing together." As

I said this, I watched my wife slowly crumple and tears begin to well at the corners of her eyes.

"Oh Jake, we only have six months to say goodbye to everything that we have made together."

My wife who had no compunction about taking a knife to an infected wound of dealing with an amputation was now faced with an amputation of her own. Considering the many shocks of the weekend, she had done remarkably well. "Listen Sweetie, we aren't saying goodbye to all the things that we have made together. We are taking a fair number of them with us, and saving the rest from destruction. It is not going to be easy or pleasant but neither was gross anatomy your freshman year in Medical school. It may even turn out to be fun. We just do not know yet what challenges we will be faced with. However, look at it this way. We have done a number on the one s that we have faced in the past. It is going to work out." How much I believed of this little speech is subject to speculation. It did not matter whether either of us believed in any of this. What mattered was that we had a shot and we were going to take it. In the meantime, we still had each other. It had always been enough. She managed a little smile, as that determined look crept back into her eyes.

"You're right sweets. We'll muddle through."

A few minutes later, we were all gathered in my study that had become the unofficial headquarters of the project. Tom and Margaret were sitting on the couch with Bob. Jack was in my reading chair and Madelyne was sitting by me at the computer desk. I had loaded up my world atlas program and had the United States displayed. "I think that it is time to make some basic decisions and plans. When we sell this house, which seems rather likely, we will have to be somewhere else until we leave the planet. It would only be better if it were somewhere where we could assemble our launch vehicle. It has got to be someplace far enough from civilization that we don't pose a threat to others but close enough were we can get essential things delivered."

"There is more to it than that Daddy. The closer we can get to the equator the more we will be able to lift into orbit using the rotation of the Earth to give us a boost."

"Sure Margaret, but how are we going to get our boosters shipped to South America of Africa, much less get the additional hardware we might need. I think we are stuck with the original space faring nations."

"Jack, are you seriously considering someplace beside the United States?" My eldest son just did not think like me.

"Dad, the good old USA is one of the most advanced nations on Earth. It is also one of the most taxed, regulated and watched. On top of that I don't think we will get an importation permit for a couple of Energiya boosters even as exotic scrap."

"Are you saying that we are going to have to move lock, stock and barrel to the Asian republics of the former USSR?"

"Dad, That wouldn't work either. We need access to the markets of this country in order to finance this venture." Jack clearly had something in mind that I was not going to like. However, we did not have a lot of time to be coy.

"All right son. What is your solution to these seemingly inconsistent requirements?

"In order to avoid the difficulties of no money and too much regulation, I propose that we lift the water from the old USSR. Enough of the right color of money will buy what ever cooperation we need from the locals."

It was worse than I thought. "You are saying that we should attempt to launch from two different locations. From your area of expertise, doesn't that mean that we will have twice the security problems?"

"Only if our activities are viewed as related."

I do not know much about secrecy, government surveillance or economics beyond keeping my checkbook balanced. Still, in this instance, I was hesitant to follow the advice of someone who obviously did. I guess that even though my son went into danger every day, I did not want to be the one to send him. "OK, what about getting the hardware ready in two separate places separated by half the world?"

"What do you know about the Energiya rockets in the first place Dad? Besides that, you do not speak or read Russian. I think I can find the people to do the job over there. They are not accustomed to knowing what they are working on any way. That's just not the way their system worked."

"So what do the rest of you think?" I had to hand it to him; he had a number of good arguments. Although I could not think of an alternative plan, perhaps one of the highly intelligent people in this room might. Of course, it was Bob that spoke up.

"I think that Jack is right. I was worried about how we were going to get a nuclear reactor into orbit, much less the uh, special explosives that we are going to need. Jack, I have been taking Russian for a couple of years, what about me joining you over there for the flight up?" It just kept getting worse.

"Maybe for the flight up but certainly not at first. You may speak a little Russian but you do not know the ropes and the early negotiations will be a bit tricky and no offense, I do not want you in the way. Besides, I have a job for you on this side that is more important than anything that you could do overseas. Remember that secret code we worked up to keep Margaret from knowing what we were talking about when we were kids?"

"Sure Jack, but what does that have to do with anything?"

"That code was based on some experiences that we shared but that no one else knew about. As such, it is virtually unbreakable as codes go because no one knows about us in that degree of detail. I will need to be in the former USSR and other places as I cannot just quit my job and retain the access that we need. I will need someone here who can make the securities transactions we will need to make the capital acquisition phase of this deal work. I not only can't be here to do it but if I personally did the deals the jig would be up pretty quick."

"So I stay here and help with the trading aspect of this plan with coded instructions from you."

"Close but no cigar Bobby. Because of the amounts that you will be trading and the fact that cash will be used in a number of them, you will have to relocate between New York and Chicago, as you will have to be able to get between then at a moments notice. I think that being in Chicago may be the best spot but New York will also be a place you become acquainted with at least for the next few months."

I actually had not given the financial aspects of this project much thought. I had just determined that Jack pretty much does what he says he can do and let it go at that but there was obviously more to it than a few quick phone calls to a broker.

"OK, I guess I could do that. It seems kind of trivial but I am going to hate giving up the band."

"I looked around the room and thought about all the things that we were going to have to give up and the fact that my family were now thinking of these things themselves. The entire effort was an incredible sacrifice but the prospect was exciting as well. Moreover, the need was clear. "Margaret, What do you think about your brother's plan?"

"I think that Jack's arguments are convincing but like every other discussion we have had the last couple of days it raise more problems that need to be considered. We are now talking about rendezvous and docking in low Earth orbit with two or more spacecraft. That is a good trick for Astronauts with thousands of hours in simulators much less for six ordinary Joes four of whom have some limited piloting experience. If we manage that first hurdle we are going to have to load our water and light our candle pretty quick if we don't want to burn up or be shot down in the midst of our preparations." She was absolutely right but I did not have the necessary knowledge base to concern myself with solving those problems just yet. Time to bring all that up and burn those bridges later on in the design phase.

"Margie, you are right and I hope you can figure something out. The best that I can do is get us to orbit if everything works out as planned and they never do. I am going to count on us to get the little details figured out in time." She looked like she had just had a big bite of a lemon. She blinked and nodded. She was going to grow up a lot in the next few weeks. It looked like she was going to have some help and for the first time I began to appreciate that.

"What are we going to eat?" It was about time that my dear Madelyne had something to say. Tom had sat there during the whole discussion with a distant look on his face. Having gained an appreciation of his intellect only this morning I was curious about what he was cooking up. Madelyne having not gotten an immediate response repeated herself. "Well, What are we going to eat?"

"Once again, this is not an area that I intend to explore right now. We seem to have made the major logistical decisions and the details will have to wait for the detailed configuration. I think that your interest in this matter will provide an impetus toward solving the problem of feeding us indefinitely and the matter of life support in general." I was pleased that she was thinking ahead. She was the natural person to handle the physiological side of the design requirements.

"OK, Jake, you incredible blowhard. I will be happy to be the chief cook and bottle washer on this little camping trip as I said yesterday or the day before. I already have a thousand thoughts on the matter and I am confident that if you can deliver on your promises, that I can deliver the bread and bologna sandwiches. I am thinking of more immediate concerns. What are we going to eat for lunch today? It is on into the afternoon and although the Eggs Benedict this morning was delicious, it was a long time ago and I for one am getting hungry. So why don't we table this discussion with our objectives as stated and go out for a change and eat lunch?"

Once again, my wife was right.

We drove on into town after a minor amount of straightening up for the realtor to show the house. One of the bigger hotels had a Sunday brunch that they carried on into the afternoon with Champaign and an excellent buffet and it was a merry group that arrived at the Justice of the Peace's home for the marriage ceremony. OK, I cried a little more than Madelyne but she has a very professional demeanor. We had called for a limousine to pick us up from the hotel and we let Margaret and Tom drive away in that. We had filched some birdseed from the feeder in Drew Stewart's yard and threw it at them as they got in the car. As impromptu weddings go, I guess it went well. I could not help feeling a little hollow knowing that I had just seen my only daughter married. It really did not help a bit that I had come to like and respect Tom. My little girl was gone.

    Tom and Margaret were going to head straight back to the house and head out for California. We called a cab to take us back to the hotel to get our car. Drew lived at the edge of town so it was a few minutes before we got there. There was an incredible line of cars in front of us as we tried to leave the hotels underground parking lot so overall it was at least an hour and a half before we drove up our drive to our house on the hill. Tom and Margaret were gone. They had left a note instructing us to sell Margaret's car along with the title and registration. I had a better idea. I gave it to Bob who was soon off to check out of his school and settle his affairs. Jack and I had a long chat about the expected timetable. He told me that he would do what he could about that. We set up a means of staying in contact which was the first time that we had ever had a deal like that with Jack. He packed a few things and told us to sell the rest or get rid of it anyway we wished and left to parts unknown. Madelyne found a note and a contract from Steve Griffin saying that the Irvings had agreed to meet our price and that he would be by in the morning to pick it up. When things start happening, they can happen very fast.

    Madelyne and I were in the kitchen cleaning up the remains of the disaster this morning. The easy way that we worked together gave me new strength to face the challenges that waited in the wings. I suppose that maybe I had been getting a little set in my ways and that change would do me good. I just never would have planned this much change.

"Do you think that the Irvings would be interested in any of the furniture?"

Madelyne knew them much better than I did or at least she knew John and had talked to his wife on one more occasion than I. "I'd hesitate to guess, but John commented on the furnishings as well as the design when they were over here. It certainly would not hurt to ask. We can't take it with us."

"That's what I was thinking. I guess we could take a few small items and more than that to Texas but it sure looks good here."

"Everything looks good here Mad. That's why we need to give it up - to try to keep it that way."

"I know, Jake. It does not make it any easier- it just makes it possible. Its real hard on me Jake." She looked down at the plate in her hands." This was my mother's china. She always wanted me to have it." As she said this, the tears required by the weekend's events began and we both grieved the loss of our world and the little things that made it our own. I do not remember how long we stood there in the comfort of each other's arms. It was long enough.

"Let's go out on the deck and have a look." I broke our embrace and led the way out the back door. The day's unusual warmth was having its rational consequence. The clouds that I had seen out to the northwest earlier had blown up and there were gust of wind that blew the fallen leaves around and from the trees in a crackling sweep of motion. There in the west a fork of lightening was followed a few seconds later by a first rumble and clap of thunder. The next gust of wind brought a few drops of rain to our already wet faces. Madelyne and I looked at each other and smiled. We had always loved thunderstorms and a storm was coming. A storm was coming.

Chapter Seven
A Brief Stop at The Hardware Store

T minus 00:00:13:10:00

Jack finished his story to a hushed audience of two. It had taken him almost an hour to relate the events of last year in sufficient detail to flesh out a convincing tale.

"And, as we speak, on the other side of the world, your parents and the rest of your family are about to blast off in space shuttle tanks with solid rocket boosters?" Katerina had a way of getting directly to the point.

"Dad let me know that much in our last communication. They will actually launch before the launch tomorrow at Baikonur. The object will be to rendezvous in low Earth orbit with the water launched yesterday and the launch tomorrow - I mean, later today."

"And the plan was for you to do the guidance of the Soyuz to these dockings?" Perhaps she did not have to sound so disdainful.

"I have more piloting experience than my brother Bob has."

"And you are of opinion that this will enable you to dock with spacecraft in orbit assembled by amateurs?"

"As I hope I have made clear, we feel that this is the only chance for the world as we know it to survive."

"I see." Katerina sat and considered the story of this strangely compelling man from the other side of the world. The issues as she understood them were clear. Did she assist these impossibly naïve saviors or allow them to proceed without her assistance and probably fail, at what was conceivably, the most important job members of the human race had ever attempted. The large amount of detail in his story had convinced her that this was no con game to get nuclear weapons to hold nations hostage for money. Truth has a funny sound. It sounds utterly implausible until considered in the light of the most human details. She found herself believing the story and almost being able to see the human characters about which Jack had spoken. She also saw the unbelievable innocence that led these intelligent, but ignorant, people to think that they could beat this monster on their own, without any assistance from strangers. She considered her thousands of hours in a simulator and Jack's flying experience and broke into a belly laugh. She laughed and laughed until tears came to her eyes and the wound on her head began to ache.

"So you don't believe me." Jack was hurt and feared his mission was doomed to failure. Without the nukes, there was no hope that the overall mission could succeed.

"No, I believe every detail you have spoken. It is this that makes me laugh." Katerina wiped the tears from her eyes and looked into the face of the shocked Jack. "You will need more than bombs and good intentions to save the world, Mr. Knight. You will need someone who can actually fly and dock the Soyuz. It is not like flying a plane or docking a party barge. It is also funny that, of all the people in the world you would have to talk to about this amazing mission, I am perhaps the only one that can help you accomplish the job. Was this part of your deliberations before you intervened last night?"

Jack had a momentary look of discomfort on his face. "I learned everything I could about you before our "chance" meeting last night, Commissar Yerisivloskaya. I knew that you were a cosmonaut. That was never a conscious part of my thinking last night - if you could call it thinking. I never intended to tell you any of this. I cannot afford to fail so I improvised as the circumstances warranted. It seemed the only way to get my part of the job done was to tell you why I needed these weapons."

"My Katerina, you actually believe this stupid story of stupid Americans in their stupid country far away?" Nina had understood virtually every word but had no concept of the matters discussed.

"Yes Nina, the story is stupid enough to be completely true, and it seems internally consistent. It appears this man who saved my life may also intend to try to save the whole world." Katerina would still occasionally break into chuckles.

"So you will help me get the nuclear weapons?" Jack's outlook had begun to improve.

"No, Mr. Knight, you misunderstand. I will personally take these weapons to this asteroid."

Katerina drove while Jack sat in the front seat beside her. Her grandmother sat in the back seat with a small parcel of goods removed from her apartment. A similar parcel from her own apartment resided in the trunk of the car.

"Mr. Knight, we are on our way to pick up your "goods". If I find out that you have lied to me in the slightest significant degree, your death will be painful and slow." She slowed down and made a left turn into a narrow street. "Not that I am able to guarantee your safety in any case. The competition clearly is aware of your intentions. It was less than discrete to discuss your intentions with your informant."

"I had to let the scumbag know what I was looking for or he couldn't tell me where to look. By the way, I am getting very tired of your threats. If you didn't believe in our purposes you could have sent me to deal with your shredders on my own –no muss, no fuss." Jack was searching the area around the apparently deserted office building. The previous arrangements had provided for the movement of his special hardware to this location. He was not supposed to pick it up until tomorrow morning, but nothing else was going according to his plan. Why should this? He had not counted on two more persons in the caravan. The final checks on the booster and its payload would be occurring as he spoke. He had thought of a possible way to get all of them to the ship in low earth orbit but he did not like to consider it in any detail.

"If I didn't believe in you I would still be along to insure the proper disposition of the "merchandise." Katerina stopped and then backed up to a loading dock. "Besides, if I didn't come along your precious plan would be doomed to failure from the outset."

"I think I could handle your boys here at the shop now that I know the way business is done here in beautiful Alma Ata." Jack reached into his jacket pocket and checked the status of his pistol for the seventh time.

Katerina noted this and smiled mysteriously." Perhaps." She got out of the car and started for the side door. "Nina, stay in the car." Jack got out and followed her lead.

The dock was attached to a three-story building with few windows. Largely decrepit, it still had very good doors and locks. There was a light just beside the door placed just right to illuminate the face of whoever came there, along with a peephole in the door. Katerina pushed a key into the lock and, as the door partially opened, she reached into the space and did something before she finished opening it the rest of the way.

"I set a little trap for strangers," she said as she walked into the bay of what would best be termed a very small warehouse. Unlike many warehouses, a person would have been relatively comfortable eating off any of the shiny white surfaces presented. Lights, when they came on, illuminated very white walls, floor and ceiling in exquisite detail. There was a small series of numbered steel doors with the subtle look of bank vaults. There were no protruding edges, and the average razor blade would not have fit between the edges. "Your parcels should be in number 23." Katerina stopped before a door with the number "23" prominently displayed on it and then stepped to the left of it and inserted another key into the lock of number 22. The door opened and they stepped into a small room much like the one they had left. In the right hand wall was an obvious bank vault door. There was a numeric keypad set into it.

"I thought you said the goods were in number 23?" Jack had a suspicious sound in his voice.

"This is number 23. None of the odd numbered doors open, but inserting a key sets off alarms. Inconvenient, noisy and probably dangerous for us." She entered a seven-digit number on the keypad and the thick heavy door began to open. As it opened, a fluorescent light flicked on inside the cramped hole and four small suitcases were revealed. Katerina and Jack each picked up two and lifted them out of the vault. They were relatively heavy but no more than might be expected for an overseas flight. Katerina set hers down and closed the vault door. She picked them back up and walked out of the small room. When out, she set her bags down again and closed the door with the 22 on it. She then walked back to the door where they had come into the little warehouse. She closed the door behind her and they put the suitcases in the trunk of the car. When they had gotten back into the car, Katerina started the engine and they drove out of the dock.

"That's all there is to it?" Jack sounded sarcastic.

"Yes, that is all there is to it. However, I might point out that any deviation from exactly what we did would have resulted in casualties. A step in the wrong direction would have been enough." She drove in silence for a few minutes. "Also, the most dangerous part is yet to come."

They rode in silence as they headed for the edge of town. The rot of the new economy was depressingly clear as they passed through what appeared to be one large slum.

"The new capital is about a hundred miles away. The leaders of the new republic thought it would be better to leave the mistakes of the past behind. This included Almaty." Major Yerisivloskaya clearly had little but distain for the new regime.

"It all looks ugly to me!" Nina remembered the empty plains of her nomadic heritage. The thrown-together "make do" architecture of the Soviet era had no appeal to her.

"I think that the new capital is being built primarily to attract foreign investment and to impress visiting dignitaries. I passed through there on my way to Baikonur. It seemed impressive in an artificial sort of way." Jack had no idea why he felt obliged to weigh in on this seemingly unimportant issue.

"Yes, exactly. I think that sums the new capital up perfectly. Impressive in an artificial sort of way, like a plastic palm tree in the lobby of a business that is too cheap to invest in the real thing." Katerina was a little more impressed with this man who had convinced her that she must leave her world in order to save it. Actually, she had begun to think that he was not that bad looking. The deer in the headlights naiveté was also somewhat endearing and packaged with deadly skills. She wrenched herself back to the immediate problems at hand. "Did you pay off Major Kostolinkavitch?"

"I had thought I would be able to conclude my business with you, Commissar. Does everyone in this entire country have their hand out for a bribe?"

"Perhaps most of those with some little bit of authority. It is beside the point. Kostolinkavitch controls the road to Baikonur."

"Does he have a toll booth or something?"

Katerina's laugh echoed in the small space of the Russian-made car. "No, Mr. Knight. He has many bad guys like the ones you helped me kill last evening. They are at some wonderful ambush points along the road to Baikonur."

"Is it too late to pay him off?"

"Yes. For one thing, you chose to ally yourself with me. That, by itself, would be reason enough for him to kill you. Also, we recently picked up some items he would very much like to have."

Jack considered his options. "We did well last night because they had no idea I would become involved and they were not the best shooters I have ever seen. I do not think we would do as well in an ambush situation. We have lost all of the element of surprise."

"Perhaps we shouldn't drive." Katerina had a sneaky sort of idea. "Does your flying experience include helicopters?"

Chapter Eight
The Bowels of Texas

T-Minus 00:06:19:23:45

It is difficult to determine which I have the least regard for - the hot, flat part of Texas or the snowbirds who plague it in the winter. Although my experience with either is limited, I prefer to keep it that way. I am not sure whether this antipathy is mutual, but with luck, we will not be here long enough to find out. This time of year has long been odious to me. The kids have been back in school long enough to infect each other and their parents with those wonderful viruses that lead to the sinusitis and bronchitis which kept my doors open and my immune system working in high gear for so long. Actually, it had not been that much of a pain to leave my practice. Much of the challenge was gone. Add to that the incredible power and greed of the insurance companies and the government intervention in the practice of medicine, and it really was not that hard to leave it behind. I guess some of my patients will miss me and I some of them. I was actually able to sell the practice to a local hospital that moved in a young doctor right out of his training and owing more than he will make the first year for his schooling. I would not want to trade places with him. I put the money into our general fund and wished him well.

We have located outside the beautiful community of McAllen, Texas in a warehouse so old and ramshackle that my husband had at one point intended to bill the owners for its demolition but, after reflection, decided that it wasn't up to his usual standards and didn't feel right about it. He is a lot softer-hearted than I am. Then again, that is one of the reasons I married him. He knows more about so many different things than anyone else I know about. He is one of the most brilliant people I have ever met and one of the most dense. He finally caught on about that weekend back in October after my Jack explained it to him. Tom and Margaret had practically been living together for two years, and he thinks that she is dating lots of other guys. This is in spite of the fact that no names were ever forthcoming. Things did straighten out when he actually gave the kid a chance. Those two are actually cut from the same piece of cloth. I felt that Tom would be a good man for Margaret when I first met him, but Jake is much too slow about people to notice things like that, even if he is ready for the information, which in this case he was not. I knew that I had to bring matters to a head and get the thing settled, and so told the kids to be home that weekend. I had no idea what else Margaret would bring home with her. I had no clue that things could happen so rapidly. I had intended to marry Margaret off to Tom but I did not intend to sell my house and take off to tilt with some celestial windmill. So much for good intentions.

    Here I am in the early part of December in a tumble down warehouse. I cannot say a whole lot about the surrounding countryside, but where we are situated is about as ugly as a toxic waste dump. Jake did this on purpose, but it does not make it any more fun to look at. Jake put us out here because no one lives within five or six miles, and no one wants to.

    He took lots of care to find this particular section of creation. The warehouse was originally nineteen floors of industrial supplies, oil-drilling equipment, and other filthy stuff. However, the design did not withstand the test of time and the weight of tons of steel. At one end of the building they had an accident when a goodly piece of derrick fell through the topmost floor and the floor below that and the floor below that and so on; so that they were left with a bunch of debris in a pile at the bottom of a really tall room - the floors remaining like giant dirty shelves on one side of a tall filthy closet. Jake was all fired up because the big elevators that they used to get the goodly piece of derrick to the top floor were still working. Needless to say, a different engineer than the one who drew the plan for the building designed them. The rail spur and the incredibly small sum the owners wanted to lease the real property and "improvements" also fired him up.

We were now in the scrap business. I have to hand it to Jake. He was actually making money in the scrap business. Not as much as a consulting design engineer at his level is used to, but it paid the rent and the utilities and provided a convenient cover for our real activities. In addition, it allowed him to deal directly with the people who were providing us with our rocket engines. We were paying top dollar for them - as scrap. Being in the scrap business, we sent out as many rail cars as we got in. However, when we got in three space shuttle external tanks, we did ship out scrap aluminum - just not the same aluminum. I will get to that.

We were living in what used to be the office spaces of the warehouse. I have stayed in worse places but not while married to Jake. The first week or so we all cleaned and scrubbed and Tom installed a shower in the bathroom where the line of urinals used to be. I didn't appreciate the industrial grade fluorescent lighting in our "bedroom", the lack of a bathtub, real kitchen etc. but I had camped out in worse conditions and enjoyed it. I have gotten very creative with the microwave and hot plate that constitutes our cooking equipment. Jake even pitched in when I could drag him away from the computer - and that was not very often. He was working about eighteen hours a day in the design process. He would come to me from time to time and ask weird questions about oxygen pressures and nitrogen mix and average water consumption and waste production. I would either give him an answer or tell him I would look it up and get back to him; whereupon he would stand at my shoulder and look at me like a little child that needs to go to the restroom until he had his information. Then he might grab Tom and they would disappear into the back room with the computer for another five or six hours until he came back with another question. Now, this did not drive me as crazy as you might think. Jake has always been this way when he has been on a heavy design project. I was used to it. Jake had me doing research on life support systems. When he told me he wanted a totally closed system, I had no more idea what he was talking about than I have of non-Euclidian topology. As it turns out, I now know about as much as anyone who has not made a career of it does. It is a very simple idea that can be very complicated in its execution. The simplest system is a fish in a bottle with some water, a plant and a snail. There are other things in the bottle like algae; bacteria etc. but the major features are the fish, snail and plant. The fish eats some of the plant and some of the bacteria. It and the snail take oxygen out of the water and put carbon dioxide into the water along with other waste products. The plant takes the carbon dioxide out of the water and puts oxygen into the water. The snail eats the rest of the fish's waste and whatever algae start to grow on the sides of the bottle. The only input into the bottle is sunlight. Everything works out until one of the creatures dies or the sunlight is cut off. We had in mind a system like this, only more complicated. We had plenty of power. We just had to take the right plants and animals along. My little garden at home had never been intended to feed us. The huge aeroponic garden in the ship was going to have to at least supplement our diets even on the way out to Belial as well as take the CO_2 out of our air. Later we would have to depend on it altogether. We were not going to run out of oxygen, as Jake assured me that we would have plenty of that as a by-product of our Ion/fusion rocket. Nevertheless, unless we were able to grow enough green plants we were going to have trouble. I felt like I could do it, but Jake was being a real nerd and saying that I could not take any potting soil. We would see about that. Growing plants without soil was not part of my previous experience, but he assured me that I would grow to love it after some time.

    Jake and Tom refined their design to the point where construction commenced. They had erected two cranes inside the cavernous space where the construction was to take place. They had then taken three of the external tanks and fastened them together at the points opposite of where the tanks had attached to the space shuttle. Then they welded a docking adapter to this framework that connected the bottoms of the three liquid hydrogen tanks together. They put another hatch behind this one after about six feet so it would function as an airlock. They welded another triangular piece of aluminum near the top and welded the seams between the three tanks. They pumped air into the resulting triangular chamber at what Jake said was five atmospheres. Then they watched a little gauge for three days hoping a needle would not budge. It did not. They had then ripped out some of the stuff in the "innertanks" and rotated the SRB Beam one hundred and eighty degrees each. I did not this know when we started, but each of the external tanks had three major pieces. The top piece was the liquid oxygen tank, then the intertank; and finally, the liquid hydrogen tank. The whole tank was 158 feet long and almost twenty-eight feet wide. The biggest part was the liquid hydrogen tank. Jake explained to me that I could grow plants in two of the liquid hydrogen tanks. When I started out, I thought he meant a little round patch like at the bottom of a silo. "No! No! Mad! I mean that you can fill the whole thing! You have to lose that earthbound terrestrial viewpoint! At the most, this fusion torch Tom and I are building will be capable of pushing our mass at two tenths of a gravity. We will have a little bit of up and down but, at most, you will weigh eleven or twelve pounds." I really could not imagine weighing that little and I began to be concerned about the effects of so little stress on the human body. Yet another load on the old donkey. So anyway, now I was putting lots of shelving and water hoses with high intensity lighting into big dark tubes. I was absolutely forbidden to drill a hole into the outer wall. The tube had another tube going straight down the center that Jake called the liquid hydrogen siphon. It was seventeen inches in diameter and was wonderfully convenient for hanging shelves and lights on. I was putting misters every few feet but they were of a higher caliber than is typical. These plants would be handling the solid waste as well. There would be no toilet paper on the trip, or so Jake had repeatedly told me. We would be washing ourselves after doing our business. Jake had designed a special solar furnace into which waste and urine would be put. Jake's creation generated a sterile dry powder and steam which powered the agricultural pumps. The dry powder was then mixed with the water the plants got after the introduction of selected strains of nitrogen-fixing bacteria. The big thing that Jake was worried about was whether there would be enough carbon dioxide to let the plants grow efficiently. I gently pointed out that we would not, in most cases, be eating the entire plant. If we needed more carbon dioxide we could put a little of our excess oxygen into Jakes special furnace along with food scraps and vegetable matter and have as much carbon dioxide as we desired. He looked a little bit sheepish, as he sometimes can, and ran off saying something about modifying his design to include all kinds of waste; and seemed as happy as if I had given him a new toy.

    Jake and Tom's work was also proceeding apace. They had succeeded in attaching the six solid rocket boosters to the sides of the three external tanks. The pointy parts of the tanks were down toward the ground and the stubby ends were pointed up. They had spent two weeks at least on this big nosecone that they had to put on the front of the three tanks to streamline it. It was made of some very thin plastic with carbon fiber reinforcement. Fifty-five feet across and some forty-five feet long, it weighed only about five hundred pounds. Jake and Tom handled it like a big eggshell. Jake said he had added "a bit" of thrust to the design by a modification to the nozzle of each of the solid rocket boosters. He also had slowed down three of the six boosters so that they would burn four minutes longer. He assured me that without the weight of the orbiter the solid rocket boosters would be quite enough to get our mostly-empty external tanks into low Earth orbit where we would rendezvous with the payload launched from Kazakhstan. This launch arranged and manned by my son Jack would be primarily water along with a Soyuz and some other special "hardware". We would pump the water into our reactor compartment and into the liquid oxygen tank on the habitation external tank. Yeah, we had our very own nuclear reactor. It was about the size of a bass drum box on steroids and was originally designed to run a fair sized submarine. I really was not sure how Jake had managed to get hold of it, but it would supply our power needs in the event that the fusion drive did not work. Jake and Tom were virtually certain that it would, of course. The problem with computer simulations remain that they are only as good as their programming. Although Jake and Tom are about as good as it gets, they suffer from the same blind spot that every other programmer does. - They just could not think of the things that they had not thought of.

    Naturally, the great male engineers had some feminine jobs for Margaret and me. We had some sewing to do. Naturally, we had to do the job with buckeyball monofilament on buckeyball fabric. It was as smooth as silk and as light as air, but the pieces we were sewing were kilometers in length; and we had to be incredibly precise with our stitches. Jake said that if we were as little as two millimeters off it could be the difference between success and failure. Jake can be so stuffily compulsive. The stuff was much more shear than a pair of panty hose, but when inflated and positively-charged, would not even allow a proton through. We sewed and sewed and then we sewed a lot more and then some more. We sewed four curved tapering tubes. Then we attached this thing that looked like an inner tube at the big end and a series of things that looked like inner tubes at the small end. The big end was at least twenty feet across. Of course, when we were working on it, it looked like an extremely large, very ugly dress for a giant four-legged spider. Then we had to sew smaller hoops on the bottom of the skirt, and the illusion was dispelled. The smallest one was no bigger than a doughnut. It took weeks to do all this and, just when I thought we were through, Jake had us put a zipper on it! The zipper went around the very largest tube at the "top". The mate of the zipper was attached to this aluminum dingus that looked like something that really belonged in the heating and air ducts of a good-sized building. Alternatively, maybe like something that belonged in a distillery. This thing had at least seven hundred little round pipes that came out at an angle all around the outside edge. They pointed slightly in and counterclockwise, if you looked at it from the bottom. Jake called them wave-guides. The center of the device was given over to lots of very thin, light, metal plates that were offset from one another. Jake called them "Ds" for some unknown reason. Only in the most obtuse corner of an engineer's imagination did any of them look anything like the letter "D". The entire dingus was maybe three feet thick and cone shaped, tapering about five feet from where it was attached to the bottom of the external tanks. Attaching the zipper was a real bitch because we had to work on ladders about twenty-five feet off the concrete floor. Oh, we had safety lines and nets and what have you, but it was still scary working that far off a hard floor. The fabric that we were sewing the zipper to extended over the entire assemblage of external tanks and was a very tight fit. It only extended about three inches below the bottom end of the "Synchrotron Bank", which is what Tom and Jake insisted on calling the dingus. "Fine," I said." I'll just call it the dingus for short."

After we were done with our sewing and it had passed inspection about thirty times, we very neatly folded it and put it into a thin round aluminum box that clipped onto the side of the external tanks. The box was only six inches thick but over twenty-five feet across. It was an incredible pain to get it clipped on to the special frame the boys made. The box had to weigh at least a hundred times as much as the fabric that Maggie and I put into it. Jake said that it was important to protect it for the ride into low Earth orbit.

Jake and Tom spent days in the bottom of the external tank with one of my gardens in it working on electronics and tubing and such. They did all this work before Jake and Tom put the tiny little fuel rods in. They spent as little time as possible doing this while wearing special radiation suits, and thereafter, this section of the tank and the empty space near it were off limits. The interior of the habitation tank was smaller on the side of the other tank because of the shielding that Jake and Tom put in. There was a thin sheet of lead but then a very thick piece of translucent plastic that Jake said was actually more effective than the lead. Jake also put similar shielding between the garden and the reactor chamber. For some obscure reason, I got to be the "Radiation Health Officer". I laughed and laughed when Jake told me about this. "Radiation Health? Isn't that like jumbo shrimp or military intelligence?"

"It is a good point, Sweetie. I am also serious. Although it is essentially bookkeeping, someone has to keep up with all the radiation exposure that we get. The object is to get as little as possible, of course, but also to keep a record because we have to consider the effects cumulative. I think that we will all be getting much less than a dangerous level, but some of us should get as little as possible. There is a very good reason that there are not any women on nuclear submarines. So, unless you want our grandchildren to be green with tentacles…"

"Ok, Jake, I'll keep the books. As far as all that goes and as near as science can tell me, I am done with the baby making business. That was the point of all that hygiene stuff disappearing from our bathroom closet. Margaret is, as far as I know our, only concern in that department."

Chapter Nine
The View From Baikonur

T Minus 00:00:06:24:12

Bob Knight tapped his foot. He walked to the window of his borrowed office and looked out. The early morning light was just beginning to come over the top of the eastern mountains in the distance. Out over the huge circular pit, the immense Energiya booster loomed over the huge booster clamps topped by the large tank and tiny Soyuz. The cryogenic fuel and oxidizer were boiling away from their respective tanks as the tanks reached operating temperature. Fueling continued. Where in the hell was Jack?

Bob had overseen the first launch from this office. It had gone off without a hitch. What a rush! The roar of the monster rocket and the swift retraction of the docking clamps as the four-footed beast had taken to the sky still filled his mind's eye with a vision of fury released. He had watched the water play over the red hot metal of the clamps as the star-like exhaust had driven the big tube of water into orbit. Real money works amazingly well to grease the wheels of progress, even in central Asia. The ground crews were overjoyed to be working again. So far, nothing out of the ordinary - if you call launching huge rockets ordinary - had occurred at Baikonur. Something unexpected must have occurred elsewhere in Kazakhstan. Where in the hell was Jack?

The beautiful Balalaika he had "bought" for such an exorbitant price that it constituted a bribe, leaned against the couch that slumped against the wall. It gleamed in the early morning light. Bob had already spent an hour or so playing with it. It tuned a little like a mandolin and a little like a banjo; and so making a song on it required an exercise in patient exploration. The whole thing, with the rapid little picks on a single string, was going to be a little tough to master. The triangular body with the relatively short neck, along with an incredible amount of mother of pearl inlay, was so foreign and inviting to the eye and hand. He was surprised by the relatively low and easy action, and the shallow little body had an amazingly solid tone. It was not cheaply made and, although he had paid at least twenty times its reasonable price in rubles, he felt it was money well spent. The previous owner had never learned to play it because his duties as chief of security at the Baikonur Cosmodrome precluded the necessary leisure time. The instrument had spent most of its life out of its case propped where it currently leaned against the couch. The tiny office with its spectacular, though distant, view was a courtesy provided by the former owner. Along with other favors appreciated by its current occupant, the lack of probing questions into the purposes of the rich American entrepreneurs was the most significant.

Bob had seen Jack only briefly when he had arrived two days before. Jack had made most of the arrangements and had left the operators of the base with the impression that Bob was the favored son of the boss of the entire project, and therefore, to be coddled. The fact that he had brought a huge amount of cash along had done nothing to dispel the very slight misimpression. The major transfers had of course been made through banks in Japan and Switzerland after funneling them through Paris. The obvious fact that they were brothers had gone unremarked. Bob had spent the money like water on the best food and wine. It was not going to be of much use where he was going; he intended to take none of it. Actually, it was uncomfortable to have in his many pockets. He had introduced Nataly to the joys of Bourbon Whiskey in addition to the prodigious amounts of vodka he routinely imbibed. The ensuing deep discussion that followed had provided Bob with the opportunity to pick up the balalaika and begin to noodle with it. He had actually been impressed with the instrument, so his admiration was unfeigned. The bargaining after the fine meal had been rather one-sided. Bob had insisted, that as the instrument was Nataly's personal property and not available here in central Asia, he must be properly compensated. The amount that Nataly had ultimately agreed to accept had been equivalent to his annual official salary.

"It is a small price for such a beautiful instrument, and my expense accountant will not notice it." Bob had cradled his new acquisition and enjoyed the slick feel of its lacquered finish.

Nataly had looked on a little blearily, as the Wild Turkey which he had sampled lustily had packed a bit more punch than the eighty proof vodka to which he was accustomed. "It was the best instrument that I could afford, and that model is no longer manufactured. It is happier in your hands. Most of the time, it has been idle in its case. You are a real musician. I just tried to play it from time to time when I needed to remind myself of the sounds of home." He took another swallow of the Wild Turkey and looked at his almost-empty glass. "This is a fine drink. It has great integrity."

Bob smiled to himself at the memory. He had spent most of the meal explaining the cover for the water project. "We will dock with a launch from the United States. After we get the projectile ready, we will explode a canister of water in the airlessness and cold of space. The resulting ice cloud will damage or destroy an impacting ballistic missile. It is relatively inexpensive and does not require the accuracy of a direct hit. It is, of course, a simple idea; but the targeting and actual dispersal method is proprietary. It is going to take a number of experiments under actual conditions to work out the fine points. I believe we are closer than the chief designer thinks. I think that most of this water will become the biggest ever ice-cube in orbit." Bob had adopted a bragging demeanor while relating the big "secret purpose" behind the launches from two continents.

Truthfully, a reliable and relatively inexpensive missile defense system would be worth several billion American defense dollars and his dad had applied for patents on the ideas as part of the cover for the real purpose. Several defense companies had been quite interested in the filing and had proved the hardest people to elude in the pursuit of saving the world. Competition is always the most ruthless where there is real money to be made. The office of White Knights, Inc. in New York had - through their lawyers - obtained a restraining order against Martin Marietta, Lockheed, and Boeing in order to prevent harassment of the non-existent "employees". The lawyers were then put in charge of the negotiations. A receptionist took phone calls, most of which were never returned. Bob occasionally dropped by the office, which had an old couch he slept on but was otherwise an empty, locked room behind the receptionist's desk. Martha, the receptionist, the wife of an old friend of Jake's, was a late middle-aged black woman who really believed in any project Jake thought was worthwhile. Her husband had been killed in an accident the previous fall and left her financially dependent on Social Security. She was not ready to just lie down and take the dole. She had really needed a change of scene, and the move to New York had provided her with just what she and White Knights, Inc. needed. Whatever money was left after the launches, and any monies that came from the new patents, were already in trust in her name. Jake had explained the danger of the job to her before the office had been rented and let her know that she would be included in any windfall that resulted, while never actually letting her know what it was all about. This was as much for Martha's protection as to protect the secrecy on which the future of the entire world depended. She took her job seriously and knew only that the company was involved in national defense and that various competitors would be trying to find out whatever they could about anything that they could. Martha had gotten quite maternal about Bob. She had known him since before he could walk and always wanted to know whether he was eating or getting enough sleep. "Mr. Robert, those clothes look like you slept in them! Now you just leave them outside the door and get you a nice nap on the couch after you eat this sandwich. I will take care of that! What would your Momma say? Go on now! Wash your hands!"

She was not quite as bad as his real mother about these same issues and had more of a sense of humor about why he kept the hours he did. Before he took the cab to LaGuardia, he had given her a big hug and a peck on the cheek. "Martha, I suspect that there is going to be some real trouble in the next week or so and I will not be here to help out. If the bad guys come to the door, do not rely on that restraining order. You call the police and get them over here, OK?"

"You do not need to worry about me Mr. Robert. I was handling pushy goombahs at your Daddy's job sites since before you and your sister were born. I will be fine. Now, I don't know if I like you flying off to some foreign country where they are not even Christian! I know how independent you are but. If you get in a tight spot, you just call your Auntie Martha; and my Arthur and I will be on a plane before they get the door locked good!" Martha's son Arthur was about six foot five and built like a buzz saw. Bob never wanted to be on the opposite side of an argument from Martha and Arthur. He had known Arthur all his life as well and, although Arthur was four years older and they ran in different circles, counted him as an old friend.

"Martha, you know Arthur is in the playoffs and I do not want him to lose his shot. You just do what I said and call the police if anyone tries to bust in on you." This insistence on Martha calling the police was part of the plan for her protection. It would be very difficult to prove that she was involved in a plot to put nuclear weapons in orbit if she called the police when the FBI came to execute a search warrant. He had gone down and gotten in the cab for the airport. He knew that Martha and Arthur would understand as the events played themselves out but he did not want to put her through the short-term trouble that he knew was coming. They were all going to go through some trouble and there was no way around it.

Bob bent over and picked up his balalaika. The flight over to Paris had been as boring as a transatlantic flight can be. He had had to leave the airport in order to cash out the bearer bond he carried. He had returned to the airport with a bit over three hundred thousand dollars in cash. As Jack had instructed, he carried it in multiple secret places on his person. It made it uncomfortable to bend over or sit in a narrow seat on an airplane. Bob had not bothered to look, but he thought he had developed a chafe. Yet another hazard of carrying around too much money, and one not often discussed in polite company. He heard the sound of a helicopter nearby. He began working on the only theme he knew that was unmistakably played on this instrument. It was the haunting tune from *Dr. Zhivago* – "Somewhere My Love". That rapid picking thing was going to be tough, but it was clearly essential for the thing to sound right. He was picking away as Nataly walked in.

"Robert, my friend, I have interesting news." Bob's pulse went up eighteen points.

"What is it, Nataly?"

"Your associate, Mr. Jack Knight, has returned to Baikonur.

Strangely, he brings two more members of your crew. I say this because they are both women and one is wounded!"

"Two women?" What was Jack planning?

"Yes, two women. One is well known cosmonaut of my personal acquaintance. But Robert, point is that Soyuz carries only three."

Chapter Ten

Blasting Out Of Texas

T-minus 00:00:10:00

Jake sat in the control couch and watched as the minutes ticked by. Unlike a liquid fueled rocket, a solid rocket booster required no last minute fueling. The fuel had been put in as a thick paste in separate sections of the solid rocket casing as it had been spun in a special centrifuge. This eliminated any bubbles and positioned the fuel all the way along the casing wall, leaving a tiny pore at the exact center where the igniter was placed. It would be good for a year or more at constant humidity. As it totally dried out, it had a tendency to crack and separate. "Yeah," thought Jake, "that is exactly what I need to be thinking about right now."

Tom had come up with the perfect idea for getting the roof out of the way. He had developed a crop of nanomachines that he sprayed onto the ceiling just over the booster rocket/external tank assemblage. The little machines had nibbled away at the area over the ship until a thin remnant was all that remained. They had build sealed multiple doors into the area and sprayed silicone over the walls and what was left of the overhead. It was kept aloft by air pressure. When the solid rocket boosters ignited, the sham of a roof would be blown away like a thin layer of dust by the sudden increase of pressure. Booster rocket/external tank assemblage! Was that a real name for a rocket ship?

"Maddy, what should we name this ship?"

Madelyne looked over at her husband and considered his question. "It sure isn't very pretty. I mean it seems very functional and all that, but it looks like the north end of a southbound horse. I guess it ought to have a name and not some sort of dumb acronym."

"I think it has a nice symmetry. The three tanks and the six booster rockets all arranged in a circular pattern." Tom had spent too many hours on this thing to have it criticized like that.

"I think Mom's right. Those aluminum plates at the top and bottom with those tapered ends sticking out beyond give it a sort of puckered look." Margaret remembered long hours looking up at the end of it while she sewed on the zipper to the dingus.

"So you think my beautiful ship looks like a horse's ass?" Jake thought back to a certain conversation with Tom only nine months ago. "OK, let's call it Trigger."

"You want to name it after Roy Roger's horse?" Madelyne considered that he could have picked out something worse.

"Sure. Fine. Who is Roy Rogers?" Margaret was much too young to remember the cowboy star.

"It has a nice direct sound - The Trigger. It will also have to be our horse to get us where we are going." Tom was beginning to have other things on his mind as the clock ticked down.

They had put the control section at the very bottom of the main habitation tank. This reduced as much as possible the length of wires that would be needed to tie all the electrical systems together. The roughly hemispherical floor had been largely filled with polyurethane pierced by a sealable hatch that provided access to the lower section of the ship. Beneath them were the three liquid oxygen tanks that would be filled with water. The one on the left, from their perspective, had the nuclear reactor in it. It was shut down, as their electrical needs were more than adequately met by several large fuel cells that combined hydrogen with oxygen and produced electricity. The reactor could be started up later when they needed the vast amount of power it would take to start the dingus. Meanwhile they did not need the dose of radiation that running the reactor would entail.

Above them, connected by a slender aluminum rod through a round hole in the ceiling, was the rest of the habitation tank. They had erected expanded aluminum floors every ten feet or so divided into the sections that could be shoved through the one thirty-inch hatch. These were then covered with a thin sheet of opaque plastic in different colors. There were seven decks installed in the tank.

Red level was where the control section was and, with the extra shielding and other control systems installed, was nearly fifteen feet in height. The top section - Violet - was also extended in height and was used for access to the farming tanks and storage of essential equipment they would need to stay on an asteroid indefinitely without Terrestrial support. Orange level was given over to the galley and common area. Yellow level was the scientific support area and sick bay. It was isolated from the other sections by an access sheet that sealed with a zipper in an otherwise opaque tube that extended from floor to ceiling around the almost ever-present siphon pipe that was used to hang almost everything; this pipe was also used as a ladder except in red level, where it had been removed. There it had been replaced with an aluminum rod that terminated in an aluminum plate welded into the end of the siphon. This supported the siphon during the ascent to orbit and allowed a handrail into the upper sections. On the side of red level away from the control section were the sanitary facilities. They had all been carefully coached in their use by Jake, and instructions were posted all over the inside of the ten by ten cube. Jake had proudly explained how advanced it was over what the astronauts had had to deal with on the space shuttles. Madelyn and Margaret were thoroughly convinced it was the worst thing about space travel.

Green level was outfitted with a special microgravity gym on which Madelyne had insisted. There were of course no weights to lift. Blue and Indigo levels were used for private quarters. All crewmembers had their own private space. There were two hundred pounds allotted to each crewmember for just "stuff". It could be anything that the member thought necessary, as long as it was properly stowed. There was a double layer of opaque plastic around the pie shaped sections with a two-inch layer of expanded foam insulation between them to cut down on transmitted noise. It was all the privacy that they could afford even with such a large space. There were four cabins on each level. The extra two were used for last minute storage and whatnots. There was an entire crate of duct tape strapped down in there.

The ship computer housed in yellow level administered the actual ignition and guidance. All the crewmembers had wireless access through their PDAs, which most had handy all the time. Jake's was actually mounted in a plastic rack just above his face where he could keep an eye on their countdown. When the last minute arrived, he consigned himself to his creator and after forty seconds began to speak. "Here we go folks. Fifteen, fourteen, thirteen, twelve, eleven, ten, nine, eight, seven, six, five, four, three, two, one, ignition, liftoff!" The last word was crushed out of his lips as a gigantic hand began to mash him into the skimpy foam of his acceleration couch. Jake had programmed his PDA to switch to a split view from the fore and aft cameras. The tiny image only four inches from his eyes was perfectly adequate to show that they had left the warehouse in flames. The fore camera showed a billow of dust as the ceiling blew away, and then the blue skies of Texas. The PDA switched to telemetry for a few seconds and showed that all six of the SRBs had ignited at much the same time and that they were being accelerated at a bit over seven gravities.

The PDA switched back to cameras and now the Gulf of Mexico was a big blueness off to the east. Two minutes and they were already traveling at over ten thousand miles an hour. Almost halfway there, Jake thought, as he struggled to breath. His normal weight of two hundred pounds suddenly increased to over fourteen hundred has that effect on a person. The fore camera showed a darkening blue. The aft camera showed mostly blue now, but the long thin island of Cuba was just at the edge of the tiny picture. Apparently, it was a beautiful day in the keys as well.

Six minutes into the flight and half of their SRBs were due to separate. Jake watched the countdown in the small screen of his PDA and would have held his breath in anticipation if such a pointless exercise had been possible under current conditions. It was not. There was a sharp crack as the countdown reached zero. The aft camera duly showed the almost spent casings begin their fall into the mid-Atlantic ocean. The modified nozzles on the other three SRBs continued to operate at about seventy five percent of the ones just separated, and the weight on Jakes chest lightened up markedly.

Jake could have talked then if he had wanted to but the creaking and groaning of the ship had him wondering if his and Tom's welds would hold and remain airtight as the stress of their acceleration was redistributed. Jake still weighed six hundred pounds, but it was a big improvement in the way he felt. The special acceleration suits they had gotten second hand from the Air Force obviously had done their job. He had remained conscious during the heaviest acceleration of the entire journey. Coming up on ten minutes into the flight and the SRBs had exhausted most of their fuel. The next separation would tell the tale.

"Countdown to final SRB separation. Ten, nine, eight, seven, six, five, four, three, two, one. Mark." There was another duller crack, and soon the last of their major rocket boosters were seen falling behind them to land in burnt cinders over a large area in the Indian Ocean. The only rockets left operating were small JATO units in a special rack mounted over the Dingus that kicked in after SRB separation. The push was much less than a single gravity. The PDA above Jake's face reported that they had achieved a velocity of over eighteen thousand miles an hour and a height of over three hundred miles. The JATO units went silent and, after a pop that went unheard in red level, they dropped off to burn up in the atmosphere. All weight left, and they pushed up against their restraining straps.

"Count off." Jake needed to hear the voices of his family.

"Madelyne."

"Margaret."

"Tom."

No one really sounded peppy. They had suffered almost eight gravities for six minutes and three gravities for another four minutes. They had had about two minutes of the sixth of a gravity acceleration from the JATO units to start breathing regularly again, when suddenly they were for the first time in their lives in free fall. They had not eaten for twelve hours and so had empty stomachs. This was at Madelyne's insistence. It appeared to have been a good idea. No one was actively sick but all were more than a little queasy.

"Secure from acceleration stations. I think we had better start to get used to this. Remember Maddy's instructions. No sudden turns. Look at something solid and upright from your point of view. No flying until everyone gets hungry." Jake began to loosen his restraining harness slowly and carefully. Suddenly he saw his daughter floating above his head. She was floating slowly toward the overhead with her arms sensibly out stretched to protect her face and head from the impending collision. She pushed off too quickly and more rapidly reversed her course and whacked her rear end against her acceleration couch.

"Oh! I should have held on to my straps. The foam padding had enough loft to push me against the ceiling!" She arched her back and grabbed the nearest fixed object which happened to be her father's leg.

"Are you hurt, sweetie?" Jake himself had held on to his harness when he had removed it. He felt bruised and beaten, and about twenty years older than he had twenty minutes before. He now floated above it distracted from his own discomfort by his daughter's adventures. He gingerly levered her over to her own couch.

"Just my pride, " she said.

"Then you shouldn't let your pride hit first!" Madelyne zoomed over to the aluminum pole and caught herself looking like she was doing a horizontal pull-up. She began to pull herself into orange level. "I feel better!"

The initial disorientation had begun to pass. After freeing his PDA from its rack, Jake carefully followed Tom and the women into orange level. "Where are you two going?" Tom had finally remembered how to talk.

"I don't know about you guys. I just want to see out!" Margaret followed her mother over to the single port that Jake and Tom had allowed in the outer wall of the external tank. It was about twenty-four inches in diameter and opposite from the food storage and preparation area. Handholds surrounded it and they all grouped around this window into the universe. As previously determined by their trajectory and orientation, which had been perfect as far as their instruments had been able to determine, the port looked out upon Earth. They were passing over the Sahara desert. The shadows cast by the dunes stretched back along their course and stood out in sharp relief.

White Knights Inc.

The line of the terminator was just ahead and, while they watched, they passed into night.

Chapter Eleven
A Long Cold Ride In The Dark

T – minus 00:00:00:03:34:12

The Helicopter pad was silent and deserted. The four-seater helicopter was put away for the night, with one end of the main rotor strapped down to the tail. The pad was sharply illuminated with no hint of the few remaining stars visible through the cold blaze of the mercury vapor lights. The four fugitives from Almaty made no pretence of stealth but drove directly to the pad. It had taken only a moment at the gate and a flash of Katerina's badge to grant them admission to the otherwise secure airstrip. "A phone now rings in Major Kostolinkavitch's house." Katerina said as they opened the little car's doors and unloaded.

"Nina, get into the back seat. Mr. Knight, please un-strap the rotor while I preflight." Katerina left no doubt who was in charge of this phase of the mission. Clipping out orders, as if to enlisted personnel, she hurriedly placed the four suitcases in the back seat. Nina had she and Katerina's parcel in her lap and struggled to strap in.

Jack ran to the back of the helicopter and, after learning what parts could be stepped upon and what parts could not, managed to un-strap the rotor in time for Katerina to start the engine. The rotor began a slow rotation that rapidly accelerated as the engine caught. The loose clothing Jack wore began to be flattened to his skin and flapped away behind. He shielded his eyes from flying dust. He climbed into the right seat and put on the headset. The sound from the rotor and the engine was already deafening. "Commissar, have you often flown helicopters?"

"I have perhaps a hundred hours or so since my qualification. I should not have much trouble flying between here and Baikonur. I would have preferred a gunship for this short hop. At least it is pressurized."

"What about your car?" Jack eyed the still shiny Russian model as the helicopter took to the air.

"It will not be of any use where we are going and the freight is prohibitive. It will disappear much as we will. I hope its next owner will care as little for it as I did." Katerina turned her attention to the task of piloting.

They cleared the city, the lake, and its outlying installations quickly and were the only aircraft visible flying west in the lightening sky. "I do not like this particular solitude. I am going to take this craft as high as it will fly. At least we will be a smaller target for Kostolinkavitch's brigands." Katerina made a conscious effort to unclench her jaw. Nina looked out of the back window. Jack looked out of the front and side windows and thought that it was going to be impossible to return any fire that they received.

"The little yurts and houses - they look like tiny dots! I camped down there for the first and nicest part of my life and now, for the first time, I am flying above it all." Nina was obviously enjoying her first flight. She was grinning like a small elderly chimpanzee as the farmsteads and camps rushed by so far underneath. Katerina smiled and thought of a nomad girl flying through the sky.

Jack caught the first flicker of muzzle flash with his peripheral vision. It was impossible to hear the reports of the automatic weapons fire. Tracer rounds flew past the like fire flies outside of a car window, except they were vertical rather than horizontal. Katerina took evasive action, and the helicopter veered sickeningly to the left. She corrected, and the engine roared as the little craft fought for altitude.

The helicopter struggled on, and everyone breathed a little easier as it left the attackers behind. From their altitude, the early sun began to appear from behind the eastern mountains, coloring the peaks ahead with the colors of daylight. A long patch of gleaming blue revealed Lake Balkhash curving away behind them. Soon the muted reddish browns of the Betpak-Dala Desert bloomed beneath them. There in the distance they could see the gleam of what remained of the Aral Sea.

There was a sharp crack and shriek of metal tearing. Suddenly the cabin's air became thinner, and the smell of blood became noticeable. "Nina!"

Jack looked into the back seat and saw the elderly woman bleeding from her left shoulder. He reached into his jacket pocket and handed her his handkerchief to press against her wound. "I think I am all right. It is bleeding a lot, but I don't think it hit a bone." She looked worse than her voice would have indicated.

"Hold pressure on it! I'll see if I can get us to Baikonur." Katerina slewed the copter, evading further fire, and went to full throttle. There, just north of Turayatum, was the little town of Baikonur and the complex that was the Baikonur Cosmodrome.

"What in the world is going on, Jack? I thought that you would be coming back yesterday. – And who are these women?" Bob was a little excited. The helipad was forty steps away. They followed Katerina and Nina, who were being pushed on a stretcher. "Damn, these bags are heavy!"

"Bob, you know I never do anything except on purpose. These ladies are the real key to our success. Do not make it look hard to carry. These are the special clothes I told you I could only find in central Asia. I would like to get them stowed on the Soyuz first - if we can. By the way, can we get into our space suits soon? I would like to inspect the water container and get a little acclimatized before we lift." Jack's voice sounded a lot more concerned that his face let on. Bob knew immediately that things were not going as planned and that the entire mission was in extreme jeopardy.

"That should not be much of a problem. The director of security and I have become good friends. I really like the guy, although I think he drinks too much." Just at that moment, Nataly walked up and spoke to Katerina and Nina on the stretcher. "Here he is now."

"Bob, It is good to see you and Mr. Knight together again. I have spoken with Major Yerisivloskaya. She believes that the countdown can continue as planned. That is good news for all of us. Can I help you with that?" He started to reach for one of the small suitcases.

"Nah, Nataly, that will not be necessary. I would appreciate it if you would put the balalaika into its case and help us get it and everything stowed in the Soyuz. My associate, Mr. Knight would like to be fitted with his spacesuit. He would like to inspect the water container. I think he is a little nervous about the ride. What is the condition of our older traveling companion?"

"I am not sure, but she is being taken to see our base physician. I am sure Dr. Yousef can patch her up. She is the best."

"Excellent. I know our pilot will be pleased that her grandmother will have such care." Jack was clearly relieved that Nina would have a real doctor to look at her wound.

"Do not worry, Mr. Knight. Dr. Yousef will take good care of her patient. Shall we transport to the Energiya?"

The small party loaded into a small van and drove the two-mile trip to the launch pad as soon as Nataly had gotten the balalaika and its case from his office. "I took the liberty of loosening the strings before I put it into its case, Bob."

"Thank you, Nataly. I have always made a point of doing that before any air travel and never had a problem with my stringed instruments."

"Yes, it has something to do with the reduced air pressure. I hope you will take care of my little balalaika." The party arrived at the huge elevator that would take them to the tiny Soyuz at the top of the immense rocket.

"You can count on it. I think that I will be the first human to play a balalaika in orbit." The metal door closed and they were lifted toward the space capsule.

"No, but you will be the first American."

"Really! Who else played?"

"Bob, there were many long and empty hours on Mir, and there was a balalaika on board when it burned up in the atmosphere. It is possible that you will be the first human to play one well." They reached the top of the big elevator's path, and the hatch of the Soyuz was in front of them as the interior door retracted. Nataly un-dogged the hatch. "I think that there will be room enough in this storage compartment behind the pilot's head." The compartment was in fact just deep enough, and the suitcases fit upright and the balalaika fit just above. It was a tight fit. "It is better than I thought," said Nataly. "A tight fit is best so that things will not have room to move on the ride into orbit." He closed the compartment and sealed the hatch. "It can be a little rough, or so I am told." He chuckled as the interior door of the elevator closed, and they started down.

"Hold it right there, Chief!" The elevator had just come level with the inspection hatch of the water container. Jack looked the hatch over. It was about thirty inches across and had manual seals. "Can it be opened from the inside?"

"Why would you need to know this, Mr. Knight?" An edge of suspicion had come into Nataly's voice.

"It may be necessary to use this container for more than water when we reach orbit." Bob had a sudden tingling of horror. Jack's voice was totally unaffected.

"I see." Nataly sounded relieved. "There are some safety seals on the inside that could be opened. They were placed there during construction to prevent a construction worker from being trapped on the inside. They could serve a purpose, but they are clumsy compared to these. Also, there is no light source inside the container. All construction workers had portable lights on hardhats while they worked. Also not filled with water at that time. Is this information helpful?"

"Yes, Thank you very much." The elevator resumed its descent.

The base's infirmary was well supplied and as modern as any facility in central Asia - and more than most. Nina was on an operating table, and Dr. Yousef was working on Nina's right shoulder. Nina seemed to be awake, and was busily telling the doctor how well she was doing at any given point. "That doesn't look good! How did you get your license? Do you have a license? Oh! That hurt! What kind of a monster are you anyway..." She did not ever quit talking during the entire procedure.

After she was through, Dr. Yousef walked away from the table with Nina hurling insults over her shoulder. "I don't think a single bullet will be enough to kill that harridan! Oh, sorry, I realize that she is your grandmother." Katerina smiled at the doctor's words.

"I don't think my Nina would mind being called a harridan even if she knew what it meant! She has had a very hard life and it has made her suspicious of strangers. How serious is her injury?" Katerina's concern reached only her eyes.

"It could have been much worse. The bullet entered her back just above her scapula and exited below the clavicle in the front. It nicked an artery just beneath the clavicle but missed the brachial plexus as well as her lung. She will probably recover fully. She has lost a lot of blood. I managed to sew the nicked artery closed and debrided the entrance and exit wounds before I closed them. It is going to be very sore for several weeks. She will also be weak from her loss of blood. I am always concerned about any wound in a person of her age."

"Is she fit to fly?" Katerina looked grim.

"No, not really. She would probably survive it. She would not feel good for some time. Her ability to adapt is also less than someone younger." Dr. Yousef sounded as grim as Katerina looked.

"She will survive it, and I'll wager that she will be much more adaptive than you would guess."

"Then you are set on her going on this little trip?"

"Yes, she must go." At that moment Jack, Bob, and Nataly entered the infirmary.

"Very well, I will dress her wounds in such a way as to make it possible to wear a suit." The doctor returned to her patient, and Nina's protestations were again heard in the infirmary.

"Is everything going to be all right?" Jack looked as if he was uncertain what he wanted the answer to be.

"Yes. It looks like we can launch on schedule." Katerina was getting her first good look at Bob.

"Major Yerisivloskaya, may I present my younger brother, Robert Knight?"

"Certainly, Mr. Knight, it is a pleasure to meet you. Your elder brother has told me exactly nothing about you, other than he has more flying experience than you do." Katerina smiled in a somewhat predatory way as she considered this infant attempting to dock the Soyuz.

"That is almost exactly what he has told me about you, Major, other than that part about flying and all." Bob smiled sheepishly at the tall attractive redhead with the scary look on her face."

"Major, what is your plan for the extra crewman?" Nataly was again beginning to have nasty suspicions about this very strange crew.

"Mr. Knight has made it very clear that this is not an area of my concern. I will pilot the Soyuz to a safe docking with the American spacecraft. I have reason to trust this American as being as good as his word."

"Mr. Knight, you have not informed me about any such plan."

"I'll talk to you about it as we suit up Chief."

T-Minus 00:00:00:00:10:00

The countdown resumed as the elevator descended. It seemed that the elevator had stalled for a few minutes on the way up. Apparently, Mr. Knight wanted to inspect the water container again on the way up. Nataly watched from his place in the control room as the elevator reached the bottom and the gantry began to withdraw. He was uncomfortable at the huge wad of cash that Bob had pressed into his hand as they were suiting up. It made an uncomfortable lump in his back pocket. It was more money than he had ever owned in his entire life. He recalled the last moments in the suiting room. "Nataly, my friend, take this. I will have no use for it where I am going. I do want a little favor if you will. Don't let anyone stop this countdown once it recommences."

"Bob, my friend, you do not have to further buy my cooperation. I am more than amply compensated. I am certain that I do not like your brother's nearly suicidal plan."

"It was the best we could do under the circumstances. I do not like it either. If Jack thinks he can do it, he probably can. He is funny that way."

"I still don't like it."

"That is to your credit, Nataly. I will miss you. I don't think that you should drink so much."

"I only drink because I hate my job." He had eyed the huge wad of thousand ruble notes and said. "Perhaps, I'll retire. Someplace warm where the women are scantily clad."

"Perhaps you will." Bob had laughed and climbed into the van for transport to the waiting rocket.

"Starting final countdown. One minute. Fifty-nine, fifty-eight, fifty-seven, fifty-six, fifty-five, fifty-four." A phone rang at Nataly's place. He answered it.

"Mr. Dimitri?"

"Yes, this is Nataly Dimitri." The voice on the other end of the line sounded very frightened. The countdown continued in the background. "Thirty-seven, thirty-six, thirty-five, thirty-four."

"I have a Major Kostolinkavitch here at the gate, Mr. Dimitri."

"Yes, yes, I know of Kostolinkavitch - Formerly of KGB, now some sort of clandestine entrepreneur. What does he want?" "Twenty-seven, twenty-six, twenty-five, twenty-four."

"Major Kostolinkavitch is very insistent to talk to you personally."

"Fine, put him on but keep your gun on him." "Fifteen, fourteen, thirteen, twelve, eleven." Nataly kept his eyes on the distant rocket.

"Dimitri! You have got to stop that rocket!" "Seven, six, five, four."

"Why would I want to do that?" "Three, two, one."

"Because it has nuclear weapons on board!" "Ignition, liftoff!" The distant rocket shuddered and began to rise. The docking clamps retracted, and the rocket practically leaped into the sky. The thunder of the exhaust finally reached the control room with the banshee shriek of the huge rocket.

"It has what?" Nataly, unconsciously reached for the range safety button, which would destroy the rocket and the lives of his friends.

"Nuclear weapons! I tried to stop them from getting here but my attempts failed. You must destroy that rocket!" Nataly's finger twitched. He knew that something was wrong with this launch. "You are certain?" He was fully bribed, but letting nuclear weapons into Earth orbit was the act of a maniac.

"I am certain! Now do your job!" Nataly hesitated only another few seconds while he reviewed his own recollections and recalled the four strangely heavy suitcases they had placed on the Soyuz. He crossed himself, as his Russian Orthodox heritage moved him to do, and pressed the button. There was a distant explosion.

T-Minus 00:00:00:00:10:00

The water temperature was not immediately apparent as Jack splashed into the thirty-inch hatch so far above the ground. With the excursion type suit on, he weighed almost four hundred pounds and sank like a stone to the bottom of the tank. The suit was designed for vacuum and not for water. Soon the water began to suck the heat out of his body despite the efforts of the suit heater. Water is eighteen hundred times better at conducting heat than air. Air was as much better at conducting heat than vacuum. Although the water temperature was only about sixty degrees or so, it was still almost forty degrees colder than Jack; and he and his suit heater tried mightily to heat up enough water to fill a small swimming pool. The total blackness was not relieved by his suit's external light, as the lights had nothing to illuminate in the otherwise featureless tank. The dark and cold had become the only things in Jack's life when suddenly a huge weight pressed him down against the bulky backpack that contained his air supply and batteries. His legs extended beyond the lower edge of the excursion backpack and were pressed into the most uncomfortable position that Jack had ever experienced. The cold dark beckoned now, filled with agony beyond his previous imaginings. He felt as if he were being torn in half. All the blood, which should have been in his head, rushed to his legs and feet. Jack drifted swiftly into unconsciousness.

T-Minus 00:00:00:00:10:00

Katerina sat in the middle with Bob and Nina on either side. The tiny capsule was crammed with what appeared to be old-fashioned instruments to Bob. Katerina worked at the countdown checklist. From time to time, her thoughts turned involuntarily to the man getting very cold in the dark water behind her. "Coming up on the final minute. Is everyone secured?"

"I think I am strapped in as well as I can be." Nina had regained her good humor as soon as she had left Dr. Yousef's infirmary.

"Yeah, I am buckled down." Bob did not attempt not to think about his brother in the water container. He said a little prayer for his brother and one for the ultimate success of the mission.

"Coming up on final countdown. On my mark, Fifteen, fourteen, thirteen, twelve, eleven, ten, nine, eight, seven, six, five, four, three, two, one, ignition, liftoff!" The last word was mashed out between clenched teeth as the largest single stage engine in the world lifted them away. No screens were visible to this crew, no frills of any kind - just the crushing acceleration to remind them that they were on the way to space. On the way they were. "Four seconds away from main stage separation. On my mark, five, four, three, two, one, mark!" There was a sharp crack and, in their minds, they saw the huge booster tumbling away behind them. The second stage booster kicked in, and they were again pressed into the acceleration couches. Suddenly there was a huge boom transmitted poorly through the thin atmosphere.

"That sounded like the range safety ordinance. I wonder that we were not destroyed as well."

"Perhaps because I bribed a technician to disconnect it yesterday. I was hoping that he had managed the main booster as well. That was much too close." Bob was thinking again about the power of real money - on where the water hits the wheel.

"He may have tried. There is a back up system on the Energiya booster because of its great destructive potential. Coming up on second stage separation. On my mark, five, four, three, two, one, mark!" There was a duller crack and all weight left them.

Chapter Twelve
A Little Light Housekeeping

T+00:00:00: 35:12

Katerina Yerisivloskaya maneuvered the Soyuz and its trailing tank of water into position along side of the huge tripartite spacecraft. It was more than a little tricky to engage the bayonet valve on the side of the tank with the female mate on the side of the Trigger. Hours of simulation made the real thing relatively difficult but possible under the demanding circumstances. There was a sharp click and suddenly she could feel the water being sucked into the evacuated tanks of the trigger. She allowed herself a moment to consider the occupant of the water container.

She looked to her left and saw that Nina had not yet regained consciousness. She was breathing normally and Katerina felt that the only thing possible under the circumstances was to wait until she could get Nina out of the spacesuit to check her over. She turned to her right and looked at Bob. He was alert and had a concerned look on his face but remained quiet. Katerina really appreciated his calm, as it had allowed her to concentrate on the task of unloading the water when she needed all her attention. Bob noted her regard and interpreted this as her permission to speak. "How long do you think it will be before we can find out about Jack?"

"I am not sure. That pipe emptying the tank is about sixteen inches in diameter, and it is being pulled by a hard vacuum. Not as long as you might think considering the volume of the container."

"Do you think that he will be all right?"

"Your brother is a very tough man. I doubt he was able to remain conscious but, if he survived the cold, he should have survived the ride. We are doing the best we can for him right now by taking the water from around him. That will help him by letting his suit catch up with heating him up to a reasonable temperature. When the tank is empty, I will dock at the forward end of this huge spacecraft. I will evacuate you and Nina and personally open the hatch on the container. Then we will see."

Jack Knight floated in the cold darkness for several eternities. The first thing he noticed beyond the cold was the fact that his low back was not as painful as it had been before he blacked out. Oh, it still hurt but it was not like being broken in half anymore. He was totally disoriented in the dark and cold. He could hear things through the water that sounded like rockets firing from time to time but was unable to associate any motion with the thrust. There was a loud click, and then there was some motion. There was a rushing sound that Jack could not associate with darkness and cold. There seemed to be some sort of movement. He was being swept along in some sort of current. The sound of rushing water grew steadily louder until it almost drove out the sensation of cold. Suddenly there was a sharp thump as his helmet clunked against a grate. The sound of rushing water had reached its fortissimo.

He pushed against the grate and tried to get to his feet, but there was no appreciable up or down sensation. He was in space! It all came quickly back as he recalled the desperate effort to get all four of them into space and his decision to try the ride in the container of water. The only force he had to push against was the tenuous force of the water being pushed into the tank by the tiny bit of atmospheric pressure in the container of water. The tank was largely empty now with only his feet to above his knees still immersed. If it could be called that, as he stood up, he was pulled free of the surface of the water by his sudden acceleration and propelled toward the other end of the tank. The tank was still in absolute darkness as he slowly drifted toward the end away from the sound of water. His body slowly began to warm up, although the outside of the suit was still wet in the humid but thinning air of the almost empty tank. The sounds gradually diminished as the air in the tank was evacuated by the greater volume of the three liquid oxygen tanks. His hands were still numb, and he could not feel the walls of the tank through the thickness of the excursion suit. The water must have shorted out the lights on his helmet. Luckily, the water had not penetrated into the electronics operating his air and heat. Even though it was darker than the inside of a coalmine in the tank, he was beginning to feel better than he had since climbing into the tank and its numbingly cold water. Suddenly, the wall of the tank whacked him on the back, and he was flung across the tank into the other wall. Katerina must be maneuvering the Soyuz, with the tank attached, to dock with the space shuttle external tank assemblage. He hoped his family had come up with a better name than that. He was suddenly looking forward to seeing light again.

A pressure suit is much more comfortable than a strait jacket but, as far as things to wear, that is about it. They are hot, claustrophobic, and noisy under the best of conditions; and wherever it is possible to itch, it will itch. It will not be possible to scratch anywhere. Jake oriented himself where he could hang onto one of the tethers in the triangular passage and waited for the inner door pressure to equalize. He had no idea who would be coming in, although the odds favored his sons.

The radio silence had been part of the original plan, but it was un-nerving to not have contact at this point in the mission. They knew that the Soyuz had arrived when the gauges showed water in the tanks. They were able to hear the docking when it occurred. Jake had already been putting the pressure suit on. The crew of the Trigger had been setting things up for space. Madelyne had been in her garden setting her sprouts in their hangers with the assistance of Margaret. Margaret, who was in charge of navigation, had spent about five minutes determining that they were exactly where they were supposed to be and headed off with Madelyne to get the garden growing. Tom was doing the final checks on the reactor before bringing it on line. Jake was answering the door. The pressure suit was a precaution upon which their preflight protocol had insisted. It was sensible and very uncomfortable. Although he could not actually be in any danger, the suit was to allow him to assist others if they required it.

There was a dull clank communicated through the air around the pressure suit, and the inner door began to open. Jake had a sense of unreality exacerbated by the micro-gravity, when an elderly woman in a Soviet-era spacesuit was pushed through the lock by his youngest son. She was unconscious, and Jake immediately assisted his son in bringing her into the lock and closing the door after them. "Where is Jack?"

Jake's voice carried through the helmets and air but was muffled by the barriers. "He is in the water container."

"He is where?!" Jake had spoken much louder this time.

"He is in the water container. Katerina has gone to get him out."

"Who is Katerina?!" Jake was practically yelling now.

"She is our pilot."

"Why is Jack in the water container?!" The yelling seemed to make Jake feel better, although he still had a profound sense of unreality.

"There was only room for three in the Soyuz. We had to bring Nina."

"Who is Nina?!" The answers seemed to make sense but not to Jake.

"This is Nina. She is Katerina's grandmother. She was wounded on the way to the Cosmodrome. She has not woken up since we blasted off. We need to get Mom to have a look at her. I'm worried about her."

"What about Jack?" Jake took Nina's other arm and they began to steer the unconscious woman down the Triangular passage toward the inner hatch.

"Katerina will take care of Jack."

Katerina Yerisivloskaya watched as the outer hatch door closed behind Bob and Nina. When she was sure that the lock was cycling, she began the checklist for EVA. Although she was not wearing an excursion suit, it was equipped with an umbilical that should allow her enough freedom to reach the hatch of the water container. When she reached the point on the checklist where she unsealed the hatch door of the Soyuz, she paused only long enough to make sure everything was properly sealed and attached. There was still pressure in the inside of the capsule when she opened the hatch and the unnoticed but tiny scraps of whatever blew into low Earth Orbit. She released her harness and started out into the immensity. The water tank was immediately behind the Soyuz as the huge spacecraft orbited the Earth. Katerina, despite thousands of hours in simulators, had never been in space. It was one of the most incredible moments in her life. The Earth hung like a curved mountain off to her left. The Pacific Ocean was like a great turquoise curtain, and the Hawaiian Islands looked like oddly shaped beads on a beautiful necklace. The clouds danced in unpredictable patterns over the surface of the waters. The sun was high in the sky, and the light was sharp and hard in the vacuum of space. The shadows were black with crisp edges.

There was the hatch. The stars away from the Sun were hard points of light. Katerina pushed herself over to the hatch and tried to anchor herself enough to unseal it. Unlike her experience on the surface, it was difficult to unlatch the closures. There, in the light of the stars, she finally was able to open the hatch. There was a brief moment of total darkness as the hatch opened and, framed in the hatch, was the face of Jack. His suit looked beaten up and stained by the water. When he emerged from the dark tank into the light of the sun, she watched as he gleamed and sparkled in the sunlight. He held on to the edges of the hatch, and Katerina noticed that the sparkles were due to a coating of ice all over his suit.

Katerina grabbed his suit and snapped a tether to it. She helped him over to the hatch of the Soyuz and pushed him in. She pulled herself in afterward. After the hatch was sealed, she initiated the protocol to repressurize the cabin. After the cabin pressure had equalized, she started the sequence to open the outer hatch of the Trigger. When the hatch opened, she pushed Jack into it and closed it after her. Because the pressures were not very different, it was only a few moments before the inner hatch opened, and they were in the Triangular passage. She closed the hatch behind them and propelled Jack down the Triangular passage to the hatch into the living quarters. She opened it and nudged Jack into Violet level on the Trigger; and there was Madelyne, Margaret, Tom, Jake and Bob. They all assisted the two space adventurers with the removal of their suits so that conversation was possible.

"Welcome aboard, Major Yerisivloskaya. I am Madelyne Knight. This is my daughter, Margaret, and her husband, Tom White. This is my husband, Jake, and I believe you have already met my sons, Jack and Bob."

Katerina looked them over, and a strange sense of having been there before shook her certainty that she had never seen these people. She then recalled that Jack had spoken at length about all of them. "Please, call me Katerina.

Mr. Jack Knight has told me about all of you at length, or we would not be here having this conversation. "Where is my Nina?" Her thoughts returned to the wizened little woman who had not been conscious when she saw her last.

"Nina is in the sick bay on yellow level. I started an IV and left her loosely secured to the exam table when I heard you and Jack coming aboard." Madelyne looked again at her eldest son, looking quite confused and beaten up, and considered that there was another reason to go back to yellow level. She turned and started "down" the siphon toward yellow level. There was of course no real up or down in the micro-gravity of low Earth orbit, but she still thought of violet level as being up because it had been that way in Texas. She assisted Jack down the siphon and through the plastic isolation barrier into the tiny sick bay of the Trigger. She helped him onto the sole remaining exam "table". It was a very lightly built table compared to the ones she had become accustomed to on Earth. Here in orbit, it would do fine. She secured him to the table and started checking his vital signs. His blood pressure was low, and his body temperature was only ninety-four and a fraction degrees. No wonder he seemed confused and lethargic. He was hypothermic! She warmed a couple of liters of lactated Ringer's solution in the microwave oven and started an IV. She then wrapped him in several layers of blanket and let him rest. He had remained conscious, and she was sure that he would recover completely. She returned her attention back to the other table and was unsurprised to see a strange tableau unfold.

"Katerina, why am I here in this unfamiliar room filled with strangers?" Nina spoke her native Kazakh.

"We are in orbit, Nina. You passed out during the acceleration. This nice doctor has helped you to awaken." Katerina held onto her grandmother's arm so that she would not drift away during this important conversation.

"Why are they flying around? Am I not really dead?"

"No, Nina, you are not dead. We are in space where the pull of gravity is very slight. That is why I must hold on to your arm to keep from drifting away myself."

"Where is the young foreigner who got us involved in this crazy business?" The people floating around her largely blocked Nina's view.

"He is your roommate. He injured himself taking the ride into orbit in a big container of water." Katerina glanced over at Jack who was beginning to shiver.

"Why would he do that?" Nina had her suspicious look back on her face.

"I think he knew that I would not come without you and he needed my help."

"Why did I have to come with you, again?"

"If you had remained, Major Kostolinkavitch would have had you killed - after he had you tortured, of course. " Katerina thought back to the flight up and realized that these people needed to know what had happened on the ascent.

"My new friends," she said, "I feel that you need to know that the authorities at Baikonur know that we have taken nuclear weapons into orbit. It is only a short matter of time before they attempt to neutralize us as a threat to world security. They attempted to destroy us with the range safety ordinance. Luckily, your son Bob here bribed the technician to disconnect the device on the upper stage."

"Katerina, how long will it take to rendezvous with the other large water container?" Jake suddenly stepped forward to lead.

"Not too long, perhaps three to four hours – once I jettison the empty one attached to the back of the Soyuz." Katerina considered where the other container was in orbit and the corrections that would have to be made with the attitude and control rockets of the Soyuz.

"Tom, how long will it take to attach the particle control shroud to the dingus and begin our acceleration out of orbit?"

"The reactor is ready to be brought on line now. That part is just a matter of minutes. It all depends on how quickly we can put the dress on the dingus. I have never tried to zip a fifty five foot zipper in micro-gravity." Tom reached up to push his glasses back up on his nose and then realized that they had not slipped. He had a moment of self-consciousness, put his hand down, and caused himself to drift in the opposite direction from his hand motion.

"I have had training in doing such things, but I will need to be briefed on exactly what needs to be done." Katerina actually looked forward to walking in space again. "I think that I will need at least one more person to help me - regardless of the task - for safety."

"Perhaps, I can be of assistance again when I warm up a little more." Jack had regained the ability to speak, although his voice was broken by the rhythm of his shivering.

"We will need to wait until after we get the additional water before we put the dress on, otherwise it will get in the way when we try to maneuver. "Margaret had clearly thought of the kilometers of fabric billowing behind the ship as they rotated, pitched, yawed, and ultimately, wound the shear fabric thoroughly around them.

"Good point, Margaret. I guess the first thing to do is discard the empty can and go collect our other container. Tom, consolidate the water we have taken on board into a single tank and evacuate the other two to prepare for loading the rest of the water. Bob, would you assist Katerina in getting rid of the empty container? Madelyne, Margaret needs to calculate our course changes. If your charges here are stabilized, you and I can continue planting your victory garden while they recover. Does anyone have any suggestions or objections? Are there any problems that we have not addressed?"

"Katerina, are you going to leave me here with these people?" Nina had been left out of the conversation as it had taken place in English.

"Yes, Nina. You will need to stay here for a little while. There are some things that need to be done before we really settle in. Bob has told me that we will have our own quarters on Indigo Level. When you are well enough, you can go and check them out." Katerina turned to Jack, still shivering slightly on the exam table, swathed in blankets. "Well. Mr. Knight, I guess I was right about you. You were telling the truth."

"It would be a little late to find out otherwise, wouldn't it? Thank you for believing in this mission and me. Thank you for helping us get this far, Major Yerisivloskaya. And please, call me Jack." Jack looked her in the eyes, which were floating above him from where he was strapped on the table.

"I actually had no real doubts. It was much too bizarre a story to be made up, Jack. You must also call me Katerina." Katerina smiled, as she had not before during she and Jack's short association. Jack's shivering lessened perceptibly.

The attachment bolts exploded with a sharp crack heard inside the Soyuz, and the empty tank started its tumble down into the atmosphere. Katerina had oriented the trigger in such a way that the small acceleration of the bolts was enough to cause re-entry after an orbit or two. When the tank was well clear, she reoriented the craft to dock with the larger container of water ahead of them in orbit. It would take perhaps two hours with the course corrections in order to match orbits with the container.

Katerina and Bob were in shirtsleeves as the seals had been tested and found to be holding well. The hatches were open all the way back to the inner door in the Triangular Passage. They headed back to the crew quarters, closing the hatches behind them. "Is this ship more difficult to maneuver than the Soyuz and water container, Katerina?" Bob carefully checked the seal of the Soyuz hatch while Katerina looked on approvingly.

"Not really. It is much longer and heavier, but moves more slowly and surely. I think I will be able to get our water without difficulty." Katerina was pleased that she had managed the dockings as easily as she had.

"You make it look easy. We were very lucky that Jack met you and got you and Nina to come along." Bob finished with the inner hatch, and they started down the Triangular Passage toward the Violet Level hatch.

"Your brother is very convincing. I hope he is fully recovered. I think he took a big risk with the ride in the water tank we just threw away. He will need to have his wits about him when we take our little EVA."

"He'll be ready. He is as tough as they come and gets over things quickly. Whose idea was it for him to ride in the tank?" Bob already knew the answer to this but wanted to hear it from Katerina.

"His, of course. I would not have even thought of it as a possibility. This is a disadvantage to formal training. You learn there is only one right way to do anything, and it shackles your mind so that you do not see other possibilities."

"I figured it was his idea, and he not telling us about it before he climbed in, had him written all over it. He just didn't want me to worry."

"Actually, he planned well. I thought Sergei in the suiting room would go mad when Jack kept insisting on an excursion suit. He had no clue what was planned. He thought Jack was just an eccentric American with more money than good sense." Katerina smiled as she recalled the look on Sergei's face. They closed the hatch to Violet Level behind them and used the siphon to pull themselves to Orange Level where the crew was gathered.

The others were all oriented in various positions having a snack and a sip. They were talking and laughing except for Nina, who was hanging in front of the view port, looking at the Earth as it rotated below. The light from the planet gave her face an elfin glow that with the expression of childlike wonder, made her look years younger.

"Nina, it is some view, is it not. Are you sorry I dragged you along on this little trip?"

"No, my Katerina. I never expected to see such wonders in my life. Even if we were all killed soon, I would not regret this trip. I feel so strong and light. I have not felt this way for years – if I ever felt this way." She smiled down at the planet of her birth. "I feel like I have left so little behind."

"What do you think of our crewmates?" Katerina gestured with her eyes toward the family acting like they were on a picnic.

"I think they are soft and pampered. To think that they would take in a strange woman like myself who doesn't even speak their language and treat her as if she could do something for them – it is beyond even the exaggerated hospitality of my father's people."

"These soft people intend to leave that beautiful planet you can't take your eyes away from and go to the farthest reaches of space to try to save it. It has a quality of selfless purpose that I can admire. I've found so little to admire in the last fifteen years or so in our corner of the world." Katerina considered Major Kostolinkavitch with his tiny piggy eyes and looked at Jack getting a hug from his sister.

"I think that they will make some money from this venture if they can, my Katerina."

"Is that so wrong? I have lost faith in the principles of Lenin and Marx, and I never though you had any faith in them."

"No, it is not wrong at all. I just wonder whether they will be able to hold on to what they win. They took in an old woman with nothing to contribute. It does not bode well for when the negotiations get intense." Nina looked at the family and a worried expression came into her eyes.

"I will help them with these negotiations, should we be able to arrange things so that negotiations make sense. I think that you must begin to learn their language. You may be more of an asset than our crewmates can guess. You will need to be able to share your wisdom with them."

"It will take forever to learn this tongue. You will be there to translate for me." Nina looked concerned.

"Yes, I will be there. However, Nina I cannot always translate for you. I might disagree!" Katerina laughed and, pushing off the bulkhead, she joined the group in the food service area.

Nina watched her grandchild move effortlessly to join this group and smiled. She pushed off with her uninjured shoulder and caught herself on one of the many straps from floor to ceiling. She reached out to the rack of plastic tubes of food. She turned to Bob who was nearby. "What do you call this in English" She used her not so good Russian.

"That is a container of pureed broccoli. I call it "Crap"".

"Crap." Nina tore off the end and sucked some of the greenish goo into her mouth. She grimaced. "Crap," she repeated and meant it.

Chapter Thirteen
A Crazy Time To Be In Space

The acquisition of the additional water went without incident. The three liquid oxygen tanks at the base of the Trigger were now almost full of water. Jack continued to improve. He had pain in his lower back, which became somewhat chronic. It did respond to exercise and stretching, but it gave him an occasional tweak. Madelyne and the rest of the crew got the little sprouts hung in their tiny braces in the two cylindrical farms. Jake had insisted that they complete this task before resting, after extremely long days. He had noted some accumulation of carbon dioxide in the short time all eight of the crew had been aboard. He made the point saying, "Would you rather sleep or breath?" The waste disposal system began to work, and everything seemed to work out exactly as Tom and Jake had planned. A test run of the Dingus was performed and the Trigger attained a higher altitude. Jake and Tom remained the only crew that referred to the Synchrotron Bank as anything but the Dingus. The thrust generated had been only a few hundredths of a gravity. Jake and Tom had been elated that it was able push this much mass as fast as that. It took almost twelve hours of this gentle acceleration to get the Trigger to about five hundred miles above the Earth. This made their orbiting speed seem slower, although they were moving faster. This was because they moved in a bigger circle around the Earth. They were far above the atmosphere now, and they could see most of a continent with one look. Asia, of course, took longer. The smaller islands were now hard to see. During the acceleration, they had had some tiny bit of up and down. Jake had weighed almost two and a half pounds. He felt like a balloon. Their sinuses had all filled up, as there was no gravity to assist the drainage. They had to urinate frequently, as their bodies considered the extra fluid in their upper bodies as too much water. They had to drink a lot to keep from becoming dehydrated. They all began the exercise protocol upon which Madelyne insisted. There was only room for two in the tiny gym at any one time so they divided into teams. Jake and Madelyne, Tom and Margaret, Jack and Bob, Katerina and Nina were the teams assigned by Madelyne, who demanded that they grade one another on their performance and cooperation. She had ruined their first breakfast by giving them the gruesome details of just how bad things would be if they did not comply fully with the program.

Jake and Tom had prepared a brief for Katerina and Jack as to how the Dingus needed to be dressed. They called the Dingus the Synchrotron Bank, and the Dress was the Proton Control and Acceleration Shroud. The pan shaped container for the dress was attached to the external tank that did not have the reactor or the crew compartment in it. They had wanted to minimize the welds on each of the tanks, and this tank had the least stuff on it; so it got the cosmic compact. Margaret had started calling it that as she and Madelyne folded the Dress to stow it. It had a hinged lid, as it could not be discarded when the Dress was removed. The Dress would have to be stowed again when they arrived at Belial. The kilometers of monomolecular fabric would surely get in the way when they tried to dock with an asteroid. They might need their fusion drive again sometime, so they had to put it away when they got through playing with it.

"The Shroud Storage Container is very simple to open." Jake said. "All that is needed is to remove the cotter pin in this hasp and the container will open on its own, as the top is spring loaded. The pin itself is chained to the locking ring of the hasp." Jake smiled as if he wanted his mother to give him a cookie.

"What is the mass of the container lid?" Katerina was taking notes on her PDA, which she had strapped to her wrist like a huge geeky watch.

"It is fourteen gauge aluminum and is twenty five feet across. The rim attached to the outside of the top plate is eleven-gauge aluminum and is four inches in height. This closes over the bottom for the security of the contents. The entire unit masses less than three hundred kilograms." Jake recalled the incredibly painstaking weld that attached that rim to the top plate.

"What is the tension on the spring?" Katerina had a concerned look on her face.

"Gosh, Katerina, you got me there. When we put the shroud into it before lifting it, it took a little bit of a shove to close it enough to latch it. We didn't actually measure the tension on the spring." Jake had a look on his face that suggested that perhaps the newcomer was asking frivolous questions.

"And this container was lying flat on the ground?" The look of concern had matured into a worried look.

"Well sure, it was too flimsy to support its weight on its side."

"This lid is a very dangerous thing for a cosmonaut to open, Jake."

"I see what she is talking about, Jake. We had the weight of the lid to help us close it in Texas, and that was not quite enough to compress that titanium spring welded to the other side of the lid. We both had to press on the lid pretty hard to slip that hasp over the locking ring. That means that without gravity to assist by pulling down on that lid, only its just released mass will slow down the snapping open of the twenty-five foot lid. Once it starts moving, it will tend to stay moving until it reaches its maximum degree of freedom. It would be plenty of acceleration to fling an Astronaut into deep space and perhaps even snap his or her (looking at Katerina) tether. In my mind, I can see Jack coasting up to this gentle looking pin and pulling it and surprise! It leaps up and snaps his neck." Tom had indeed figured out the worried look on Katerina's face.

Jake Knight looked as if he had been slapped. His face colored redly and he thought of all the times he had accused Madelyne of planetary chauvinism. The error that Katerina had noticed without even seeing the container might have cost the mission the two of the crew most qualified to prepare the ship to actually get underway. Jake looked at his son and Katerina and shuddered. He felt like a fool.

"OK, call me stupid, but I don't think the problem is as serious as you big brains seem to believe. The mass of the lid is the same now as it was on Earth. It is going to require a good bit of force to accelerate this mass, and it will not be instantaneous by any physics I understand." Jack did not like that look on his dad's face.

"Jack my friend, you are confusing mass with force. Mass is unchanged. Force of gravity is absent. The mass of the lid will resist acceleration. This property of mass is inertia. The lid was closed on Earth by seven hundred pounds of force, plus the efforts of your burly father and brother-in-law. All this will not be present when we pull the pin from the hasp this time. It is a problem with the English system that uses units of force interchangeably for units of mass. No English speaking person in my acquaintance uses the word "slugs".

"Exactly! We could feed a bit of cord through the hasp before we remove the pin and have the other end fed through an attachment eyelet and have some sort of brake on the cord to control the speed of opening." Tom had already been thinking of some practical and quick ways to keep this spring-loaded monster from being dangerous.

"If we leave the lid up will it not flex and wobble under acceleration?" Jake was trying to envision his beautiful spaceship with a thing like a cooling waffle iron sticking out the side.

"Not really. It will become very slightly closed during the first few seconds of acceleration. When the acceleration becomes constant, at the levels we believe we can attain, it will surely be open. It might make some sort of sound when it finishes opening that might be disconcerting if we were not expecting it." Tom was drawing on his PDA as he spoke. "I think I have it. I can use two nuts at the end of a short tube as a brake. If you off set the huts just a bit and rotate the tube, the friction can be varied over a large range from almost none to a great deal. I can glue this little gadget together while we are working through the rest of the spacewalk." He showed his design to Jake and then to Katerina and Jack. It was simple and practical. "I'll design an electrically operated hoist to close this when we put the shroud away."

"OK, now that we have identified that unforeseen bit of trouble, lets work through the rest of the necessaries and then get on with the job." Jake had recovered his composure. "To remove the shroud from the container there are four Velcro closures at the compass points. The Zipper is facing up from the container. The beginning is here. If this can be brought to this position on the Synchrotron Bank, and if one of you can brace themselves against the other while they hold on to these attachment eyelets, it should be possible to zip the entire length."

" It is almost eighty feet around the bottom of the Dingus. We will have to switch off from time to time to avoid unnecessary fatigue in our zipping hand. We will be clipped to the ship and to each other. This part of the mission will be tedious but not too dangerous." Katerina was again looking forward to the bright hard sparkle of distant stars.

"It should not be necessary to do anything about straightening out the shroud. We used the Synchrotron Bank for twelve hours to get us up to this high Earth orbit. We should have built up a considerable negative charge. I do not think it will be dangerous to you as long as you remain grounded relative to the ship." Jake was looking forward to lighting the torch to see if the fusion drive would work.

"I think I have got the brake and cord together for you. First, clip this end to the hasp. Then clip this end to the eyelet nearest the hasp on the side of Trigger. When you first pull the pin, keep the tube brake a little more than sideways against the axis of cord motion. It should allow you to control the rate of opening precisely." Katerina, Jack and Jake all regarded the simple construction of cord, tube, and metal nuts glued together, with approval. It appeared as if it would work perfectly under any conditions. "I have included about a foot and a half of extra cord. This should give you plenty of leeway regarding your choice of eyelet, and yet not be so excessive as to snarl." Tom smiled.

The team would keep in contact with Margaret, who had patched their suit radios into the main communication system. This would be the first time the strict radio silence would be broken. The entire crew had discussed the pros and cons of this. Jake had not wanted to do it, as it would provide a good fix to those watching from the ground below and perhaps allow a lock-on of weapons already in orbit. They had no clue of the types of weapons that the various space-faring powers had in orbit, although they had a strong suspicion that there were satellite killers in orbit with them. They were tied into the World Wide Web through the entertainment satellites in geosynchronous orbit above them. They were also passively listening to the radio and television broadcasts. The official story was that the blast off from Texas had reached orbit but that the crew had all perished in their homemade spacecraft. The launch from Baikonur was also described as a coincidental launch of an experimental satellite that had been destroyed automatically by the range safety device, when it strayed off course before reaching orbit. The two launches were not seen as connected in the civilian broadcasts they were able to intercept. The official attempts at communication on the military wavelengths had included various threats of destruction if their unconditional surrender was not immediately forthcoming. The fact that they had not already been destroyed was an indication to the crew that the people on the ground did not know exactly where the "terrorists" were. Why anyone in orbit would trust someone on the ground offering terms for their survival was not conceivable.

The decision made, they made some provision for the worst-case scenario. The attitude controls of the Soyuz were set to allow for aiming the Dingus at whatever started tracking them. It was automatic except for actually turning on the dingus. This was to insure that no one was in the path of the Dingus when it started. It was set up where Jake in Red Level could turn it on with his PDA. The Soyuz would be evacuated at the time to allow the spacewalkers to get to where they needed to go and to give them a place to come back into the Trigger. The Trigger's own radars would be on passive mode unless the attitude controls of the Soyuz were activated.

Katerina and Jack went to Violet Level with Bob and Margaret to suit up. "Keep talk to an absolute minimum when the radios are activated, Jack. I fear that I agree with Jake about why we have not already been destroyed." Katerina pulled on her right glove, sealed it, and had Bob check the fit.

"I got over the ooh and ah thing when I went into that tank of water, Katerina. I will not say anything if I do not have to. I'm afraid that just having the carrier going will be enough for some of the equipment that the United States has." He finished putting on his gloves and started checking his equipment before fastening his helmet. Jack's excursion suit had been gone over completely by Jake and Tom, and the small shorts repaired. It should operate perfectly now that it was not expected to survive extended immersion in water.

"I think you are right, my friend. If we could trail a wire through hatches, it would be safer. Unforgiving vacuum will not allow this." Katerina finished with her left glove and began the systems checks that Jack had just finished on his own suit. After she and Jack had checked their own suits, they checked each other's. Then it was time to go.

Tom was in the Triangular Passage with his brake and line. He attached it to Katerina's suit with a Velcro strap out of the way. He then tapped them each on the helmet and went back into Violet Level. He dogged the hatch behind him. Katerina and Jack made their way through the lock at the docking adapter. They entered the Soyuz and closed the inner hatch. Katerina began the protocol to depressurize the capsule to begin their walk. They listened to the pump pull the air out of the craft and, when the sound was sensible only as a distant vibration, gathered their tethers and opened the outer hatch. The stars waited.

Katerina led the way to the aft section of the Trigger. Jack followed carefully and, looking up once, decided that perhaps he was not really over that ooh and ah thing, as he was stunned and shocked by the harsh beauty of the greater universe. They quickly reached the Cosmic Compact, and Katerina secured herself. She carefully attached the clips on the hasp and eyelet less than a foot away from the hasp and pin. When she was ready to apply the brake, she motioned for Jack to remove the pin.

Jack carefully grabbed the pin by its restraining chain and slowly began to pull it from the locking ring. The amount of resistance was much greater than he anticipated. He paused and took time out to secure himself to nearby eyelets. Katerina smiled approvingly but did not loosen her grip on the brake. Jack resumed his pull on the pin and, with not having to brace himself, found it a much easier task. When the pin cleared the locking ring, there was a sudden movement as the hasp sprang off the locking ring, and the lid leaped to the limit that Katerina had allowed it to open. It occurred in much less than a second. As the large lid quivered at the end of the braked cord, Jack was suddenly very glad that Katerina had foreseen this problem. When the lid had damped its motion, Katerina slowly rotated the brake toward the axis of the cord's movement. The lid slowly and regally opened fully.

Katerina was very pleased with the cleverness of the simple brake design and allowed the remaining cord to slip from the tube, which she reattached to a Velcro strap on her suit. She reached forward and detached the closure from the Dress in the container. It was her first time to see something that was a fabric but consisted of, at most, five to ten single molecules. Jack detached himself and made his way across the container to the area at the hinge. He detached the Velcro strap and looked back at Katerina. She was moving toward the "East" point and so he worked his way over to the "West" side. He carefully detached the strap and held on to the Dress at the zipper. He looked over at Katerina, and they each started moving farther aft toward the Dingus.

Jake and Tom had had the foresight to position the Dress so that no major rotation was necessary. Katerina moved across the bottom of the Dingus and secured herself to an eyelet. Jack secured himself to a handy eyelet and looked back at Katerina. There were several Velcro stays around the outside diameter of the Dingus. When these were secured, the zipper lined up perfectly. She then motioned toward the beginning of the zipper and She and Jack met there and anchored themselves, while Katerina began to mate the sides of the zipper. She was initially unable to do it, as the fabric of the dress had begun to billow out away from the ship, and it pushed her upside down. Jack choked down a nervous laugh and helped her reorient herself with respect to the zipper. With the ends mated, it was clear that the entire operation would have to be carried out left-handed. The zipper zipped from right to left. It was unexpectedly difficult to pull the heavy zipper with the left hand across the body and out to the left side. With the fabric of the Dress billowing farther and farther out from the ship, it was not possible to be over the Dingus while the zipper was closed. The zipper was nearly eighty feet long. Jack and Katerina slowly zipped and reattached and zipped and reattached. They switched off when the left hands of either began to cramp. The Dress stood out from the ship like a huge drape of exotic fungus - black, curved, and indistinct in the sudden night their orbit took them. Time passed slowly as they slowly worked around the Dingus. Katerina was taken by the surreal quality of zipping a huge four-legged dress in the moonlight of high Earth orbit. The only sound was that of her ragged breathing. Jack worked in the same silence and was breathing hard from the effort of holding himself and Katerina still against the side of the dingus. He was using muscles that he had not known he had, and they were beginning to complain. Then unexpectedly, they arrived back where they had started. They took a moment to breath and reattached themselves to the base of the external tank the habitation was and surveyed their work. The Dress looked as it never had. It appeared stiff and shiny black in the sunrise that appeared as they watched. They attached the four control cables to the ring clips, spaced at even intervals around the tripartite ship. There was a cable to be attached over the reactor compartment, and Jack waved Katerina back and snapped it himself. They looked everything over again. Then they started back toward the Soyuz. Katerina looked at Jack and indicated that he was to make the announcement.

"We have dressed the Dingus! I repeat, we have dressed the Dingus and are on our way back in!" As Jack said this, he had a sudden feeling of unease and looked behind them. He was horrified to see a sudden jet in the distant night behind them.

"Get out of there! We are being painted by radar and a missile is incoming!" Margaret's voice sounded scared.

Jack and Katerina hurried toward the Soyuz. Suddenly the ship moved underneath them as it slewed its rear toward the unseen threat. If they had not been tethered to the ship, they would have been lost.

The attitude control rockets on the sides made swift adjustments, and the forward end of the ship made large movements, rotating around the huge mass of water stored in the liquid oxygen tanks at the base. Jack and Katerina attached more tethers and steadied themselves against the aluminum skin of the Trigger. The kilometers of black fabric stretching out from behind the ship rippled and readjusted itself as the Dingus fired up. The increased negative charge stretched the fabric more than previously, and it appeared a hard shiny surface behind them. There was a sudden pull as the relativistic protons added thrust to the Trigger. The Soyuz was now clearly up and the Dingus was down. What was level was now vertical, and the motions of the ship, as it moved its deadly particle beam toward the threat, gave Jack severe vertigo. He felt like he was going to fall and be batted off the Trigger at the same time. Back behind the Trigger, there was an eerie glow down towards where Jack had seen the brief flare of a jet. It was pink at the edge and green towards the center. It was probably the incredibly thin atmosphere being ionized, Jack thought, as he struggled to hold on to the tethers.

There was a brief moment of lessening of the thrust and they were in free fall again. "Jack, Katerina, get back into the ship! The missile that was nearby has apparently been neutralized. However, it may be on silent running for all we know. The radar has stopped, but the thing is still coming our way. We need to change course as soon as possible and get underway!" Margaret was talking to herself after the first few words as Jack and Katerina struggled to get back into the open hatch of the Soyuz.

They had just gotten the hatch closed behind them, when they were thrown against the walls of the capsule as the attitude control rockets fired again. The capsule began to pressurize, and they began to be able to hear the clicking of relays in the ancient electronics of the Soyuz, as the external computer in the Trigger ordered quick firings of the rockets. Weight returned, and they settled against the bulkheads in the capsule. They started the protocol to open the inner hatch. It was now down below them.

The Hatch opened, and they found the unfamiliar handholds that allowed them to climb down into the docking adapter. They lifted the hatch of the Soyuz and sealed it behind them. The lock cycled, and they open the outer hatch of Trigger. The Triangular Passage yawned beneath them like some strange well. They climbed down the passage and opened the hatch into Violet Level. There, they were able to stand for the first time in several days. They hurriedly assisted each other removing their suits and stowed them carefully.

"Do you think this is a course change, or are we trying to kill another missile?" Jack started toward the siphon and started down toward the now obviously lower parts of the ship.

"I am not sure, of course, having no more information than you do. If I were to guess, I would suggest that it is another attack." Katerina found the use of her voice again, although tired from the efforts of putting the drive together.

"I am headed down to Red Level to check things out." Jack sounded a little ragged from his exertions.

It seemed almost like climbing down a tower. Jack weighed only about six pounds, but the up and down was enough to make the siphon a steep climb.

"I am tired as well." Katerina had followed Jack and was above him on the siphon. "You did very well for someone without training. I suspect you will pay for your efforts later."

Jack looked up at Katerina and marveled at the steadiness of her climbing. The jumpsuit she had worn beneath her space suit was tight enough to show the good conditioning she had maintained despite not being in the program for several years. "I am sure of it. What is your secret?"

"It is not working against yourself. I learned it in a water tank."

"What I learned in the water tank, you do not want to know."

"My water tank was warm and well-lit, and I had a special harness that helped to simulate microgravity. I spent many hours there. It was a very brave thing you did. Perhaps a little foolish, but very brave. I am glad you came out OK" Jack and Katerina arrived at the aluminum pole that took them down to Red Level.

"I can't remember how long I was in the tank. The main thing I remember is you getting me out." They slid down the pole to Red Level.

The crew was buckled in. An additional two acceleration couches had been constructed from available materials and were more lightly made, not having to withstand seven gravities. Jake had his PDA mounted in its rack. Margaret had hers in her hand. She was calculating various trajectories to take them away from the Earth. Madelyne was actually almost asleep. She was lying in her couch and, if she was not asleep, she was in deep meditation. Nina was sitting up and looking around. She had learned a few words of English to go along with her not so good Russian. She had not learned to use her PDA and so depended on Bob, who had become her English teacher, to keep her up on the struggle to leave the planet. Bob was leaning over and talking quietly. From time to time, he would consult his own PDA. Tom and Margaret were side by side holding hands and just waiting to see how things worked out. Margaret looked considerably calmer than her voice had revealed over their radio link. Tom looked like he was worried about something, but not necessarily what was going on at the time. Jack and Katerina took the last two acceleration couches, which were directly behind Jake. Katerina took out her PDA and used it to recall the last twenty minutes of history aboard the Trigger.

"I was correct, we have been under continued attack. Luckily, the launches have all originated from the same place on Earth. We have been able to destroy their electronics as soon as they left the atmosphere. Only the single satellite killer was close enough to have any impact on this exchange. The Dingus makes a very good weapon at this altitude." Katerina was happy about not being blown up and dead.

"Jack, you were right. My little ion rocket is a weapon where it is. The Proton Control and Acceleration Shroud seems to focus the beam very nicely. The beam is now intense enough to reach a few kilometers into the atmosphere." Jake seemed to find this very satisfying. "Where are we in our plan to actually leave the planet, Maggie?"

"We have managed to direct most of our thrust into our line of flight, Daddy. As I figure it, the Dress has increased the thrust of the dingus by an additional twenty percent. Our thrust is now about eight hundredths of a gravity. Did you expect it to push this hard?" Margaret was updating her position information from the GPS satellites for as long as she could.

"No, not really. I had expected the shroud to assist the Synchrotron Bank by twenty percent, but I was surprised by how well it worked by itself when we tried it yesterday."

"We can leave most anytime now, but we will still be in orbit around earth for the next eighteen to twenty-four hours, at our current rate of acceleration."

"As long as they keep shooting at us, it is very dangerous to remain in this region of space. I am thinking that now that we have got all our buttons buttoned and our zippers zipped, we should leave as soon as possible. Good job, Katerina and Jack. Very well done!"

"Thanks Dad. Katerina did the real stuff. I begin to think the smartest thing I did was to convince her to come along to give us a hand."

"Jack, I could not have done that spacewalk without your assistance. We make a very good team in space. I am personally very proud to be included in this most important mission of all space travel. I am most grateful not to have to leave my Nina behind to suffer and die. This was your doing altogether. I thank you for this most wonderful adventure, where perhaps my training and dreams can be of real benefit. Thank you all for making my Nina and myself so welcome in your family."

There was a moment of silence as the entire crew listened to this little speech. "You are most welcome, Katerina, and without your assistance, we would not have the special hardware that will be necessary to carry out our mission. I like what I see of Nina and, as she learns our language, I know I will like her more. You are both splendid additions to our crew." Madelyne never opened her eyes and spoke this as if she had been thinking for some time how to say what everyone else in the crew felt.

Tom was looking over at Jake. "Jake, I think it is time to find out what the Trigger can do. Why don't we put the pedal to the metal?" The last sentence was spoken as if it was something that Tom had heard on television. Everyone laughed, and the tension was broken.

"Let's do it by the numbers, dears. Propulsion?" inquired Jake.

"The reactor is at about forty percent of full power, said Tom. I will bring it up when we shorten the control cables to bring the beams into collision mode."

"Excellent. Life Support? How does your garden grow?"

"All is well in the garden," replied Madelyne. "All the hot air just vented will make things grow even faster. The carbon dioxide levels have been declining for the last three hours. We are as good to go as I can manage."

"Navigation?"

"We are in an orbit of increasing size as we speak. Depending on our acceleration, we will leave the Earth Moon system in the next two days or so. The ability to accelerate constantly has all manner of advantages. We can light your candle as soon as you are ready, Daddy."

"Bosun?"

"Dad, everything is stowed as securely as we can manage. We are processing our waste efficiently as far as I can tell. We appear to have adequate stores. We are as ready as I can manage at this time." Bob had discovered he was the Bosun more properly spelled 'boatswain" - although never pronounced that way - when he and the rest of the crew had arrived with the water and the Soyuz.

"Guns?"

"The tactical nuclear weapons have been inspected and appear to be in good working order. All small arms are properly stowed. The particle beam weapon appears to be operating within nominal parameters." Jack was in charge of these things but would have other duties as directed by everyone else.

"Medical?"

"Jake shut up and push the button or whatever! Get us out of here! This battle is making me nervous!" Madelyne had yet to open her eyes.

Jake had not been married for thirty-seven years without learning when action was required. He reached up, took his PDA, and entered the instructions to shorten the control cables by what he and Tom had calculated would be the optimal angle for initiating fusion. Everyone had set their PDAs to show the view from the aft camera. At first, all they felt was a slight increase in the vibration as the motor winches brought the tapering tubes of the dress so that their outlets faced one another more. Tom entered instructions on his PDA to bring up the power of the reactor to about eighty percent of maximum. There was, at first, a decrease in thrust as the beams axis was altered into a position less than directly behind the Trigger. As the reactor power increased, and the beams started to collide, they all noticed a few faint sparks in the aft view that had shown the pink and green ray reaching out toward Earth. As the beams became more and more incident, the sparks became more frequent - until they were a faint source of actual light, and not just the flickering of fireflies on a summer evening. The thrust continued to fall off, and everyone held their breath, as they wondered whether this farfetched experiment would be more than a faint light show. Then there was a tiny sun behind them, and they were pressed into their couches like never before. It was almost like real weight. "Jake, we are pushing at almost two tenths of a gravity! I am getting overload readings on the power circuit, so I am backing off on reactor levels."

The weight did not increase, but there was a strange sense of solidity to their feeling of weight.

"The power levels from the fusion are still increasing. I am going to shut the reactor down!" There was a sudden decrease in the vibration of the reactor. The sudden decrease in the noise on Red Level was almost deafening. Then they heard it. It started low and seemed to occupy all octaves on the musical scale. It was a sweet basso. It was a thrilling tenor. It was an enthralling soprano and a soothing alto. And the crew of the Trigger lay on their couches watching the blue white brilliance of a tiny jewel-like sun behind them and listened to it sing.

Chapter Fourteen
Like Ducks in a Shooting Gallery

The authorities in the United States were nothing if not determined, or maybe it was plain ignorance and that old American adage "if some is good then much more is probably better". The firings continued as long as they had space ready rockets. They kept killing missile after missile. This put very stringent limitations on possible course changes. As they orbited higher and higher, their now active radars picked up missiles as they passed over the space down orbit from the United States. The crew of the renegade interplanetary spacecraft Trigger were all still at their stations on Red Level.

Right after their fusion drive had ignited, there had been a visible blackout throughout the entire hemisphere they could see with the aft camera. All the radio stations and TV stations just stopped and the net was off line. Tom and Jake were certain that, it was the result of the electromagnetic pulse or EMP that was now powering their ship. Jake had hoped that, without the uncontrolled release of fusion that the EMP would be limited to the spacecraft and the dress: so much for a stealthy get away

"I wonder what this will do to our investments?" Bob had been in charge of handling this from his office in New York.

"Probably not too much as those choices were based on the short and long term spending goals of the larger multinational corporations." Jack had used his position in whatever government agency he worked for to make those choices and had broken many laws on the uses of that privileged information. "I guess that we are all white collar criminals now." He announced to no one in particular. "I don't suppose that I should have even divulged the source of my information. Zap! There goes another one!" He actually seemed a little morose.

Katerina just grinned at the display on her PDA, and when she heard the catch in Jack's voice, she sat up in the gentle thrust of the fusion drive and grabbed Jack by the shoulder. "And this is important to you now? What foolishness! The crew of this ship, by taking on the responsibility that they have, has stepped into the shoes of a large sovereign power. We are no longer subject to the - How do you say it? - Mickey Mouse rules that bind ordinary citizens. We do what is necessary. If I did not believe this, I would still be in Alma Ata wondering when the rapacious ambitions of Major Kostolinkavitch would succeed in ending my miserable existence. I feel so invigorated that these petty griefs that seem to drag you down so thoroughly, are jokes to me now. You, of all people, are responsible for our being here now. The technological wizards your family seems to sprout like weeds are not so important. The money that made the technological miracle we ride in possible and a reality resulted from your insights into the value of the information that you possessed. The fact that you were able to actually obtain nuclear weapons from a person who was convinced that no possible good could result from anyone having them is another accomplishment that you seem to be - How do you say – glossing over? That this same person had the training necessary to accomplish all of your goals – this was all a big accident? I have ocean front property to sell you in central Asia also!"

Katerina's rant ended with a belly laugh that destroyed whatever serious intent she had. It was violent enough to actually lift her from her couch. The resulting spectacle generated enough humor to lift the White Knights from the torpor that had infected them since the planet of their birth had been trying to kill them. They were really getting away with it! The missiles were not reaching them. They had a rocket capable of reaching the orbit of Jupiter in a surprisingly short time. No one on board couldn't recover from the wounds that they had received in getting to where they were in a high escape orbit. The laughs started with Katerina, but they spread to Bob first, then to Madelyne and Margaret, and then Tom and Jake, and finally – Jack. His face had been so serious for so long that it seemed to stretch as the unbelievable humor of concerning himself with having committed securities violations finally got him square in the funny bone.

    They all laughed and bounced off their couches as the automatic responses of their computer to the continued threats from Earth rotated the Trigger to drown the hardened electronics of the oncoming missiles in relativistic protons and helium nuclei. This rendered the now disabled missiles into very expensive and dangerous space debris. They became very much a waste at this point, as they could no longer match the acceleration of the Trigger. The only danger the crew of the Trigger faced was a missile that was launched from ahead of them and hit them from the side. Thankfully, there were none that fit that description. They were now more than a thousand miles from the surface of the Earth. The Earth still had satellites above them in geosynchronous orbit at twenty two thousand miles. These had spent a day or two getting there with the puny chemical rockets that were light enough to lift into low earth orbit. Nina finally caught the bug and laughed even though she had no idea of what she was laughing about. It was just that everyone else was laughing. Even her Katerina was laughing, and she was such a serious child. Then Nina realized how serious she herself had been since the first third of the twentieth century. She had not laughed much in a real way since the Russians had come. That was so long ago. Perhaps, it was time to forgive that drunken fool, Nicholai. He had been dead for sixty-seven years. It was time to forgive him and let him go. She smiled at Katerina, and Katerina smiled back.

"It may be a little early for such things as celebrations, but perhaps it is not. We have reached a milestone in the course of our mission. We have succeeded in leaving the Earth with potent enough medicine to perhaps save it. It may be that we can never go home again, but at least now there is a real chance that there will be a home to go home to. I have a little bit of spirits stored away in one of the lockers on the deck above. Bob, as the Captain of the only interplanetary ship in this region of space, I hereby declare that you have reached the age of majority. You may partake if you wish." After the speech, Jake Knight launched himself to the aluminum pole and hoisted himself into Orange Level to get a certain bottle and some cups.

When he returned, the first interplanetary party in the history of the children of Earth began. For some physiological reason known best by Madelyne, the tiny quantities of single malt Scotch that the crew consumed seemed to raise their already high spirits into a new plane. Madelyne fetched some snacks from the foods stored above and some soft drinks. It was such a novelty to actually be able to drink out of a cup again, and the entire crew noticed that their voices had started to sound more like themselves again. Nina did not take any of the alcohol. She noticed that these people did not seem to get belligerent and angry the way she recalled that Nicholai had done so many years ago - so perhaps that had been yet another personal failing that he had.

Katerina and Jack told the story of their space walk to the entire crowd. They used their hands and switched off so that the entire silent time had been well explained. Jack told the story of the flare of rocket exhaust he had seen behind them, and the terrifying ride under acceleration on the outside of the Trigger's hull. The incredible immensity of the star-filled blackness had awed and given him a sense of how small the entire solar system was. Katerina had just enjoyed the entire time. It was everything she had dreamed of and trained for - and more. An hour, perhaps two, had passed when the voices fell into silence, and the fatigue of the day's labors began to be felt over the adrenaline rush of simple survival in such an impossible place. The party broke up and, after setting several alarms to wake them should an emergency occur, went off to their separate quarters and put themselves to bed.

'When they were all lying on their beds and all the noise of people had died down, they heard the wonderful chord that the fusion drive made as it converted hydrogen into helium.

Then, out in the emptiness about five hundred miles away, a low yield hydrogen bomb exploded. The electromagnetic pulse traveling at the speed of light spread out in a spherical wave front. When it encountered the Dress, it disrupted the standing wave that powered the fusion and the Trigger. The tiny little star winked out like a candle in a storm. The reactor had been shut down and automatic circuits switched in the fuel cells that had powered the Trigger on the way to orbit. When the acceleration stopped, so did the feeling of weight that held the sleeping people in their beds on the Trigger.

The first thing that Jake Knight noticed was that Madelyne was no longer next to him and that the overhead was. He tried to turn on the lights with his PDA, and then noticed that the computer had shut down. Then he figured out that he was in free fall.

"Madelyne, are you awake?" He fumbled in the darkness for his jumpsuit.

"I'm awake. What could shut down our drive like this?" Madelyne did not bother with her clothes but went to the compartment where some emergency equipment was kept. She reached in, found the flashlight, and switched it on. Jake had one foot in the wrong leg of his jump suit and was flailing around the wedge-shaped room trying to dress himself. "Jake, I think that you have got that on wrong."

"Hold that light for me. Then, I'll hold it for you." Jake managed to get his jump suit over his legs and arms and zip it up. He took the flashlight from Madelyne and helped her dress herself. The pair made their way down to Yellow Level and found Tom and Margaret working with the computer to get it on line. They both looked like they had been ridden hard and put up wet.

"I think it was some sort of a power surge, Jake. The surge protector has to be manually reset. The computer is booting. We will probably have to update its astronomical fix." Tom was working at the desk and had strapped himself to the little stool there, so he could use the keyboard.

"Tom, I am going back down to red level to try to reset the shroud to its initial configuration. I will work with the manual controls. When you have the computer back on line we will need to bring up the reactor. The only thing I can think of that is potent enough to shut down our drive is an electromagnetic pulse from a nuclear weapon. It does not seem to have been nearby. Next time they might get lucky. Don't bring up the radar, and resume radio silence." Jake went on down to Red Level and started manually switching the motor winches to gradually allow the shroud to lengthen. When he had allowed them to reach their maximum length, he checked his PDA and noted the controls were back on line. He started the protocol for a cold start of the nuclear reactor. The pumps started and he watched the power levels begin to rise. Jack and Katerina came down the pole and took note of the proceedings. Katerina went back to her quarters to make sure that Nina was secured for acceleration. Tom and Margaret came down the pole as Madelyne brought up the rear. Soon Katerina and Nina returned, and everyone got into the couches that they had occupied before.

"Tom, is the computer back online?"

"Sure Jake, The computer knew where we were when it shut down. We did not change course. - We just stopped accelerating. This changes our trajectory but is not an appreciable change in our course."

"I am going to restart the Synchrotron Bank without restarting the fusion rocket. I don't know if they figured out that the EMP would take us off line or whether that was just a lucky shot. I would prefer not to hang around to find out. I do not want to give them a better idea of where we are. That little star is a bit conspicuous." Jake entered orders on his PDA, and the Dingus started spewing relativistic protons. There was the now familiar beginning of weight. The view from the aft camera showed only the huge black expanse of the Dress. There was no ionization trail this far from Earth.

There was a sudden roar of the attitude control rockets on the Soyuz and with it the realization that the Earth was still shooting at them.

They had not been secured on their couches but just lying on them. The few pounds of weight they had were not enough to secure them from the slewing of the rocket as it aimed itself at an oncoming missile. They were all thrown against the bulkhead. Jack recovered himself first, grabbed Nina and pressed her into a couch, then strapped her in. Everyone else got themselves onto their couches and secured themselves to them. Nina's shoulder had begun to bleed again. It was just a little staining on her jumpsuit, but she looked as if she were hurting from the impact with the metal bulkhead. Katerina looked on worriedly but flashed a grateful smile at Jack.

"I guess they know where we are after all." Jake had sustained a small cut above his left eyebrow, but it did not seem to be anything serious. "I don't think there is any point in the attempt at stealth." He entered more orders on his PDA, and the nuclear reactor increased in volume and power. The crew waited in their bunks for the slight increase in noise associated with the control cables but could not hear them above the roar of the reactor's pumps. "I just fed in the previous settings for the fusion drive along with instructions for the reactor to shut itself down when the power rises above a certain level. I think I just want to hear that thing sing until they can not shoot at us anymore."

"I think we might be able to get a little more out of this thing, Jake. I am going to lengthen the collision path a bit and simultaneously increase the proton flux. I am going to increase the reactor power to near maximum." Tom entered a modification of Jake's instructions on his PDA. The crew all watched as the tiny fireflies of light began. They watched as it brightened and brightened, then there was a jolt and a push as the tiny semi-stellar mass ignited. It looked different this time. It was sort of smeared out in length and much more blue white in color. The reactor pumps slowly decreased the noise they made. The thrust was slightly more than before, but there was an unpleasant wail just at the edge of their ability to hear. It was nauseating. It was nails on the blackboard. It was the grief of old women. It was time to change it back to the way it was before.

Both Jake and Tom struggled to enter the same adjustment to their PDAs at the same time, but it would not accept orders from two at once. Tom noticed what Jake was trying to do and stopped his own entries. The monstrous screeching wail faded and was gradually replaced by the wonderful chord everyone had heard previously. It was a drink of cool water. It was bread to a hungry person. It was a huge improvement. Everyone relaxed and savored the wonderful sound. The thrust also relaxed to about what one would feel on the moon.

There was a sudden roar from the attitude control rockets in the Soyuz, and the Trigger aimed its deadly tail at another missile trying to murder them. This time, they were all strapped in and felt only the exhilarating rush of a thrilling amusement park ride. This was, however, real in all respects – and therefore much more exciting.

"I think that we are getting more from that little star than a ride where we need to go. I want to study the effect it has on us all and the plants too. It is more than a very pleasant sound. It makes me feel younger and more interested in what is going on, yet not as fearful as my intellect would indicate I should be." Madelyne did not have her eyes shut as she frequently did when under extreme stress.

"Mom, do you think it is some sort of intoxication? Margaret was studying her PDA as if it would tell her the answers to her questions. She was merely looking at the image of the tiny star from their aft camera.

"No, it does not feel like any sort of impairment. I just feel a contented sort of excitement."

"It is a feeling of ecstasy." Katerina was as enthralled as the others. "I did not feel it as acutely when I went up to Indigo Level to sleep. Perhaps, it is a matter of proximity."

"I didn't feel it as much either. I had thought that it was only the effect of that little bit of alcohol I had. I do not think it was the alcohol now." Jack was also watching the little star in the image on his PDA.

"When I listen, my shoulder hurts less, and I am less concerned about it." Nina had joined the conversation in her not very good Russian.

"That's the sort of thing I am talking about! I need to study this phenomenon!" Madelyne was quite excited by the idea of looking at this occurrence objectively.

"Mom, did you understand what Nina said?" Bob had a quizzical sound in his voice.

"Sure, she said her shoulder was feeling better. I thought everyone understood that." Madelyne was a little short with her youngest son.

Tom and Margaret nodded as well, as if they did not understand what Bob was getting at. Jake looked at Jack and Katerina, who were beginning to look suspicious as well.

"But Mom, you don't speak Russian."

That particular type of insight was not repeatable, although it seemed much easier to catch what another person was really talking about on Red Level. It seemed to be mainly a sense of well being that enhanced whatever was being experienced. No physical basis for it could be determined. Listening to a recording of the drive still sounded good, or at least soothing, but it did not give the same sense of well-being that actually being on Red Level had.

Jake and Tom taught all crewmembers how to restart the drive should the thermonuclear attack be repeated. The little bit of setback caused by the attack was insignificant in the larger view.

The attacks continued intermittently. As they all originated on Earth, the defensive weapon always continued to put more distance between the Trigger and those who would destroy her. The need to change the aim of the particle beam occurred less and less frequently over the next ten to twelve hours. During that time about sixty kilometers a second had been added to the Trigger's relative velocity. Constant acceleration has a tendency to add up even when not used in the most efficient manner. Everyone slept and ate down in Red Level the first day or so of the escape from Earth. When the orbit had increased to more than ten thousand miles or so, the EMP from the tiny star no longer had any effect on the power grid on Earth. Radio and television stations resumed their broadcasts. The truth was not to be obtained there. The official accounts ranged from attempts to destroy a satellite that could not safely re-enter the atmosphere to sunspots to unexplained cometary debris. Apparently, everyone on Earth could dimly see the little star-like object that was the propulsion system. Everyone on the hemisphere facing them had seen the nuclear blast that took the propulsion offline. It had had no effect on the local power grid, as it was already off because of the fusion drive. As the distance increased, so did talk about the actual cause of all the blackouts. The Net recovered more quickly than the radio and television broadcasts. This actually seemed to strengthen the Net as a primary source of information. The information thereon soon included a fairly detailed version of the actual events. This version seemed to inspire more confidence than the vague official blathering. It was hotly debated what their purposes were. Some thought that they were escaping some religious persecution. Some thought that they were really on a quest for world domination and had been driven off by the concerted efforts of the governments that tried to kill them. Others merely dissected the events themselves and did not attempt to assign motives to eight people that very few knew. There was an interview with Martha, who had been arrested during the first twelve hours after the blastoff from Texas. Apparently, the strategy for her ultimate protection had worked as she was soon released. She was the Knights' steadfast supporter and did not believe that they were involved in doing anything wrong.

"If Mr. Jake Knight is risking his life and that of his family, you can be sure it is not for some stupid reason!" Martha would not immediately get the proceeds of the trust Bob had set up for her but they would come when the transactions could in no longer in any way be attributed to our still secret, but undoubtedly, nefarious purpose.

There was also an interview with Nataly Dimitri, who appeared to be somewhere like Tahiti. "I don't know what they are up to. They seemed like nice people to me." He was sober now with none of the bleary slurring that had obscured his speech before. He was neatly, but not extravagantly, dressed, sitting at a shaded table overlooking a tropical ocean. "I am glad that I was not able to destroy them although I did my best to. I do not think that they mean anyone any harm. Now, if you will excuse me." He stood up and walked away from the interviewer, who continued to shout inane questions at his back.

There were pictures of the burned up warehouse in Texas with "experts" sifting through the ashes looking for clues. The owner had appeared but refused to be interviewed on camera. As an insurance policy had covered his loss, he really had no grudge against the Knights and did not pretend to have one.

The President of the United States held a press conference in which he appeared to answer any question posed, but a semantic analysis revealed that he actually said nothing. He just radiated confidence and the appearance of being in total control of the situation.

Dr. Irving and his wife were shown trying to explain the brass marker on the floor of their living room. They had no idea of its purpose but denied it had been used for any satanic rites. Jake and Madelyne enjoyed that interview the most, as they got to see their old home again and laugh at the ignorance of the people to whom they had sold it.

Eventually, most of the crew found one reason or another why they had to leave Red Level. Madelyne wanted to check on her gardens. Tom and Margaret went to check the computers on Yellow Level. Nina and Katerina went to Green Level to redress Nina's wound. Jack and Bob wandered up to their separate quarters to put some things away and arrange their things.

Jake Knight remained on watch down in Red Level and considered how far they had come in less than eleven months. After six hours passed with no further attacks, he arranged one final course correction to take the Trigger toward the asteroid that was on a collision course with Earth. The news on the Net and on the broadcast media had never mentioned the asteroid. It seemed that the policy of secrecy had worked to everyone's advantage. The governments still appeared to be in charge of the Earth as much as they had ever been. The Trigger had departed with many fireworks and a grand, if not benign, send off. The efforts of Jake and Tom to break a technological barrier that precluded practical interplanetary flight had been broken in a dramatic way. As Jake had read the news, it seemed that there was a new interest in Space and Space Travel. Although there had been the usual hardships and confusion with the blackouts and net outages, no wars had broken out yet. Some old institutions had lost more ground on the way to their ultimate dissolution. Some new institutions had gained the ground that the old ones lost and expanded their sphere of influence. Jake knew intuitively that nothing fundamental had changed – yet.

Chapter Fifteen
There Is A Reason Why They Call It Space

There are things that are more boring than space travel. There must be. I have heard it is like the practice of Anesthesiology. Hours of crashing boredom punctuated with moments of over the top excitement. There is no Anesthesiologist who would not prefer to be bored. We had already traveled millions of miles and would never come close to any celestial body other than Belial. Space is empty like that.

Tom and I have settled into some sort of routine, and we have been married a few months less than a year. I like it. Although we have separate cabins, we sleep in one but socialize and store things in the other. I feel much more comfortable about our relationship than I ever did while we were dating. It's not because he is stuck on a ship with me millions of miles from anywhere else. It is a feeling of serenity and peace that I never had before. Oh, Tom is not perfect. He forgets important things and ignores obvious hints. He does consistently make me feel special, and that makes up for a lot.

We left the Earth /Moon system about a week or so ago. It took us several days to curve around them to the point where we acquired enough velocity to escape the pull of their mass. We got within a hundred thousand miles of the moon on our last pass. It looked bigger and brighter than it does in October but not so much as it should to be that much closer. The Dingus and its Dress keep pushing us at a constant acceleration equivalent to the gravity one would feel on the surface of the moon. It is plenty to keep things in their place most of the time and yet we all feel so light. It is impossible to walk normally. The acceleration, which allows us to stand normally, is not nearly enough to give the bottom of our feet sufficient friction to let us walk in a normal manner. Instead, we sort of hop on the balls of our feet. It was extremely tough on our calf muscles for the first few days, and then we got used to it.

We all work out every twenty-four hours. Personally, although I worked out regularly two or three times a week on Earth, I am getting to be much more fit than I have ever been before. Tom is looking better than ever. The routine is brutal. There is this machine like an elliptical exerciser, except it has this thing like a yoke that fits around one's shoulders. It is attached by springs to the base of the unit. The springs are pulling the person down against the pedals just as if they were being pulled by gravity. There is this spring with a belt attached to it fixed to the wall. It is our scale here in microgravity. The person is attached to the end of this spring and the partner counts the number of oscillations per minute. The slower the oscillations are, the more mass the person has. The strength of the springs on the yoke is calculated to be equivalent to our weight on Earth. I find out that I have actually gained a little mass, although my clothing fits more loosely. I think I like this. We also do weight lifting without weights. We pull and push against different kinds of resistance: Plastic composite bows, rubber bands and springs. It feels just like lifting weights and makes me just as sore later. The resistance keeps increasing. Mom keeps track of all of our progress and gives us what for if she thinks we are slacking off. She and Dad look better than they have in years. Daddy whines about it, but I think he secretly likes the results.

Some of us look no different whatsoever. I am speaking, of course, about my brother Jack and our pilot, Katerina Yerisivloskaya. Jack has always looked good because he works hard at it. Katerina is a knockout. I even catch Tom looking at her when she is in the compartment. I look at her myself. She is about three inches taller than I am with thick red hair that many women would kill for and perfect proportions. I cannot be sure how old she is, and I will never ask. I am guessing mid-thirties because of all the things she has done. She has been wonderful, pitching in like everyone else and gradually improving her already good English. Sometimes, she gets a look in her eye that is scary. She and Jack have not shared just how they met, but she had a couple of minor wounds when she came on board. I just do not get how Jack talked her into coming along. Perhaps it was the lure of space. I know she always wanted to go to space. I think Jack actually convinced her that we were going to save the world. That is a big inducement, certainly. I do not like to think how things might have turned out if she had not been with us.

Daddy and Tom have been crawling all over the ship checking this and measuring that. There was a small problem with the furnace that dehydrates our waste. There was a buildup of a hard substance at the exit pipe. It was baked on like a clay pot. Daddy looked it over and tried to chip it off, which did not work too well. Then he upped the temperature in the furnace and added a little more oxygen to the mix, and it disappeared. He gradually backed off on the oxygen until it started to build up again. He upped the oxygen again and watched for signs of corrosion. "We can not have our ship corroding away out here. It might be a bit tough to get it fixed." Stuff like that kept him and Tom busies most of the time.

All of us had shifts in Red Level just being sure everything went OK. Truthfully, we did not have to stay in Red Level, as the only controls were our wireless PDAs. They were our eyes and ears on the ship. They were communication devices. They were entertainment and research equipment. There is a single very powerful computer on Trigger. All of the PDAs were tied into this one computer and therefore to each other. They have a small video camera on the faceplate that can be used to transmit video images or take still pictures. They have no keyboard and no hard drive. The use very little power because of their lack of any moving parts. They have recharging bases that they had to be placed in every few days. It was convenient to recharge them while we slept. Information or instructions could be input by stylus or by speaking. Even Nina was inseparable from hers when she got over her initial distrust of the foreign equipment. She used hers to learn anything she could about whatever she had not known about. She was coming along with her English and made a point of engaging each of us in conversations daily. She and Katerina stayed in a single stateroom together.

Katerina spent many of her hours up in the Soyuz looking out of the tiny port and keeping it maintained. The attitude control rockets of this particular Soyuz burned methyl alcohol and used liquid oxygen as an oxidizer. Daddy had specified this in his order for the Soyuz. He set up a special still in which he placed some of the stems and leaves from the plants we were growing and made use of a catalyst to make methyl alcohol. He carefully distilled this to refill the fuel tanks. There was always oxygen available from the Dingus. He did not use it to try to make ethyl alcohol, as he was too much of a snob to drink moonshine. Daddy's plan had been very comprehensive. He had brought along a barrel of single malt Scotch.

Mom was primarily watching out for our health and well-being by making us exercise; and she grew crops, which we all tended in the farm tanks. The primary staple was soybeans. We were all going to learn how to love tofu. We have many other fruits and vegetables, but no trees. Tubers, grains, vines, legumes and berries, we have lots. We supplemented our diet from our freezers. Our freezers used the cold of deep space to keep things cold. I made the mistake of reaching in with my bare hand and got a superficial case of frostbite. Cooking was done with a light oven that had very bright halogen lights. It was great for toasting. To heat up things that were not flat, we had a microwave oven. We stopped eating the contents of the plastic goop tubes as soon as we were under constant acceleration. They were stowed for when we did not have up and down anymore.

Bob spent much of his time with Jake and Tom doing the things that had to be done on the ship to keep it going. He had plenty of time to play his guitar and the little instrument he got at Baikonur. We all got together at shift change and talked, sang, played games, and planned our next big step. Jack and Katerina were clearly attracted to one another. I am not sure that either of them was aware of it, other than in some abstract and peripheral way. It was obvious to everyone else.

Jack had determined that the nuclear devices were each about six kilotons each - plenty of punch for something the size of a small suitcase. I was still not sure it would be enough to change the course of a six-mile wide asteroid. Jake and Tom were concerned about how to keep the asteroid all in one piece with a nearby nuclear explosion.

Although the orbit of Jupiter is where we all tended to think Belial was, it was actually nowhere near Jupiter right now and would not be when we reached it. Jupiter's orbit is between six hundred and fifty million and almost a billion kilometers from Earth's orbit. This is in straight lines, which is how most people want to think about the distances between planets. Actually, straight lines occur only in the imagination of mathematicians. There is no such thing except as a mathematical abstraction. Oh, there are things that look straight. However, even light does not travel in straight lines. It is bent and slowed down by whatever medium in which it travels. Even when it travels in a vacuum, it is bent by the presence of a mass like a star, planet, moon, asteroid or grain of space dust. Ok, it is practically straight except when you look past large masses the size of the sun or more. The best way to think about distances between planets depends on what you are doing with the information. For us, we were traveling like every other orbiting body in the solar system - in a curved path. After we were through escaping from the mass of the

Earth and Moon, we were now escaping from the mass of the sun. Just as the mass of the Earth, and then the Earth and the Moon combined, had caused our path to curve around them, now the mass of the sun was causing our orbital path to curve. What we needed to do was to arrive at Belial going in the same direction at the same orbital velocity it had. To do this, we had to actually go far beyond the orbit of Jupiter and then come back toward the sun below the imaginary flat surface that is the plane of the ecliptic. It was a very long curve, almost twice the length of the maximum straight-line distance between the earth and Jupiter. The last third of it or so we would be slowing our relative velocity. The Trigger was still at least a month and a half from turnover. At that time, we would use the attitude control rockets of the Soyuz to turn the Trigger end over end to where our rocket would be pointing ahead of us instead of behind us. By the time that we would shut off the drive, we would not be more than a mile or so from Belial and would not be moving with respect to it.

    Meanwhile, we worked out various schemes to keep the asteroid in one piece while we exploded hydrogen bombs on its surface. It did not help that we needed to be there, and that the explosions would be dangerous for us as well. We also had to think about our futures. We intended to claim this asteroid as our own property and that of our children. We could not expect to spend our entire lives on the Trigger, although it was pretty comfortable overall. Tom had several ideas on how to separate out the various components of Belial into pure forms using his nanotechnology. There were major design problems, as we did not know of what materials the asteroid consisted. We tried to generalize from what we knew of asteroids in general. We could probably count on nickel/ iron, silicates and some percentage of carbonaceous composition. We all hoped there would be water ice, nitrogen compounds like ammonia, and perhaps some other interesting minerals.

To listen to our talk at shift change we probably sounded like every group of prospectors who rode the clipper ships out to the gold rushes of the Klondike and California. We were more sophisticated, and the gold was not our primary purpose, but it was of importance to us all. We knew that if we succeeded, we would go down in history, but we did not want to go down. We all had dreams of saving the world and then selling them pieces of what had so threatened them.

Katerina seemed to grasp how difficult this negotiation was going to be. She had mentioned the United Nations Treaty concerning the Moon and other Celestial Bodies. She had been briefed on this treaty, as it had been the Russian's idea that they did not want the United States to think they owned the Moon because Neil Armstrong had landed on it. The language of the Treaty disposed of the entire external universe as the "Common Heritage of Mankind" - whatever that meant. Katerina seemed to think that it meant whatever the big governments on Earth wanted it to mean. She did not think this Treaty would be used for our benefit. It would be a fight to leave, and a fight to come back. "Hail the Saviors of the Earth! By the way, you owe back taxes. There is also the little matter of those millions of dollars worth of missiles we tried to kill you with, who is going to pay for that? We were within our rights to defend ourselves. - You must know that. We are all rational people here, are we not?" No, it was not going to be a joyful homecoming, regardless of the outcome of the quest.

Bob just worked at playing his music and taught Nina how to speak not very good English to add to her not very good Russian. Mom tried to keep all our bodies and souls together. Jake, Tom, and I tried to figure out how we would keep the asteroid together. Jack and Katerina found whatever they could do to keep busy, keep fit, and not think about being lonely. There is no need for a pilot when the ship is out at sea or in deep space. You do not need a secret agent when there is no foreign government or multinational corporation to keep track of. They threw themselves into their assigned duties and taught themselves new skills. Mostly, they waited.

Chapter Sixteen
We Have Twenty Cubic Miles of What?

Days of lunar gravity pass slowly. There is a semi-timeless quality to the way things move, when they weigh one-sixth of what they usually do but have the same mass. Things fall so slowly that the high gravity humans seemed to be able to snatch impossible saves out of the air all the time. The crew continued to work out regularly, and their strength and reflexes did not diminish, as Madelyne had planned. Margaret used the small telescope that she had insisted upon to study the hunk of rock, ice, and metal they had decided to keep for themselves. And that is precisely what it seemed to be - rock, ice, and metal. It was impossible to tell what kind of rock it was, but it had a low albedo. This means that it did not reflect back very much of the light that shone upon it. This excited everyone, as it allowed the possibility that it contained complex hydrocarbons, which would make their lives much easier as time passed. It also could cause a plethora of problems. Margaret's observations, unhindered by the atmosphere of Earth, allowed her tiny ten inch aperture telescope to perform on a level with the big observatories on Earth. She had taken digital images of their target and discovered a periodic change in its brightness as it rotated in its orbit. She had accumulated enough observations to give her a good idea of the shape and brightness of the sinister object. It was vaguely potato-shaped and had no independent satellites. There were lighter areas and darker areas and, based on observations of similar asteroids, she had figured out a probable composition of thirty eight percent rock, twenty two percent water ice, and forty percent nickel iron. This could not be much better from the standpoint of what they were going to get, but raised serious doubts as to whether they could get it. The problem as Jake and Tom saw it was whether it would shatter when stressed. There was also the question of whether four six Kiloton nuclear weapons, however intelligently placed, would make enough change in the orbit to save the Earth. The news was not all bad.

As Nina continued to learn not so good English to add to her not so good Russian, Madelyn, Jake, Margaret, and Tom were all trying to meet her halfway, and were adding not so good Russian to their English. They were now harvesting soybeans, carrots, and other beans to add to the greens they had already harvested. Margaret had learned to process the soybeans into tofu. The recipes were beginning to get interesting. There were other problems.

The waste disposal system had begun to develop a few glitches about three weeks into the flight. The furnace had developed a minor leak that vented fumes back into their breathing air. They had initially shut down the furnace, but the waste began to build up. They finally had to actually shut down the drive and make a space walk to conclude the repair. This had taken a day out of their acceleration and required a complete re-calculation of the trajectory. It was worth it to get the smell out of the air. It was like a combination of a house fire and a broken sewer. The enriched oxygen mixture had corroded a vent pipe at the elevated temperature present at the furnace. Tom and Jake determined that if they raised the temperature and reduced the oxygen content, they could decrease the corrosion to almost nothing. The original pipe, however, must be replaced. This required a space walk. Jack and Katerina were the most experienced and so got another opportunity to float with the ship in the stars. The Earth was millions of miles away by this time, and the Trigger was alone with the Sun and the other bright stars. Jack and Katerina had to reach the furnace on the outside of Red Level. It was not a difficult trek, and only a single pipe had to be replaced. The whole thing took thirty minutes from start to finish. It took a few hours to make the pipe on Violet Level. The entire crew had to be in space suits while the pipe was replaced, as there was a pressure leak when they loosened the pipe and pulled it out. The pressure in the habitation tank dropped by about ten percent. The farm tanks could be shut off from the habitation tank, and so the loss was from only a third of their total atmosphere. Jake and Tom were primarily concerned with the nitrogen loss, as they had no reserve from which to replace it. The oxygen was not an issue. They all counted it a loss that they would have to live with, as the smell could not be tolerated. Jack and Katerina had just enjoyed fixing it. The loss of the odor was a big benefit for everyone. The intrepid space adventurers re-calculated their trajectory, restarted their drive, and went on.

Tom had resumed his research on nanotechnology on Yellow Level. He already had dissassemblers that could break down most forms of rock and metal, but the presence of water gummed up the works. The job really required a larger set of machines, which could handle actual chunks of ice. Water molecules by themselves had the unfortunate tendency to stick to things. There were almost four and a half cubic miles of water to be dealt with. It was not going to be a small job. Luckily, there would be about eight cubic miles of stainless steel to make a container for it. Not to mention a bit over seven and a half cubic miles of rock to arrange artistically around it. It left a born and bred designer with too many options. There was also the issue that he did not want to spend the rest of his life in the space available on Trigger. It was a pleasant enough space for a voyage of a few months, but years under these same circumstances were inconceivable. His work in the past had primarily dealt with nanotechnology used in conjunction with biological systems. It was going to be an extremely important area of knowledge. It did not have much application in situations where cubic miles of material needed to be manipulated. He needed an engineer.

Jake had been feeling useless since Katerina had figured out the problem with the shroud container. He was taking extra time in the gym to finally try to rid him of the eternal spare tire when Tom found him.

He had just finished the second set of crunches. They were an entirely different exercise in lunar gravity. The bench was set up to supply resistance lost with the pull of a full gravity.

"Jake, what are you up to? Tom hopped into the half cylinder on green level where the gym was located.

"Almost thirty pounds with twenty reps. I probably need to increase the resistance and reduce the number of reps. I should talk to Madelyne about it." Jake admired the shape that the younger people on the ship seemed to manage so easily.

"No, Jake. I mean what are you involved with intellectually right now. I have some serious problems that I could use your experience and insight on." Tom and Jake still had moments when they could not seem to make sense to each other. They were becoming less frequent, but they still occurred regularly.

"Tom, I don't know anything about nanotechnology. You are into something that has happened after most of my education and career. The best I could do is carry your tools and hand them to you when you asked."

"Jake, I am talking about real engineering. I can make little machines that that can take things apart and put them back together atom by atom, but not one of them could pick up a soybean on the Trigger if it fell to the floor. How do you expect me to work effectively with cubic miles of material on an atom by atom basis?"

"Well, you have your little machines make bigger machines."

"OK, sure, I had gotten that far. But what manner of machines do I have my little machines build?"

"Borers, compactors, welders, stampers... Come on Tom, you know this little litany."

"No, Jake. I do not. What are we going to do with these hundreds of trillions of tons of stuff, assuming that we do succeed in changing its orbit? Nobody is going to want to buy rough rock or metal, even if it is in Cis-Lunar Space."

"Sure they will, Tom. They will need it for things like shielding from cosmic rays and other radiation."

"Why haven't you brought up this little radiation problem before?"

Tom had this mental image of iron nuclei slamming through his body at sixty percent of the speed of light.

"Because, it is not much of a problem on the Trigger, Tom. Remember that layer of cloth that I insisted we have covering the entire outside of the Trigger except for the Soyuz and its docking adapter?"

"Sure Jake. It was a major pain in the rear quarter to get it on there and make it tight enough to suit you. I still have dreams about hanging upside down a hundred feet above the concrete floor trying to tie tighter knots!"

"You wouldn't want it to blow off now, would you?"

"Damn, Jake! You keep saying that in my dreams too. It's maddening!"

"Well Tom, I haven't felt this good since our little escape party. Did you not realize what that thin sheet of Buckminster Fullerene cloth does when it is energized by the kind of electromagnetic pulse that is pushing this ship?" Jake allowed himself a real smile for the first time in days.

"I can work through this! OK. Super-conducting cloth with a high voltage, alternating current at millions of hertz, sustaining a standing wave able to fuse protons a mile or so away. Radio waves?"

"Work backwards, Tom. What pushes the protons together?"

"A very intense magnetic field at the squeeze point and the incredible velocity of the protons."

"Right. My daughter was right. - You can be taught. An intense magnetic field that encloses the entire Trigger; although, it is somewhat attenuated at the very front of the ship where it cannot double back on itself because of the Soyuz. It acts much like a solenoid that encloses the whole ship. Ionized particles crossing a magnetic field generate their own magnetic fields that push them aside because it takes less energy to curve around than to go straight through. The main radiation we have to worry about on the Trigger, when it is underway, are neutrons from our own reactor; which is well shielded and off as often as I can manage it."

Tom, seeing the beautiful simplicity of the plan, once again recalled why he had sought out Jake for collaboration. "Beautiful Jake, simple and elegant! I supposed that you had a real good reason for that cloth, but I never put it all together. So, OK Captain Big Brain, it's time for you to get out of your little retreat here and come up to Yellow where the real work needs to be done!"

Jake and Tom left the little gym and went from Green to Yellow Level. Tom showed Jake the range of molecule-sized machines he had at his command. "So these little guys here remove one atom at a time of whatever is indicated?"

"Pretty much. They mainly move atoms. They can work at one layer at a time."

"And this little guy here, he puts atoms wherever you want?"

"They are better at taking them longer distances."

"I don't think you have much of a problem here, Tom. The way I see it, you just need to get them a little more specialized and to work cooperatively. If you can get this one and this on to attach together and have more of these lining up, you could use it to cut thick pieces into precise sections. If you had them arrange themselves into a round patch, you could have an excellent drill or borer." Jake was thinking of just how precise the little holes could be.

"But what about how to organize the material in the first place?"

"First you come up with a design for what you want to build, then you figure out how to do it. What about a pair of O'Neill cylinders?"

"What are O'Neill cylinders?"

"Don't they teach you youngsters any history? At the dawn of the space age, back in the seventies of the last century, there was a physicist at the Institute for Advanced Studies at Princeton who was primarily known for inventing particle storage rings. He began to ask his students whether the Earth was really the ideal environment to carry on industrial activities. If it was not, where would the ideal place be, and how would you go about living there comfortably? One of the neater designs that came out of these collaborative brain ferments was this thing called an O'Neill cylinder. They were twenty miles long and almost two miles across and were attached in pairs that rotated in opposite directions to help them with canceling out the gyroscopic precession so that their mirrors could bring the sun into them without too much station keeping. If they rotated once a minute, a person standing in the sun on the inside would have the feeling of one

Earth gravity with minimal, though noticeable, coriolis force. The idea is to provide a nice place to live and work, using the materials that were to be found in Space. A couple of million people could live in one of these things, if they didn't mind being a little crowded together and importing most of their food. They were about perfect for a few hundred thousand or so. Here, let me call some of these pictures up from the database."

"I have never heard of this guy. What kind of industry did he have in mind?"

"History again. Back in the mid–seventies there was a period of time when the Organization of Oil Exporting Countries stopped selling to the United States. It was called the Arab Oil Embargo. O'Neill was interested in making that a less attractive ploy by reducing the cost of energy to almost nothing. He wanted to come up with a source of renewable energy that did not depend on Oil. He came up with the idea of solar power satellites. They were huge photovoltaic arrays that floated in geosynchronous orbit over single spots on Earth, where there would be antenna farms that converted the microwave energy beamed down from the satellites into electricity for the power grid. Stupidly expensive to start up and, when the industrial capacity came up, pennies the kilowatt hour."

"It was a very large dream."

"Yes it was. It was an engineer's fantasy."

"Let's make one of these O'Neill cylinders. I had the thought of hollowing out this asteroid and spinning it, but we would always have little problems with making the closed cycle work with all the leaks that would inevitably develop."

"Sort of a big job to start when we get there, Tom. I think it is a very good long-term goal. We have got to get this thing stabilized so it doesn't break up when we explode a nuke right by it."

"I think I have that figured out."

"What is your plan?"

"I think the right thing to do is set some of these little guys to making cable. It occurs to me that a whole lot of stainless steel cable would help to keep our little asteroid from falling to pieces while we are pushing it around."

"How do you plan to wrap it all around an asteroid?"

"I was planning to seed the entire surface with preliminary assemblers and then have them reproduce themselves for a couple of days then they link up and turn themselves into cable units. After they link up, they can act almost like a fine circulatory system. They hand off atoms to one another until every one of the assemblers has enough to do their job."

"That should give us a few days to plan our blasts and get ourselves settled in on the opposite side of the asteroid. I think your plan is workable, and the only issue is whether we will have enough punch to make the course correction. Lets make your final plans for this much and then turn our attention to our future home." Jake and Tom could not have been happier.

Margaret and Madelyne were in Farm Two where they were growing greens and potatoes as well as things like tomatoes and onions. Not all of the crops were doing so well. Part of the problem was some sort of root rot that affected the tomatoes and the berries in general. Margaret pulled another dead tomato plant out of the rack and began to gather all the sick ones she had culled into a bundle for the waste processor. Madelyne was inspecting the other crops. "I think that this stuff is spreading. Cull the plants immediately around the ones that are obviously affected as well as the ones you have already pulled. Wait, I'll help you." Together they made relatively quick work of the sick plants and their neighbors.

"I don't know when you have been this quiet, Margaret - so how are you and Tom getting on." Madelyne looked at her only daughter and considered how much work seemed to have fallen on them because assignments on the ship had largely followed the roles they had made for themselves in their lives on Earth.

"Oh, things couldn't be better. We are always dead tired when we go to bed but we have an easy affection that is very comfortable. Actually, I wonder what you think of Jack and Katerina." Margaret got a little catty grin on her face.

"They are a pair all right, but I really don't think either of them knows it yet."

"Yeah, I don't get it. Can't Jack get a clue?"

"Well, under these circumstances, if it doesn't work out, it was never supposed to. Jack will make his move eventually." Madelyne and Margaret gathered their huge but light burdens of dead, dying, and possibly infected plants and made their way to Red Level for disposal.

Chapter Seventeen
Yes, It Is A Very Big Rock

They were all in free fall again. They were eating goo from tubes again. - The stuff that Nina continued to call crap. It had been fifty-three days since the eight crewmembers of the Trigger had left Earth orbit and headed away from the sun to the dark places in the Big Empty. Only thirteen days ago, they had turned the Trigger end over end and started their deceleration to rendezvous with the rock they all called Belial. They had reached a top speed of over fifty-four hundred kilometers a second. To put this into perspective, it takes seventy-four seconds to cross the distance between the Earth and the Moon at this speed. They had to slow down to meet the asteroid. They came up from behind the big rock and, when Jake shut the dingus off, they were going a paltry fourteen hundred and fifty-four kilometers per minute. They did not feel like they were moving at all, of course - unless the feeling of always falling is movement. They did not anymore. Jack and Katerina had gone out the first hour or so after they stopped and struggled the Dress back into the Cosmic Compact. It all seemed so easy with no one shooting at them.

Belial was about a two-mile journey away. This was about the minimum safe distance. Belial turned end over end about every ten minutes and rotated along its long axis about every twenty minutes. Belial was eleven and twenty-seven hundredths kilometers in length and six and ninety two hundredths kilometers in maximum width. It looked much like a potato. It contained about 295 cubic kilometers of material. It had a bit more than 409 square kilometers of surface area.

The Sun was a very bright star that cast shadows. Its light had very little warmth this far away. Jack and Katerina watched the slow tumble of their new home as they made their way back to the Soyuz. "That tumble is going to make things a little dicey as far as docking with that rock goes." Jack was feeling a little discouraged when he could actually see the magnitude of the task that faced them.

"I am a little more concerned about the rotation." Katerina could also feel the magnitude of their self-assigned task weighing her down.

"Let's recruit some of the big brains to see if we can simplify this task a bit." Jack allowed Katerina to enter the Soyuz first and then pulled the hatch closed behind him and waited for the atmosphere to equalize.

After they had closed the inner hatch behind them, they allowed themselves the luxury of removing their helmets and breathing the somewhat fresher air of the Trigger. They made their way through the hatch into Violet Level and began to struggle out of their excursion suits. No one was on Violet Level to help them, which seemed a little out of the ordinary. They continued to make a very good team, assisting one another without unnecessary words. When they were both down to the undersuits and they had racked the bulky excursion suits in their storage spots, it did not seem too strange for Jack to reach out and pull Katerina into a tight hug. The long kiss that followed did not seem so odd either.

When they separated slightly and looked at one another's faces, a new understanding seemed to have been reached without negotiation. The sunny smiles that bloomed unbidden on their faces, seen for the first time by the other, were more evidence of a new dimension of their relationship. A door had opened, and the serious world left on the other side of that door was hundreds of thousands of miles away. "I wonder why it took this long for us to arrive here." Jack could only wonder why it had taken him this long to see what was right before his eyes.

"Things take as long as they take. We had to be friends and trust one another, or this would never have happened." Katerina reached out and tweaked his nose before pushing herself away and streaking down the siphon to pull her down to where the others waited. Jack bounced off the opposite bulkhead and followed her down.

The rest of the crew was down on Green Level, looking out the port and talking in between consulting the computer via the ever-present PDAs. No one even so much as looked up as the spacewalking team entered.

"I like the look of 3M4." Margaret was studying the display of her PDA.

"That one looks a little jagged to me." Tom was also looking at the display of his PDA.

"It's so close to the ice deposit, and it's right on the axis near the center of moment." Margaret looked up from her display and at the huge tumbling stone out of the port. "Do you really see a better one?"

"I think that 1P3 has promise."

"That is too close to blast area one."

"It has got to be at least three kilometers!"

"That is way too close. I want at least ten kilometers between me and any thermonuclear device however small."

"It's not like you are going to be that close when it goes off!"

"Sorry, Mister. You may know a whole lot about chemistry and nanotech, but that does not give you any basis for an opinion regarding what residue may be present after a nuclear bomb goes off in the neighborhood. I really think that ten kilometers may be too close, but there is only so much asteroid to work with."

There was something about the last thing that his little sister had to say about Belial and his own recollections of the immense rock tumbling heedlessly through the great black void that hit Jack firmly in the funny bone, and a belly laugh escaped. ""Only so much asteroid to work with." Oh, Sis. That is rich!"

"There are our intrepid space adventurers! Returned from the black abyss unheralded and unassisted." Madelyne left her spot at the port and grabbed her eldest son in a hug, which somehow also ensnared Katerina who had been floating nearby. When the hug was returned by both of the "intrepid Space Adventurers" Madelyne had an instant of confusion as she realized that something fundamental had changed. She gave Katerina a quick peck on the cheek and watched as Katerina blushed. Madelyne left her son and Katerina looking a little confused and rejoined Nina and Bob at the port. Margaret looked up from her PDA's display and caught the devilish grin on her Mother's face. She looked back at Jack and Katerina and frowned in puzzlement, having missed the slight change in body language that had been so obvious to her mother at close quarters.

"I guess we ought to bring you guys up to speed on the planning, as you will both be having a large role to play. We did a scan of Belial and divided it into quadrants. We decided to begin at the pointiest end with A and end with Z at the opposite end. We then divided the circumference into six sections, as that gave us almost square areas near the middle. The biggest crater in one of these quadrants is designated one and so on, down to 9H6, which is only a hundred and fifty meters across. We are pretty much ignoring features smaller than that at this point. We are planning the first explosion to modify the orbit and to help us lose the awful tumble and rotation. We have to get the most bangs for our buck.

"The explosion will have to be most carefully timed and located." Katerina immediately got the point of the weird conversation now that she knew the basics. "The discussion now centers around were we should dock with the asteroid after we have stopped its tumble."

"Exactly! We also did a deep scan with the radars and got a fair appreciation of where the major resource concentrations are. We are primarily interested in ice and whatever carbonaceous concentration there may be. Metal, silicon, and oxygen do not appear to be much of a problem.

"When can we take the Soyuz over for a seeding mission?" Jake had largely been silent.

"Anytime you are ready! We would need to top up the liquid oxygen tanks, but the fuel tanks have been full for weeks." Katerina, as pilot, had made maintenance of the Soyuz one of her primary priorities.

"We need to attach a little sprayer that Tom and I made first and fill it with the little assembler bugs that Tom has made up. We need to spray as much of the surface as we can."

"I do not think that will be much of a problem. How much thrust does your little sprayer develop?"

"Minimal, as it is low velocity. We do not want the stuff to bounce. It is powered by compressed oxygen at low pressure. We will need to get within a hundred yards of the asteroid so that the little guys will be captured by its weak gravity and settle onto its surface."

"At one hundred yards or so we will also be captured by the gravity of Belial. It will be an interesting exercise in station keeping."

"Interesting! It will be like crop-dusting somewhere the size and contour of Manhattan! " Jack felt the danger somehow more sharply than he had an hour ago.

"No, It will not. We will use the current motions of the asteroid to do our flying for us. This plan will also never put us out of radio contact with Trigger. If we calculate an operating time equivalent to one entire cycle of its motion, we should also have even coverage of the little robots. Jack, you still suffer from a terrestrial viewpoint. It will not be like crop-dusting at all. All we have to do is maintain the proper separation." She smiled fondly at Jack.

"How will the spray rig be mounted on the Soyuz? How will it be controlled from inside the craft?" Jack had not dispelled his skepticism.

"We can solve these problems by inspecting the rig and working together." Tom led the way to the workshop where he and Jake had assembled their simple device.

The solutions were all very low tech, involving duct tape and manual cables extending through an open hatch.

Jack and Katerina wore their suits for the second time in less than twelve hours, as they carefully undocked from the Trigger and made the short trip to the tumbling rock next door. Katerina slowly approached the rock while keeping the Trigger directly behind her craft. The smooth looking rock revealed its rough edges as they approached.

"Damn, It looks like a badly maintained grindstone from this close! I can make out a few colors now at least. It doesn't look so uniformly gray."

"Closest approach in one minute, Jack. Test the rig. "Katerina never took her eyes off the rock or her hands away from the controls.

As Jack pressed the cable release, it seemed a million sparkles of diamond dust blew in an expanding cloud away from the big nozzle of the low-pressure sprayer toward the surface of the asteroid only a football field length away. The tiny particles seemed to settle down to form an iridescent haze just above the surface. "It seems to be working fine, Katerina."

"How is the supply of assemblers holding out?" Katerina made an adjustment to their altitude that rocked Jack out of his contemplation of the rough surface of the asteroid.

"I cannot really tell. Tom said we would have just about enough compressed oxygen to blow a hundred and fifty percent of them out, and we still have almost as much pressure as when I started two minutes ago."

"We will just have to see how far it goes." Katerina made another adjustment to their altitude. This pattern continued for about another twenty minutes.

"The stream seems to be thinning up some, Katerina."

"Good. This is getting tiresome and my hands are beginning to cramp."

"That seems to be the last of them. The little sparkles are all gone."

"Let it run itself out as I slowly back away from this rock." She took another ten minutes to retreat to a half a mile from the tumbling rock.

"The oxygen tank is now officially empty. The last tiny sparkle was at least five minutes ago."

"Throw that cable control out and close the hatch." The Soyuz retreated toward the Trigger. Katerina easily docked with the adapter on the Trigger. "Practice makes perfect."

"Let's get out of these excursion suits and let them dry out for a while." Jack said as they entered Violet Level and started removing the bulky suits. Once again, there was no one to greet and assist them. Jack's sense of order asserted that this time it was no accident. "Lets go to my quarters and I will rub those cramps out of your hands." Jack looked at Katerina, who grinned back at him.

"Among other things." She said. Jack and Katerina slipped down the siphon to Blue Level and were not seen by the other crewmembers for almost twelve hours.

Chapter Eighteen
It's a Blast Really

The new situation between Katerina and Jack drew no more comments than would have been expected in such a small group. Well, Nina did have a few choice statements to make in Kazakh. She did tend to smile when she said them in a thoroughly aggrieved tone of voice. As the only other person who understood Kazakh was Jack, and with Bob picking up only every third word or so, it had a small audience. Katerina simply started staying in Jack's quarters. It was a small addition to the enormous amount of time they spent together already.

Preparations continued for the first blast to change the orbit and take the tumble out of Belial's motion. Jake, Tom, and Margaret continually refined their solution to the exact timing and placement of the blast. The main area of uncertainty was a result of the weapons yield. - It could not be precisely predicted. What they were doing consisted of considering the minimum and maximum yields of similar weapons. They were able to measure the neutron flux and knew to a tenth of a milligram the weight of fissionable material the bomb contained. Using this information, they were able to get within twenty percent of the theoretical yield. The actual yield depended on the efficiency of the shaped charges of plastic explosive and the Tritium content of the chamber surrounding the plutonium sphere; plus other variables that they could not even begin to predict. They knew they could not get it exactly right, but they wanted to be as close as they could get. They only had four bombs to work with.

The timing was not one of the issues. They had a window every ninety-six minutes. The only real issue was exactly how far above the surface of the asteroid the bomb should be. Most of the change in acceleration that would occur would be from vaporization and out gassing from the surface from the heat of the fusion bomb. The best guess at the yield was important to figure the optimum distance from the surface. If the bomb were too close, not enough surface area would be exposed to the heat of the bomb. If it were too far away, it would not heat it enough to get a nice big push.

For Jack and Katerina, the issue was how to get it to exactly where the planners wanted and have it explode at exactly the right moment. The solutions all were within a few hundred meters of the surface. They intended to toss the little suitcase out of the *Soyuz* at a precise time on a precise approach vector but, because it all depended on human reflexes, it would only be as precise as they could make it. Later explosions would undoubtedly be more precise, as they would actually be on the surface of the asteroid. This time it would be somewhat quick and dirty. Everyone hoped it would be enough.

The crew was down on Red Level talking about setting off the bomb. Everyone was floating somewhere oblivious to everyone else's orientation. It was an unnoticed change from the first time this crew had been in free fall. Everyone had initially tried to keep everyone else in an upright orientation. Now it did not matter to anyone.

"The middle of the sweet spot is between 1000 and 500 meters above this point right here. Above that, and it will be too far away; and below that, it will be too close. We have to figure out some more accurate method of putting our device where we want it when it explodes. Somehow, the idea of Jack just tossing it out the hatch of the *Soyuz* just does not make it for me. No offence, Jack."

"None taken, little sis. I know I could have a countdown, and I trust Katerina's driving, but it seems like a nonchalant manner of delivering one of only four weapons that we have."

"This entire mission was jerry-rigged from its outset," Jake rubbed his chin and looked over at Margaret. "Here we are where classical mechanics works without many of the fudge factors, and we can't somehow use that to our advantage?"

"We could put some sort of spring-loaded device on the outside of the Soyuz and radio control its release. That probably would not be too difficult. The fact that we have no way of knowing exactly how much mass the Soyuz contains makes that not so trivial a problem. It will use some of the energy of the spring being pushed in the opposite direction."

"We will do a couple of test firings with similar masses and not bother to do calculations. We will measure this effect exactly and not depend on inaccurate assumed numbers." Katerina pulled her PDA off her wrist and began to sketch out the mounting possibilities on the side of the Soyuz."

Jake started to consider the various devices that could act like a spring. "We could use compressed oxygen. I think we are a little low on springs. We do have some electrically-controlled gas valves we could rig for this purpose."

The team ultimately decided on a bladder of Mylar on the underside of a sheet of insulating plastic with a small piece of Velcro in its center to hold the payload until launched. The shortest opening/closing cycle of the electrically controlled valve (.6 seconds) put about a half a liter of compressed oxygen into the Mylar bladder. It rapidly expanded and accelerated the payload with enough force to break the hold of the Velcro and allow the valise to be propelled toward Belial in a predictable manner. The most difficult part of the entire exercise turned out to be finding two small enough parcels that massed as much as the bomb that they didn't mind losing into space. It turned out that they were able to manage only one such parcel, and it had to be retrieved as it ultimately contained a number of metal items that the crew did not feel that they could lose. They tried the device out several times inside the Triangular Passage before doing more than a few vacuum tests. It turned out that one layer of Mylar was not strong enough to withstand the internal pressure of a half a liter of oxygen in a hard vacuum. They first doubled and then tripled the layers of Mylar. The entire building and testing process lasted almost a week. Katerina ultimately halted the tests as the Soyuz fuel needed was limited by the speed of fermentation. It was fun, but time consuming, to fire the load and then chase it. By then, they could get the forty-two kilogram parcel accelerated to within two percent of ten meters per second. It just had to be close enough.

The final plan was to use the mass of the asteroid as a shield against the nuclear blast. The Soyuz would maneuver to the opposite side of the asteroid and release the bomb at a precise time. After it released the bomb, the Soyuz would return to the same side of the asteroid as the Trigger. If everything went off as planned, the only thing any of the crew would see of the blast would be a change in the tumble of the asteroid, along with a small change in its orbit. It had been ten days since the seeding mission, and everyone hoped that the little cables would keep their new home from breaking into pieces.

That evening they made a small ceremony of returning items placed in the parcel all undamaged by their space adventures. "And last and possibly least, here are Bob's toenail clippers!" There was a small round of applause as Jake presented the gold-plated clippers to his youngest child. Bob accepted the clippers with an expression of genuine joy to the laughter of the assembled crew.

"Hey, one of you guys ever try to trim your toenails with a pocket knife before? I don't think any of you brains could have replaced these if they had been lost in space! Besides, did any of you catch a glimpse of Dad's face when he pulled out his jewelers pliers?" There were calls of "hear, hear!" "Right On!" from the various crew and a discrete "Point Taken." From Jake.

"I wonder how many of you realize that this may be the last night that we are on this ship as a space going vessel. This time tomorrow we may have set down on an alien planet that will become our home. By the way, has anyone figured out how we are going to do that?" In the sudden silence that followed Madelyne's pronouncement, it was pretty clear that the matter of landing the over one hundred foot long space ship on Belial had been largely ignored.

"Well, we still have the Dingus to help us slow down, and the gravitation of this asteroid is pretty negligible." Tom was clearly unhappy with his little speech as soon as it left his mouth. His wife soon gave him good reason.

"Negligible is a word that people use when they can't do the math! How fast do you think we will be going when we touch down? We haven't had to worry too much about space keeping several miles away from Belial, but if we were much closer we would have to be using the rockets of the Soyuz several times a day, with non-negligible burns, to keep us from crashing. Besides, the last time I looked we didn't have anything like landing gear on the base of the Trigger. I am not so sure that the Dingus would survive in a serviceable condition as we thumped down with it underneath."

"Good point, Margaret. The Dingus is a fine little rocket. Overall, it is the best rocket for the long stretch that mankind has ever developed. It was never designed to fight off the presence of a nearby large celestial body. I have a few ideas but I want to hear what everyone else has to say.

"Who says the best way to come down is tail first? I know that if we don't, our quarters will have an up and down that they were never intended for."

"That gets some of the issues out for discussion. Thanks, Bob. Anyone else?" Jake had stepped into the middle of the discussion and assumed leadership, which he had not tried to do in several weeks.

"The Soyuz would not have any trouble with the puny gravity of the asteroid." Katerina was swift to note the strengths of her primary responsibility.

"Yes, but we might want to use it again sometime. I don't believe that you could reliably dock with a space craft on even a small planetoid." Any chance of docking would have to occur from a straight up and down configuration, and I don't think I would want to risk it, even then, except under extreme circumstances."

"Well, I for one do not intend to hang upside down trying use that damn potty. It works adequately under the circumstances, but it wouldn't take a whole lot to make it unuseable." Madelyne was practical as ever.

"Well, I for one think that the orientation issue has been decided. We need to come down tail first. The next issues involve the landing gear. It needs to be stable and strong, but not so strong as it would have to be if we were so foolish as to try to land on a planet substantially bigger than Belial. It needs to be able to absorb some of the jolt of landing and should allow for the attachment of our landing rockets."

"We have landing rockets?" It was the first time that Nina had opened her mouth since the little ceremony had begun.

"Yes, we do." Jake smiled at Katerina's grandmother. "I had actually given a fair amount of thought to how we would actually land on this asteroid. There was a reason that I just happened to have extra electrically-controlled gas valves on board."

"You are going to use compressed oxygen?" Margaret had clearly been considering this problem and overlooked the most obvious answer.

"Yes, I had a feeling that we would find a use for it besides as a backup for our breathing supply. We aren't running the Dingus in the near future, but I hope we will be able to make up the deficit from local materials. Has anyone noticed those lengths of aluminum tube in the triangular passageway?"

"Sure Dad, I thought that they were left from when these were still external fuel tanks. I just didn't think you took the time to remove them because of the rush job." Bob had not been present when the Trigger was constructed.

"Au contraire, Mon Freir! We cut them off the outside edge before we even set the tanks upright; then carried them to the other side and attached them into the brackets they now occupy along with a few other similar miscellaneous pipe lengths. It was a miserable day and a half, but I had forgotten until just now." Tom winced at the recollection.

"They are the same pipes used for our siphon and originally carried oxygen down to the inlet on the bottom of the space shuttle. I added a few other pieces to allow assembly into three telescoping tubes. I thought we could attach them to the brackets where the solid rocket boosters attached to the tanks. We could fill them with a little compressed oxygen and attach some cable to keep them from splaying out when we land. They could absorb the shock of landing and allow us to remain upright as the assembly has requested."

"Why did you even bring this up if you had already solved the problem?" Jack was feeling a bit sullen, as he had had so little to contribute to the discussion.

"From time to time everyone wants a little recognition for their abilities and foresight. Besides, I rather enjoyed the looks of horror on your faces when this came up."

"Even if you created a kit that just snaps on, it is going to take some time to get it on." Jack was trying to get a bit of his own back, now that it looked as if the entire actual task was going to fall into his and Katerina's laps.

"I was hoping we could make this a family affair. You and Katerina have done all of the space walking on this little trip and soon we will all be working in vacuum. Once we set off this bomb, it will actually be several weeks before we need to do it again. We will have a bit of time to train ourselves for the tasks ahead. Besides, I really want to be ready when it comes time to land on that rock. We only get one chance, with no way to test the equipment before actual use. " Jake's voice had taken on a serious note before he finished this little speech. What he had not said was that if the mission failed most of the people of Earth would die. The entire mission had been rushed and jury-rigged and with very little latitude for clumsiness and error. Jake was beginning to feel the weight of the terrible responsibility. They had made it this far against the odds. Like a golf swing, the most important part of this mission would be the follow through.

The crew went to their quarters soon after. Bob did not waste anytime "knocking" at Jack and Katerina's quarters. "Knock, Knock" Bob said. "I really miss wood in my surroundings. It's amazing what you take for granted." Jack had opened the enclosure and Bob had floated in.

"What's up, Bob?" Jack floated just inside the door, and Katerina floated in the larger part of the room brushing her hair, which she had released from the bun she wore most of the day. Her red hair floated in a cloud around her face as the brushing caused a static electricity buildup. Bob had never seen anything like it.

"Gosh, Katerina, I have never seen your hair down before. I mean as much as anything can be down in microgravity. It's wonderful!"

"I have often been told it is my most attractive feature. I don't get tired of hearing it." She laughed as she finished her brushing and put the brush away.

"OK, Bob I know you didn't just drop by to look at Katerina's hair. Although I can think of worse things to do." Jack turned and smiled at Katerina.

"I think that I will go to say goodnight to my Nina. I don't want my hair to distract the brothers from what would seem to be a serious conversation." Laughing, she launched herself through the still open door behind Bob. Jack watched her floating progress as he sealed the door behind her.

"OK, Bob you have my complete attention. What's on your mind?"

"I can't really say, but it seemed to me that you were angry about something at dinner."

"Oh, I wasn't really mad, but I sometimes get tired of the way that Dad goes on and on. It's nothing new, I have occasionally felt that way for years."

"I think that Dad needs our cheerful support more than he ever has right now, Jack. We have all made our contributions but without Dad's clear thinking, we would not even have a chance to do what we came here to do. I think it is beginning to get to him right now."

"I can't fault your thinking Bob, but I don't think I had much of an impact on the discussion."

"Isn't that what was really bothering you?"

"That was clearly part of it. Then he had to say that the spacewalking thing was going to be shared. I guess that I am having a tough time figuring out what my role in this crew really is. I had a real job back on Earth and now I am just a retired spy in a spaceship that I can't hope to completely understand, smack in the face of nowhere. What is worse, here I would stay if I had to make any of the real decisions."

"Are you forgetting who you are talking to, man? I am an amateur musician who knows fewer languages than you do. I am not even a retired spy. I was a full time student before I started jerking to the strings you pulled from somewhere out in the world. If I hadn't had a receptionist, I don't know if I could have handled what little I did."

"Hey Bob, don't put yourself down. I wasn't doing anything as complex as that when I was just twenty years old. You did your job perfectly, without a bobble, the first time you tried."

"Like anyone ever traveled to orbit in a big tank of water! How do you top that? If I had had a clue what you intended to do I would have tried to take your place. I am a great deal more expendable."

"Bob, I know you would have taken my place if I had left it up to you. There are only six of us. None of us is expendable. As much as I hate to say it, you wouldn't have survived the trip in the tank. I barely did and I am bigger by twenty or thirty pounds than you are. That water would have sucked the heat out of you even faster than it did me. We all came up here the only way we could."

"Well, Jack, if I have a point, its that I feel this mission will succeed only if everyone does whatever they can to see that it does. They are going to do it better if they have a good attitude about it. I wanted to let you know that you don't need to search for a role on this ship. If your looking for a job, try to keep that redheaded pilot happy. She has to land us on that asteroid. You are a lucky man, brother."

Jack looked at his younger brother and realized that Bob was telling him the truth; exactly what he needed to hear. He had been thinking as if he was still on Earth and had to fall into some sort of job. He already had a job. He was saving the world as an entrepreneurial exercise. The most beautiful woman for a billion miles was his girlfriend. It was the best possible place to be at the best possible time. A slow smile crept over his face. "Thanks Bob."

"Don't even think about it Jack. I'll get going and turn in myself. Big day tomorrow." Bob turned in the air and headed down the siphon to his own quarters.

"They all are, aren't they?" Jack spoke to his brother's receding form and considered what he was going to do when Katerina got back. Another big smile crept over his face.

The next day began about seven and half hours later. Jack and Katerina spent an hour or so checking their equipment. They did not set the timer on the bomb until they were on the other side of the asteroid. Jack opened the hatch and put the bomb in the launcher, making sure that the Velcro was engaged. Katerina slowly guided the Soyuz to the exact spot that they needed to be over, and the mechanism threw the bomb at Belial. It went off about four hundred and fifty meters above the surface. By the time it went off, Jack and Katerina were on the Trigger side of the asteroid. They noticed that the shady side of the asteroid was suddenly a little closer, and the tumble was practically gone. They did not hear the huge blast or see the center of the sun brightness but some people on Earth did.

Chapter Nineteen
First Steps on a New World

Jack and Katerina found themselves not only in charge of assembling the landing gear, but also vicious instructors of the rest of the family in how not to die in vacuum. It was not so much that the family didn't want to learn, but it was so outside their normal experience, that some of the lessons needed to be driven home by being so humiliating that you never wanted to make that same mistake again. There were some surprises. Bob and Nina took to it as if they had been doing it for years. Nina had spent the voyage recovering from her wound and gaining strength that she had thought lost to her past. She somehow quickly learned exactly how to put the excursion suit on and check it before Madelyne and Jake even got the lower part of the suit on. Jake was the worst. If he could have been any worse, he would have been killed the first day they actually faced vacuum. As it was, his bungle aborted the entire exercise, and he never forgot to check his boots again.

Later that night, when Jake put his aching muscles to rest, he winced as he recalled the scathing put down he suffered at the hands of Katerina Yerisivloskaya. She had addressed him as if he were a salesman on the first day on the job that had gone out to the customers with his pants unzipped. Jack had directed his own sometimes-harsh comments primarily to his mother and sister. He knew it was madness before he started, but he had let Katerina bully him into it. He would pay, oh yes, he would pay.

Bob picked up the rigorous protocols almost as rapidly as Nina. He and Nina had been teaching each other their respective languages. They spent most of the early training sessions floating while the rest of the class was hammered into shape. They chattered back and forth in Kazakh, English and not so good Russian. Tom learned reasonably quickly, only to find himself in the doghouse with Margaret, who did not pick it up with as much speed. He had gotten an early dressing down from Katerina who then softened the blow with a compliment regarding his progress. The fact that Margaret overheard it, and that he made the mistake of bringing it up later in their private quarters, was the cause of some particularly cold and quiet nights. For Margaret, who had never been an average student, the entire exercise was her worst nightmare.

 Eventually the entire family could be relied on to put their suits on and check them properly. The first excursion was one of fear and wonder. They just traveled down the Trigger to examine the attachment points for the tubular landing gear. During the next trips, they each carried something to assist in assembling the hardware on the Solid Rocket Booster attachment brackets. They assembled the attachment points with Jack and Katerina watching as each did his job more or less perfectly. Jake was responsible for checking the work itself. He was pleased that his design seemed to work without having to reengineer. That ended their first day of work in hard vacuum. The next few days were spent on the ship moving the three large oxygen tanks from their location at the bottom of the second external tank. They weighed almost nothing but massed a couple of hundred kilograms apiece. This made handling them difficult and dangerous. They worked very slowly in suits to move the tanks to the Triangular passageway, where they attached them to the landing struts as the telescoping tubes came to be called. It just made more sense to use nuts and bolts in a place where they could be retrieved if they floated away. There were only so many of them to use for the job. They also fabricated the actual landing pads. These were round aluminum plates, which were welded to the bottom of the landing struts.

"Ok Dad, I give up. When are you going to produce the gaskets and O rings to seal the compressed oxygen in the struts?" Margaret was deeply tired. She had not been sleeping too well.

"I didn't plan on using them. Too complicated, and they would require some fine machining on a bigger lathe than we could bring with us. I am going to use Miracle Goop instead." Jake and Tom, with the assistance of everyone else on board, were about to assemble the short tube into the long tube. It required the entire length of the Triangular Passageway and for the inner airlock hatch to be open. This was another good reason to be in vacuum suits.

"Miracle Goop?" Jake disappeared into Violet Level and returned a few minutes later with a five gallon bucket of this material that looked like grease, but seemed even more slimy.

"It is a silicon based heavy grease that isn't volatile and doesn't get much stiffer a hundred and forty below zero. You know, Miracle Goop." After this little advertisement, Jake proceeded to put generous quantities of the goop on the end of the smaller pipe and assisted the others in inserting it into the longer larger pipe. It was a tight fit, and would have been impossible if the pipes had had any weight.

"Dad, do you happen to know the type of lubricant that is used in your electrically controlled gas valves?" Margaret had her own suspicions.

"I think it is petroleum based. It seemed to do alright in our bomb launcher."

"But that was open for less than a second, Dad. These may be open for minutes. If one wouldn't close again, it could topple the Trigger down on the surface of Belial."

"Why wouldn't it close again?"

"Because it is going to get really cold, Dad. When that compressed oxygen comes through the outlet side of the valve, it is going to expand really rapidly, and the energy to do that is going to come from the metal of this valve."

"Now you see why I wasn't considered a rocket scientist. I had not thought about this until you brought it up."

"We can do something about it at this point. You were going to have electricity to this valve anyway, why not put a little heating circuit on it that is on at the same time the valve is open?"

"A brilliantly simple solution to this unforeseen problem, Margaret. That shouldn't be too difficult. I had better go down to the workshop and get started. It would be better to install them here in the Triangular Passage than trying to do it on a spacewalk."

The contraptions he came up with after a couple of hours, consisted of small coils of wire that fit tightly around the outside of the valves. The devices were wired into the control circuit and then attached with duct tape. It was very ugly.

"Well, I don't want them to get hot. I just want to keep them warm enough to open and close properly." Jake actually sounded apologetic about how ugly his rig was.

"It will be fine, Dad. Who is going to look? Margaret put her vacuum suited arm around her father and hugged him. The motion caused their helmeted heads to bang together, which was audible to everyone in the passageway. Everyone chuckled at the display of affection gone awry.

"I don't think we can assemble more than one of these at a time in this passageway. Why don't we put this one on?" Katerina had developed a plan to tether the Soyuz to the Trigger that would allow them to undock the smaller spacecraft and unblock the airlock so that the landing struts could be taken outside the ship. They had carefully measured before attaching the oxygen tank to the strut. It would fit through, but just barely. It took about thirty minutes for the vacuum pumps in the airlock to evacuate the entire Triangular Passageway. This was the first time this had been done on the trip. They had to override a safety that would not have allowed the pump to function with the inner door open. "Why don't we install this strut and return and assemble the others without re-pressurizing this passageway? We will continue until we have all three attached, or we start to run low on air."

The rest of this evolution went on until it was completed, and this was just before their breathable air entered the safety margins. Katerina docked the Soyuz, and the Triangular Passageway was repressurized, allowing them to open the hatch into Violet Level. It was an exhausted, but triumphant, crew that tethered their damp excursion suits into the drying rack. The conversion of the Trigger from deep space vessel to asteroid lander had been completed. No one was in the mood to try to land without a rest period. They decided to celebrate the accomplishments so far. The crew cleaned themselves up and put on their cleanest jumpsuits. They ate flavored paste from tubes, drank juice from plastic bags, and talked about the last day in absolute microgravity for the foreseeable future. There would be some gravity on the surface of Belial. It would not be much, but it would provide and up and down. They toasted the accomplishment of coming so far so fast and the real possibility that they would actually save the Earth. Then they flew like falling monkeys to their separate quarters and rested.

The following "day" found them all worried about the coming maneuver. It was something that they had all dreaded. Taking off had been dangerous for them all, and landing was every bit as chancy. They broke their fast, got into their vacuum suits, and began the orbital changes that would ultimately bring them down on the surface of Belial. Using the rockets on the Soyuz, Katerina reoriented the Trigger so that their makeshift landing gear was directed toward the asteroid. Another quick burst from the rockets on the Soyuz started the Trigger into the shallow gravity well of the asteroid. After these changes, Katerina made her way back down the siphon to Red Level to wait with the others for the landing to come. The approach was very gradual, and the Trigger did not begin to accelerate until the surface was only five hundred meters below the landing tripod. When their rate of descent had increased to more than ten meters per second, the three oxygen cylinders all opened up at the same instant, and a short burst of compressed oxygen slowed their approach to half that. The surface of the asteroid was now very close as seen through the real camera. The place that they approached was a dimple of a crater with rather steep sides but a relatively flat bottom. They had chosen to land on the sun-exposed side of the asteroid, so that if the spot they had picked out proved to have hidden problems, they might have a chance to choose another one. At an altitude of a hundred twenty-five meters or so, they had seen no problems; and another short burst of compressed oxygen slowed their descent again. A few seconds later they were only fifty meters above the surface, and another longer burst of compressed oxygen slowed their descent just a little. A second or so later the compressed oxygen rockets fired a longer burst. They shut off one last time. After a second or two they opened up and did not stop until all three of the plates on the ends of the legs of the tripod had made contact with the strangely veined surface of Belial. The Trigger settled down on the telescoping legs, and for the first time in history, living creatures from Earth had soft-landed on another world other than Earth's Moon. There had been scarcely a bump.

Within a minute of touchdown, the entire crew was against the port for their first view of an alien world. Alien it was, with strange lines crisscrossed over the landscape. They gleamed in the distant sunlight like metal blood vessels. They were piled up like different sizes of spaghetti on a rough gray plate, crossing and re-crossing each other with no apparent order. It was totally unlike any natural landscape anyone had ever seen.

"The little machines have certainly done their job." Tom looked pleased but puzzled as well. "I would have thought that they would have made do with a single layer. But then again, I would also have expected a single size of cable. I can barely see any normal surface at all."

"I cannot see any normal surface at all. When I look as straight down as I can, I think that instead of surface regolith, I see smaller and smaller tubes or cables, or whatever they are!" Katerina thought the entire appearance more than just odd; it was unearthly in the most profound way.

"I do not think we need to worry about setting off nuclear weapons next to this mass of cable. If that stuff has any strength at all, it is more likely to unravel than to break apart." Jake was mostly approving, if somewhat taken aback, by the incredibly bizarre appearance of their new home. "What sort of endpoint did you program into your little machines?

"None. I just hoped that enough cable would be made to do the job." Tom was still scratching his head at how weird the surface looked.

"Well, that explains it. We are looking at an iterative process taken to an illogical extreme. Given enough time, all of the metal in this entire asteroid will be in the form of cables across its surface - with all other materials contained within its hollowed out husk."

"How long would that take?" Madelyne finally thought of a sensible question to ask.

"The process is limited only by the energy available. The energy driving the process is sunlight. So the rate would depend on the incident sunlight and the available surface area." Tom had his PDA out and was entering calculations with his stylus. "Actually, I think the rate is increasing as we speak. Every minute, we are getting closer to the sun, so the energy per unit area is increasing. Add to that the fact that these cables - because they have a three-dimensional shape, compared to a flat surface - are actually increasing the surface area of the asteroid. The shape of the curve indicates that the acceleration of the process is geometric. The only way to actually predict the endpoint is to measure the rate of growth of cable and consider the absolute mass of metal the machines have to work with. Just estimating though, it will take a lot less than a year."

"Did you actually install any safeguards?" Jake was looking at the landscape with what amounted to suspicion now.

"It will not break down anything with carbon in it. That is a basic prohibition. It prevents the little assemblers and dissasemblers from being the worst plague the universe has ever known." Tom was still looking at shiny cable outside the port.

"It wouldn't have any problems with finished aluminum then, would it?"

"No, it would turn it into cable as quickly as it did any other metal." Tom had begun to look a little alarmed.

"Then, unless we suddenly develop the ability to breath vacuum, we had better cover the Trigger with some sort of carbon because it will otherwise be just more cable on the surface of an otherwise deserted asteroid! "

Chapter Twenty
Old Gray Belial, Ain't What She Used To Be

It actually didn't take a motivated crew long to design and fabricate a sprayer to cover the exposed metal parts of the Trigger with a thin covering of a non-volatile hydrocarbon solvent that they had intended to use for other purposes. They had, of course, sprayed their excursion suits before they went outside to prevent any migration of the suddenly dangerous nanotech from inside the Trigger. By the time Katerina and Jack arrived on the actual surface of Belial, the aluminum plates on the landing struts had already been cannibalized to some extent. They seemed to have sprouted a few cables. The joint above did not seem to have been involved yet, and wouldn't be if the carbon-based solvent did as they hoped it would. They had sprayed thoroughly as they descended, and this delay may have actually compromised the bottom-most aspect of the ships landing struts. When they got to the actual surface, Katerina knew that the Trigger would never lift again. The landing plates had already been overgrown with a shiny growth of cable. At closer inspection, the landscape seemed to writhe and squirm as the metal from the interior made its way onto the surface. The Trigger seemed to be sinking into the surface of a shiny metal sponge. It was not that the Trigger was sinking, but rather that the surface was rising around it.

"Katerina, this is too weird! I knew that we would be on an alien world but I didn't anticipate it would look much different than the old pictures from the Moon!"

"I know what you mean. I just hope our little paint sprayer will keep our ship from being destroyed."

"If Tom says this will work, I really have no doubt that it will. He did design the little machines that are turning this entire asteroid into a gigantic brillo pad."

Katerina had handed the sprayer to Jack and was leaning over trying to see the surface of the asteroid that they had landed on. The cables got thinner and thinner as they approached the surface. The surface itself had the appearance of cotton with an unearthly metallic sheen. The smaller cables joined to form larger cables and these joined to form still larger cables. The largest cables were at the very surface and were almost an inch in diameter. Katerina removed a cutter from her tool belt and carefully snipped a piece of one of the larger cables and levered it into a black plastic bottle that Tom had provided. The cut piece was hexagonal with a somewhat complex cross sectional structure including a hollow in the exact center.

"Let's hope that we can figure out how to turn this strange course of events to our advantage." Katerina started climbing the strut, and they made their way back into the Trigger against the gentle pull of Belial.

"I never expected to see a specimen this big. It is a wonderful example of cooperative manufacturing of large components from microscopic components. " Tom had been very enthusiastic when he obtained the sample from Katerina. She and Jack had decontaminated and returned to the interior of the ship. The sample itself was in a plastic box having been sprayed with solvent. Tom was looking at it with a small microscope. "Most of the sections of the fiber are inert metal depot. This thin layer around the lumen is still active, along with this layer in these medullary rays. I'm betting that if this piece got some light it would shrink and elongate."

"Does any of this help us figure out what we are going to do about all this cable that is going to eventually cover our little ship and imprison us in a cocoon of metal fibers?" Katerina regarded the fiber like a tumor removed from a dear friend.

"Oh, that's not going to be much of a problem now that I know how the little machines are working. I am going to let them continue the way they are working now until the process begins to slow down - which I now calculate to be about a month and a half away. Then, I am going to modify their programming a bit to allow our little engines to manufacture the larger components of our new home for us."

"Are you pursuing the O'Neill Cylinder concept that we talked about a month or two ago?" Jake seemed calm compared with his son and the former Soviet agent.

"No, it is an elegant design, but I don't see exactly how to make two cylinders happen through an iterative process. I am going for the Bernal Sphere design."

"Of course, that would be the most straightforward way to proceed."

"What the hell are you two talking about? Margaret had not spoken more than thirty words since they had set down on Belial some hours before, and now her patience was at an end.

"Well Dear, the O'Neill Cylinder and the Bernal Sphere are large designs for space habitats that Jake and I discussed a month or two ago on the trip out for our long term comfort and safety. We didn't figure that we would want to live out our lives crammed into the Trigger. Tom was quickly calling up some pictures on his PDA and some of his preliminary design work based on the basic properties of Belial.

"And it did not occur to you that this kind of major decision should have been brought up with the rest of us?" There was a quiet intensity in Margaret's voice that did not bode well for Tom's immediate future.

"I really didn't think we would be this far along toward a design on the day that we landed." Tom had begun to look a little nervous.

"When were you going to bring up this little project of yours?"

"Oh, I would have brought it up in plenty of time to get everyone's input." Jake had slowly backed away from the debacle occurring and had his hand over his face like the mythical ostrich with its head in the sand. Tom looked a little more nervous but clearly had no idea of how pathetic he really sounded. Katerina, Madelyne, and even Nina were standing behind Margaret with their arms crossed. Bob and Jack were trying hard to disappear into the background. It was not working any better for them than it was for Jake.

"Tom White! You have the temerity to tell me that you were going to get everyone's input after you have turned what appeared to be a perfectly good asteroid into a knotted ball of metal snakes!" Margaret then turned her flaming viewpoint onto her father. "And you helped him, filling his head full of your big ideas without once just mentioning to the rest of us that you had something like this in mind! You think that these are the actions of a responsible adult! What in the universe are you guys on!" At this, she turned in the miniscule gravity of Belial and bounced/swam out. Katerina, Madelyne and Nina gave their male crewmates a withering glance and followed her out.

Tom watched the female contingent of the crew file out with a shocked expression on his face. Jake looked almost as bad. Jack and Bob just had concerned expressions but with an edge of worry as well.

"Tom, didn't I teach you better than that? Now we are all in the dip with you. Remember; always apologize before it escalates to this extent. I blame myself. You have just had it too easy." Jake moved quickly to get the blame assigned to Tom before everyone had a chance to think things through.

"Shut up, Dad. Tom may have screwed up; but as you said, he really did not know better. This particular explosion from my little sister can be directly traced to your door."

Jack had already worked out the problem. The problem was scientist types who did not think other people had enough sense to understand what they were talking about, so they did not even bother to discuss it. "What we need now is a concrete plan to present to our ladies that will demonstrate the risks and benefits of your designs. The trick is going to be to leave enough leeway in the design to allow improvements to be suggested. As Maggie said, we are a little late to quibble over the basic outline."

"Well, there are thousands of things that still need to be worked out. My design, as you put it, leaves us with a big hollow ball with rock and water on the inside. At this point, it is not even airtight. Even with thousands of layers of fibers, it will be much like a thatched roof. Frankly, to be this far along is simply shocking. I had not accounted for how much better things work without an atmosphere to interfere with manufacturing processes."

"Okay, it's a start. Let's see some pretty pictures."

It was a sober looking group of men who made their way down to Red Level several hours later. The women of the crew were quietly looking out at the alien landscape and talking intently. They were also ignoring the men who came down the siphon. Jack had determined that he needed to be the mediator and main spokesman.

"Okay, I know you ladies are all upset by the pace of our little reconstruction project, and we would all like to apologize here at the outset for not including you in Tom and Jake's preliminary deliberations. The truth is that Tom had no clue how efficiently his little machines would operate and reproduce themselves in the airless and energy rich environment of Belial. The truth is also that, although Tom loves our little Rocket ship, he never considered living on it forever. His initial intent was to stabilize the asteroid so we would not break it up trying to change its orbit. I think that we can all agree that he succeeded in this and that this is no longer one of our concerns. Which brings us up to the minute. Now we need to decide the shape of our new home. Tom has, by his actions, taken much of the guesswork out of this process. We are going to live in a giant sphere. That much has already been determined. However, many details remain to be worked out. We have prepared a number of possible configurations of the final design that we need to arrive at a consensus regarding. At this time I would invite your attention to the screens on your PDAs." Jack's little speech had been delivered with such a serious and forceful manner that no one in the room hesitated for even an instant looking into the screen of their PDAs.

There on the tiny but high resolution screens appeared photographic quality images of huge vistas with lakes and mountains, streams and meadows with trees that reached toward the sky. And in the sky, there were people flying with wings under their own power. The Sun was a ring at one end of the huge spherical space. It cast short shadows all the way to the opposite end of the sphere. There, great elevators rose all the way to the central axis of rotation. On the shady end of the sphere were located the great labs and manufacturing plants with the appropriate docking facilities for the fleet of interplanetary ships that came for relaxation and trade. At the sunny end of the sphere were towering mountains that rose to the level of the sun coming in from the huge circular window. Between the opposite poles of the sphere was a remarkable selection of landscapes ranging from flat farmland to rolling forested hills. Small herds of grazing animals could be seen with occasional flocks of birds. Across the great distance to the opposite side of the sphere could be seen lakes and forests suspended as if by magic on the sky above. A few thin clouds floated between the two seemingly separated worlds. A glance at the gently curving horizon showed that it was a continuous strip all around the inside of the inverse world. The reflected sun gleamed and sparkled off the lakes all around the arc of the world. Here and there, connected by bicycle paths, were houses and cottages made of stone and glass.

At this point, Tom made his way to the center of Red Level near the siphon. "Now, it doesn't have to exactly this way. It could be more regular, and the different types of terrain could have obvious separation to have a more rational land use. I chose this particular configuration because I thought it was pretty. I guess that the feeling of randomness gives a more Earthlike look. But, we can make it any way that you all want it."

Margaret looked at Katerina and Madelyne. They looked back at Margaret, who glanced over at Nina. She looked back at Margaret and gave a quick nod. Katerina and Madelyne both nodded as well. Margaret made her way over to Tom. "Tom White, if you change anything in this plan in the smallest particular, I will never - and I mean never - forgive you!" At this point she grabbed Tom, and a few tears leaked from her closed eyes. "It is the most beautiful thing that I have ever seen."

Chapter Twenty-One
You Can't Just Toss Nuclear Weapons

The crest of excitement regarding the new space habitat that the crew was making for themselves did nothing to abate the need to save the planet they came from. They still had more than four years before the predicted impact, but the best calculations still predicted that the Earth would be destroyed along with whatever their asteroid became.

In the meantime, it was changing rapidly. The shiny hexagonal metal cables now were level with the bottom of the viewport, and no evidence remained of the surface that they had landed upon. The hydrocarbon coating that Jack and Katerina had sprayed on the Trigger did its job completely. There were no new cables growing out of the metal of the spaceship, but the surrounding area was a different story. The ship now occupied a pit in the surface of intertwined cables. The largest cables were now almost a foot in diameter. All the work the crew had done to map the surface of the asteroid had been a total waste of their precious time, as that surface no longer existed.

Margaret and Katerina had spent the better part of the ninety or so hours since the landing trying to determine how to recalculate where and how to set off the next blast to maximize the change in the orbital parameters. Part of the problem was the change in the actual shape of the asteroid. A greater and greater proportion of the total mass was being deposited on the surface. This changed not only the center of mass but also the center of moments. Since the Trigger had landed, the crew no longer had a perspective that allowed them to precisely determine these parameters by direct observation. Margaret was put into the position of having to figure this out from astronomical observations. Additionally, the process was constantly changing, and the rate of change was accelerating. Eventually, it came down to a meeting of Margaret, Jake, and Tom on Red Level. Far from being a heated argument, this meeting of the main mathematicians on the Trigger was a group of people trying to just define all the variables that needed to be accounted for in their quest to save the Earth. They badly needed to make their last three weapons count.

"I am afraid it will be impossible to calculate exactly the rate of mass redistribution. The process is accelerating as I predicted; however, it varies depending on how much sunlight actually hits the surface. Additionally, the surface area is growing. Although the rate of surface area growth is decreasing as the caliber of the cable increases. The shape of the asteroid is at this point still a factor - as it is still much more oblate than it is spherical. It is becoming more spherical all the time." Jack picked that moment to appear at the bottom of the siphon followed closely by Katerina.

"So what you're saying is that Belial is still shaped more like a potato than it is a ball." Jack knew all those words but it seemed a waste of his time to actually use them.

"Pretty much, Jack. The issue is, of course, how fast that is changing." Jack and Tom had developed a great deal of mutual respect over the course of their association. They deferred to one another in their respective fields of expertise.

"I just wonder how important it is in the long run. If I recall correctly, the sooner we make our course corrections, the more effective they will be. Is that right?"

Celestial mechanics being her forte, Margaret addressed her brother's question. "Yes Jack, you are remembering correctly. A little bit of change out here is worth a great deal more than fifty or a hundred times as much later in the orbit. That was the whole point of getting out here as soon as we could manage. The problem is that, when it is David against

Goliath, we have to aim our little stone just right to actually make this work. And to complicate matters, we only have three stones left."

"Bear with me a minute. If the longer we wait the less effect our bombs have, what percentage is there to waiting until our numbers all make sense, if the delay is causing us to lose yardage for delay of game. The point I am trying so poorly to make is that, at what point do precise calculations reach the point of diminished returns? You guys have been down here most of the last three days and seem no closer to arriving at your answer than you were at the end of the first day. It seems to me that you are wasting your time just trying to frame the correct question. From what I have overheard, it sounds like you agree that an exact solution is impossible to calculate because you can't accurately predict all the variables. Does that sum it up?"

All of the advanced mathematicians on Red Level looked at one another and recognized that the best solution would gain them only a percent or two, whereas delay was costing them almost that much every day. Jake turned to his learned colleagues and daughter and son-in-law. "I think that Jack has raised an important point. Personally, I think that I was intrigued by the complexity of the issues and lost sight of the purpose of the inquiry. When it comes right down to it, the only important variables are the vector and our personal safety."

"I think that there is at least one more issue that must be addressed. How do we get the bomb to wherever we decide to set it off? I don't think our little launcher that we used for the first one would work now that we are down here on the surface. I personally don't wish to be anywhere near the explosion. I might point out that travel on foot across this surface, if you could call it a surface, is impossible." Jack had a mental image of he and Katerina trying to carry one of the valises through the tangle that constituted the outside of Belial. "I just can't feature it."

"Katerina, would you please join us on Red Level?" Jake had spoken into his PDA.

"I am in Farm Two cylinder, so I will be a few minutes delayed."

A few minutes later when the main space technicians were gathered in Red Level, the discussion turned to the various means that they had to deliver the bomb to where and when it was needed.

"I think the projectile idea is out. It would be easy enough to orbit something here on Belial, but with the parameters constantly changing in an inconstant manner, it would be impossible to figure out where it would go off. It could have disastrous consequences. In retrospect, it was incredibly foolish to land until we had expended all of our nuclear weapons." Jake was still of the opinion that it would have to be walked to point zero.

"If it would be easy enough to orbit something, why not use Soyuz?" Katerina was always looking for an excuse to use her piloting skills.

"The same reason we had the last time we brought this up. The docking ring was designed to use in open space, not on the surface of an asteroid. I don't think a pilot, having even the extraordinary talent that you possess, would be able to redock here on the surface of Belial." Jake did not believe that it was possible to do even in the tenuous gravity that was found here.

"Agreed. We will have to land nearby." The new argument echoed in the sudden silence on Red Level.

"How would you get back to the Trigger?"

"We would walk of course."

"We have three more bombs. How much fuel will be left after taking off and landing on this asteroid? The Soyuz wasn't designed to work against this much gravity."

"Effectively, none."

"Is there any safety margin?"

"No, Not Really."

"Well, I think you have your answer."

"I do not think that we can afford much in the way of a safety margin. If we intend to save our home planet and therefore ourselves, it will be necessary for further risks to be taken. We did not get to this point in the mission by playing it safe. I have heard no other suggestions as to how else we can accomplish what needs to be done."

"We could reduce the mass of the Soyuz as much as possible. If we can no longer dock with the Trigger, It does not make much sense to carry the mass of the hatches. There may well be more extras that we can leave off." Jack was looking over a diagram of the Soyuz on his PDA.

"The atmosphere pumps would not serve much purpose in a space ship without doors." Katerina was also looking at a diagram of the Soyuz on her PDA.

"The docking adapter wouldn't seem to have much point if no further docking is anticipated" Jake was now looking at his own PDA.

After further consideration, it became clear to the crew that the Soyuz could be lightened by at least thirty-five percent. The stripped down Soyuz would have some margin for error.

"We still have not figured out where to put the remaining bombs." Jack hated to bring up practical stuff, especially when things seemed to be going so well.

"I have been thinking about that while we have been tearing up our Soyuz. Although minor features like craters have been effectively eliminated by the little nanomachines, big feature would actually be emphasized by adding more to them." Tom brought up one of the previous images of Belial before his handiwork had changed it forever. "There was a major prominence here on the other side of the asteroid. It should still be visually higher than all the surrounding terrain."

"That would do perfectly! Although my calculations will not be exact, they will be close enough to make a difference. Is it possible to use two of the devices at the same time?" Margaret had been frantically calculating during the entire discussion.

"It is possible to tie the firing mechanisms to a single timer so that they will go off at the same time. I thought that the point was that separate explosions would be more effective in changing our course." Jack still had the Soyuz on his PDA but began to consider how to set off both bombs at the same time and to tie the valises together so that the wiring would not come apart.

"Well, we actually have already done that with the first explosion. The best place for a big correction is right about now. That will leave one more bomb to make a smaller, more precise, correction if we will still need it." Margaret was looking at her ephemeris program. "We will now collide with the Earth in the middle of the Indian Ocean a few seconds later than I previously calculated."

"Well, that is wonderful news." Katerina said dryly.

"It is at least fifteen hundred miles better than before. When you are dealing with this much mass, that is a significant difference."

"I do not mean to impugn our progress, it is just that it seems so little after all we have been through so far." Katerina was thinking about how much like death Jack had looked after he came out of the water tank. She gave him a fond look, which he returned with a ready smile that would never have graced his face this time last year.

"If we need to make this little correction soon, we had better get about remodeling our Soyuz." Jack turned and swam to the siphon, heading toward Violet Level. The others followed quickly, and work soon commenced.

It took the better part of three days of working in excursion suits to make the needed modifications to the Soyuz. What could not be brought through the hatch into the evacuated Triangular Passageway was unceremoniously tossed into the waiting mass of cables a few meters away, where it soon became a part of their new home. On the evening of the second day, Jack and Katerina worked on the two bombs wiring the firing mechanisms together and removing one of the timers. The bulky package of the two valises was attached to the modified pneumatic launcher on the outside of the Russian Space vehicle.

Only a single couch remained inside, and the pilot of the Soyuz modified the launching mechanism to allow its use. Only Katerina would be going on this bombing mission. Jack had resisted this idea strenuously, but the rest of the crew had vetoed him. He simply could not contribute enough to the mission to justify his mass on the Soyuz. With a single person aboard and the possibility of carrying additional fuel to the Soyuz after this trip, it was possible that the last bomb could be delivered like these two - assuming that everything worked perfectly.

The night before the mission, the crew gathered in Red Level and had a big meal with toasts and tears and as much celebration as was possible under the somewhat grim circumstances. Here on Belial, it was possible to drink out of a glass or cup if one was very careful. Food would remain on a plate if not accelerated precipitously. It took practice and patience which all of the crew had learned. After two long days in pressure suits, the exhausted crew soon headed for their sleeping quarters. Jack and Katerina closed the partition behind them in what had become their quarters and made their preparations for sleep.

"If something goes wrong tomorrow, I will come looking for you, bomb or no bomb." Jack folded Katerina into an embrace that set them both into a gentle spin. He and Katerina were almost the same height, and Katerina looked him directly in the eyes.

"I know this, you big American Cowboy. I will allow nothing to go wrong. I am enjoying this adventure far too much to let it go easily. Besides, I cannot leave this group of amateurs to finish this important work. You all need me too much to not be around to take care of serious business."

"You talk about serious business. Well, I am going to show you some serious business." What happened next is best left to the imagination.

The next morning, ship time, final preparations were made. A quick breakfast, tea, and then the timer on the bomb was set. The explosion would occur when the high part of the asteroid was aimed precisely toward the direction the asteroid needed to be farthest from in order to miss the Earth later in its orbit. Katerina would have about two hours to deliver the bomb and get back to the shelter of the Trigger before it went off. When all the hatches that remained between the Trigger and the Soyuz were closed, Katerina spoke a short countdown before using the attitude control rockets to push the capsule into a stable orbit around the asteroid. The asteroid rotated beneath her. Radio contact with the Trigger was lost almost immediately as a result of the metal cables surrounding the ship. Katerina realized that it was the first time she had been out of contact with her crewmates and by herself. It was literally the first time that she had been really alone for months. It was not a very good feeling to be alone here in the big empty with the cabled surface of Belial and the stripped down Soyuz her only separation from that very alien place. It took about twenty minutes to reach the area of the asteroid where the prominence was supposed to be. The entire surface of the asteroid was an amazingly uniform jumble of shiny metal cable. Navigation was made much more difficult.

There were several areas, which seemed taller than other parts. Katerina eventually chose the one that seemed the tallest and farthest away from the location of the Trigger. When she had made her choice, she had to wait another orbit to effectively launch the weapon in the right direction. This required an additional fifty minutes. The launching mechanism worked perfectly, and the bomb started its parabolic course toward the highest point on the asteroid opposite of the location of the Trigger. It should explode when it was just a few dozen feet above the surface. Katerina changed course to take her back to the Trigger. It was then that she realized she would not be back at the ship before the bomb exploded. It would be about forty minutes before she returned to the area of the asteroid where the Trigger was located. She would be in the process of landing when the bombs went off. It was less than ideal, but at least she would have the asteroid between herself and the thermonuclear explosion. It would likely complicate her landing. The result of the explosion would be to accelerate the asteroid in her direction when she was on the opposite side of it. She adjusted her orbit to place her over the Trigger when she ran out of velocity relative to the surface and a few hundred meters above it.

Meanwhile, back on Trigger, there was a fair amount of nail biting taking place. They had been out of radio contact for almost two hours when the crew all gathered on Red Level to await Katerina's return and the coming explosion. An eerie silence had descended on everyone as they all watched their countdown clocks. At T – minus one minute and ten seconds there was a crackle on the radio.

"Trigger, Trigger, Trigger this is Soyuz. Come in."

'Well, you took your sweet time getting back. Are you down?" The relief in Jack's voice was evident.

"No, I am several hundred meters above. It took two passes to deliver the weapon properly. You should shut down your sensitive electronics."

"Why? We are on the opposite side of the asteroid from the blast, aren't we?"

"You are in electrical contact with the metallic spheroid adjacent to the thermonuclear weapon blast. The electromagnetic pulse could be a conduct-" The count reached zero, and there was a mighty shove beneath their feet, and all the lights went out.

"-ed. Shut everything down." Katerina heard herself say as the surface of Belial rushed toward the bottom of the Soyuz and the carrier wave was lost in a blast of static. Katerina braked with the rockets and tried to control her descent to maintain a proper attitude. She was still firing her rockets when the bottom of the Soyuz contacted the upper cables, and the fall was arrested abruptly.

Chapter Twenty-Two
Lost on Belial

Katerina Yerisivloskaya looked out the open cockpit hatch at the alien surface of Belial. The landing during the blast had been a mistake. The Soyuz had been pushed off course by the change in the rotation of the asteroid beneath her. She might be a mile or more from the Trigger. The radio seemed to be working but could have been broken for all the benefit it produced. The metallic cables were incredibly effective in absorbing radio waves. Here on the so featured as to be featureless surface of Belial, although individual cables were shiny on the surface, the overall impression in the light of the incredibly distant sun was one of the darkness between them. It looked as if they were flat black with occasional little patches of paint peeling off and glinting in the starlight.

A compass would not work this close to such large concentrations of Ferro metallic material. Katerina herself was somewhat surprised that she herself seemed totally uninjured given the violence of the crash. Even without the hatches, the angle she had come in had not allowed any of the heavy cables to enter the cockpit. The flexibility of the cable itself probably accounted for the rest of her luck.

Katerina carefully unstrapped herself and began a check of the Soyuz. She had burned all her fuel on the way down, which was probably just as well as it made it a little less likely to explode. There were still breathables in the storage tanks, and she took the time to equalize her oxygen tank with the one on board, which gave her an additional twenty minutes including what she already had in her suit tank. All in all, she now had about fifty minutes or so to find her way back to the Trigger.

It might be a somewhat interesting trick. Without the Soyuz, the height of the cables now exceeded the height of the Trigger. The surface, with its entangling layers of different sized cables looked much the same in all directions. She climbed out of the Soyuz and climbed to the top of it to see if she could see any evidence of which direction she should attempt. The ubiquitous cable had largely absorbed even the taller hills of the surface. There was a slight rolling quality to the landscape as it curved sharply away at a mile or so. Somehow, the nuclear explosion had bumped up the rate of the growth of the cable. In retrospect, perhaps, it had been accelerated by the first one as well. The little nanomachines that made the cables up had been designed to get their energy from ambient light. Perhaps they were not terribly particular regarding the wavelengths they could use. That could be a neat thing at times, but this was not one of those times. She looked all around her, and as the light changed with the now relatively gentle roll of the asteroid, she began to feel that there was an especially dark spot about a mile from the top of the Soyuz. That coincided with her recollection of how much the asteroid would have rotated while she was trying to land. The issue became how she would possibly maintain any straight direction once she left the orienting top of the doomed Soyuz. Breadcrumbs would not work even if she had some breadcrumbs. They would just trickle down into the space between the cables. A line might work if she had one long enough; however, all such items had been removed during the stripping of the Soyuz. Katerina looked at her dwindling oxygen and, considering her new life in the stars, determined that she did not want to give it up. The stars! That was the key. She carefully memorized the stars passing over her as the asteroid rotated and considered the line between her and where she suspected the Trigger to be. She watched until she was reasonably sure that she could navigate toward the possible declivity where she hoped the Trigger was. She had spent some time watching the stars; so on her way down she stopped and equalized her oxygen pressure again. Without stopping, she started out across the uncertain cablescape of Belial. It was incredibly difficult to travel in a straight line across, under and around the metal cables that the surface of Belial had become. The gravity was very slight but enough to make some of the choices a bit vertiginous. It was quite a distance down to what remained of the surface and the growth of cable was not uniform. Additionally she had to be certain that she kept the little bump that was the Soyuz directly behind her. She had been traveling twenty minutes when she noticed that the Soyuz was no longer visible. The declivity was still somewhat apparent. There being no choice, she continued toward where she thought she needed to go. The pressure in her oxygen tank steadily dropped. She carefully guided herself with her stellar clues as the asteroid rolled in the sky. The same sequence over and over again. The stars slid by overhead heedless of Katerina's serious danger.

When she was down to her last three minutes of air, she suddenly came upon an abyss in the cables and saw the Trigger in its center. It was a long way down. The cables got thinner as she descended into the pit. It got darker and darker to the point that she had difficulty making out when she had reached the bottom of the pit. She stumbled and fell as she tried to grasp the strut and begin her ascent. According to her gauges, she had no oxygen remaining and her breath came faster and faster as the carbon dioxide built up in her helmet. She was soaked with sweat from the exertions of crossing the unpredictable surface of Belial and her rapid breathing had dehydrated her. She was almost to the top of what seemed to be the oddly truncated height of the trigger, trying to reach the Airlock leading into the Triangular Passageway, when she became aware of how lightheaded she was. She had fallen across the top of the hatch when she realized that she could not use her hands anymore. Each breath was less and less satisfying to the point that it was now a physical pain to breathe, and yet she must! She just needed one more breath - just one more breath. Katerina Yerisivloskaya lost consciousness.

Jack Knight was just about to lose his mind. Just as he had almost gotten used to the fact that he might have to live his life without Katerina he had heard her begin her climb up the side of the Trigger and had hurriedly gotten into his excursion suit to try to help her in. He was severely hampered by the fact that the EMP had shut down the nuclear reactor, and battery power was being used to power the air circulation through the farms. Jake and Tom were almost ready to restart the computer when he scrambled up to Violet Level. The electric air pumps were not working, and the Triangular Passageway had been evacuated prior to the Soyuz blasting off. No one had thought to re-pressurize it during the emergency. Jack was struggling against the safety interlock that kept the hatch from opening on a vacuum. He knew that the hatch on the outside was closed and that there would be plenty of air to fill the Triangular Passageway even if he opened the door. The trouble was that there was a very good reason the hatch would not ordinarily open when the outside passage was a hard vacuum. Jack was in a hurry and had already determined that he could not force the door. He carefully recalled where all the thickest metal was on the other side of that hatch and made a small fixable hole with a large caliber handgun. The explosion in the small confined space deafened him. The air blasted through the hole and the safety interlock released as the pressure began to equalize on the other side of the hatch. Jack gave a cursory glance at the hole on the other side of the passageway and trusted that perhaps it had not penetrated all the way through to the vacuum on the outside of the Trigger. Regardless, it could be fixed soon enough. Jack climbed up to the external airlock, where previously the Soyuz had stood guard, and opened the inside door. He manually operated the pump motor to evacuate the air in the airlock. He unlatched the outside hatch and Katerina fell into his arms. He quickly laid her down on the top of the inner hatch, closed the outer hatch, and pumped an atmosphere into the airlock. As quickly as he could open the inner hatch, he quickly removed Katerina's helmet. The fetid air in her helmet almost made him lightheaded and he noted that Katerina was not breathing. He braced her against the opposite side of the airlock and removed his own helmet. The air in the lock was thin but breathable. He took a deep breath, grabbed her nose, cocked her head back, and blew into her mouth as hard as he could. It was impossible to tell whether she was breathing inside of the suit, but he could tell that he had gotten some in, because it blew back into his face. He took another deep breath and blew into her mouth as hard as he could, and was again rewarded with a breath of warm fetid air across his face. He quickly felt of her neck and decided that he could feel a pulse. He took another deep breath and rescue-breathed for Katerina again. At that moment, power came up, the automatic pumps kicked in, and the pressure began to come up. Jack's ears popped and he gave Katerina another breath and then quickly took her into a fireman's carry down to the hatch to Violet Level. His sister met him in the hatch and helped him carry the still unconscious Katerina down to the infirmary. The air in the ship was noticeably thinner than usual; and as Madelyne, assisted by Jack and Margaret, removed Katerina from her suit, Tom flew up the siphon carrying one of the curved patches that were kept in a well-marked cupboard on Red Level. Katerina started becoming agitated and combative when they tried to put a mask on her face.

"Try to hold her down so that she does not hurt herself. I think that I am going to have to intubate her to get her brain oxygen level up as quickly as I can. I am going to sedate and paralyze her, so we will have to breath for her. She has an open airway and no evidence of injury other than having run out of air, of course. Everyone get ready!"

Madelyne filled a hypodermic needle with two different medications from the crash cart and prepped an area of Katerina's arm. She quickly injected the medications, turned back to the cart, and grabbed the laryngoscope and a sterile plastic tube. At that moment, Katerina's efforts at breathing stopped; and Madelyne quickly anchored her coveralls to the table at Katerina's head, levered the scope into her airway, slid the tube in behind it, and attached the bag with its pure oxygen supply. She squeezed the bag, and Katerina's chest rose. She was listening through her stethoscope at the left base of Katerina's anterior chest and, satisfied with what she heard, shot a syringe of air into the inflating ring on the airway to improve the seal and secure it in its current position. She squeezed the bag again and watched as Katerina's chest rose. She was listening at her stomach and again seemed to be satisfied.

"Ok, Jack - grab this bag and squeeze it every time you see her chest fall all the way. Let us get her secured on the table, and I need to start an IV line immediately." There was a distant "thunk" and suddenly all their ears popped again. The air pressure immediately began to come up. Madelyn prepped an area on the right side of Katerina's neck, inserted a large caliber tube over the needle into Katerina's internal jugular vein, attached it to an intravenous pump, and started an electrolyte and glucose flow. Jack was bagging Katerina at what Madelyne considered a reasonable rate. Madelyne prepped an area on Katerina's right wrist and, after palpating a pulse, inserted a short fine gauge needle into Katerina's radial artery, withdrew some bright red blood, and grabbed Margaret's hand.

"Here, hold a lot of pressure here while I run these gasses." Margaret stepped forward and held a piece of gauze against the area of Katerina's wrist that Madelyne had punctured. Madelyne swam across the compartment and injected the blood into a small device that hissed and clicked. She watched a small liquid crystal display and winced. She opened another cabinet and added a bag of bicarbonate to the flow into Katerina's neck.

"She is incredibly acidotic, but with the oxygenation and the electrolytes, we will probably be able to turn that around. We are just incredibly lucky that her heart had not stopped as well as her breathing. Jack, keep doing what you are doing, and I think we can put a dressing on that radial artery stick. Wait, we are going to be doing this for a while. I am going to set an arterial tap so that I don't have to keep sticking her." Madelyne grabbed another set of sterile gloves and, after prepping and draping Katerina's wrist, inserted a catheter into the radial artery and secured it with a couple of stitches in Katerina's wrist. She then drew off another arterial sample and did another pH and blood gas. She seemed more than a little pleased with the result.

"Ok, Jack, step back and let me handle this. Get out of your suit and clean up. You need to get a little distance. If Tom and Jake are done repairing the holes that you put in the side of the ship, send them down here to spell Margaret after she takes over for me in a minute or two. We will probably be doing this for several hours at least. I wanted to bring a respirator but your dad would not hear of it. He did not want to spare the weight. He will one day learn to listen to me. Meanwhile I will give him such a forearm workout that he won't be able to grip anything for a week without a reminder of why he should listen to me." She had slowed down the frequency of the bagging when she took over from Jack. She pulled Margaret into service and indicated that she needed to keep the same rate that she had. "Go on, get out of here. You are beginning to make me nervous and irritated, and the one thing that you do not want to meet right now is me nervous and irritated. Send Bob too but keep Nina down on Red Level, if you can. Tell her that as far as you can tell, Katerina is going to be okay. For one thing, that's the truth. For another, if I can get you out of here, I might actually be able to make that happen. The biggest thing I am worried about right now is if she has suffered too much brain damage. I have got to normalize this low pH as quickly as I can without going too fast. It is going to be very ticky and will require every bit of concentration that I can bring to it. I will do absolutely the best I can for her, son. I love her too. Go on, get out. Send the others in, and go talk to Nina."

Jack turned away from the scene with his mind filled with the image of his love strapped to a table unmoving and stuck full of tubes.

As soon as Jack had left the compartment, Madelyne started a Foley catheter to catch the urine that she hoped Katerina would soon be producing. She had not wanted to do that with Jack in the room, regardless of Katerina and Jack's relationship. She also had not wanted to discuss the possibility of kidney and heart damage before she really had to. She and Margaret gowned and covered Katerina as well as they could before anybody else got there. Jake and Tom soon came into the infirmary, shortly followed by Bob.

"Ok, Gentlemen. Welcome to my situation. For the next several hours, you will do as I say. Exactly as I say, and exactly the way I say to do it. You will not make comments, and you will not ask me how things are going. When I tell you something that I am ready to tell you, you will carry that information, and that information alone, down to Jack and Nina. Okay, you're first Jake. Take over for Margaret while I do another gas. If anyone starts feeling wimpy, get the hell out of my infirmary!"

Jack had first gone to Violet Level and shucked his excursion suit, which for some reason had an unusual smell. It was after he wiped himself down before donning his ship suit that he realized that it was the smell of fear.

Jack swam down to Red Level where Nina waited and, without hesitation, gathered her into a tight hug. She looked as if she had been crying for an hour, which was pretty close to the elapsed time they had calculated would be the end of Katerina's air, based on her suit air alone. After the first ten minutes or so, Madelyne had to give her a little something for her nerves. She had stopped railing against heaven and the government in Kazakh in two partial languages, and had sort of shriveled up and quietly sobbed.

"Mom told me to tell you that as far as we know, Katerina will be okay. Then she kicked me out. They are breathing for her, and before that she was trying to breath for herself, but I think that was caused by some medicine that Mom gave her. She was not breathing when I got her helmet off, and I was breathing for her until Mom and Margaret started helping me. I shot a hole in the side of the ship so that I could get the hatch open to bring her inside. I probably shot up a few of our plants in the process."

"Of course you did, you big American Cowboy, of course you did." Nina almost smiled as she said this in her best-improved English and fell asleep in Jack's arms. Jack just held Nina and let her sleep. From time to time, he closed his eyes, and prayed.

Chapter Twenty-Three
Sometimes the Big Stuff Doesn't Matter

The vigil continued until the paralyzing agent wore off. At that point, Katerina started to breath on her own. She was still unconscious and largely unresponsive. Madelyne kept the endotrachael tube in and hooked it to the oxygen supply. Katerina had continued to produce urine and, after a time, Madelyne started to do the arterial blood gasses every eight hours or so. The acidosis caused by breathing all that carbon dioxide had been corrected. Still, Katerina did not wake up.

There was someone with her all the time. After the crew was able to let her breathe on her own, Madelyne sent everyone but Margaret off to sleep. She herself stretched out on the deck with some cover and took a four-hour nap. Margaret worked through her PDA to determine how much the twin nuclear explosions had changed the orbit of Belial. It was very difficult for her to concentrate on this task. With Katerina lying unconscious a few steps away, it really did not seem so very important. The orbit was going to be what it was, and that could be determined at most any time. Margaret mainly was working on this to keep herself from thinking about Katerina.

Madelyne had been very pleased when Katerina had started to breath on her own. She had still been fairly certain that she had suffered brain damage from the anoxia. After working for seven hours without a break, Madelyne had been able to just lie down and fall to sleep. It was not like that for her daughter. She had been there the entire seven hours as well but had been in a corner of the compartment for a fair percentage of that time just watching. She had taken her turns at helping Katerina breathe; but her husband, younger brother, and father had performed most of that duty.

Margaret had admired Katerina from the moment they had met, and they had gradually developed an ability to talk about important things with one another. She did not consider herself Katerina's confidante by any means; but they were, despite their difference in age, at about the same level in their personal relationships with members of the other sex. When there is only one person to discuss certain things with as an equal for a billion miles, it has an impact. She had offered her insight into Jack's personality in the hope that this tall redhead from another world and culture could actually make her brother happy. She had never seen her brother so complete and comfortable in his own skin.

After almost precisely four hours, Madelyne woke up and folded her cover. "Margaret, you might as well get back to your quarters and get some rest. If I need anything, I will call on your PDA."

"Why doesn't she wake up, Mom? She has got plenty of oxygen now, and you corrected the metabolic problem."

"Her brain is swollen inside her skull from the anoxic insult, dear. I just hope that, if she ever wakes up, the damage is not so bad as it seems it might be now. I hope that if it is that bad, she gets pneumonia and dies. We haven't got the resources to take care of someone with severe brain damage. Personally, I cannot imagine someone with the personal power that Katerina possessed in such abundance, needing to be restrained, soiling herself and having to be fed." Madelyne ran her hand through her wild hair and got a drink of water.

Margaret finally caught the full impact of how injured Katerina might be and stumbled out of the Infirmary up the siphon to the quarters that she shared with Tom. The tears came quietly, as many things do when others can overhear everything. Tom rolled uncomfortably in his sleep as Margaret joined him in bed. Heedless of her husband's comfort, she latched on to him and used him like a rag, soaking the shoulder and collar of his tee shirt with the helpless tears of mourning for what might have been.

"It's going to be okay, sweetie. Come on, it will all work out all right." Tom ran his big hand over his wife's head and hugged her tightly.

"I don't know what to pray for, Tom. It seems too much to hope for that Katerina will really be altogether well if she even wakes up. Mom says it might actually be better if she didn't even wake up if her brain is severely injured."

"Is it really that bad? I thought when she started breathing on her own that she was out of the woods."

"After you all left, Mom and I had a short conversation before she fell asleep. She said that Katerina's injury was like a near drowning, worsened by the heat and the dehydration. She says we have no idea how long Katerina's brain was without oxygen. She says probably less than three and a half minutes, but more than one or two. If Jack had not blown a hole in the side of the ship getting that hatch open, she would have been dead. And if she spends the rest of her life drooling on herself tied to a chair that might have been the best thing that could have happened." Margaret lost her voice in new tears.

"Is Madelyne in the mood to talk about this with me?"

"She had a good nap, unlike you, if your rolling around was any indication of how you slept. She is as upset about all this as I am. She just has too much to do to focus on the horror of it all."

"You get some sleep if you can, Sweetie. I am going down to the infirmary to talk to your mom. Now, while her mind is somewhat fresh, is probably the best time to do it." Tom pulled on his ship suit and closed the compartment partition behind him as he headed for the siphon to take him down to the infirmary.

Tom found Madelyne checking Katerina's blood pressure and quietly looked over the notes that Madelyne had kept during the time since they had started trying to save her life. Madelyne looked up as if annoyed. "I thought you would be sleeping, Tom. Didn't I wear you out enough?" Madelyne managed a wan smile at her lame attempt at humor.

"I slept some, though rather poorly. I had an idea I wanted to discuss with you regarding Katerina's care."

"Let's not. I think that I have done everything that can and should be done for Katerina, at least within the bounds of the generally accepted standard of medical care. I don't want to spend any time attempting to second-guess myself. I'm sure that there will be plenty of time later for me to do that." Madelyne's elegant face looked twenty years older than she had the day before, and this was probably a result of the grimness of her expression.

"What I have to offer is not near to the generally accepted standards of care. Are you familiar with what I was doing back at the University?"

"Tom, I know your work in the most general terms. It is clearly amazing stuff based on the bizarre alteration you performed on our asteroid in such a short time."

"Oh, that was old stuff, just carried out on a massive level which proceeded faster than I could have predicted. The stuff I was working on just before that weekend when Margaret and I got married was a lot more subtle. I am sending some of the last data to your PDA as we speak. It may have some benefit for Katerina, although it has never been used on a human being before. If you can spare the time from the work you are doing for Katerina you might just glance over it and see if you think it might be helpful. I don't have any big axe to grind to leap to human experimentation with my work but, from what Margaret told me between sobs, it may be that any benefit would be an advantage. It is possible that the benefit would be major. I have no way of evaluating this in the light of medical care. Just call me if any of this stuff doesn't make sense to you or you have a question. If you don't mention it to me again, that will be enough of an answer for me." Tom left the infirmary and headed down to Red Level to clean up and see if he could help anywhere else while Maggie tried to sleep.

Madelyne was torn between just putting her PDA back in her sleeve pocket and actually looking over the nonsense that Tom had thrust into her hand. Cellular level homeostasis - that sounded sort of appropriate. What a strange approach to medicine, little machines! Looking for the slightest glimmer of new hope, Madelyne read on.

Jake found her there about two hours later. He had spent around five or six hours trying to rest, and had finally given it up as a waste of time. Madelyne looked like she had been mugged. Jake grabbed her hairbrush and, coming up behind her, had begun to try to reduce the tangled mess.

"Jake, did you know about this work that Tom was doing before he came into the family? Do that again and try not to pull my scalp off, you hideous man."

"He and I have talked about some of his work, but he knows that I am an engineer; and when my eyes started to glaze over when he started talking about animal experiments, I think that he got the weird idea that I wasn't interested. Put your chin down a little. This rat's nest has to be straightened out before it wanders off.

"Well, it is some pretty interesting stuff. He developed some of his little machines that were based on carbon. They apparently could work within normal animal metabolism and keep the animals themselves safe, at least on the cellular level. He had gotten it refined to the point that his animals actually did better with than without it. Now you just brush that right side again, mister, and this time go slower." Madelyne was beginning to relax for the first time in most of two days. There is a point when you have done the best you can do, and all that remains is to allow nature to take its course. Madelyne was way past there into the next phase where you keep looking for one more thing to do.

Jake watched as Katerina's chest rose and fell and stuck the brush in his pocket and began to rub Madelyne's neck. "Do you really think any of this may help our Katerina?" Jake himself had watched his wife over enough years to know that she had very little hope for Katerina except for something outside of her medical experience. He began to work down the upper part of her back and shoulders.

"I am satisfied that there is nothing else we can do, and I really don't think she would wake up without us doing something. Her pressure has been dropping a little for the past hour or so, and frankly, I was a little glad. I just can't face Jack without doing the most that can be done, regardless of whether I really think it will help or not." Madelyne paged Tom on her PDA. Tom arrived in the infirmary within five minutes.

"Tom how long would it take to set his up?"

"I have the last batch from the assembler at the University. When you paged me, I collected it from the lab and came straight down here. I will need some of her blood and, more specifically, some white cells to expose the diamontoids to the major histocompatability complex. It will only take about ten minutes once we get the right cells isolated. After that, we can inject it or put it into her endotrachael tube. I have never done this with a human subject before, and I don't have any idea how long it will take before we know whether it will help or not." Tom was talking very fast and he looked both excited and alarmed as he spoke.

"Here is some blood. Let's get this going as soon as possible. It doesn't look like anything about it would hurt her more than she is already. It may offer her some benefit. Who knows, some may be enough." Madelyne assisted Tom to extract some white cells and put them into the little vial he had. After ten minutes or so, she put some normal saline into the vial and then drew it out again carefully, removing everything in the vial. Then she injected the saline with its invisible contents into Katerina's central line.

"Now, call Jack and have him come up here. We are going to wait some more."

Chapter Twenty-Four
Usually it is the Little Things that Matter Most

There was a roaring in her ears. It was so loud that it seemed to be interfering with her thinking. What had she been thinking about? Wait! Had she been thinking at all? That incredibly loud roaring, what was that sound? It did have a certain intermittent quality. It got louder and then softer. She knew that sound! It was the sound of breathing. Why was it so stupidly loud? There was a timeless shift in her perception and she realized it was the sound of her own breathing.

She tried to open her eyes but everything was so heavy; it was so hard to move. The sound of her breathing seemed to recede as other sensations clamored for her recognition. She could not move much because she seemed to be restrained. She appeared to be tied down. There was something in her mouth. She could feel her lips and teeth but she could not close her mouth. It was nightmarish. She began to struggle against her restraints and whatever it was in her mouth. She was suddenly overcome with a profound lethargy and a feeling that none of this mattered much; and during this uncertain interval, the object was removed from her mouth to be replaced by some sort of mask that covered her mouth and nose. The feeling of lethargy departed like fog on a bright fall morning. She was still restrained, and she could not open her eyes.

There was a tearing sensation, and whatever had kept her right eye shut was removed. She opened her eye to have it assaulted by a bright pitiless light that seemed to roam around the back of her eyeball like a searchlight. It was removed, and another tearing sensation announced the removal of the restraint from her left eye followed by the same intense glare that roamed around the back of her eye. The horrible light was removed, and the world seemed to recede into darkness, a darkness dominated by bright blue spots. The blue spots gradually faded, leaving a blurry muddle.

Katerina could feel a soft touch across her eyelid on the right and some of the blurriness departed with the gentle touch. It was then that she began to notice other sounds. The same gentle touch traveled across her left eyelid and she began to understand the sounds were someone trying to talk to her.

"Katerina, can you hear me? If you can hear me, squeeze this hand. Good. Very good. Now squeeze this other hand. Excellent! Now pull me toward you. Wonderful. Now push me away. Good very good! Now, the other hand. Pull me toward you. Now, push me away. Wonderful, wonderful. Now pull this toe up toward your face. Good. Now push down against my hand. Good. Other foot. Pull! Good! Push! Good. Do you feel me touching you here? Just nod sweetie. Good, now here? You are doing so well!"

The silly series of exercises seemed to go on and on. Katerina discovered that she could not speak. All she could manage was a coarse croaking.

There was a gap in her recollections. She could not really remember getting back to the Trigger, but could only see a mental image of looking down on it from the hedge of cables that surrounded it. She sort of remembered a stumble at the strut. Her vision and hearing continued to sharpen until she felt that she had never ever seen or heard so clearly. What came in the most clearly was the incredible joy that the people around her were feeling. She must have been really sick. Nina was crying openly, and Jack was trying not to let his blubbering show. Really, she couldn't see a dry eye in the room but there were plenty of big smiles.

"How long have I been out of it?" Katerina croaked painfully.

"You got back about a week ago, Sweetie; and we have been so worried. I want you to sleep now for a time while I get some of this stuff out of you, so that you will be able to move around normally when you wake up more. Your voice will feel better then too, so you will be able to tell us all about it. We have a few things that we need to tell you about as well." Katerina realized that Madelyne was speaking and that she was doing something with a tube off to her right. The night came down like a waterfall and swept Katerina into a dreamless sleep.

When she awoke again, she was in the quarters that she shared with Jack. Jack was snoring next to her as if he had not slept in a week. She found out later that that was pretty close to the facts. She quietly got up, dressed, and made her way down to Red Level. There seemed to be snores from all over the ship. She made herself some coffee and winced when the hot liquid hit her still sore throat. She had bandages on her neck and wrist. The wounds beneath were slightly sore but nothing that diverted her attention. She had a little soreness elsewhere, including her privates, for some good reason she was sure. But all things considered, she felt unusually well. She marveled at the care these familiar strangers who had become her family had obviously lavished on her during her illness. She was beginning to tire of her solitude when Jack made his way down the siphon. He rushed across the intervening space and grabbed her in a tight embrace that was most unlike his usual almost shy approach.

"Katerina Yerisivloskaya will you stay with me the rest of my life? Will you marry me? I do not know how our mission will turn out, and that does not matter to me. I only know that I do not want to live without you in my life." Jack had never been the least bit vocal with his affection, and the three sentences he had just spoken were every bit of conversation that she had ever heard from him on this matter.

"Silly American Booby, I will marry you. I knew you would eventually get around to asking. I was willing to wait. We are two of a kind, you know. I had despaired of ever meeting someone I could actually respect and care for. But in the aftermath of a firefight in the dirty streets of Almaty, there you were. Wading in as if you did that everyday. I saw the shock in your eyes when you killed for me. A girl learns to appreciate that sort of thing. We will arrange it when it is convenient for our family." Katerina's voice sounded a little quivery but strong enough to make herself heard.

As if on cue, the rest of the crew flowed down the siphon. They surrounded the couple, pounded on Jack's back, kissed and hugged Katerina. In the miniscule gravity of Belial, these operations had them bouncing around the room. The effect was like a group of otters cavorting in a pool of crystal water. There were laughter and tears, jokes and stories. Katerina's coffee got cold and another pot from their dwindling store was made. It became a time for telling stories and bringing Katerina up to date with the events that occurred while she was unconscious.

"And so you are telling me that I have millions of tiny machines in my body right now?" Katerina could not get over this part of her recovery.

"Probably billions." Tom was on the hot seat while being interrogated by Katerina.

"And they will always be there?

"They will if I do not turn them off, and that will actually take some time, as I brought the machines but not the turn off sequences machines. I can make them, but unlike the machines themselves, I do not have them already made."

"Does my life depend on them?"

"I do not think that it does anymore. I do believe that the repairs they helped with are responsible for you waking up from the coma that you were in four days ago. How are you feeling now?"

"I feel very well. In fact, I feel better than I have in some time. My vision seems clearer and my hearing more acute." Katerina had also noticed that the coffee was not making her feel jittery like it usually did when she had more than a single cup. It was more like a sustained feeling of excitation.

"You are clearly stronger than you have any right to be after an injury like you had." Madelyne noted that her patient seemed to be thinking much more clearly than any patient she had ever seen wake up from a coma before.

"I feel as if I just woke up from a normal sleep but better rested than I have since I was in my twenties." Katerina was looking at the back of her hand as she held her coffee container and it seemed to her that it looked younger. As she looked around the rest of the compartment at her crewmates, they also seemed to look younger and more vital than she recalled.

"There is more." Tom looked like a little kid with a brand new toy that was turning out to be more fun than he had anticipated. "The little machines are contagious. After I put them into your IV, within the next eighteen hours, everyone had had a dose. You are farther along than the rest of us, as you got the biggest dose directly. We seem to have gotten it from the air that you exhaled. I did not expect this, as I never tested for it. I injected all of my laboratory animals when I was in my lab on Earth and would never have detected any subject-to-subject transfer, as all the animals within the enclosure had already been exposed. Apparently, as humans, our DNA is so self-similar that the minute differences between our major histocompatability complexes, that would trigger an immune response if this were an ordinary antigen, are not different enough to cause problems with the nanomachines. Of course there is the matter of our blood type. We only have one blood type on Belial. Somehow, through some bizarre chance, we all have O positive blood." Tom grinned.

"Well, I guess the next question is how do the rest of you feel? Even if this is not a permanent change, I feel good enough to hope it continues." Katerina was sure she liked the way she was feeling now. She was also sure that she had never seen her Nina look so young.

"I think that I can speak for the rest of us in saying that we have all noticed some improvements as well. The main things that I have noticed in myself seem to be a sharpening in my senses. I have started not wearing my glasses. I also have noticed that the stiffness in my fingers, that I have not bothered to tell anyone about, is totally gone." Madelyne smiled as she rubbed her hands together.

"What I have noticed is that my spare tire seems to be diminished. I have more energy." Jake was also smiling as he rubbed his abdomen.

"I have not noticed much of anything except that some colors are a little different than before, and I do not seem to need as much light as I did to see." Bob, as the youngest, was still enjoying that first bloom of youth.

"I have not noticed very much either. I do seem to be stronger and I guess a little more coordinated although, in spite of what Jack says, I have never been clumsy. I just never cared for athletics." Margaret looked at her older brother and gave him the evil eye as she always did when he seemed to imply that she was a klutz. Jack was totally oblivious, as he looked at Katerina awake and whole.

Tom looked at his wife very fondly and turned his gaze back to the others in the compartment. "I think that if things continue to go this well, we will let our little experiment in the human-machine interface continue. I will, of course, continue my work with the construction of the shut down sequence machines so we will have them if things begin to go wrong."

"Is anyone else hungry? I feel like I have not eaten in a week." Jack finally tore his attention away from his fiancé, and everyone in the compartment laughed.

"I am hungry, too. I move that we suspend the wedding plans until after lunch. Is there a second? Jake looked around the crew on Red Level.

"I second that." Bob replied more quickly than anyone else could.

"All in favor, say 'aye'," Jake, said just before a quick succession of seven 'ayes'. "Motion carries. Let's break out the good stuff." Jake headed toward the freezer and started asking for everyone's preference from the more select menu items. Everyone took their turns with the microwave and settled into various comfortable positions around the room while Jake broke out their ever more scarce store of wine. When he had supplied everyone with a small portion, he raised his container. "A toast to the happy couple."

"The happy couple" was spoken loudly around the compartment, and everyone drained their little containers. The meal continued with occasional burst of conversation and laughter.

As the meal began to reach its conclusion, Jake looked at Katerina and Jack. "When would you like me to conduct the ceremony? I think that even though we are not in free space, we can extend my authority as Captain of the Trigger to include the power to perform marriages here on Belial. Is there a motion?"

"I move that the Captain's authority to perform marriage ceremonies be extended to here on the surface of Belial until an obvious civil authority arises. As if we would ever allow that to happen!" Bob did not even grin as he altered his Father's intent.

"I second Bob's motion." Jack clearly had an interest in the question, as his own marriage was at issue.

"All in favor say 'aye'." There were again seven 'ayes' in rapid succession. "Motion carries. Once again, I ask you, now that I am duly empowered, when you would like this ceremony to take place?" Jake carefully did not look at his oldest son but at his fiancé.

" How about right after lunch? I have never wanted a big wedding, but there are certain formalities that should be observed. We are sufficiently far from my parents in Russia that I must ask Bob to give me away. I would like Margaret to be my Matron of Honor."

"Well, if Bob is going to give you away, and Dad is going to perform the ceremony, Tom must be my best man." Jack turned and grinned at Tom, and Tom nodded.

"It sounds like everyone is going to be in the wedding but Nina and I." Madelyne graced everyone in the compartment with a mock frown.

"No, my future Mother–in-law, you must assume the role given you in this play. You and Nina must sit in the first row and sob quietly." Katerina gathered her grandmother and mother-in –law to be in a big hug.

"All right, I will sit on the front row and cry, but I do not promise to be quiet."

Jake took Jack aside to his quarters. Katerina and Margaret went to Margaret's quarters, and the others cleaned up Red Level. "Jack, your grandmother would have liked you to have this. If it does not fit, I can probably size it for you." Jake removed a small golden ring with a diamond solitaire from his drawer, where it and some other small bits of jewelry waited in a small plastic bag. "She would have been very proud of you, and I think she would have approved of your choice of a wife once she had gotten over the fact that you were marrying a foreigner." Jake laughed at his own recollection of his mother's prejudices. "Come to think of it, we are all foreigners here." Jake and Tom went down the siphon to Green Level where the ceremony would take place.

In Margaret and Tom's quarters, Margaret was digging through her own drawers and first pulled out a blue garter. This will have to do for something old, blue, and borrowed. I do not think that a dress is going to work in this gravity and I do not think I brought one in any case. I do want you to have this for your something new. Our coloration is similar so I think that it will look as good in your hair as it does in mine. Tom got it for me on our short trip to the mountains of Mexico after we got married. He got me so many other things that I have never worn it after trying it on." Margaret pulled out a malachite and silver hair binder with an ebony stick. "The Mexican women we saw wearing things like this always put their hair on top of their heads when they dressed up. Probably, it got the hair off their necks and kept them cooler. It was hot down there during the day. I think that it would also do for a ponytail if you wanted to use it for that. Let me help you put it up for now. You have such a pretty neck."

"We have similar customs, but these are not like ours exactly. I think that your customs will do for today, and it seems like fun." Katerina had slipped out of her ship suit and was pulling the old blue garter up her leg to above her knee. "Jack will enjoy finding this later." She laughed.

Margaret was combing Katerina's hair; and when she was satisfied, twisted it once and put it on top of Katerina's head in an attractive knot, secured by the malachite and silver curve penetrated by the pointed ebony rod. Margaret pulled out a small mirror and handed it to Katerina, who had just finished pulling her ship suit back on. Katerina looked at her reflection in the hand mirror and clearly approved. She grabbed Margaret in a tight hug. "Thank you so much. It is beautiful!" She and Margaret headed down the siphon to Green Level where everyone else waited.

Bob had combed his hair, which was an unusual occurrence. Not that it made any lasting impression to comb his hair anymore. He waited near the siphon as Margaret and Katerina arrived. Margaret swam to the bulkhead where her Father and brother waited at the viewport. The scene out the port was largely unchanged, with cables of various sizes in tangled growth a meter or two beyond the glass. Madelyne and Nina sat together on one of tables. Tom stood near Jack. When Margaret arrived at the bulkhead near the viewport, she stood to the left of her brother. At that point, Tom punched in a command on his PDA and the familiar Wedding March played tinnily from the tiny speakers. Bob and Katerina clumsily swam toward the viewport with Katerina trying to hang on to Bob's arm. The resulting gyrations would have been humorous under any other circumstances, but here, today, they seemed charming. When they reached the others, Jake asked, "Who gives this woman to be married?"

"I do, acting as a proxy for her parents who are a billion miles away." This line that Bob delivered in all seriousness broke the party up into peals of laughter.

When the giggles had subsided, Jake continued. "From the time of the sailing ships, Captains have had the authority to conduct whatever ceremonies that the crew of their ship or passengers required. This happily included the authority to marry members of the crew or passengers who were so lucky as to require this service. Now, the seas that we sail are not water but the vaster spaces between the planets and stars. Therefore, although the circumstances are different, they partake of the same essence with our distance from other duly designated authorities. Although we are grounded on an asteroid, we are moving as if still under power or sail from one region of our

Solar system to another part, and I have been authorized by our crew to retain the authority that would be traditionally mine in open ocean or, as I see it, open space. Therefore, I now ask if anyone in this company knows of any reason why this man and this woman cannot be joined in the bonds of Holy Matrimony. If so, speak now or forever hold your peace." The traditional challenge given, Jake waited about ten seconds before continuing. "There are many customs regarding marriage in human culture throughout the world. They range from being as simple as the couple jumping over a sword or a broom to elaborate ceremonies which last for days on end and culminate in the groom crunching a glass under his boot. The essence of marriage, however, remains remarkably consistent across our home planet. A man and a woman promise to combine their assets and live their lives together. The interest of the state is primarily concerned with the welfare of any children born or of protecting the weaker from the stronger in the event of conflict. We are by ourselves, and no state or government is going to be involved in the foreseeable future. There being no state or government to accept his responsibility, we must, as we have for the last several years, look entirely to ourselves. This would seem to require more than the assent of the parties of the marriage, and so I now ask this company if they will assist this couple during their lives together with the welfare of any children born and in the case of conflict help protect the weaker from the stronger?"

There was a moment of silence and then the others in the compartment all nodded or spoke in assent. Then Jake continued, "Ekaterina Terescova Yerisivloskaya do you take this man, Jack Knight, to be your husband? To have and to hold, to love and cherish, honor and regard during your life?"

There was not a second of hesitation before Katerina answered, "I will."

"Jack Palladin Knight, do you take this woman, Ekaterina Yerisivloskaya, to be your wife? To have and to hold, to love and cherish, honor and regard during your life?"

"I will."

"Tom, if you will give Jack the ring." Tom unzipped one of the pockets on his ship suit and removed the ring that Jake had given Jack less than an hour ago.

Jack took Katerina's left hand and put the ring on her fourth finger. It actually fit very well. Katerina looked at the unexpected gift and smiled not only for its beauty but also for its value as a family heirloom. She grabbed Jack's face and kissed him on the lips.

" With the authority conferred upon me, I pronounce you husband and wife. You may kiss the bride." Jake said unnecessarily. The laughter and tears were immediate.

The assembly dissolved into hugs, kisses, and congratulations. A bottle of Champaign appeared as if from nowhere; and after Tom popped the cork, which almost hit Jake in the face; there were more toasts and music from the tiny speakers on the ubiquitous PDAs. More intoxicating liquids soon appeared, and the company tried to dance in the microgravity of Belial. After the laughter this generated subsided, the group went down the siphon for another light snack.

The talk eventually came back to how well every one felt and how well they were seeing and hearing. Tom told about how they were all making diamond in the metabolically active cells in their bodies, and that they would eventually have difficulty even cutting their hair.

"That could become inconvenient. I do not know if I would really like this man if his face was all haired over." Jack and Katerina could not keep their hands off one another. They were both on one couch on Red Level.

"Oh, I think we could fashion a diamond coated razor or two if it became important." As soon as he said this, Tom developed that distant expression that he got when he was working. Margaret looked on fondly and idly ran her fingers through his hair. Jake and Madelyn were also sharing a couch and, while primarily looking at Jack and Katerina, spared an occasional look of concern for Bob. He and Nina were talking in the three not so good languages that they shared and continued to try and improve their respective skills.

Katerina looked around the compartment at her family and smiled. She thought back to the desperate struggle to get back to the Trigger after setting off the last explosion. It occurred to her that she had not heard the most important news yet. "I think I have heard enough about the physical changes we have undergone. It all sounds very good, but what is important right now is whether we succeeded in our mission. Will we miss the Earth?"

Margaret looked a little uncomfortable for the first time since Katerina had been awake. "We will indeed. That last double blast was much more effective than our first one. I do not understand it fully yet, but the metallic surface of Belial was much more effective at absorbing the force of the blast. The surface itself seemed to flex and propel us farther than we calculated the maximum effect to be. Apparently, from the cloud of metallic debris that was in our wake, we vaporized a few tens of meters of metal from the blast area."

"That is wonderful news! We have succeeded! We have saved the Earth!" Katerina didn't understand the noticeably longer faces in the compartment.

"We have saved the Earth, and that is very good news surely. The problem is with the rest of our little plan. We had intended the asteroid to be captured by the Earth-Moon system and to orbit around them forever. The trouble is that we have overcompensated. It is obviously very difficult to steer an asteroid with nuclear weapons. We will miss the Earth and pass between the Earth and Moon in such a way that our gravitational interaction with the system will be minimized. We will pass through and not even slow down; and about four months after our nearest approach, Belial will impact with the sun.

Chapter Twenty-five
A Little Bit of Miscalculation Goes a Long Way

"We are going to impact with the sun?" Katerina's mouth had dropped open when Margaret had let this last little tidbit fall from her lips.

That's the way it looks right now, but we still have one nuclear weapon. We can probably steer us into the capture we had in mind. Tom has some idea about a light sail that he hasn't bothered to explain to me. The problem, as we see it, is whether it is worth the risk to Earth." Margaret had grabbed Katerina's hand and was stroking it, causing them both to rotate in place.

"Of course it is worth the risk! We do not have to die to save the Earth. Remember, that last blast was twice as powerful as the first one. "

"Actually, it was almost three times as powerful. It is the unpredictability that has us worried. What if we made this little correction and hit the Earth? We are going to take a little time to figure out how to do this without endangering the Earth again."

Katerina thought about this. Everything that Margaret said had made sense. It was a little bit too much though to have come so far and survived so many dangers to suffer and die because of a little miscalculation.

"There is also the delivery problem. The Soyuz is history. The ever-changing surface of Belial is impossible to navigate, despite the miracle that you accomplished, Katerina. You didn't exactly come out of it unscathed." Jake was looking at his brand new daughter–in –law with a mixture of fondness and fear as he recalled her in a coma.

Madelyne did not like the direction this conversation was going. "Let us agree to table this discussion, here on my daughter-in-law's wedding night. There will be time to make things right when we have time to do a little figuring. Katerina is just out of a coma today, and we are already loading her up with the extreme problems that we have come to expect her to solve for us. We need to give her a little time to acclimate."

As far as Katerina was concerned, it was a little late to be worried about upsetting her on her wedding day. She was confident that they would be able to solve this problem as they had solved all the others. It was, after all, only one more thing to be worried about. She determined to be relaxed and happy on the wedding day that she had never hoped to see. There was more alcohol and dancing, and the crew eventually retired to their respective compartments to rest for another set of hazards.

The next day, or waking period, as day and night had long since lost any meaning on Belial, the crew met on Red Level to eat and talk about whatever would come next. There was the usual talk of inconsequential things, as the crew made their largely separate ways to Red Level. Katerina and Jack swam in last. The modest amount of alcohol made available the previous evening had not been enough to cause any fogginess in this crew of dedicated individuals. The mess was provided with coffee in a diluted form. It was hot and contained a discernable quantity of caffeine. It, along with the assembly of the crew, signaled the new beginning of effort. Jake, as the titular head of the clan, started the action.

"How are our farms doing?" Jake's question, directed at his wife, was largely ceremonial as everyone worked a few shifts in the farm cylinders and therefore knew pretty much how things were going.

"Most of our food crops are growing well. I am a little concerned about our wheat, as it does not seem to want to want to produce without soil. The tomatoes and peppers are particularly exciting, as we have not had any of these since we took off. The squash is also looking good, though it is behind the peppers. We lost all of the eggplant to some fungus that killed it. I am going to wait to replant it when I have an opening at the top of one of the cylinders." Madelyne was very proud of her cylindrical gardens.

"Power?" Again, Jake's question directed at Tom was largely rhetorical, as Jake was mainly responsible for the reactor.

"The reactor is purring along at reduced power, as our requirements are so low now that the drive isn't being used. " Tom had not actually been near the reactor since he could access all the readouts from his PDA.

"Galley?" Jake directed his question at his daughter. Everyone on the Trigger wore multiple hats. Jake was merely asking questions of the people who had taken on the primary responsibility in any given area.

"We are doing pretty well, Dad. Although we had only accounted for six persons in our packing, we added enough excess capacity that our two unplanned crewmembers are not significantly affecting our food supply. This is largely the result of the fresh supplemental items provided by our farms. In addition, we do not expend as much energy here in a microgravity environment. We seem to be eating less."

"This brings up a problem that we need to deal with." Madelyne interjected. "We are indeed eating less and, although we have not really noticed it, we are losing both bone and lean body mass."

"Will it take a full Earth gravity to prevent this problem?" Jake had not given this problem any thought at all.

"I noticed it while we were under acceleration. Clearly twenty percent is not adequate. The problem has worsened since we stopped accelerating. The natural gravitational field of Belial is largely negligible. It is equivalent to the acceleration we had with the Dingus without its dress. It is nice to have an up and down that is not costing us, but in terms of our long term health, it is not doing us any good."

"Once we get the Bernal Sphere going, we will have normal weight if we choose. It will come at the price of a slight, but noticeable, coriolis force." Tom was clearly excited about his big engineering project. "I would guess we are months away from this, but I would not have expected us to be this far along if you had asked me two weeks ago."

Margaret was looking at her husband with a strange mixture of fondness and exasperation. "If you actually intended to remodel this asteroid in the shortest amount of time possible, how much time would it take?"

"I am not entirely sure. The little machines that I made to create the cable were rather more productive than I would have assumed. If I modified these same machines so that they would not have to reproduce themselves, the time could be greatly reduced. The main thing I am having to try to get my mind around is that the actual quantity of materials is not as impossible as they initially appeared. The main issues are to simplify the process so that no human, or rather, very little human attention is required for the process, I spent a few days modifying a few machines such that they could, as Jake advised, work cooperatively. In the space of forty days or so, they have moved cubic miles of metal from the deepest interior of this asteroid to its surface. The day before yesterday, I measured the height of the cables around the Trigger and, at nearly eighteen meters above the top, it is almost fifty meters in depth. If the process is uniform, and I have every confidence that it is, there can be only so much metal left on the inside."

Bob meanwhile had been playing with his PDA and suddenly announced," That is almost a hundred and sixty five feet!" Bob had never been entirely comfortable with the metric system.

"Yes it is, Bob. If my somewhat rough estimation of the surface area of this asteroid was correct, we are nearing the eight cubic miles of metal that I estimated the asteroid to contain. The process should end within the next few days. What I really ought to do is reprogram the nanomachines network to start working on the rock, leaving a network of metal in place to facilitate moving the silicates around." Tom's face had taken on a dreamy expression as he considered moving over seven cubic miles of silicates one atom at a time.

"How did you overcome your little water problem?" Jake recalled Tom's concerns about water and how the molecules tended to stick to the little nanomachines and gum up the works.

"When I thought about it again, I realized that I didn't have to work with the water itself, but rather with ice. One of the things that these little machines do is to reorder matter atom by atom. They have been doing this for the last forty days or so and, as a result, the interior of this asteroid is so cold that the small amount of helium present is a liquid. It is refrigeration on a scale never before attempted."

"Ok, brother-in-law, I get that the inside of the asteroid would be cold because it always has been. Why would it now be colder?" Bob was primarily a humanities student in college.

"Let me handle this, Tom." Margaret took her younger brother's shoulders and oriented his face toward hers. "The reason the inside is colder than before has to do with the three laws of Thermodynamics. I am a little surprised that you have not encountered them before."

"Oh yeah, I remember them. The first one is that you cannot win. The second one is that you cannot break even, and the third one is that you cannot ever get close to breaking even." Bob grinned at his recollection of his chemistry professor's face when he had restated the three laws of thermodynamics as he just had.

Margaret also smiled at this and said, "Those are the ones, and you have summed them up nicely. However, your simplification leaves out the pertinent section having to do with entropy. There is a certain amount of energy in organization. Reactions can go forward without exogenous energy if they tend to leave things less organized than they were before the reaction. Tom's little machines leave things much more orderly than they were before. They are able to do this because they get energy from the sunlight falling on the increased surface area of this asteroid. However, not all the energy comes from the sun. Some of it comes from the retained heat of the interior of the asteroid. Consequently, as the reaction progresses toward greater order, the interior gets colder and colder."

"OK, now I get it. That does lead to another question. Where are we going to get the energy needed to melt almost five cubic miles of super cooled ice?" Bob suddenly had a worried look on his face.

Tom also looked worried but then appeared to put it out of his mind. "We will have it when we need it. I have not figured out exactly where it will come from, but we will have when we need it. I have got a few ideas that would take care of the problem."

"Tom still has not answered my question. How long would it take to get things arranged the way you showed me in those pictures?" Margaret was not going to let Tom wiggle out of a firm answer.

"It will take me a couple of days to modify the nanomachines' programming to go after the silicates. The products will be various metallic salts and silicon along with a generous portion of oxygen. I intend to use a fair amount of this to make quartz for our big window. I will leave some of it as rock, and make sand and soil out of the rest. The shape of the asteroid is already changing into a sphere. This is the result of conservation of momentum and the tendency of any liquid to take the shape of a sphere in free fall. I know that those metal cables out there are not a liquid, but they have enough freedom of movement in relation to one another to act pretty much like one. We will end up with a certain amount of spin because it is spinning now. We will know when the asteroid is spherical because the spin rate will start to stabilize. I do not know if anyone else has noticed that we are spinning faster than we were a week ago, but it is picking up as the shape becomes more regular and the long axis gets shorter. I think that the important thing to be aware of is that the outside of the asteroid is going to separate from the contents when the metal extraction process is completed. It may, in fact, be possible that the Trigger will fall towards the center of the asteroid when this happens."

"The Last time I looked, the cables were thoroughly involved with the landing pads." Jack was certain that falling through the surface would not be an immediate concern.

"I really do not think the primary process has completed. It would not be an issue until that time. I just need to get busy with the programming of phase two." Tom grabbed a food packet and started toward Yellow Level.

"Tom White, you will answer my question before you touch that siphon, or you will live to regret it!" Margaret would not be put off indefinitely.

"The primary construction could be completed in three months, assuming a random distribution of soil and water. I need to set my machines up to determine the axis of rotation at this location so there is no chance of us falling into the darkness below. I have also got to begin planning external facilities that would not require us to move the Trigger again, yet allow us to have commerce with those that we hope one day be our customers. It is going to be quite chaotic for some time." Tom disappeared up the siphon to Yellow Level.

Margaret had her PDA out and was running a series of calculations. She sniffed and looked over at Jake. "Dad, I need for you to go with Tom and help him figure out how to tell the little nanomachines that we need a big curved sheet of very shiny metal connected by cables that we can shorten or lengthen. He already knows why he wants to do this."

"Any particular shape that you would care for?" Jake already knew the answer, but he just wanted to hear her say it.

"Whatever is easiest and quickest will be fine. It will need to be at least two hundred kilometers across." Margaret barely looked up from her PDA.

"I will tell Tom that we need five hundred and see how he handles that." Jake made his way up the siphon toward Yellow Level.

"Would someone be so kind as to tell me what is going on?" Madelyne's tone was such that no one on board would dare not be so kind.

"We are going to hold that last nuclear weapon in reserve. We are going to try to sail our beautiful sphere into the spot where we want her to be. I just asked Daddy to tell Tom to make a light sail." Margaret was still busy with the calculations.

"A light sail? Don't be ridiculous! Nothing five hundred kilometers across could possibly be considered light!" Madelyne would brook no nonsense.

"Not light in the sense that it has negligible mass, although the total mass when it is only a few molecules thick might surprise you. It is a sail that uses light instead of wind." Margaret still did not look up from her calculations.

"Oh. That is different, I guess." Madelyne headed toward the farm cylinders through Violet Level. Bob and Nina followed her for their shift in the garden.

Jack and Katerina looked at one another, and then Jack asked Margaret, "What are we supposed to do? We seem to be off the schedule."

For the first time Margaret looked up, "That is no accident. You are to do whatever you like for the next week or so. We arranged the schedule so that you and Katerina can have as much of a honeymoon as we can manage here on Belial. We all figure that Katerina needs some time to recover from her injury and you are the logical candidate to help her do it." Margaret smiled and went back to her calculations.

Jack looked at Katerina and they made a beeline to the siphon and their quarters on the otherwise deserted Blue Level.

Chapter Twenty-six
Things That Go Around

The light sail had begun to grow. It looked like some sort of alien leaf that kept getting bigger and bigger. For a time it shaded the hole that had grown around the Trigger until it was far enough away that its shade was occasional.

The gravity of Belial had decreased. Although the mass of the asteroid was almost exactly what it had been when the Trigger had landed, it was now spread through a volume almost three times what it had been. This had decreased the apparent surface gravity of Belial to one ninth of what it had been when the Trigger had landed. There had been Belial quakes when the interior had broken away from the metallic outside. There had been all manner of rumblings and jolts.

Suddenly, almost the entire tiny amount of weight they had gotten used to went away. The floor seemed to just fall away, and things started floating. No one could feel it, but that's when the stuff left at the core actually broke loose. The Trigger was now attached to the outside of a rotating ball. The centrifugal force now caused items and people to gradually drift toward the outer bulkhead. The axis of rotation passed directly perpendicular to and through the Triangular Passageway. The crashes and bangs of cubic miles of ice and rock colliding with the walls of the sphere were largely lost on the occupants of the Trigger as they were conducted through the solid surfaces in the ship. The atmosphere inside the ship was not a great medium for the transmission of shockwaves. It was probably just as well.

The little group who was responsible for saving the world sat or rather floated around on Red Level and discussed what needed to be done next. Jack was trying to brush

Katerina's huge hair. It stuck out almost a yard from her head and was a hazard.

"It is probably safe on the inside of Belial now, at least from the standpoint of falling asteroidal material." Tom White had an amazing capacity for understatement.

"Safe, if you don't mind temperatures at which Helium is a liquid! Personally, that seems a little chilly to me." Margaret had some issues with her husband's cavalier attitude toward the incredible amount of work and energy (literally) that needed to be put into the construction of their new home.

"I have some very concrete ideas for how to warm it up in there, dear."

"I don't want to hear anything about setting off our last nuclear weapon inside of our new home! It is impossible! And so unsanitary!"

"I concur with my daughter, Tom. They were fine on the outside but not where I may live to see grandchildren – my grandchildren." Madelyne had some issues with her son–in–law's apparent attitude about nuclear weapons in the house.

"Tom never even mentioned using nuclear weapons to supply the initial heat for our new home, did you Tom? Give the man a break, will you gals?" Jake was secretly glad that the girls had broached the subject and disposed of it without him having to get involved.

"I had something a bit more benign in mind. Thank you very much for the sterling vote of confidence. But before we even try to warm it up in there, the little nanomachines have got to finish their work. They can handle ice but not liquid water. There are rocks inside of there that are so big they would interfere with normal commerce, much less proper drainage. My little guys are at work breaking down the big ones into smaller ones. They are extracting some useful minerals for our later use, as well as working on the eye."

"The eye? What are you talking about, Tom?" Jack was still brushing Katerina's hair. Velcro anchored them both to the little table.

"The eye of Belial sounds so much more interesting than the big window, don't you think Jack?"

"Granted, it sounds much more interesting than the big window of Belial. Where did you intend to put it?" It was incredible to Jack just how tangled long hair could get in near zero G.

It will go to the area where the acceleration is least. The acceleration is going to increase you know. Just because we have redistributed the mass doesn't mean that we have lost any of the momentum that the system had before we changed its shape."

"Wait a minute, Tom, haven't you got that backwards? Haven't we redistributed the mass to the outside? Isn't that like an ice-skater throwing her arms wide to slow down her rotation? It seems like we have increased the moment arm."

"Sure we have, Jake. But it is not simple rotation that we are dealing with. Remember, we had rotation and tumble on Belial before we changed it into a more efficient rotator. All of that will be additive, and we will end up with a single faster rotation in a single plane, although we will have some degree of precession. The light sail is rotating as well and pulling gently away from the sun. When we retract that, as we will when we reach where we need to be, it will be like the ice skater pulling in her arms.

"That will be some time in the future, right? There will be plenty of time to prepare for this?" Katerina really already knew the answer, but wanted the answer just to put some of the others minds at ease.

"Oh yes, months and months will pass before the rotation will cause the centrifugal force to exceed that of gravity."

"It seems to me that we need to turn the ship over." Madelyne looked up from her needlework. "If we need to get to the inside of this hollow ball eventually, it makes sense to me that we need a door and a place to live while the inside becomes livable. Why don't we turn the ship end for end? Then we would have the airlock nearest the surface. We could use it to go to and from the inside of Belial."

"Here at the zero axis there won't be much in the way of atmosphere on the other side of that door."

"Don't we have enough atmosphere to fill up the whole thing?" Bob had been quietly reading until this last pronouncement from his brother in law.

"No, not really. We will have plenty of oxygen but the bulk of the air we are accustomed to is nitrogen. Unless there are a lot more nitrogen compounds inside than I think we can count on, we will be lucky to manage a low pressure atmosphere that peters out a kilometer or so above the inner surface."

"Why wouldn't there be as much nitrogen as on Earth? I mean, it all came from the same place, right? Why wouldn't there be tons and tons of methane and other nitrogenous compounds on the inside? The atmosphere of Titan is almost all methane, and Belial came from farther out. I don't think it has had a significant opportunity to outgas." Jake had to put his two bits in. Besides, no one actually knew what awaited them on the inside of Belial. His guess was as good as anyone else's.

"I don't guess I had thought of it that way. I was thinking in terms of the meteorites that have been found on Earth. The complete absence of volatile materials could be artifacts of their size and their passage though the atmosphere. There could be considerable nitrogen inside this metal ball! The same sort of things found in the spectra of star-forming nebulae. There could be things like cyanide and petroleum inside there!"

"And this is good news?" Nina's English had improved to the point that she would occasionally contribute comments in the dominant language of the ship.

"Yes, Nina it is very good news. The presence of carbon and nitrogen in Belial would almost certainly make it possible to grow plants with the addition of sunlight. If we can grow plants, we can grow animals – like ourselves."

"So what else do we need to set up housekeeping inside Belial?" Madelyne was all about getting down to the basics, especially when it was about her or her children's health and comfort.

"There are three big things and one fairly small thing. First and largest is energy. We need to raise the temperature inside Belial to the point that water is a liquid and the liquefied gases inside are gases. If we are lucky, the resulting atmosphere will be a poisonous mix of water vapor, methane, and ammonia with trace amounts of oxygen, argon, helium, and carbon dioxide - if my assumptions are correct.

Second, we need to convert that inside to an environment conducive to our kind of life. I might be able to do this with some modifications to the nanomachines that make up the outside metal shell of our new home.

The third problem, as I see it, is to keep it that way. Without plants and animals the gases will have the tendency to revert to their former conditions.

The fairly small thing is to have access to the inside. This is complicated by the fact that eventually we will want to have commerce with our fellow humans. The only docking ring that we possess is firmly attached to the top of our ship. For obvious reasons, the only possible place for someone to dock with Belial, as we have remodeled it, is at the zero axis. The only obstacle there is the rotation, which can be easily matched. The problem is that the zero axis will be several kilometers above the inner surface. I personally am a little afraid of unenclosed heights. It doesn't seem too welcoming to open the inside door of an airlock to find a vertiginous drop of several miles with only the gentle curve of the inside of the sphere to break it up! It should be a relatively simple matter to reverse the airlock so that it points out, and some ships from Earth could dock. But how will we get down? I am leaving that for your consideration."

"What if you used some of the same type of programming that you a currently using for the lightsail to make a series of circular ledges on the inside of Belial, so that we have steps down to the bottom?" Bob leaped into the discussion with what appeared to be the obvious solution.

"That would probably work fine, but I perceive another problem that perhaps you have not considered. When we left Earth, we were not well liked. If you recall, the governments of Earth tried very hard to destroy us with nuclear weapons. No doubt, they watched our detonations and have surmised our plan. What makes you believe that they will recognize our claim to Belial? Remember, we are international terrorists." Katerina had her own opinions of human nature, having little to do with the milk of human kindness. There was a long silence on Red Level as the crew absorbed this bit of new intelligence.

"They will have the ability to reach us without any major technological advances. Probably, the rocket scientists on the bad guys' payroll will have analyzed our drive signature, if you will, and will have been able to reproduce everything we have done and be there when we arrive." Jack also had a dim view of the benevolence of the governments on Earth.

"We have the Dingus and it's dress. That would give anyone a bit of trouble, wouldn't it? Belial has already withstood the impact of nuclear weapons. Surely we can defend our new home with these assets." Madelyne had also been thinking of the people of Earth, and not necessarily about how grateful they would be for the job her family had done saving the planet.

"We will need to be able to aim it, and targets in space are small and distant. We will also need to be able to talk to them. We can't be assured of harmful intentions, and eventually we will want to have commerce with them." Jake had his own ideas about setting up initial relations with Earth.

"We have been in a communication blackout since this hole formed around us." Margaret was a little concerned about what was happening on her home planet.

"There is also the lightsail. It could focus a very hot sunbeam on something incoming. It just can't change its focus or direction very quickly. It is almost five hundred kilometers in diameter, even though most of it is only a few atoms thick. It can't be moved quickly, or it will break up. By the way, that is how I had intended to use that energy to heat up the inside of Belial as soon as the eye becomes transparent." This last pronouncement from Tom made every one stare. "Come on guys, it was the obvious solution!"

Everyone laughed and the mood lightened perceptibly. "Obvious now that you have pointed it out Tom. I guess that is one less thing to be concerned about, and we needed a bit of good news just now, Tom. Bravo!" Jake was a little relieved at this sudden addition to the asset side of their energy budget. He had had no idea where the hundreds of millions of kilowatts were going to come from.

"So what we really need is a structure here at the zero axis that will allow us to steer the Trigger so we can point its rear end at the bad guys that we all expect. It should have access to the inside of Belial and include a docking port so the good guys that we also expect can come for visits; and a communication array so we can not only hear what bad things the bad guys are saying about us but also to get our own message out. It should also have some radar arrays so we can point the Dingus accurately." Bob was sketching something on his PDA as he said this. When he had finished, he transmitted his crude design to everyone else's PDA.

There followed an interactive session as everyone proposed refinement and other changes to Bob's very basic design. What they came up with looked like a large wheel sticking out from the center of rotation of the much larger sphere. There was a slip joint, which connected Belial to a cylinder and another to connect the cylinder to the wheel. The wheel didn't rotate, and on it were mounted all manner of docking adapters. "Is there a way to keep the whole open wheel pressurized with this slip joint? We may have to settle for pressurized sections. I don't really see that as a big problem. We could have a bulkhead inside of this cylinder where it would have atmosphere. Of course the Trigger would remain pressurized." Tom started to work on a slip joint that could maintain a vacuum.

Jack wasn't too happy with the aiming arrangement for the Trigger. "What about a deal that looks like this?" He had revised the design so that there was a semi-articulated joint instead of the gooseneck. It would allow the Trigger to point its rear end everywhere except at the sphere itself.

"That looks good, Jack. It seems to fulfill all of our requirements and looks a bit safer than that gooseneck, which would have been more difficult to fabricate in any case." Jake could never get too far from how things would be engineered.

"So how do we do this? Its not like we have sheet metal growing on trees out here." Margaret was skeptical as usual.

"Actually, we do have sheet metal growing on trees - or the nearest nanotech equivalent. What we can do will not have those nice squared off edges and corners. It will look considerably more organic, and will consist of single crystals of the local alloy." Tom modified the design to what he could accomplish by programming his tiny machines. It looked like some sort of bizarre flower growing out from the sphere.

"How long will it take to do the programming, Tom?" Jack had grown somewhat accustomed to the miracles his sister's husband could perform with his tiny little machines.

"You know our motto: The difficult we can manage this afternoon. The impossible will take a couple of days! It will take some time to plan out the terraces on the inside, but I can make these structures part of those programs. I think that, at best, the terraces will be used for emergencies. It will take a couple or three weeks to actually grow them, as most of the mobile components are going to the lightsail right now."

"Well, as usual, no one has a clue as to the logistical realities of our survival. How am I supposed to move our farm through a vacuum? Tom you mentioned that maintaining this internal environment on the inside of Belial would depend on plants and animals. How am I supposed to get them in there? And given the incredible volume of atmosphere that these plants will need to maintain, how will we be able to plant enough? Where will the carbon dioxide come from with only eight animals to make it? I want you big brains to consider the biological realities of our situation." Madelyne had listened enough to the discussion to recognize that her family needed a little wake up call.

"The wonderful thing about living things is that they tend to reproduce themselves. The trick is to help them do this as rapidly as we can manage. My thought is that we leave the farm growing on the Trigger. The ship will always need to be a means of escape. Once we are located at the zero axis, we will need very little in escape velocity to return the Trigger to space. Using the Trigger for a weapon makes some sense if we have to do that, but it is designed as a ship of exploration. There isn't any place in the entire system that we cannot reach in a month or two. I want to do a bit more of that once things have settled down a bit here in our new home." Jake had gotten their attention. Most of them had gotten used to the idea that the Trigger was where she would always be. The idea that the freedom to travel was still theirs had an almost intoxicating effect on the crew.

"Fine, we can still travel. We still need a place to come home to. That is going to take years of work, and I expect a bit of assistance from my family."

"Don't worry, Mom. We don't have any plans to leave anytime soon. It's just nice to know that we have the option. I don't think that had occurred to anyone but Dad." Bob floated over to his Mother and put his arms around her and gave her a big sloppy kiss on the cheek. The rest of the crew giggled as she pushed him away and he bounced off the bulkhead.

Chapter Twenty-seven
The Great Eye Opens

    Weeks passed and gradually the world, as experienced by the crew of the Trigger, changed. The hole around them grew more and more shallow, and then they began to be extruded from the surface of Belial. The lightsail grew like some bizarre leaf from its surface. The extrusion grew like the base of a flowerpot until the trigger was fifty feet above the surface of the sphere. Then the extrusion changed into some rounded shape that was an approximation of a wheel, except with rounded edges and radiused corners. The Trigger remained attached to the surface by a few cables that extended through the flat aluminum disks mounted at the base of the three legs extending down from the three modified Space Shuttle External Tanks that were the Trigger.

    As soon as the ship had extended above the surface of Belial, its antennae were able to focus briefly on Earth. The rotation caused the dishes to be turned away from Earth and the signal was lost. After an hour or so of disjointed snatches of radio transmissions, Jake turned it off to save wear and tear on the motors and gears that kept the Earth in the focus of the dishes. The plan called for the wheel section to stop rotating when it and the articulated joint were finished growing out of the end of the cylinder that connected them to the surface of the sphere.

    A new docking adapter was fabricated using nanotech. It was physically identical to the other at the end of the Triangular Passageway but lacked all of the Earth-made one's more advanced features. After this was completed, it was a simple matter for Tom to program one to form at regular intervals around the wheel.

Jake, Tom, and Margaret worked in the tiny shop on the Trigger, putting some new receivers and transmitters together along with a simple radar array. At least they assembled the electronic parts, which they obtained from the spare parts that Jake had prudently kept aboard in the case of failure of the installed systems. The new dishes grew organically from the side of the wheel section directly underneath the base of the Trigger after Tom sprinkled some of his little machines there. The movable joints had to be fabricated from stores. The radio and radar dishes were then cut off and the moveable parts attached to them. They were then reattached and the little ten-inch telescope installed in a nearby section.

As a compromise to Madelyne and to solve some engineering problems, the cylinder had a smaller extension that extended all the way through the wheel and was the same diameter as the docking module. An additional airlock had been manufactured from a few spare parts and some sheet metal grown for this purpose from the inside of the wheel. The new airlock rotated with the sphere and cylinder, but on the inside of the wheel. An additional small airtight section had been constructed against the section of the wheel where the dishes grew. Another airlock had been constructed as an entry into this currently dark and airless space. When the tiny machines had finished their programmed extrusions, they pulled back from a circular area at the base of the sphere where it joined the cylinder and also at the juncture of the extended part of the cylinder. The wheel was then free to rotate or not rotate with the cylinder. It gradually slowed down over several days. The central aspect of the wheel lost its atmosphere and the section leading to the outside rim had its own airtight doors and airlocks. Now space in the wheel was illuminated and pressurized to allow the installation of the equipment manufactured to give Belial radio eyes and ears. After installation, the small section where the gear was installed was mostly evacuated with the systems powered down and a nitrogen atmosphere introduced into the space. The components were not designed to operate in a vacuum, but they should do well in an inert atmosphere. When these preparations were completed, the Trigger was cut loose from its cables and it was gradually rotated end for end and docked by hand to the rotating docking module. This was, of course, the scariest part of the entire evolution. Everyone was in spacesuits and the crew had literally pulled the Trigger into the docking with cables attached to the door of the docking module. The rotation was matched by tension on the cables. When the clamps snapped, the whoops of relief from Jack, Katerina, Bob, and Jake were audible through the walls of the ship, even in the vacuum.

The cylinder and its extension through the wheel was now capable of being pressurized. When everything was in place and all the pressures equalized, a person could float in shirtsleeves from the farm sections of the Trigger to the plate of metal that separated the cylinder from the inside of Belial. Tom's little machines had been working at all the speed they could manage in the lightless, cold interior to break down the cyanide and ammonia into nitrogen, carbon, and hydrogen. After a basic level of carbon dioxide had been produced, the carbon was sequestered in inert form. In the middle of the metal plate, Jake affixed a contact thermometer. In spite of the temperature of the metal surface being increased by sunlight hitting the surface, the temperature of the metal was very low. When the chamber was first pressurized, a thin coating of frost had formed quickly on this surface while all the water in the chamber had been sucked out of the air as it condensed on the cold metal.

Meanwhile, on the other side of Belial an area of metal had become thinner and thinner, and eventually a ten-kilometer circular area of the clearest quartz had been revealed. The Eye of Belial had opened. One side of the cable connecting the lightsail to Belial had flexed, and the eye had slowly rotated around to regard the sparkling glory of the five hundred kilometer lightsail. Coincidentally, with its full regard, the lightsail had pulled its outer edges in and the five hundred kilometer wide reflected beam of sunlight had contracted to a mere ten kilometers wide. Liquefied gases and solid water had used this energy input to change their states from liquids to gases and from solids to liquids. The hammerlock of eternal cold on the interior of Belial was broken. The frost on the metal plate dripped in a lazy circular fashion, and by the time it was about to reach the wall of the can, it evaporated. When the thermometer attached to the metal plate had read eighty-nine degrees for twelve hours, Tom and Margaret had drilled a hole in the plate and installed a valve. The atmosphere had tested out at seventy-six percent nitrogen, nineteen and a fraction percent oxygen, two percent carbon dioxide, and four percent argon and helium - with small traces of the other noble gases along with water vapor. It was pressurized at about eleven and a fraction pounds per square inch. The temperature had stuck at eighty-nine degrees for a total of fifteen hours. After that it had begun to rise again. It went up two degrees every two hours until it stuck again at the boiling point of water, from which it refused to budge. After the heat had been maintained for three days, Tom relaxed the flex in the cable holding the lightsail, and the great eye turned away from the dazzling five hundred kilometer mirror and cast its daze on the still dim and distant star that had provided its current heat. The cable that was gently tugging Belial away from its rendezvous with the sun gradually carried away the heat, radiating it away from the side away from the sun. When the course had changed to where Belial would be captured by the Earth/ Moon system, the lightsail had collapsed and begun to retract. The rotation rate gradually increased until the former asteroid spun on its axis every four and a half minutes. It also precessed on its axis so that the sun illuminated the Eye for twelve and a half hours and dark for twelve and a half hours. The temperature continued to drop until it hovered between seventy-five and eight-five degrees, depending on whether the Eye was facing the sun or not.

As several weeks of watching and waiting passed and the temperature dropped and stabilized, the crew set up another garden in the Can, as the big cylinder began to be called by the crew. It was, of course, much larger than the farms in the two tanks. Some plants were grown from cuttings and others from seed. All hands were involved in the plantings with Madelyne supervising and instructing. There were grasses and vines, shrubs and saplings, weeds and herbs. Some were allowed to go to seed, while others were cut and rooted. The farm in the Can was eventually many times the size of the farms in the cylinders. It was necessary to produce more carbon dioxide to keep them growing.

When the temperature inside Belial had stabilized, the valve through the metal plate was opened and the pressures on either side began to equalize. The valve was less than an inch across so that the reduction in the pressure in the Trigger and the Can took almost ten days to reach equilibrium, with the lower pressure inside Belial. This was part of Madelyne's plan to prevent any of the crew from developing the bends.

When all the pressures were equalized and the metal plate showed a temperature of seventy degrees, Tom sprayed some of the oil he had used to inform the nanomachines to move away from whatever he coated with the oil on the metal plate and it became thinner and thinner. Eventually, after several hours, it had developed a hole in its center that had widened gradually until it involved the entire end of the Can. Initially, there was a line waiting to look through the hole but it gradually enlarged, giving the entire crew a glimpse of the inside of Belial. Just inside the huge sphere was a wide ledge that extended almost fifty meters across. Almost three meters below the first ledge was another ledge that was about twenty feet wide. The next ledge was not as far beneath the second as the second was below the first. The differences were not apparent to the eye but required fairly careful measurement to be revealed. This process gradually reduced the width and height of the ledges until near the bottom they became wide shallow steps. The effect was much like being at the center of an old forty-five RPM phonograph recording with the groove being gradually elevated toward the outside edge of the record like a shallow bowl.

The ledge was revealed as a continuous spiral ramp extending from the zero axis all the way down to the base. "I decided that a series of steps would be a disservice to anyone who was disabled and had to get down. It also allowed me to think in terms of a tracked train to move cargo up and down the ramp. It does actually require quite a bit of time to get down that way, as it is well over a hundred miles going round and round and round." As Tom said this, the entire crew's heads had rolled on their shoulders as they tried to take in the expanse of the big panorama.

As the crew carefully floated on their tethers that Jake had insisted upon, all eyes gazed into the huge open space. The distant sun revealed itself gradually dipping toward the outside edge of the immense round window ten miles away. The wall of the Can had the slightest feeling of up and down. Things tended to settle to its surface. There were clouds that hid the lowest parts of the ramp in some directions. Only when a person looked in a given direction did it seem to be down. The rest of the time it would be sideways or up. Clouds also obscured parts of the distant landscape that extended all the way around the inside of the huge sphere. As the sunlight appeared to rotate along the inside, the surface was shown to be of varying heights with areas of hills and valleys. In the lowest areas, water sparkled in the long shaft of sunlight. There were lakes, rivers, and streams. Not counting the expanse of bare metal across the sphere bordering the eye and the area of the ramp at the near end, there were nearly two hundred and fifty square miles of land and water area. Not all of the clouds were fluffy accumulations of mist. Far away across the expanse of the sphere, about eight miles away, rain could be seen falling from a huge bank of clouds. The zero axis itself had very few clouds and these were not thick enough to obscure observation of the monstrous round window across the abyss. The clouds took on a tubular appearance across the axis of the sphere. The sun was a tiny brilliant spot that was almost too bright to look at. The rest of the eye was black space with stars wheeling in concentric circles like the sun. The sphere took almost five minutes to rotate all the way around. The light of the sun was hard and intense but diffuse like the light of a distant arc welder. There were several bright points of light on either side of the sun that they later found out were Mercury and Venus. The Earth did not come up while the Sun was in view.

The air was warm and moist with the sharp scent of ozone and iron, somewhat reminiscent of the way the industrial part of Birmingham, Alabama smells after a thunderstorm. There was a light breeze. As they watched, the distant sun sank below the rim, and the entire sphere was suddenly dark. The stars and inner planets still wheeled in the Eye of Belial ten miles away.

The celebration on Red Level continued all that night, or at least until everyone had trundled off to sleep. The younger generation had stayed up a few hours after their wiser elders had called it a day. Katerina sat Velcroed to Jack while Tom and Margaret shared a bench near the table. Bob floated near the center of the compartment. Most of the social life of the ship had migrated from Green Level, with its rotating view port, down to Red Level, where the rotation was just perceptible as a tendency of things to end up on the outside bulkhead. The crew had noted that alcohol no longer had any kick for them and, other than the occasional wine with dinner, had largely discontinued using it. Tea, on the other hand, had become very intense in its effect. Subtle flavors never noted before had risen into sharp perception. The crew itself looked different. There was no extra flesh on any of them. There was no wrinkled skin and nothing sagged. Even things, which had had pleasant sag on Earth, protruded proudly into whatever clothing covered them. The crew's hair had taken on a glossy appearance with sparkling highlights. It also tended to be longer. Unless intentionally confined, it floated in a nimbus-like arrangement around their faces. Every exposed body part showed well-defined muscle groups and clear skin. Sinuses were clear, unlike their previous experience with micro-gravity. It was a very different group than the one that had left the Earth six months before.

"I don't think I like the way the sun moves around. It does not actually hit all of the ground evenly. It will make the growth of plants too dependent on position in the sphere." It was not just the esthetics of the current arrangement that bothered Margaret; it was how it would impact the practical aspects of their new home.

" I don't like it either. I know the eye is very thick, but it cannot fully shield us from the effects of a solar flare." The outside of Belial was not protected by an intense electromagnetic field like the Trigger had had when it was underway.

"We have already thought of all that." Tom said over his bulb of tea. "The new radial mirrors are already growing from the metal around the outside of the Eye. The design includes a thick metal shield between the sun and us. The outside circular mirror reflects the sun onto an inside circular mirror that then reflects it in through the eye. A conical mirror here at this end of the zero axis will reflect it to all the areas on the inside that don't see it directly. It, unfortunately, will not look like a disk anymore, but rather a ring or band of very bright light around the rim of the eye and around the outside of the cone. The mirrors will not rotate with the sphere. The sphere will continue to precess such that the mirrors will not focus the sun all the time but only twelve and a half hours a day. Our day will be twenty-five hours instead of twenty-four and it will always be like spring. We should start seeing the beginnings of the new structures in the next few days." Tom looked like a cook that had just served a great meal and was now talking about the dessert.

"OK, Tom. It looks great, but have you given any thought to practical transport between the zero axis and the area at the bottom? The big ramp is fine if you just want to spend a week or two walking up or down a gentle hill. If we were down at the base and needed to get to the Trigger quickly, how would we do it?" Katerina finished her tea and crumpled the recyclable container, tossing it toward the trash storage area where it rebounded and hit Tom on the back of the head. Whether it was a complete accident was unclear. Katerina and the others laughed. After rubbing his head for a moment and acting as if it had been horribly painful, Tom joined in.

"I don't think I really thought about it that way. It is such a small place, I never really considered rapid transit."

"Granted that the maximum distance between any two points of the habitat is a paltry twenty-four miles, it seems a little bit of a stretch to get from here to there on foot, Tom." Jack had done a few simple calculations on his PDA.

"Hmm, I guess that is a pretty good point. I guess I thought of a brisk walk getting you just about anywhere in twenty or thirty minutes. It would take more than a day to walk around the inside of Belial! Although it is only about five miles as the crow flies down to the base of the ramp, that trip is largely vertical. I had thought some about that, which is why I made the ramp so gentle. I hadn't thought about it making the path so long." Tom rubbed the back of his head again.

"It would take long enough in an elevator!" Bob finished tuning his Balaika and started on a traditional Russian dance tune. He had had plenty of time to improve on his skills during the long journey.

"A single elevator would get you to one point on the inside surface of Belial which would be twenty four or so miles from the farthest point." Jack continued playing with his PDA.

"Six would get you within seven or eight miles of anywhere inside. You could do that much distance in thirty minutes or so on a bicycle." Margaret was idly doodling with a six-spoke arrangement with a central ring that held the conical mirror. She sent the crude picture to Tom's PDA.

"So now you are talking about six elevators to travel the five or so miles to the base. The sixty miles of cable wouldn't be such a big deal. Cable I can do without much problem. The problem is the big motors it would take to hoist those cars and cables five miles up and down."

"We have plenty of air pumps and can make more. What about making them pneumatic? We could use the air compressed under one of the elevators to do most of the work to hoist another. An air pump could give the extra boost needed to reach the top. It's not like a regular elevator with stops between the top and bottom."

"The force needed to compress the air would increase as the centrifugal force of our mass increases as we move farther from the zero axis. A minimal amount of additional energy input to the system would take care of friction and leakage from the fittings." Tom had his own PDA and was working a few numbers.

"So we can use pneumatic elevators. Big deal. I'm thinking we are going to need more transport than that." Jake made his way over to the food service area and helped himself to some tea.

"Did we wake you up, Dad?" Jack disengaged himself from Katerina and, after meeting her eye, headed over to the kitchen and got himself and Katerina more tea.

"No, I woke up a few minutes ago thinking about the same thing you guys are discussing. It's all very well to think about a healthy lifestyle and all that, but we are going to need some means of getting around quicker than we can walk or ride a bike." Jake and Jack made their way back over to the group. Jack handed Katerina her tea and reattached himself.

"If things go as we have planned, there will eventually be thousands of people living in Belial. So do we want to build a bunch of ugly roads over our beautiful parkland and have a lot of stinking cars driving over them? I think not. What we have to do before we ever stick a spade in the new ground is to plan on the things that people will need. It's not just transport. It's water, power, communications and waste disposal, to name a minimum set. Sure, there should be walking and hiking trails. We just need to plan for the ugly stuff so it isn't actually ugly!" Margaret looked at her husband as if she wondered exactly what he had been thinking.

"That is exactly the kind of thing that woke me up. What we need is a plan for the entire future development of Belial. It needs to be well-considered and flexible enough to allow expansion beyond our current guesses for how many people will want to come here." Jake attached himself near Bob who was listening to the conversation while he noodled on the balalaika.

"I don't like the idea of a bunch of big bulldozers pushing stuff around in there. I think we should take the lay of the land and plan communities. Much of the surface area is covered by water. We can rule out that land as we will want fish and crabs and such in the long run." Margaret actually got a little hungry thinking about a certain lobster soup she had had in a restaurant in New London, Connecticut.

"No doubt some of that water is salty if the primordial mix is anything like what we have seen before." Madelyne came down the siphon and fixed herself some tea. She joined her husband and her youngest son.

"If there is meeting, why was not included?" Nina came down the siphon and floated over to Katerina and Jack who made room for her at the table. Jack returned to the kitchen to get her some tea.

"We just started talking, Nina. We haven't decided anything. I think we are just now getting a handle on what problems need to be solved." Katerina smoothed Nina's hair, which looked slept on. After a stroke or two, it sprang out from her head like she had her hand on a static generator. Nina, like everyone else, looked as if she had had plastic surgery and a major workout program. She smiled at her granddaughter's ministrations and pinched her granddaughter's husband on the calf. At his shocked expression, she just acted innocent.

"Fine, you ancient Cossack, but if you pinch me again, I'll pinch you back!" Nina looked pleased at Jack's outburst and had a sip of her tea with a big grin on her now not so ancient face.

"If I designed a basic tube that carried power, water, sewage, and data, it wouldn't be too difficult to program the nanomachines to make it." Tom was doodling on his PDA.

"I don't like the idea of sewage being carried in the same tube as fresh water, even if the metal is essentially a single self-repairing crystal. Accidents happen." Madelyne looked sternly at her son-in-law.

"I guess we could make sewage a local concern and treat it like we did on the Trigger. Will we have plenty of power?" Margaret was looking at some photographs that she had taken with her PDA while inside Belial.

"Oh, we will have plenty of power. The outside of the sphere still turns sunlight into electricity. The question is what will we do with the dry powder that results from heating waste products up. On the Trigger, we use it to help plants grow. How will we move it around?" Tom looked up from his PDA and looked around the group.

"Tom, I know that you and Jake can figure out all the little details, so don't bother me with them. We still need to use the waste for fertilizer, but we won't have to spray it on the roots the way we do here on the Trigger." Madelyne had finished her tea and started up the siphon. "I don't know about the rest of you, but I intend to get a little nap before I return to my agricultural duties."

"Madelyne's right. We aren't going to get all the little details figured out right now. We have another four and a half years before we reach Earth. That is plenty of time to prepare both our friendly and hostile faces." Jake and Madelyne headed up the siphon to their quarters.

"It's not just the basics we ought to plan for but the deluxe stuff as well. We are going to live here for the foreseeable future. We should be as comfortable as we can manage. By the way, what did you intend us to build our houses of? I have noticed the weather isn't always perfect inside Belial. Of course, I think it is perfect that there is weather. I just don't want to have to camp out in it. What about hot and cold water, refrigerators, and stoves - or are we thinking about trying to import all that sort of thing? Personally, I would like an update on my computer." Tom stuck his hand over Margaret's mouth and stopped the next few things she was about to ask about.

"Ok, sweetie. I get it. I have got a little homework to do." Tom took Margaret's hand and led her up the siphon.

Chapter Twenty-eight
A Few Light Housekeeping Details

Weeks passed and there appeared a total of twelve spokes with six at either end of the sphere. There was a tube connecting them and pneumatic cars that traversed the ten miles between them.

Tubes worked their way through the dirt, which was quite sterile, unlike real soil. There was a network of tubes like the pneumatic transportation from pole to pole down the zero axis. They didn't exactly follow a straight grid but traversed the areas where the lakes were not found. They did dive beneath the small rivers and creeks that crisscrossed the cylindrical landscape. There were other tubes that carried power and cold and hot water. The hot water stayed hot and the cold water stayed cold because that wonderful insulator – hard vacuum, separated the tubes they traveled in. There was another set of tubes that carried sewage to a central collection area where it was treated with high heat, and the fine dust remaining was ultimately mixed with nutrients and used to irrigate through yet another set of tubes that snaked their way beneath Belial's soil. One day the sun seemed to disappear - to be replaced a few days later by a ring of bright light that made its way above the rim and then sank beneath it as the day waned. Here and there, on the higher areas of Belial's landscape, there sprouted strange growths that were the sealed connections to the systems that traversed the sphere's inner surface, so many meters beneath the rocks and soil exposed to light and air, where someday people would live.

Tom had seven people leaning over his shoulder telling him how to do it all. Mostly they all agreed on what needed to be done and exhibited varying levels of patience with his progress. The work of reproducing plants continued, as well as the continuing work on the communications and fire control center. Jack and Katerina took another long space walk to reattach the Dress to the dingus. An extension grew from the end of the Can where the Trigger was docked. It was articulated such that the Dingus could be pointed in most directions. Its shape was determined by the solutions produced by the fire control computer in the communications center. The wheel itself grew gradually out from the Can with symmetrical extensions away from the Can. One of these contained the communications and fire control gear. They grew and grew until they extended beyond the limb of the sphere that Belial had become, so that eventually communications were reestablished with Earth. This took some time, as the extensions needed to grow over five miles. The spindly extensions were stabilized by the ring, which joined them near the ends. Another ring joined the first about two and a half miles from the Can. Elevator cars joined these external rings through the extensions from this central hub. All of these external structures gradually grew in size over the coming months along with the Can. All of the tubes and rings grew to be at least a hundred feet in diameter.

The day finally came when it was time to test the elevators and make a trip down to the inner surface of Belial. The view had gradually been occluded by the transport and the huge mirror that grew from the tube down the zero axis. Instead of a vertiginous drop at the edge of the platform extending from the Can, there was a huge cylindrical chamber with an exit to the ramp on one side. On the wall were seven hatches. On the wall just opposite the entrance from the Can was the hatch that gave entrance to the axial pneumatic. Arranged around the cylindrical wall were the hatches for the six elevators in the spokes. There were actually two hatches, as each elevator was paired. One was up when the other was down. The spokes were not vertical, but rather followed the curve of the sphere. There had been several arguments about this. One group had insisted that it wasn't safe to allow an elevator to travel a curved route. The other side of this debate had argued that the curve was so gentle that accommodation could be made to maintain the wide-open feel of the huge space. The nice view party won out. The spokes hugged the curve of the sphere. - It was a very gentle curve after all. Only a few hundred feet over a bit over four and a half miles isn't so extreme. It also gave structural support to the spokes as they were attached to the ramp. Even though they were twenty feet wide and got slightly larger at the bottom, in the immense space inside of Belial they looked very spindly.

All of the recent improvements had been accomplished by the magic of Tom's programming of the tiny machines that were still active in every way. The spokes had grown like exotic beanstalks from the bottom of the ramp until they met a ring, which had grown out from the top shelf of the ramp. Initially there was a cable, which had expanded until it was over forty-five feet wide. The other tubes had grown in a similar manner gradually over the space of weeks.

Of course, none of the intrepid travelers had actually been down to the inner surface of Belial. Up until the last few days it wouldn't have been a practical trip with hundreds of miles of ramp to traverse. The elevators that had been created were some of Tom's most creative programming. The most difficult had been the autonomous manufacture of airtight hatches. Once he got one right, the others were not a problem. The crew had tested the machinery exhaustively. They had loaded the cars with more weight than they would ever be carrying, and the elevators had worked flawlessly. The first trip down was not a pleasure trip by any stretch. Madelyne had a program for greening up the inside of Belial that required the efforts of all, willing or not. Consequently, the first ride down would be burdened by many of the seedlings and saplings that had been sprouted since the opening of Belial. The entire crew had been crowded inside a car with plants and tools and instruments. The trip down had taken about ten minutes. It was the longest elevator ride that anyone had ever taken. At the top, they had been mostly weightless; and at the bottom, they had weighed as much as they had on Earth. Add to this that no one had had more than a sixth of their weight in well over a year and a half, and being wedged into a small elevator car with hundreds of delicate plants, and the same discomfort that accompanies an elevator ride back on Earth; and it both was, and was not, the journey of discovery they had all hoped it would be.

When they stepped carefully onto the inside surface of Belial, it was definitely worth the trip. The vista was much like the view from the zero axis except that the maximum distance to the other side of the sphere had been doubled. It was very nearly ten miles over to the opposite side of the sphere. The crew found themselves at the top of a gradually sloping hill. There was another hill that was as tall as the slope they were on a few hundred meters away. They knew from the view at the top that the largest lake was on the other side of this largest hill near the end of the sphere. The landscape curved up in two directions and down and then up in the other. The soil itself was gritty and coarse with occasional glints of crystal flecks. The land rose and fell in hills and valleys with creeks and streams in the lowest places. In the lowest places of all were lakes. Some were more than a mile across and hundreds of feet deep. Tom had programmed some tropisms that educated the tubes as to where they were supposed to grow. They couldn't get too near water or be visible in valleys. The transport tubes could theoretically transport people from any part of the sphere to the Can in less than fifteen minutes. There were occasional hummocks where the transport tubes could be accessed. There was not a spot of green to be seen in any direction. There were reds and browns and blacks. There were whites and tans and silvers. There was not a speck of green.

The crew stood unsteadily in a little group with the open hatch to the elevator to their backs. It wasn't certain who had first placed his foot on the soil of Belial, as they had more or less fallen out of the open hatch in a clump. There were plants and shovels and hands, and these soon combined to change the colors of Belial. The sunring was just rising over the rim, and the conical mirror above cast the radiance down on the soon dirty hands and sweaty brows. There was a breeze that did little to cool them. As they walked down hill they got heavier. At the bottom of the hill they weighed about seven percent more than they would have on Earth. There was a strange feeling of being pulled to one side when they walked downhill. They soon realized that it was in the opposite direction of the rotation of Belial and was so slight that they soon ignored it on the many trips up and down the hill that Madelyne insisted upon.

"We can't put all our hard work right here at the base of this one spoke! Look at each spot carefully to decide if it is the perfect spot and has plenty of room to grow. It will likely be the only plant in that area for some time. I have chosen only species that are pollinated by bees. I have brought a few hundred thousand frozen bee eggs along with some very carefully selected queen eggs. I have enough for about six hives. It will take years before some of these plants reproduce themselves. Give them the best chance that they can have." Madelyne had demonstrated by choosing a tiny hillock for one of the oak saplings.

They ended up making three more trips up and down the spokes before the troops rebelled. They had chosen a different spoke each time, and the view had differed as much as it could, given the basic parameters. Lakes were closer on the second. A big lake nearer to the last and the first had the shortest view.

"Will it always be this hot?" Jack had not stopped sweating since he arrived at the bottom of the first spoke.

"No, Jack. It will gradually cool over the next few months until it drops to around sixty-five degrees at night and rises to nearly eighty during the day." Tom had spent many hours with Jake and Madelyne before working out the parameters of the habitat that would accommodate all the plants and yet be comfortable for the people.

"Will that change when people start industrial stuff inside here?" Bob was also hot from the day's labors.

"I did not think that there would be any big industries here in Belial. I was working under the assumption that all the major industries would be carried on outside in the wheel or elsewhere. It just seemed so much more practical. I had guessed that there might be cottage industries and crafts but no big factories." Tom looked at Bob quizzically.

"I wasn't thinking of big factories either. With proper training, there is no industrial process that can not be done safer, cleaner and more efficiently out in the bright sunshine of the big empty." Jake had had enough of the smell of a paper mill in the distance.

"But what will we use to build our houses? I don't know how the rest of you feel but, although I am very fond of all of you, I am tired of all of you knowing when I flush a commode." Madelyne had her own set of priorities besides the care and feeding of the plants and animals soon to inhabit Belial.

"Well eventually, we will use a lot of the same materials that we were accustomed to using on Earth. Wood, brick, plastic, and tile, along with stone and glass, will someday be available. Meanwhile, Margaret and I have done a lot of talking about this very issue. We want our new homes to be as homelike as possible; at the same time we don't have any access to the materials that will be available to later inhabitants. In addition to this, we do not exactly want to blend in with the people that come later to take advantage of our hard work and risk, so we determined to build the first buildings and fixtures out of this." At this point Tom removed a small piece of material about the size of a deck of cards from his jumpsuit pocket and handed it to Madelyne.

Madelyne turned it over and over in her hands without immediate comment. It was about the same weight as a piece of pinewood the same size. It was metallic and was very smooth to the touch. Unlike metal however, it warmed to the touch and seemed somewhat soft like wood would feel. It was multicolored with lines and whorls of copper, gold, silver and black. It looked like the wood from a metal tree. "What the hell is it Tom?"

"Mokume-Gane with a few modern touches." Tom said with a proprietary smile.

"OK, smart guy. Try again. What is Mokume-Gane?" Madelyne was not amused. Medical doctors were supposed to know everything, and this was not something that she had ever heard of - a violation of the rules if she had ever seen one.

"Mokume-Gane is a Japanese term for wood-grained metal. Denbei Shoami who lived in seventeenth century Japan invented it. He used gold, silver, copper, and other metals to simulate organic surfaces. It was used for jewelry and other high value constructions. He was a superb sword smith and this invention was just one aspect of his work, which he invented to be used as a Kizuka, or hilt, and a Tsuba, or guard, of a sword. He undoubtedly came up with this because of its strength compared with the brass or bronze tsubas made by others during the same era. The feudal lord, Satake of the Akita area near Kyoto where he worked, was so impressed that he gave Denbei the name of Shoami, which originated from the Shaoma School, which began in Kyoto in the fifteenth century. Denbei used plates of nonferrous metal, which he laminated together without solder. I have modified his design by assembling this material atom by atom in a cloud-like pattern and making foam of it. The empty space is vacuum. It is a good insulator and it is light as wood, even though it is constructed of heavy metals." Tom had taken the piece of material from Madelyne and was flipping it around in the air while he talked.

"Exactly which heavy metals was this Mokume-Gane made from?" Madelyne snatched the piece back from Tom. She had visions of her grandchildren being idiots from lead poisoning.

"The primary ingredients of this particular piece are gold, copper, silver, platinum and tantalum. I have other examples, which don't have the nice grained appearance that this one does. I was primarily interested in the appearance, but other properties were important as well. I wanted something that would not corrode under normal terrestrial conditions and that had good insulating properties. I really wanted it to be very showy though - and this polishes up nicely." Tom was very pleased at how his work had turned out.

"So we are going to build houses out of this stuff? How will we cut it, shape it, and nail it together? Are we going to have Mokume-Gane plaster and Mokume-Gane two by fours?" Madelyne didn't like surprises, especially when it involved something in which her son-in-law had to educate her.

"Oh, no. I haven't thought of old fashioned construction techniques as something that we will have time for. When we have bricks and stone and glass and wood, it will probably take on its own mystique, like homemade furniture. Everything about this mission has had a sense of urgency that required me to think in terms of the most rapid and most efficient methods I could manage. After an airtight door, a casement window was still a challenge." Tom had bent down and picked up one of the larger clear crystals that glittered occasionally in the dirt of Belial. It was about the size of his thumb. He brushed it off and handed it to Margaret. It glittered and sparkled in the light from the sunring."I am going to make the windows out of this."

"So what do you mean efficient methods? Are you going to dictate how we are going to build our homes as well as what they are made of? I, for one, would like a little input into what my new home looks like. – Thank you very much!" Madelyne was not easily appeased when it came to matters in which she considered men to have, at most, a peripheral role. She was distracted by the glints of light from the shiny, clear crystal in her daughter's hands.

"I took the liberty of reproducing as near as possible the design of your house on Earth. I had Jake draw out the basic plan a few weeks ago. I also consulted with Margaret, and we decided on a floor plan similar to yours, but also taking into consideration the house that I grew up in. In case the rest of you were wondering why I was asking you about your favorite houses over the last few weeks, now you know. I have five houses planned, and other than the fact that the edges will be rounded and they will be of one-piece construction, the houses will be as much like your dream house as I could manage. I also put them just a hundred feet or so from one another because even though I don't really want to hear someone else's toilet flush, I have gotten accustomed to having you guys nearby. They should be ready in a few weeks."

"So where are these houses that you keep talking about? I really want to see my house on the steep old hill. Are they being constructed by elves in the night?" Madelyne was on a tear.

"Now Madelyne, you know that this entire magnificent habitat was constructed from a raw asteroid by billions of microscopic machines tiny bit by bit. Is it so incredible that Tom could program his little machines to make something as simple as a modified box with plumbing? I don't think that you are being the least bit fair." Jake would put up with a great deal before getting involved.

"All right. I admit that I was going on a rampage. It's just that once I get on a roll it is difficult for me to stop. And Jake, I would appreciate it if you wouldn't let me drone on for so long. But really, Tom where are our new homes? As tired as I am, it would give me a great deal of pleasure to see where we are going to live." Madeline was scanning the curved horizon.

"Actually, they are just over that big hill across from the first spoke that we went down. We could take a tube ride and be there in about fifteen minutes. We have yet to test that system." Tom was now itching to show off his handiwork.

"I sure want to see my new house! I have never had my own house before. Now I have got someone to share it with!" Jack was thinking about the incredible house he had described to Tom. He and Katerina had spent most of an hour three weeks ago trying to one up one another in the same house. If Tom had gotten it anything close to what they had described, it would be a cross between Mad Ludwig's Castle and Biltmore House on about a one-tenth scale.

"Let's go! I want to ride the tube too!" Bob had described a simple five-room bungalow.

"OK, I think the nearest tube socket is just over here." Tom led the way around a small hillock and opened the airtight door that came into view. Inside was a car with six rows of seats. About four people could sit on each seat. There was a diagram on the forward bulkhead, which represented all of the tube sockets in the entire sphere. A pressure sensitive button represented each socket. Tom reached out and pressed one at the base of the spoke one third of the way around the sphere from where they were, which was represented by a light under the button. When everyone was seated, Jack dogged the door behind them, as he was closest, and the car began to accelerate. As the car was going in the same direction as the sphere was rotating, the weight of the passengers decreased. The ride lasted almost twelve minutes, and the car slowed to a stop beside an airtight door exactly like the one that Jack had closed behind them. He turned and opened this door, and they all climbed out of the car.

There, across the space of a football field, were the five homes that Tom had promised. They were as different as houses can be, although they were all constructed of the same materials. The house at the top of the hill was immediately apparent to everyone but Katerina and Nina - the house that belonged to Jake and Madelyne. It was mostly underground. There were, of course, no trees as there had been on Earth. The driveway was also absent. The house next door was like a Victorian house with turrets and dormers. It stood three stories tall, and its many windows sparkled in the late afternoon light. The house nearest them was a very modern design that was mostly windows and patios with multiple wings of several rooms. The walls gleamed and shone with an almost iridescent luster. All the houses appeared to have been made of gold and silver with black and copper veining. None had doors opening into the inside. The crew of the Trigger openly gaped at the incredibly opulent houses.

"Well, I see one little misstatement in your description, Tom. Although I must say that I am very impressed on the whole." Madelyne was grinning and pleased with herself to have found an inaccuracy. "You seem to have used plenty of glass in the construction."

"Oh no, Madelyne, I didn't misspeak. It will take some time to set up production of plate glass like we are all used to. Because I already had a program for it, and we were making the houses out of silver and gold, it just seemed natural to make the windows out of diamond."

The silence was deafening.

Chapter Twenty-nine
News From The Old Country

When the communications gear cleared the limb of Belial, the crew of Trigger began to get entertainment and data feeds from Earth. In the year and a half since their departure, the face of their home planet had changed as much as they themselves had.

The nuclear missile exploding in the skies above the Eastern hemisphere and the rolling blackouts caused by the electromagnetic pulse from the fusion drive of the Trigger had been used by the politicians in power at that time to institute a number of "improvements" in the United Nations. First, it was no longer a voluntary organization. Membership was mandatory for all nations. The General Assembly had been abolished in all but fact by the growing power of the Security Council and the inability of the larger group to arrive at a consensus on any real issue.

With the passage of the Sovereignty Act, the absolute authority of individual national governments had disappeared overnight. The Security Council had modified its voting rules to give greater voting power to those who contributed the most money and troops to the operation of the United Nations. The formula was complicated by the ownership of nuclear weapons, which automatically gave the individual nation's opinions greater weight. The most important factor was the contribution of troops to the many enforcement actions that the United Nations had undertaken.

The major powers on the Security Council were: The People's Republic of China, The United States of America, United Central Europe, United Western Europe, The South American Confederacy, The Greater African Union, and the

United Islamic Emirates. The obvious consolidations had taken place in the first few weeks after the Trigger had made its escape. The bloodshed had been horrific in the newly consolidated areas. Some cities had been destroyed by nuclear weapons. London and Paris had been the first to go boom. Riyadh and New Delhi quickly followed them. An Islamic revolution, which had been in its beginning stages when the Trigger had left Earth Orbit, had been completed with the reincorporation of India and Pakistan under a fundamentalist Islamic theocracy. The United Islamic Emirates included the Middle East, India, Central Asia, and Northern Africa, as well as Turkey and the Baltics. Ethnic cleansing continued North, South, East, and West. At least two billion people had died.

The survivors had been more interested in security than in the maintenance of their traditional separations and rivalries. One thing united the people of Earth. A propaganda program, begun in the first hours of the blastoffs from Texas and Baikonur, had blackened the reputations of all eight of the crew of the Trigger. Even Nina was portrayed as a savage revolutionary and former prostitute. Stories about Katerina and Jack were used to frighten small children. The excesses of Bonnie and Clyde were as nothing to their evil exploits, which included murder for entertainment. Margaret and Tom were rumored to have used stolen babies for their inhuman experiments with forbidden nanotech. Jake and Madelyne were shown to be evil profiteering capitalists who got their huge fortune from the misery of others and secret weapons laboratories. Bob was just their evil stooge. The stated purpose of the Security Council was the expeditious capture of all eight. The Chairman of the Security Council had been elected after a speech in which he promised to bring these evildoers to justice. He also promised to insure domestic stability and get the new world economy working again. As a former President of the United States, he had given many of these speeches and was aware of the need for salesmanship in government.

As everyone had expected, part of the problem had been the collapse of the world economy. All of their terrestrial investments were now worthless. They had a big laugh about that, along with the incredible personae that the propaganda apparatus had given them all.

There remained an immense amount of work to make their new homes habitable. Instead of making Tom responsible for all of the detailed programming, they spent the next few months learning how to use the incredible power of the tiny machines and the nearly unlimited materials available to produce anything that was necessary for their health and comfort. Along with the skull sweat needed to master the complicated technology, there was the nearly constant manual labor of planting trees and shrubs and grasses and vines over the hundreds of square miles of their new home. They worked with their hands during the day and with their minds and imaginations in the evenings. The easiest way to learn how to make something with nanotech was to actually do it. Tom assigned them simple projects like tables and chairs, and ultimately they pursued their own needs with his occasional advice and counsel.

Madelyne was one of the hardest tasked, as she demanded the ability to treat any injury or illness. Jake entertained himself with large works of industry mostly outside the habitat. He set up manufacturing facilities mostly in the wheel, which became the aft docking ring. Jack and Katerina, having learned a valuable lesson in how they were portrayed in the stories from home, prepared to defend Belial and its inhabitants from their cousins on Earth. They quickly decided to rely completely on defensive weaponry. This was largely on the advice of Bob, who was working out the methods of commercial intercourse with Earth. He and Jake began to work out the specialized products and services that the Belianese (As they all began to consider themselves) could supply to the ever hungry and increasingly ignorant Earth.

Margaret returned to her first love and began to explore the cosmos in earnest, having modified the outer surface of Belial into a single, huge, sensor array that just incidentally supplied all of the habitat's electrical power from the incident radiation. She designed programs that modified this constantly rotating data into something that the human mind could fathom and the human eye, observe. Jack and Katerina stole some of her work to better observe the space around Belial for hostile activity.

Nina amused herself with the design and manufacture of home furnishings. They ranged from the merely practical, like commodes and sinks, to tableware and decorative fixtures. It was an aspect of her talent and personality that had slept for the seventy-two or so years of her life and blossomed like the art of Grandma Moses. The other members of the crew, after a few attempts and subsequent recycling, turned their homes over to her artistic and practical touch. Her palate extended itself from the Mokum (as everyone called Mokume-Gane) to soft items that included fabrics in every color and texture - all constructed from metal and carbon composites. They all found themselves with soft beds and new clothing. Tom found his brain expanding just trying to answer her more and more complicated questions.

They now subsisted entirely from the fruits of the garden on Trigger and the occasional this or that from the interior of Belial. The sounds of Belial now included the buzz of bees and the hiss of the pneumatic cars as they carried plants and the workers to plant them. Gradually the distant vistas of Belial contained a hint of green. Their homes now echoed with the sounds of laughter and speech. Primarily the crew spent their evenings at Jake and Madelyne's, as this home was one of the largest and the one at which they were most comfortable. Nina had lavished most of her attentions on this residence, and the results were evidenced in a décor that seemed to echo the grandeur of the Czars balanced with the modernity of the twenty-first century. There were Mokum chairs and a Mokum table. The kitchen was similarly equipped, although stainless steel was given a central role. There was a tapestry that depicted the first views of Belial through the view port on Green Level from a day that seemed so long ago. There was primarily gold Mokum silverware on coal black placemats and platinum plates with diamond crystal ware. There was a viewscreen that occupied an entire wall that showed the Earth/Moon system, as it would currently look through a decent-sized telescope. Their arrival was still some years away and yet the central topic of conversation.

"I trust our militarily-minded mavens have made adequate provision for our continued health and safety." Jake had taken over as chairman of these little informal meetings as he frequently did when it was in his house. The table could comfortably seat twelve and fourteen in a pinch and so was very comfortable for the eight of them present.

"I think anyone who attacks us here will have some very awkward surprises should they initiate violence. I believe that we can feel very secure." Jack chose to speak because Katerina, who ate much more slowly than he, had a mouthful of food.

"And should our defenders have an unforeseen incident, will our medical facilities be up to the task?" Jake pointed looked at Madelyne who was mesmerized by the scene on the viewscreen.

"My new infirmary can handle anything from a severe chest wound to a bad burn as well as I could have on Earth – probably better. I just hope that it will not be necessary. It seems like we have made so many significant accomplishments in the last two and a half years to have to be concerned about strangers trying to hurt us." Madelyne never took her eyes from the viewscreen.

"What about our orbit, Margaret? Are we still on course? I haven't heard you say anything about it in weeks, and frankly, I think we all need to be reassured." Jake didn't look particularly uneasy.

"Daddy, we are right on, and if we were off a few fractions of an arc second, we would still be captured by the Earth/Moon System. As I currently see it, we will miss the Earth by a comfortable thousand kilometers. It should provide quite a show, without being any sort of danger to the Earth or us. I am learning some interesting things about Dark Energy that may drastically alter how we look at energy in the relatively near future. - But you didn't ask me about that, did you?" Margaret went back to some largely untranslatable figures on her PDA.

"You only need to look around you to see what Tom and Nina have been up to. It is so far removed from the simple life that we had for so long. It makes those days in flight on the Trigger seem like ancient history. I miss having a bit of meat from time to time, as I expect that we all do - except Margaret. Bob and I believe that we can cheaply sell electricity to Earth as well as advanced materials. We have programs in place that could have the first unit in production within and hour and a half of getting the order - and the security deposit, of course." With this last part, they were all looking at Bob, who was suddenly looking uncomfortable.

"Dad, I know that you think that all of our business can be conducted from here. I want to bring it to everyone's attention that I do not think that that will work. Businessmen want to look into the eyes of their trade partners and get a feeling for how the other really thinks about the value of the products or services discussed. That is how long term business relationships are created." Bob, unlike the others, had dressed up for this meeting and was attired like a modern prince of industry. It was an accurate description.

"Perhaps someday the meetings can take place here?" Jake was nothing if not fiercely adherent to his own position.

"Of course they can, Dad. But probably not really here, but rather in the luxury hotel that I have been discussing with Tom and Nina. The point is that they need to feel that we do not have an unfair advantage. It is clear to everyone that we will have an advantage, but it doesn't have to be seen as unfair." Bob had spent some time thinking about how business could ultimately be conducted on the other side of the sphere, overlooking that enormous lake that sparkled like a diamond in the ringlight. The presence of all that open water and the airy vista, in what was ostensibly a space habitat owned by a single family, was an unspoken something that he wanted to bring to the table whenever a big deal was discussed.

"The only problem, as I see it, is that any member of this family would be shot on sight and a trial held posthumously." Jake felt that he had made his point.

"Granted. That is why I wanted to discuss a propaganda program of our own. I have been working on it in my spare time. - And first, let me say thank you to everyone here who has assisted me with this, and you know who you are." Bob tapped a few commands into his PDA and the scene on the viewscreen changed. It started with the astronomy program that had demonstrated to the, then smaller, family that something must be done to avert disaster, along with a voiceover by Bob telling the story from the perspective of one who had been there. It continued with video clips of the nearly frozen Jack being pulled from the water tank by Katerina. An audio record of the fierce missile barrage with the quiet conversations down in Red Level and the frenzied activities caused by the nuclear blast. There was footage from the rear camera as they landed on Belial. There was footage of the bizarre landscape as the cables proliferated and a discussion of how the nuclear weapons had all been used. There was footage of the rescue of Katerina as she returned from the wrecked Soyuz and her revival from the brink of death, having saved Earth from a collision with an asteroid. Then the footage took an unexpected turn, and the viewer who had been informed about how these eight heroes had saved the world, now were shown the wonders and delights of Belial as if it were Disneyworld. The voiceover took on the tone of a sales pitch that seemed to imply the safety, comfort, and unlimited opportunity that awaited the lucky and gifted few that were intrepid enough to risk the rigors of primitive spaceflight. Then there was a short segment of film lifted from the TV feed of the takeoff of the Trigger from Texas. There followed exact information of where and when Belial would appear in the night skies of Earth, along with a diagram of its nearest approach and its future orbit in the Earth/Moon system. The entire presentation took only four minutes and thirty-three seconds to run. After it ran, there was a short period of silence. Bob anxiously waited for his family's opinion of his work, as none but he had seen it.

"Show it again!" Erupted from everywhere in English and bad English. Bob triggered a replay.

This time there was a longer period of silence as the crew considered the piece critically - the first showing having caught everyone off guard.

"What about the nuclear weapon that we still have?" Katerina hadn't missed the obvious misstatement.

"I figure that we won't be the only nation in the system that has that dirty little secret. The authorities in Kazakhstan will certainly know if any survived. I do not know if getting rid of the wretched thing at this point, when things are so uncertain, makes much sense. I'll leave that for the crew to decide. Do I need to correct the presentation to indicate that we have one left?" Bob looked around the room.

"It is certainly a misrepresentation. However, I am inclined to let it stand. Certainly the few persons who could say with any certainty that this presentation is not completely accurate have already spent hours on the media talking about how evil we all are. It is something we can correct later if need be. Katerina sat down knowing that the rest of the crew would agree with her and let it stand. She was uneasy about her old nemesis, Major Kostolinkavitch. If there were any snake in Almaty that had survived the battles and purges, he would be a likely candidate.

"OK, how long would it take to manufacture a replacement for Soyuz? That is really the simplest solution. Given our current skills, I can't see that as a big problem." Jake was thinking of the quickest route to solve the problem as he saw it.

"Oh, I don't guess that manufacture would take so long, but the programming would be a prolonged nightmare. The Soyuz was a rather complicated system." Tom was already doodling on his PDA.

"I'd like to propose that we put Trigger back into its original configuration, just in case we need to send someone to Earth for some as yet undefined purpose. All in favor?" Jake counted all eight hands and then said, "Motion carries. I am in favor of Bob's presentation being beamed to Earth in as many languages as we can manage. Any comments?"

"How often can we show it?" Madelyne always liked to have the last word.

Chapter Thirty
Heavy Weather

The plan to reproduce the Soyuz had hit a snag. This was because of Tom's tendency to try to improve anything he was involved in. The original Soyuz would sit three. Tom's reasoning was that since there were eight of the crew, the escape craft, or reconnaissance vessel, should at least comfortably seat all of them.

He also pointed out that they had needed to modify the Soyuz several times in order to allow it to carry out the missions they had required of it. The resulting craft was therefore several times larger, and frankly, Tom was having trouble reproducing the computer systems.

"Tom, I wonder if you have actually considered all of your options." Jake was learning to work with Tom whenever he attempted a new design. There was a definite increase in how well the project went, as they could both learn from each other.

"What do you mean, all my options?" Sometimes a different point of view was really helpful.

"What I want you to think about is what a computer actually is. Isn't is essentially an adding machine with the ability to store and access information stored in mathematical form?" Jake looked keenly at his son-in-law.

"Sure, Jake. The problem I am having involves reproducing all the tiny parts and control systems for the integrated circuits that computers use."

"That's what I mean by considering all of your options. What do your tiny nanomachines and computers have in common?"

"Well, they use iterative processing. You know, they do things a single step at a time."

"And what does this suggest to you?"

"Are you saying that I can make a computer out of my nanomachines?"

"I am doing more than that. I am suggesting that they already are. All you have to do is craft an interface and some software. Your nanomachines will have almost all the speed, and much greater capacity, than any computer of the same size currently has."

"I see what you mean now. The problem of writing the programming isn't trivial either, but perhaps I could design a translator program that would convert my existing programs to run on the new machine." He didn't notice when Jake quietly left the room.

The planting efforts had really begun to show. The grasses and creepers were of course covering larger areas than the trees and shrubs, but with the bee's assistance and the subtropical conditions, the inside surface of Belial was rapidly changing. The seedlings planted when the crew had arrived were turning into saplings, and the absence of pests and other competitors was accelerating their growth.

A week or so after Jake and Tom's conversation, the crew noticed that their PDAs stopped working for an hour or so, and when they came back on line, they were much faster. Tom had been holed up in his and Margaret's house for the last few days, and Jake had let everyone know what he was working on, so it was not a huge surprise. But when Tom showed up a few hours later with new PDAs for everyone, they were indeed surprised. The new PDAs were tiny. They came with tiny contact lenses, which once placed in the eye, disappeared. The graphic user interface was in stereo and was largely controlled by eye movement. The new displays could show any datum that Belial could generate - and that was a wide variety. Jack and Katerina were amazed at how much information and control was at their fingertips, or rather, subject to their viewpoint. Only a few commands required them to actually touch their PDAs, which were the same size as thin watches. Elegantly crafted of gold, platinum, and diamonds, they more resembled jewelry than critical control systems.

"Tom, these new systems are beautiful! Not only better than the old ones, but fun to look at! Are we still connected to the systems on the Trigger?" Madelyne was reviewing her visual display as she spoke and seemed distracted.

"The computer on Trigger is still there, but it isn't connected to anything anymore. When I get around to it, I will recycle it. When the new docking adapter was growing on the end of the triangular passageway, I took the opportunity to allow the skin of the ship to be coated with a new layer of nanomachines. They knitted a new and stronger layer of metal alloy on the inside surface that, of course, you wouldn't notice unless you really looked for it. It added a much greater structural integrity and, because of the larger surface area, more capacity. Therefore, it's a much more powerful computer than we had when we took off from Texas. Additionally, the new computer has a flexible architecture that allows it to adapt to the data flow. Our old 256 wide bit depth was inadequate to address the increased capacity that our new machines have. Our new displays have the capacity to show a forty-two-bit color image in stereo in real time. Let me show you something." Tom made a gesture with his hands in front of his eyes and everyone was treated to a stereo view of the space outside of Belial. They could look in any direction and the data was continuous in any direction they chose to look. If they looked at anything for more than the interval of time in which the eyes blink, the image was magnified.

"But that isn't even the best part. Look at this. "Tom made another gesture in front of his eyes and they were all looking at themselves. They could even look at the back of their heads.

"Are there any limitations on where we can look with this new system, Tom?" Margaret's tone was sweet.

"No dear, we can address any area within or outside the ship or habitat at virtually any magnification to the limits of the display."

"Well, Thomas Edison White, the first thing you are going to do after you temporarily disable this aspect of the system is to design a privacy mode so that we can have a bath or use the toilet without the rest of us being able to take a look at us to see what we are up to. I might point out that some of the people in our family might want some of their other activities unobserved! We lost entirely too much privacy during our months on the Trigger to give up any now!" Margaret's tone had chilled considerably. Katerina and Madelyne gave quick nods of complete assent.

Tom colored up to his hairline and down to his coverall. "Sweetie, I didn't even think of that!"

"That's what it is with you men. You never think about the obvious things!" Margaret, Madelyne, Katerina, and Nina strolled away from the male members of the crew and entered a pneumatic car and whooshed away.

Tom, Jake, Jack, and Bob just looked at one another, and Tom started working on his new assignment. Inside the pneumatic car, the scene was entirely different. "Did you see the look on Jack's face?" Katerina couldn't control her laughing.

"I couldn't take my eyes off of Tom! He was so cute!" Margaret had laughing tears in her eyes. Madelyne hadn't stopped laughing long enough to speak.

The fix that Margaret had requested took only a little over an hour for Tom to implement. It ended up much like a telephone system where the members of the crew were concerned. The new PDAs contained microphones and locators so all a crew member had to do when called vocally was to say, "Yes, receive" and the person calling would have a stereo view of that person - and the person calling would be displayed to them. A simple "yes" would be audio only.

They all laughed about it that evening over dinner at Jake and Madelyne's house after ringset. "I had no idea that my sweet little daughter's mind was so darkly twisted." Jake had enjoyed seeing his sons and son-in-law uncomfortable over something so correctable.

"How is our new craft coming?"

"It's coming real well. One of the things that I had not anticipated was that the increased capacity of the new system would allow me to essentially show it what I want, and it figures out the best and quickest way to make it happen. On the down side, the new craft will need one of us to operate it as the Trigger now does. It doesn't have any manual controls or displays. It will seat all of us and is stronger and weighs just about the same as the old model. It is capable of reentry to the Earth's atmosphere, but is incapable of orbit again. It ought to be ready for a trial trip in the next few days. I have just about decided that we don't actually need that reentry capability unless we all need to go back to Earth. What I propose is that we create some additional reentry vehicles that carry a single person only. They wouldn't be reusable in any sense of the word, and it would simplify construction. They could grow like buds off the main vessel, with a simple airtight door between them and the main cabin. I actually started doing it that way, but I felt that I should tell you about it so it wouldn't be a surprise. My remaining design issue is what are we going to call it?" Tom helped himself to another serving of Tofu with green pepper sauce.

"It is too large and pretty to be Soyuz." Katerina had another bite of potato/carrot bread.

"We could try something else out of the Roy Rogers mythos. I don't think Bullet is a big enough subject for a ship of exploration." Jake handed the diamond water pitcher to Madelyne.

"How about Nelleybell?" Madelyne took the water from her husband and filled her glass and handed the pitcher to Tom, who set it down.

"Who are this Roy Rogers and Nelleybell you are talking about? I thought that the Trigger was named for that part of a gun." Katerina sat back in her chair and looked expectantly at Jake.

"I thought that someone would have explained the name of our ship to you at some time, Katerina! Roy Rogers was the straight-shooting, singing cowboy, and Trigger was his horse. Margaret thought that the underneath part of Trigger looked like a horse's ass. Of course, the word means that part of a gun anyway, but that isn't what we were thinking about when we named the ship. It was Roy Roger's horse. Nelleybell was the old, cantankerous Jeep that Gabby Hayes drove around the desert in. He used to talk to it. Gabby Hayes was Roy Roger's sidekick." Jake took another bite of his own tofu.

"This was series of novels?" When genuinely without a clue about some Americanism, even Katerina's excellent English suffered.

" No, it was a television show during our childhoods. It was so long ago that the kids wouldn't really remember it."

White Knights Inc.

Madelyne took a sip of water. "I think that Nelleybell is a great name."

"I think pilot should have some say as to what her vessel is called."

"So what do you think the new ship should be called, Katerina? Jack carried his plate to the recycler, and when he returned, pushed his chair back from the table.

"I think Nelleybell is a fine name. I just wanted to have my say in the matter. Tom better have a little time to show me these controls, that I can't touch with my hands, before we go for any rides."

"There really isn't anything to learn, Katerina. I have been trying to show you guys this all day. The Image of your hands are used to control the new computer, just like the other one was controlled by pressure on the display on the screen of the PDAs. If you touch this box right here in your display - which I know are ghosted out right now as we haven't been using the computer since we started making dinner. That's it. Do you see the other boxes that were inside it and the labels?" The others put down what they were eating and pushed away from the table.

"Does every one have a few boxes to play with? Excellent. Touch the one you are most interested in." In each of their stereo displays the box they had touched disappeared, and the interface of whatever application appeared, and the display cleared of all the other boxes. To Katerina, It appeared that she was sitting at the controls of the Soyuz. All the controls appeared to be transparent plastic that started to glow in a different color when "touched". There was even a feeling of reality, although it could be ignored.

"OK, Tom. This is a very neat effect. How did you do it?" Katerina could actually feel the stick move in her hand.

"Let's not all forget that we are all inhabited by another set of nanomachines. From everything that I can detect, no one has had the least bit of deterioration from this mostly accidental event. Once I had given the nanos to Katerina and the rest of us caught them from the air, all I have seen is an improvement. Does anyone want to get rid of the nanos that they are carrying?"

There were no takers. "OK, what I did today was augment the nanos software and add the tiny display floating in each of your eyes. Has any one noticed that the audio output from the display is also in stereo?"

"I noticed that at first it seemed to be coming from the PDA, but within a few minutes, it seemed to be coming from everywhere." Jack had wondered about that little trick himself.

"The additional programming interfaces with the existing nanomachines network. The tiny machines in your hands are not quite capable of stopping the motion of your hand. They are plenty to give you the sensation of touch. It is really the next generation of Macintosh along with a really cool human interface." Tom scooted back up to the table and got a piece of cake for dessert.

"Are you saying that we ourselves are now the interface?" Madelyne had dropped her hands and turned toward Tom.

"Pretty much, Madelyne. Not really just interfaces, but also extensions of the network itself. Tom set his fork down.

"So you say that we are also extensions of the system? Does that mean that I can access the different individual networks that we are carrying and get the information that they can access about our bodies?" Madelyne hadn't moved much.

"Sure, now that we have these new interfaces you should have information down to the cellular, if not biochemical, level." Tom finished his cake and drank the rest of his water.

"Damn, Tom! Thank you so much." Madelyne sat down and got herself a piece of cake.

"What do you mean, Madelyne? It is just another way of controlling our computer, which consists of every surface in or on Belial or the Trigger and, within a few days, the Nelleybell. Oh, and as of this afternoon, our bodies."

"Once again Tom, you don't see the obvious stuff. You are one of the stupidest geniuses that I have ever known."

"What do you mean? Don't you really like it? I haven't used anything else for the last twenty hours and I don't see how I got along without it."

"See what I mean, Margaret. He still doesn't get it."

"Get what, mom?" Margaret had been back away from the table studying the sun in her three dimensional display.

"The fact that your wonderful husband has given me something that I have always wanted: X-Ray Vision!"

A few days later Katerina and Jack boarded the new spacecraft that everyone now called Nelleybell. The systems were as superior to the Soyuz as a computer is to an abacus.

"What do you think?" Tom was enjoying the appearance that the walls of the new craft were transparent.

"It is wonderful! I never felt like I have had as much control over any craft I have ever flown. Lets take everyone else for a little spin around the block." Katerina was already moving toward docking the Nelleybell.

After the seals had equalized, the entire crew boarded. They had been standing by in their spacesuits, which plugged into the atmosphere jacks on the craft. Katerina undocked the

Nelleybell and pulled the craft away from the docking adapter. Tom showed everyone how to adjust their displays so that the bulkheads of the craft seemed to disappear. Katerina guided the little craft around the rotating side of Belial toward the front, or rather, the bow of the huge spacecraft; because, although it had become a world to it's inhabitants, here on the outside it was clearly a huge spacecraft rotating through the big empty. The surface was now a uniform color. It was almost black, or such a dark gray that little difference could be seen, and it was perfectly smooth. The surface appeared to be smooth, but not the least bit shiny. In their augmented vision they could see that it was not really smooth, but rather covered almost entirely with a near fractal surface of feathery projections that drastically increased its surface area. As they negotiated the almost eleven miles to the bow of Belial, the huge truncated conical mirror became more and more obvious. Over the last few weeks since the sunring had risen, the most central part of the eye of Belial had developed a cataract, or really an island, in the center that occluded the central part. It never obstructed any of the sunring, but it hardened the window; and after the initial warming, the huge expanse didn't add as much light as the sunring, which was concentrated. The central tube gave access to the area, and there was a docking area there as well as on the stern. The huge mirrors, which concentrated the sunlight, passed on the starboard and for the first time since the asteroid Belial had tumbled off the side of the Trigger, the crew saw their home as a single object.

"It sure is pretty." Madelyne was also entranced with being able to see through the sides of the Nelleybell.

"I am enjoying having a bit more stereo in my display of the sun. This mile or two of separation is really improving my visualization." Margaret was looking at something different than the rest of the crew. She had been looking at the sun the last few days and had noticed an unusual group of sunspots moving around the limb. There was a suspicious area just coming into view that might be another sunspot region. Suddenly she got a wild look in her eye, and she turned to Katerina. "Turn this ship around! I have just seen a solar mass ejection! We are outside during a solar flare! We are getting pounded by hard X-Rays and Gamma radiation!"

"How much radiation are we getting?" Madelyne looked sharply at her daughter.

"That is an X9 flare! It puts out almost ten thousand times the usual amount of X-Ray radiation the Sun usually radiates. I am guessing at least thirty rem a minute!"

"We have got about four minutes then before we start to reach critical dosages!" Madelyne looked a little pale.

"It will take us at least twelve minutes to get back!" Katerina used her virtual controls to turn the Nelleybell around and start back toward the other end of Belial.

Chapter Thirty-one
Any Port in a Storm

"There is a docking port on the central axis on the sunward end of Belial! It is much closer. Will that help us?" Tom had programmed the addition when he had programmed the mirrors. It was attached to the central tube pneumatic car. None of the crew had ever visited it.

"You mean it is just on the other side of the mirrors?" Katerina had not engaged the rockets to send them toward the spaceward end of Belial.

"Sure, it is much closer, but you have never docked there. Won't that make a difference?" Jake was thinking about the shade of the huge spacecraft from the onslaught of radiation from their raging star.

"No, not really any difference except that it will be quicker. I am heading that way." Katerina changed their direction and fired a rocket. They started toward the mirrors again.

"Aren't we going too slow? It has been two minutes already!" Margaret had not taken her virtual eyes off the huge mass of plasma that the sun had just kicked into space.

"There is limit to how fast we go if we have to also slow down. This is about as fast as I dare go." Katerina had not taken her hands from the virtual controls. The rest of the crew remained silent as the craft cleared the mirrors and began to approach the central hub on the sunward side. Seconds, and then minutes, passed as they approached the lone docking port that rotated in the center of the protruding hub. Katerina deftly docked the new craft as if there was nothing wrong. The pressures equalized, and the hatch opened. The crew scrambled out. Margaret and Katerina in the lead, followed by Madelyne and Nina. Jake closed the hatch behind himself, as he was the last to leave. The crew found themselves in a duplicate of the Can except it seemed to rotate in the opposite direction. They made their way back through the Can and entered the central tube pneumatic car.

"By my timing, it took six minutes to get into this tube and the relative protection of four inches of stainless steel. That gives us all an estimated dose of one hundred eighty rem. I know from my studies that two hundred rem were considered fatal within two months. That is just the X-Ray, of course. I didn't even try to calculate the gamma rem that we got. Mom is there any way we could possibly survive the huge dose of radiation that we just got? And if we survive, will our children be damaged?" Margaret sounded bleak.

"I created a virtual dosimeter while we were trying to figure out how to get out of the sun. By my estimate, we each got at least a lethal dose. At the same time we are not unaugmented humans. We each have a nanomachine network that is constantly working to maintain homeostasis in every cell in our bodies. As we are making this little tube trip, I have been taking a few readings from each of you. Although you probably don't feel it, we all have fever. My own temperature right now is near one hundred and three. I don't feel the least bit chilled. I suspect that our tiny nanomachines are working at a, mind the pun, fever pitch to repair the damage done us by our little trip outside. Frankly, I have no idea how injured we are." Madelyne was engaged in monitoring all the information from their bodies.

"I never adjusted my display from being in Nelleybell. I can see through the walls of this car and tube as if it were glass! Wow, what a view!" In spite of the horrendous danger that they all faced, Bob was primarily still enjoying himself.

"I can't believe that you would be taken up with such trivia at a time like this!" Margaret had managed to turn her grief into anger.

"It's OK, Sis. When I start to feel bad, then I promise to feel as crummy as you do. I promise." Bob had not taken his eyes off the walls of the car.

"He's right you know. You can see right through the walls of this car. What a wonderful view!" Jake had reset his display to how they had been in the spacecraft.

"I don't know about the rest of you, but I could eat an elephant and most of a horse right now. Something about a fatal radiation dose sure makes you hungry!" Jack had also changed his display and was looking through the walls of the car and tube, but had focused on a different set of sensations.

"That is wrong. We should all be badly nauseated by now. The lining of our bowels should be about to slough off, and we should be about to have bloody diarrhea; and instead of that, I just feel like I could have a very early dinner!" Madelyne noted that their temperatures had not declined.

"Speaking of dinner, when do we eat?" Bob took his eyes off the view through the tube and car and focused his attention on his mother.

"As soon as I can get something ready to eat. In fact, I am not sure that I can even wait long enough for something to cook. We will eat the cold leftovers while I cook something else. I am going to need everyone's help when we get back to the house." The car began to slow, as it got closer to the opposite end of Belial.

"Fine, I am going to unload the refrigerator while you throw a few things in the pot. I think that the first batch of soy cheese should be about ready. I know we have some okra and beans ready to pick. Tom, you and Margaret get those. Jack, you and Katerina dig up some new potatoes. Bob, You and

Nina go pick some sweet corn. Jake and I will start the preparation and hand out some snacks while the main meal is being prepared." Madelyne prepared to mobilize the troops.

The car slowed to a stop and the family piled out and into the elevator, which began the long descent to the base of the sphere. The incredible hunger pangs intensified to the point where when they arrived back at the tiny village, Jake handed out some emergency rations he had been saving.

"I guess this is an emergency. I haven't felt this hungry since once twenty years ago when I skipped breakfast, forgot lunch, and then found out that dinner was going to be late." Jake had torn open his MRE and was sucking the au gratin potatoes out of the plastic bag before he even set the rest of the packets down. The next two and a half hours were spent much the same way with a great deal of consumption and very little conversation.

Finally, after the quantity of food equaled or surpassed what they would have eaten during four regular meals, the frenzy eased and the crew was overcome by fatigue. Without further discussion they retired to their respective quarters and, although it was hours before ringset, slept most of the next day. They awoke sore and surprisingly well rested. They were once again surprisingly hungry although this did not compare with the bizarre feasting they had required the day before. They all sat down to a meal quickly and competently prepared by the group and were actually able to talk while they ate.

"All of our temperatures have come back down to normal! You all seem to have developed a tan but, other than that, I can't even detect that you had a fatal radiation exposure early yesterday afternoon. I just hope that the damage just isn't something that I haven't learned to see." Madelyne herself looked none-the-worse for wear.

"Hey, at least you noticed that we had tans! I didn't even see that." Bob was helping his plate and from time to time checking out his tan.

"I am wondering what else may have slipped under the radar about this nanotech we are wearing. I think that I am going to put us all through a little testing and see what I can find out." Madelyne finished her brunch and the next day put them one by one through the most exhausting testing they had ever undergone. They all took IQ tests and reaction time tests. She measured their lean body mass. She found out how much weight they could lift, push, and twist. She had them reading with one eye in various lighting conditions. They all had to put puzzles together and solve riddles and then, to top it off, she found out how far and fast they could run. Then she fed them again and put them to bed.

The next morning at breakfast, Madelyne had a few results for their consideration. There was no talk of moving the Nelleybell back around to the spaceward end of Belial as the Coronal Mass ejection plasma cloud was on the outside of Belial. Margaret had her virtual vision tuned to various wavelengths that allowed her to study the highly radioactive stew that Belial swam in.

"We are all a lot quicker than we used to be. A really fast human has a reaction time of two tenths of a second. That means that they can notice a visual cue and begin to perform a response in that much time. Our average is between four and five hundredths of a second. Bob and Margaret, our youngest crewmembers, consistently scored between two and three hundredths of a second. That roughly translates to being three to eight times as fast as an unaugmented human. We also see better than we did. I don't seem to need my reading glasses anymore, and Jake was as nearsighted as you can get and be able to be corrected. He sees a bit better than the average Naval Aviator now and can outrun the average Olympic Runner. He ran two miles in twelve minutes yesterday and was talking to Jack the whole time. Don't think that I didn't listen, boys. The payback will come when you least expect it." Jake and Jack looked ruefully at one another and then turned their attention back to Madelyne.

"We also see farther into the infrared and the ultraviolet than is normal. I don't know what Katerina's and Nina's IQs were before they were augmented, but now Katerina holds the prize and Tom comes in second in that department. None of us have IQs less than genius level, and Tom and Katerina's IQs can only be compared, not really measured. We are all within ten or fifteen points, but for me that is a forty-point increase. At the same time this test isn't accurate at these levels as we all have good days and bad taking tests. If I tested us all again tomorrow, the results might be entirely different at least in terms of our relative ranking. Additionally, our stamina compares well with most marathon runners and could, in fact, be better than most. Now, the really weird stuff. Our skin is much tougher. I can still poke a needle through it, but the needles I used had diamond-coated points. No one needed a band-aid. The chemistries I performed demonstrated that none of us has any extra cholesterol, sugar, or reactive protein. Bear in mind that we all had what would ordinarily be considered lethal exposures to ionizing radiation day before yesterday. When I examined Jake, all the seborrheic keratoses and moles he had developed over the thirty-eight years that we have been married have disappeared. The scar I had from the C-Section that I had to bring Bob into the world has disappeared as well. It was gradual, but I think most of you have noticed that Jake has all his hair back and it is his actual color. I, of course, stopped coloring my hair when we blasted off. It had been actually gray for years. I cut the last of the gray off a few months ago. Additionally, I have started menstruating again. I have this sneaking suspicion that I could bear another child. Nina, I know it is personal, but could you answer whether or not you have noticed anything like that?" Madelyne looked at Nina very curiously.

"I have not, but I had the hysterectomy when I was about fifty-five. I had too much bleeding after my cycle had stopped. The government doctors said that I had some sort of growth, and it would have to be done. I don't recall being asked if I wanted surgery, but I woke up with a big scar on my belly, which has since disappeared. I don't miss the scar, but I don't miss my cycle either." Nina laughed.

"So there are limits, but the upshot is that we are quicker, stronger, smarter, and apparently younger than any other humans our age. We are not immune to hard radiation, but apparently all it does is just give us a ridiculous appetite and a suntan. I have no idea what it has done to our gametes, but I will be able to monitor that if one of us become pregnant." Madelyne sat down.

"So Margaret, how much longer do we have to stay indoors?" Jake took up his typical duties as chairman.

"Well Daddy, we are in the midst of the mother of all storms. The ion cloud that exists outside would probably kill us, even augmented, in the space of a few minutes. It should take another several days to pass." Margaret returned her attention to the storm.

"Well, according to my genius daughter, we will have to leave Nelleybell where she is for the next few days, so why don't we discuss the other aspects of our mission. Madelyne, how are we doing on our plantings?"

"As well as can be expected, given the tiny workforce. We have now gotten almost all the available species in the ground. Most everything is doing well. Some of the more tropical species are a little wimpy, given the rather week sunlight. Everything will be fine. Now, let me eat!" Madelyne dug into the tofu.

"It does seem much greener. Thanks, dear. Now how about our defenses?"

"Better and better. Mostly we are learning everyday how to do what we may need to do. Move on." Jack was also still hungry from yesterday.

"So Tom, any improvements since yesterday?" Jake looked at his son-in-law.

"Sure Jake, but primarily in our skill with the new interface. I am learning something from everyone. Let's leave it at that for now." Tom looked over at his wife who seemed to be looking at nothing in particular.

"So Bob, how do the people at home seem to be taking our efforts at reeducation?"

"It seems to be having some effect. There are fewer references to how evil we are in the media in general, and some shows actually portray us as decent human beings who should be pitied rather than feared." Bob showed a cartoon of a bigheaded person trapped in a little box on a rock, all alone in space, as it hurtles by a warm and welcoming earth.

"Are they insane? Can't they see that we have made a brave new world here? Who are they kidding?" The comments came from around the table.

"The point is that they don't seem to hate us quite as venomously as they did a few short months ago. On the down side, the news that we are not black-hearted evil criminals has done little to shore up the credibility of the new regimes. Things are even more unstable than they were before."

"Some of them are beginning to try to regain their importance by declaring war or threatening their neighbors. It is a proven ploy that governments have used for years to make themselves more relevant and palatable." Jake loved to sound out on the obvious from time to time - just to demonstrate he was actually listening.

"Right Dad, the point is that that they are indeed listening. The fact that the confederations are looking more and more unstable is a direct result of their foundation on their promises of security with us cast as the super bad guys. The fact that we did not address our message to any single government also means that they are all essentially competing directly with us for the control of that amazingly precious commodity – the truth. It has been controlled for years by government, and now there is a competitor for a share in the collective consciousness. Although the current media stories do not specifically make mention of the fact that we, as a small group, saved the world. That is big news, and it isn't being reported in the mainstream media. That means that despite our current best efforts, the fix is still in as far as the governments of the world are concerned." Jack looked deeply concerned.

"There is more in the news than that. If they are finding it necessary to back off even a little from their earlier fabrications regarding us, we have gotten more public opinion behind us than they are capable of obscuring. We are the only people who left the security of earth to save it and are still alive to tell the tale as many times as we want. We are more than an embarrassment of the facts. We are celebrities!" Katerina had a clever idea.

"What do you mean, Katerina? How does that matter when we are talking about national governments here?" Jake could not see why it was important that they were celebrities.

"We are Jesse James, the Beatles, Elvis, and Dr. Livingston all rolled into one. This time the bad guys also get to have their say. The only media that the governments don't control is on this habitat. We can have our say, and the Earth Governments can't do anything about it. Which of those governments do we actually want to go away? What if we provided people with the information they need to make rational decisions about their governments? We have the bully pulpit!" Jack caught the gist of it immediately.

"People will die if we further destabilize any of the governments." Jake wanted to get out of this making as few waves as possible.

"People are always going to die one way or another, sooner or later. My point is merely that we provide them with more than the information than the governments who lied about us. Why don't we make a point to tell the people the truth about the other lies the governments are telling? As many as we can pick out. The interior of Belial is on its way to being a green place. Perhaps we can spend some of our time observing our home planet and figuring out whatever we can and giving that information to the common people. What they do with that information is their own business!" Katerina enthused.

"I just wonder what kinds of things that we could make out from here." Bob made some gestures out in from of his face. "Wow, I can see oil leaking from oil tankers at sea! I wonder who already knows about that?"

"It's a little like that old Greek myth of rolling in the apple and seeing what happens." Margaret looked up from her studies.

"What apple? I thought that story was Judeo-Christian. By the way, it never says apple." Bob's interest in languages extended into their mythological roots.

"Right you are, Bob. But in this case, the fruit in question is indeed an apple, made of gold and bearing the inscription " For the one who is the most beautiful". It is the sort of thing that could cause an argument or two." Margaret changed the focus of her interest outside the interior of Belial.

Chapter Thirty-two
On a Clear Day We can See Everything

Immediately, the discrepancies began to mount up. Each of the crew began to assemble a personal TV show. In whatever direction their interests drew them; they began to discover problems in what was versus what was reported. If chemicals were being dumped in a river, it could be seen and the fish kill noted. If forest was being burned to allow squatters to plow rain forest land, it was clearly visible as soon as the smoke cleared. If troops were gathering at a border, their numbers and equipment could be seen.

The broadcasts were not particularly made with great care. The basic footage was assembled, and the imagery was occasionally superficially dissected with an eye toward what the truth was that had been misreported by the government-controlled media. The style was essentially conversational. There were no commercials other than views of the crew themselves and the interior of Belial. When the broadcast was not live, prerecorded shows and Bob's propaganda film was shown. There was nowhere on Earth untouched by the Eye of Belial - as the broadcasts were known.

Some of the worst governments began to fall. Generally, it wasn't violent revolution, but rather a series of peaceful votes of no confidence. Some of the smaller governments that had not falsified information or hadn't been caught were actually strengthened.

There was a violent revolution in Islam. This government had taken a paternalistic attitude and, people being people, some corruption was uncovered. Violence followed. Tolerance for greed and corruption in this theocracy ruled by ideologue clerics, proved to be very low.

The shifts in the major powers was much more glacial. The rhetoric changed long before any significant changes in the systems began. The less association the press had with the government, the less likely that anything the crew said would make any difference. In the industrialized western nations, the press was not directly controlled by the governments, but rather by large conglomerates with entrenched interests in the Houses of Parliament or the House and Senate. Associating misinformation with specific members of these governing bodies was much more tenuous. Nonetheless, the strident objections these members made when their monopoly on the truth began to be diluted was duly noted by the more discerning members of their constituencies.

The months passed, and the search algorithms used by members of the crew improved with every use. The huge computational capacity of Belial made it possible to hack banking records and other sensitive information. Individual crewmembers took more or less time with the broadcasts. Madelyne went on a tear and took out several specific politicians with photographs of clear-cut forests and excerpts from the congressional record along with evidence of large deposits to their bank accounts from logging interests, which showed their real agenda. As Belial neared Earth, it became possible to identify ships at sea and, eventually, individual car's license plates. As the acuity of information became more incisive, the reputations of some politicians, which were built on lies, disappeared. Many were ultimately arrested, convicted, and imprisoned.

It didn't take too many of these events before the factual content of all media rose significantly. The news now included details of the compromises that members of governments arranged. The near glacial shift in policy went from a paternalistic "We'll tell them what we want them to know" to a more liberal "Let's see if we can bury the truth in the wealth of detail." This didn't work very well either. When the truth is printed, even when buried in meaningless details, it is still present; and those with an objective of digging it out can do so and publish their findings. The crooked politicians were on the way out within a year.

The bloated bureaucracy of the United Nations was the last bastion of those who wanted to control the access to information. Although the new streamlined administration of the Security Council appeared to be open to calibration by members of their constituencies, the length of time that these individuals were appointed for and the control that they individually had over the General Assembly made it impossible to force any real change in their makeup. The Security Council eventually began their last ditch effort to control the truth.

The first move was made in a series of regulations that purported to standardize electronic components to more accurately allocate wavelength controls for specific purposes and to certain licensees. The radio spectrum was already cut into little pieces that could be allocated to individual companies for their exclusive use as long as they met the requirement of operating within the public interest. This set of regulations set requirements for electronic components manufactured for sale in international commerce, such that the United Nations could selectively block any frequency or band that it chose without warning. It also allowed for more effective jamming of persons or entities that were not signatories of the United Nations or were in violation of any of the provisions. The technology was called Restricted Architecture Design. Never in any of the regulations were the Belianese mentioned by name. In fact, the entire set of revisions was part of a regularly scheduled update of the International Communication Commission Regulations. The Commission was established as an organization to promote the uninterrupted exchange necessary for commerce between the member nations. It was deemed necessary to maintain order in the market of the licenses to the slices of the spectrum. The multinational corporations that were the real powerbase beneath the current leaders of the Security Council had determined that their best interests were being served by being able to buy and sell the electromagnetic spectrum, clean air and water, and the other subliminal cues to the sense of well being of every person on the planet.

The ultimate outcome of these regulations was to leave more wealth in the hands of the private people all over the world. The consumers of the products made of the restricted architecture components did not show up to buy them. The products found their way into the corporation-controlled sector of the economy, but they never gained widespread product exposure, as the communication products were less versatile than the products they were intended to replace. People kept the old gear, and it became much more valuable on the resale market. This was a new phenomenon, as these devices had become articles that were not typically repaired when they broke down. They were usually carried to a landfill somewhere after whatever simple recycling had been done. Most of it ended up in the landfill.

Now a repair market appeared, and the older devices acquired preferred status. Some mining of landfills occurred. The market share of the multinational corporations suffered.

A small change that went unnoticed did the multinational corporations manufacture that the repair market required a supply of complex integrated circuits no longer. This required that a much larger number of people had to actually understand how the modern electronics were designed and manufactured. "Chipping", as making these electronics came to be called, became a closet industry. Electronic design became an individually pursued art form.

The first of the individuals to contact Belial was a family in southern Missouri, which had many similarities to Jake and Madelyne's family. They were about ten years younger than

Jake and Madelyne with children generally the same degree younger. The two way contact occurred about the time that Belial was about thirty light minutes away from Earth. The original message from Earth had arrived with a 127-digit encryption code key. The information sent back to Earth was encrypted with the same code and was embedded in the usual broadcast. The first thing that Jack did was to insist on tighter encryption. A second 4999-digit encryption code key was chosen and relatively secure communications were established.

The Schuylers were interested in immigration. They were part of a much larger semi-secret group called the Friends of Belial. This group had been organized within one of the chat rooms on the internet that enjoyed keeping their communications with one another private and routinely used encryption programs with pre-agreed upon keys. The role of the new habitat in the coming world order was discussed and speculated upon at one of these chat room meetings, and a small portion agreed to meet personally. This group, having first investigated one another at a distance using secure channels, met at an Alabama beach resort and, after coming to some personal and financial agreements, set up the communication gear. This gear was interfaced to the net, which allowed the crew to hack the banks and other secure records of the various politicians that opposed them. By the time that Belial was forty-five light seconds from Earth, the communications were well established along with a few corporations with their own secret agendas.

All the rest of the surplus rocket equipment disappeared from any availability and other companies began to recruit engineers and craftsmen to design and build the next generation of low Earth orbit capable craft.

The designs were based on existing, well-proven technologies with whatever improvements could be included, and they became the newest target of governmental activism. Control of the airwaves was slipping away, but control of the airspace was still within their grasp. There were spectacular raids where millions of dollars worth of space equipment was seized. The surviving companies took their knowledge and equipment underground to tiny places in suburban and urban areas with better security and camouflage. Some had followed Jake and Tom's plan of hiding their enterprise in plain view. A modest few of these were discovered, but the secret network went unchecked as the raids always came a little too slow to catch the people and their personal computers.

As B Day approached, as the near miss by Belial came to be called, there was a dedicated cabal that intended to join the Belianese. The requirements of the missions were very difficult. The craft that intended to rendezvous with Belial had to be in a near polar orbit and match its relative velocity - nearly twenty-three thousand miles per hour - relative to a line tangent to the Earth's surface. The actual transit of Belial would require twenty-two minutes and was a maximum of five hundred and twenty miles from the South Pole and a minimum of forty miles from the North Pole. It was an incredibly near miss.

It was this near miss that would curve the orbit of Belial and rob it of some of its relative velocity. This encounter set up a second close encounter with the Earth's Moon which, although not as near a miss, curved the orbit even more and robbed Belial of more of its relative velocity and allowed the habitat to be gravitationally captured by the Earth/Moon system. It would circle the Earth five times for each two times it circled the Moon; a so-called five to two resonant orbit. This would, with no course corrections be stable for several hundred years.

These orbital dynamics were very hard to match, and the resulting launch windows from any given location was required to be within a second or two to be feasible. None of the other rocket plans sent to Belial to be checked were nearly as complicated as the Trigger. The craft did not need to sustain life for many months but rather hours or, at most, a day and a half. The plans for rescue of these brave souls required the crew of Belial to design a module that could allow much more ambitious changes in the relative velocity of the Nelleybell. Tom and Katerina put their heads together with Jake and they came up with an easily-produced unit that contained a large number of solid rockets similar to the JATO units the Trigger had used to reach Low Earth Orbit. They were smaller and lighter but packed just as much a punch as the JATOs, and there were forty of them in each of the detachable modules, which stacked and attached to a special bracket, which formed on the Nelleybell. These modules would allow the Nelleybell to match orbits with all of the planned escapees and had a hundred and ninety percent safety margin for the worst-case scenario. There were a total of seven flights planned from the surface of Earth. A total of twenty persons had elected to join Belial at great personal cost and risk to themselves. There were four families from North America and two from Europe and one from Central Asia.

The crew had studied every available datum, which existed about each potential new crewmember. They undertook personal correspondence with those with whom their own personalities and passions were most consonant.

The changes in the international market destabilized two of the larger multinational companies. This resulted in a flurry of mergers and adverse acquisitions, which undermined the vested powerbase of certain members of the Security Council. The actions of these individuals, who, above all other things, desired control over their fellow man, had backfired. They had less control after the change in the regulations than they had had before they took action. The regulations were quietly repealed, and the merged companies returned to competitiveness in the altered marketplace. A new and final plan began to be discussed. The free access to information had diluted the collective powers of the states and those shady powers enjoyed by the Multinationals. The new plan required another rendezvous with Belial. One that the Multinational planners had no intention of the crew surviving. The Security Council had its own plans. They intended that the United Nations would control the airspace over the planet regardless of the cost to those who might choose to leave.

Chapter Thirty-three
B Day

July 23 looked to be a beautiful day on Earth, or at least most of it. The crew had become very familiar with their home planet's moods. It was the dead of winter in the Southern Hemisphere toward which the habitat, known throughout the world as Belial, would begin its close encounter this afternoon. It was the middle of summer in the Northern Hemisphere, where they would have their closest approach before two-thirty PM Eastern Standard Time this afternoon.

The crew gathered at Jake and Madelyne's house for a special send-off breakfast and last minute briefing. Madelyne had made her famous pancakes on which various crewmembers had smeared grape jelly. Maple syrup was still many years in the future as a local crop. Without butter, they were otherwise a bit dry.

"So what time does the Nelleybell leave?" Jake Knight actually knew this quite well. He just wanted to be sure that everyone else did.

"We will disconnect from the dock at one PM. That will give us plenty of time to be at the first rendezvous point at two thirty-five after the closest approach at two twenty-two and forty seconds. Please Jake, let me worry about these little details. It is important to me for you to be in proper position as well." Katerina finished her pancakes and picked up her tea. It was some of the first tea grown in Belial, and everyone pretended to like it as much as coffee, which would be available sometime in the next year or so. It was difficult to leave enough leaves on their little trees to keep growing.

"I will be in the Trigger with the drive up and communications running to tell me where to point it." Everyone knew what had happened the last time the crew had been this close to Earth, and they did not intend to stand by and let the United Nations have their way with the people blasting off to join them. The relativistic ions from the rocket were plenty to scramble the electronics of any missile, and the radiation dose in the beam was rapidly fatal to anything alive.

"I have no doubt that the UN has some surprises for us that will reveal themselves to us in the next twelve hours or so. I am confident, that if we all do what we need to do, they won't have anything that can overcome our defenses." Jack finished his tea and stood up. "If any of their goons should make it as far as Belial, there will be some unpleasant surprises."

The plans required seven separate rendezvous and docking missions and three separate trips out from Belial and back for Nelleybell. These dockings had gotten to be a snap for Katerina and even for Jack. It helped a lot to be able to see through the spacecraft in order to more accurately control the process. The first of the missions would take place, as Katerina had said, at one PM. There would be a second at three-thirty and the last at five forty-five. The last stragglers were coming up from Kazakhstan and would not be able to be recovered until after the nearest approach when Belial would be on its way to the moon. The timing of the launch windows had caused there to be three separate little clusters of the flights - a cluster from each of the continents. The way things had worked out; the largest group would be the four launches from North America. This would require some of the new arrivals to be strapped into the reentry modules, as there were a total of twelve in those four flights. This required Nelleybell to transfer twelve persons and their contributions to Belial, as well as Katerina and Jack. It would be packed to the rafters, and no one would have the luxury of removing their suit. The space inside the craft was simply too small to allow it.

The second group from Europe consisted of six persons in two separate flights. This flight allowed more cargo room and had been supplied to match. There were animals on these flights as well as people.

The last group from Kazakhstan consisted of only two people and three fairly large animals. Cattle were coming to the open range of Belial.

Jack and Katerina spent the rest of the morning checking their equipment. The reentry modules would be claustrophobic for whoever was put into them, as they had no port or instrumentation visible on the inside at all. They had been designed for augmented humans who would be able to control them and see through them. For an unaugmented human it would be much like being strapped into a black box. Jack and Katerina understood that the travelers they were picking up had brought sedatives for themselves when they drew the short straws. Mercifully, the ride wouldn't last long.

At just before one PM, Jack and Katerina strapped themselves in and undocked from the aft docking ring of Belial and fired retro rockets to lower their orbit.

Although they had been looking at it for days, the immensity of the Earth beneath them was breathtaking. They could see things with their unaided eyes that had required substantial magnification since that day almost five years before when they themselves had left Earth.

"It is difficult to keep your eyes off of it, isn't it?" Katerina divided her attention between the view outside and the virtual instrumentation.

"Who said I had to keep my eyes off of it? You're driving. I am just waiting for the attractive flight attendant to bring me my soft drink and peanuts!" Jack settled into his acceleration couch as if the pretty flight attendant would appear and fluff his pillow.

"You are clearly asking for trouble, cowboy! Take the controls! I must visit the tiny cubicle in the rear of the plane." Katerina laughed at the expression on her husband's face.

"You were supposed to do your business before we left home. I wonder if we have a coffee can?" Jack and Katerina were both laughing now at the mental image of someone trying to urinate into a coffee can in microgravity.

"How long 'til we get there, Mommy?" Jack was keeping up the joke as long as Katerina would let him. Truthfully, they were both nervous about meeting the first new people in five years.

"I have set up for the first docking in about ten minutes. I can just see them at about seven o'clock rising up from the surface. No sigh of hostile fire yet. Jake, can you see anything that we can't?" Jake, with the entire surface area of Belial at his disposal, could practically see insects flying in what was left of the rain forest of Brazil.

"I think these guys got off without a hitch. I watched their blastoff about forty-five minutes ago with the others staggered over about a fifteen-minute interval - two from Texas and two from Florida as we had planned. I don't see any other rocket trails just yet, but the day is young. I'll be standing by." Jake was on the Trigger.

The docking went flawlessly, which was no surprise given how many times Katerina had done it in the last five years. Jack was the one waiting to undog the hatch when the pressures equalized. A short man swam aboard and examined Jack through their respective helmets. "Hello. I am Bart Schuyler - Permission to come aboard? This is my wife Eloise and my daughter Lisa." A tall woman swam aboard assisting a small figure less than three feet tall.

"Hello. My name is Jack Knight and this is my wife Katerina Yerisivloskaya. Welcome aboard. Do you have any additional cargo to shift?"

"We have got a couple of small duffle bags. Could you hand them out to me, dear?" Bart disappeared back into his craft and, almost immediately, two stiff white bags were pushed into the interior of Nelleybell. Jack caught them and strapped them out of the way. Bart made his way back into Nelleybell, and Jack strapped him, Eloise, and Lisa into couches. Jack dogged the hatch and strapped himself back in next to Katerina. Katerina undocked from the senior Schuyler's craft and made a burn for the next rendezvous.

"It sure is dark in here. I can't see my hand in front of my face." Eloise was seated in front of the single port in Nelleybell along with Bart.

"We have displays that make everything pretty much as bright as daylight for us. I didn't take the darkness into consideration here inside of Nelleybell. I just thought the reentry craft would be dark." Jack could see shadows cast by the starlight coming in through the port behind the Schuylers. Occasionally the port would coincide with the full Earth off the port bow. The light that came in looked dazzling. It was just another way that the crew was different from regular folks like the Schuylers.

The next rendezvous went off without a hitch, just ten minutes after the undocking from the first.

"My eyes are getting accustomed to this murk. What are you using to steer us with?" Bart was a systems control engineer in his previous life on Earth, and the control systems of the Nelleybell were as far out of his experience as a steering wheel and pedals were for a stagecoach driver.

"We have virtual controls. They exist only in my display. I could sit anywhere in the craft to make this docking."

Katerina completed the docking about the time that she said the word. Jack undogged the hatch, and another three space suited figures made their way into Nelleybell.

"This is our other daughter, Susan and our son, Stephen. This is Justin, he is the oldest child of the Spencer's who we will pick up next, if I am straight on the schedule." Susan looked to be the oldest at about twenty-something. Stephen and Justin appeared to be no more than barely teenagers.

"Is there any additional cargo to shift? I am Jack, and this is Katerina, our pilot."

"There is the rabbit hutch and one bag. I'll get them. "Susan disappeared through the hatch, and a circular wire cage covered with paper appeared, followed by another stiff duffle. Susan came back through the hatch and dogged it behind her. Stephen and Justin had both opened their helmets and looked like they were going to be ill. Jack reached into the cargo pocket of his suit and removed two patches and a small bottle of pills.

"Put these behind your ears, guys. Let one of these dissolve under your tongue. I am going to have to put you into two of the reentry modules. It will be very dark in there; so if you catch a nap, no one will complain. If you do get sick, which I doubt now that you have a little medicine on board, open your visors like you have now. Above all, don't worry about it. I had a queeze or two when we hit microgravity the first time. That's right, strap yourselves in. Good! I am going to have to close these hatches, OK? You can still talk to the rest of us and listen in on the com channel." Susan and Jack had assisted the boys, and they had looked a little better when the hatches closed. Susan and Jack strapped themselves back in. Katerina had used the time to stow the cargo.

"Are we all ready?" Katerina listened to the series of ayes, some of which were heartier than others, and undocked from the second craft and initiated the burn to reach the third. "We will reach the third craft in less than five minutes."

"There is a missile closing with you off the port aft. I think that if you stick to your schedule, it won't be much of a problem. I can't get a good shot with Trigger because you are in the way." Jake sounded very calm but he was docked to Belial.

Katerina mainly noticed how quiet everyone on Nelleybell was. The docking, once again, was trouble free, and it was a matter of minutes before Jack had opened the hatch to find three strangers. The new arrivals were Trish and Marvin Spencer along with their daughter, Patricia. The Spencers had brought chickens and a rooster, along with the obligatory stuffed duffle. Trish and Patricia were soon banished to reentry modules. Snores were coming from the modules where Stephen and Justin slumbered. The chickens and the duffle were strapped into the dwindling space available in the cabin of Nelleybell. Lisa had also nodded off and was strapped into the last reentry module. The entire operation of removing the Spencers and their cargo had taken less than four minutes.

"I am initiating the last of the little burns to set up our last rendezvous of this leg of the rescue. Everyone ready? Here we go!" The last burn was almost a minute long.

Behind them came the silent flare of a missile explosion. They were miles away when it exploded, but the flare of the explosion caught Jack and Katerina by surprise. "Hey Jake, that was a little close for comfort. How about a little warning next time?"

"Sorry Nelleybell, that one came up from the cloud deck about thirty seconds after you started your burn. I got the next three but there is only so quick that the old girl will swing. I'll try to keep you better informed, but I was a little busy. Trigger out." Jake had sounded a little harried.

It took almost ten minutes to match orbits with the last launch and another three to dock with it. This time the hatch opened on Dr. Nathan Lawrence and his wife, Dr. Nancy Simons. They had brought their infant daughter, Stephanie, along with three cats and a huge bag of cat food. The cats were in a very foul mood. Stephanie was in a very poor mood as well. She didn't understand why she had to be confined to something that looked like a beach ball with a little bottle attached. The screams that reached the interior of Nelleybell were evidence of an excellent set of lungs. Those unlucky enough to have run out of suit air were treated to the mingled odors of confined humanity, chickens, rabbits, and cats that had been ill. The interior of Nelleybell resembled a high tech bus in the backcountry of central Mexico.

"I just blasted another four missiles from Virginia. They are way off course, and I don't think that they will be of any concern to you, but I thought you would like to know. Trigger out." Jake sounded like an airline pilot talking about the Grand Canyon off the right side of the plane. Jack and Katerina could see them now if they looked real hard, but with the crowded cabin their attention had been elsewhere – not that it would have made any difference.

"I hope everyone is strapped in. I am Katerina Yerisivloskaya, and this is my husband, Jack. We will now kick away from this launch craft and make a quick trip to Belial." The burn this time lasted for more than five minutes and was followed by two more burns of three minutes each, all in a twelve-minute period. Instead of a gentle nudge, these burns indicated the need of Nelleybell to catch up with Belial. The Earth had been passing by underneath Nelleybell but was getting closer and closer. Belial was reaching its nearest approach near the North Pole when Nelleybell docked at the aft docking ring, and Jack and Katerina assisted twelve new crewmembers to disembark with their livestock and baggage. Stephen and Justin were still heavily -sedated and would not rouse. Madelyne and Margaret were at the docking ring to assist the newcomers down to the inner surface of Belial, and each towed a teenage boy. The helmets were off the suits by this time, and the predominant expression was one of open-mouthed wonder.

As soon as the spacecraft was empty of passengers and debris, the outer acceleration module was released from the stack to be recycled. Some of the bulkheads had to be wiped off. Air and propellant tanks were replenished and, after a complete systems check, the Nelleybell cast off to begin the second leg of the rescue mission.

The North Pole was receding in the darkness as Belial curved around Earth on the night side of the planet where the next two rescues would occur. The loss of momentum caused the habitat to shift from a strictly polar orbit to one closer to the plane of the Ecliptic. The velocity still greatly exceeded escape velocity, but the escape from only forty miles above the planet gave the second and third groups of refugees the opportunity to be rescued at altitudes between two hundred and five hundred miles above the dark side of the Earth.

Cities glowed softly in arabesques and patchworks and, where clouds obscured the ground and sea, electrical discharges from cloud to cloud and from cloud to the surface could be seen silently sparkling below.

"I must admit that, although I knew intellectually that there would be farm animals on all of these flights, the reality was incredibly strange. I had to wipe chicken crap off the seats and bulkheads." Jack was spellbound by the view of the planet below, but his mind was still occupied with the crowded flight just completed.

"The correct international term is guano. However, I am willing to accept chicken crap as acceptable usage in this instance." Jack and Katerina both laughed. There was still a bit of an aerosol residue in the cabin and, given the nature of the next group of rescuees, it was bound to get worse before it got better.

"I think that I could get used to picking people up from these little junk launch craft, but it could smell a lot less like the state fair without the fried food." Jack turned his gaze to the next craft that they would be docking with. They saw the launches of missiles this time but could also see the shaft of ionizing radiation that fluoresced the atmosphere at the spot where the missiles emerged. "Thanks, Dad. Way to watch em!"

The docking required only two minutes, and that was only because Katerina didn't want to shake up the occupants more than she had to.

Katerina opened the hatch to admit Honore' and Isolde Martine along with their son, Jean. Messr. and Madam Martine were in their early forties, and Jean was about ten years of age. They had with them three small sheep crammed into a restraint that resembled a plastic dog kennel padded with old clothing. Honore' brusquely introduced himself and his family while clearly trying to find a place to fasten the sheep. Then he lost his temper.

"What is the intention behind the darkness of your craft? Turn on additional light immediately!" Honore' angrily pushed the container of sheep deeper into the Nelleybell and waited at the hatch with his wife and son who remained silent.

"There is no additional lighting and, unless you want to get back aboard that aluminum waste can you came up on, you will shut up and strap yourself and family into acceleration couches without further delay. This train is leaving the station!" Katerina's remark in flawless French left no doubt that she had had some history with a rude French person at some time in her life on Earth. Meanwhile the container of sheep collided with Jack's midsection as he unstrapped to assist Katerina. The collision pushed him into a bulkhead behind him. He quickly secured the sheep and swam aft to aid Katerina.

"I know that this has been a frightening day for you, Messr. Martine, but giving the pilot orders upon entering her craft, with the pilot being my wife, is the sort of behavior that would put you on my bad side. I suggest that unless you want to reenter the atmosphere in your craft, a maneuver for which it is not designed, you will follow her orders immediately and without comment. This little misunderstanding will be straightened out when we return to Belial." Jack's reinforcement of the possibility of being abandoned to survive or die in their own craft had the same effect as a swift kick to the stomach for Honore'. He quickly strapped his wife and son in acceleration couches before strapping himself in. He said nothing further during the trip.

The little disagreement, as short as it was, had put them a minute behind schedule. This required the burn to reach the next craft to be more violent than originally planned. Thrusters were required at the rendezvous as well. This made the docking more difficult but it was accomplished with Katerina's usual skill.

Jack, having learned that it was best for the schedule, made a point of signaling Katerina to remain secured and undogged the hatch himself. This time the hatch opened to admit Malcolm and Molly McGinnis and their daughter, Dianne. Malcolm and Molly were in their early thirties, and Dianne was about seven. While also taken aback by the darkness in the cabin of the Nelleybell, the McGinnis's took the lack of illumination in stride and allowed themselves to be guided to couches and were strapped in by Jack to whom the cabin was at a comfortable reading level. Dianne made up for the taciturnity of the other occupants of Nelleybell with an almost endless stream of questions in an almost opaque Scottish brogue that were quietly answered by Molly.

"I thought that there would only be two of you on this craft, Malcolm. Is the other flight scrubbed?" Katerina was already figuring it out both ways.

"No, thank you very much, Mum. The luggage and livestock were sent up on their own. I had planned to ride up with them, but Molly prevailed upon me to change the plan at the last minute. Will it be a problem?" Malcolm was clearly troubled at not having informed the crew of the change.

"No, Malcolm. It is no extra trouble." Katerina initiated the burn for the next rendezvous. It was a series of sharp jolts that had the effect of stopping Dianne and Mollie's dialog. "I think I agree with Molly about the choice. I wouldn't want Jack to ride by himself. Not that I ever intend to teach him to drive!" The little dig at Jack caused everyone, even Honore' and Isolde, to giggle; and the tension in the cabin of Nelleybell relaxed considerably.

The next rendezvous and docking went as planned - very quickly. Jack and Malcolm unstrapped and opened both hatches. There was a series of fairly heavy boxes and some foam containers. "Where is the livestock?" Jack secured the boxes as Malcolm handed them to him.

"In the boxes. There are worms and their soil and the foam containers contain many wild bird eggs. And this is a small cask of single malt Scotch Whiskey that I brought along at Jake's insistence!"

The long series of hard pushes eventually brought the Nelleybell back to the aft docking ring of Belial. Honore's face was a little florid when they disembarked, but he insisted on kissing Katerina's hand and shaking Jack's with a little bow before he let them get on to the business of refurbishing Nelleybell for the last rescue of the couple from central Asia. Jack laughed and clapped him on the back, and everyone felt better. Bob and Nina came along to help everyone down to the inner surface of Belial. Jean latched on to Nina, who had begun to speak really bad French.

Jack and Katerina removed the debris from Nelleybell and recycled the second acceleration module. Topping up the atmosphere and propellant tanks took only a few minutes, and the Nelleybell undocked from the aft docking ring of Belial and fired a burst that would drop them into a lower orbit to allow them to rendezvous and dock with what appeared to be a Soyuz from central Asia.

"I know almost nothing about this couple. What do you know about them, Jack?"

"Vasily and Valentina Klauswitz were somehow interested in an orbital flight for some time but made arrangements through the network to join us. They are in their later fifties but still fit and well educated. He is a computer engineer, and she has some advanced degree in food science. They were able to obtain the booster and Soyuz before the market dried up last year. He apparently has money from some inventions, and her from her family. They seem decent enough in their writings and photographs. They speak very good English, and that is the extent of what I know about Vasily and Valentina."

Katerina laughed. "I guess that is about as much as I know about any of the others. There is something about their names that is unusual. Their given names are so Russian and their family name is German. I do not think that is terribly unlikely, but there is something about their names that look almost made up. I don't guess my own name is all that common." Katerina concentrated on her piloting, and soon the Nelleybell was docked with the Soyuz, which appeared to be of an older vintage than the one that she had crashed on Belial. Jack opened the hatch and admitted a very large man in a full excursion suit. He motioned behind him, and another space-suited figure entered the cabin of the Nelleybell. The second figure was carrying a machine pistol, which he aimed at Jack and Katerina.

"The large man who had first entered took his helmet off. "It is such a pleasure to be able to scratch one's nose after so many hours. It is also a big pleasure to see you both again!" He reached into his cargo pocket and removed another machine pistol, which he aimed only at Jack. Katerina turned in her couch and gazed in frank horror at the smiling face of Major Kostolinkavitch.

Chapter Thirty-four
Welcome to Belial

"Well Illya, it's come to this. I suppose you intend to kill us now. Katerina had unstrapped herself and now floated next to her husband in the cabin of the Nelleybell.

"Please, Major. You mustn't think that I would allow things to end so quickly. Besides, I want to see for myself the wonder that you and your associates have created before I destroy it. It would be such a shame for you to miss out on any of the proceedings that I have planned."

"You do not suffer under any misapprehensions relating to any assistance that you might receive from me, do you?" Katerina and Major Kostolinkavitch both spoke Russian - a language that Jack knew quite well.

"Of course you will assist me in any way that I require. It might be uncomfortable to travel from here to your rogue asteroid with this excursion suit all buttoned up, but if a hole or holes should develop in the side of your fine vessel, say, from automatic weapons fire, I feel sure that my associate and I could tolerate it without difficulty. I am not altogether sure your friend, Jack Knight, would do as well. Oh, yes. I know who he is, as well as who you have become, Major Yerisivloskaya. I do not think that we will be having significant disagreements about your cooperation with my program." Kostolinkavitch laughed and, even through his suit, the ripples of adipose tissue bounced and jiggled in the microgravity like some obscene parody of Santa Claus.

"I think we better do as he asks, Katerina. I don't care for the idea of being shot and dumped out the airlock." Jack spoke English.

"I think we could take him and his friend before they had a clue that we were going to!" Katerina also spoke English.

"Please do not force me to act out the little scenario I just sketched out for you, Major. I assure you I might enjoy it quite a bit and certainly more that your husband would. I didn't expect him to be such a coward, but nevertheless, although I do not speak English, I understand it well enough. My friend Vasily doesn't speak anything, as he had an unfortunate run in with some Islamic fundamentalists who cut his tongue out. They were about to finish the job when I came to his rescue. He is very good company, especially when discretion is required." Kostolinkavitch laughed again.

Katerina looked very grim as she looked at Jack, who smiled back at her as if there was no problem whatsoever. "OK Major, we will do as you ask for this time." Katerina looked as though she had eaten something nasty.

"There is the other matter of our craft. We have exhausted all of our primary propellant, and it is necessary that it arrive at your new home. I have had an opportunity to see how you have planned other operations in the past, so I cannot help but believe you have excess capacity. The Soyuz masses a bit more than half of what this craft must mass. Our acceleration window is rapidly closing. I suggest that we make our burn as soon as possible." The huge fat Major motioned his Vasily, who had not opened his helmet, to strap in and strapped himself in behind Katerina and Jack.

"I must close the hatch between the two craft during our acceleration. I don't trust any seal under thrust." Katerina looked at Kostolinkavitch who motioned to Jack with his machine pistol. "I must also talk to Belial and let them know that we will be bringing back more than we had originally intended." Katerina reached for the virtual control that operated the transceiver.

"Oh, I don't think that that will be necessary." Kostolinkavitch gestured meaningfully with his pistol. Katerina drew her hand back.

"Hey Major! I can't believe that you actually brought the calves! They must have made quite a racket on the way up!" Jack had seen the animals through the open hatch of the Soyuz while he closed it. He strapped himself back into his couch beside Katerina.

"Oh yes. It was quite unpleasant, and the temptation to cut their throats was almost overpowering. If I had not been sure that the stench resulting would not have also been overpowering, they would already be dead. They will die soon enough. It was necessary to provide the "Eye of Belial" with images of them being loaded. Who would take cattle on a guerilla mission? It added markedly to our credibility. Now, let's get on with our little journey to your asteroid."

"Brace yourselves. This going to be quite a kick, and it's going on for quite some time." Katerina really didn't care about the comfort of these particular passengers. She didn't want to find herself or Jack shot in the back because of a surprise jolt. There was a massive kick in the pants as the acceleration rapidly expended itself. The acceleration was such that it was impossible to hold on to something as heavy as a machine pistol, so Major Kostolinkavitch and his associate set the big hand weapons down on the deck next to them braced against a cross member. They were in easy reach.

The ride was rough and, because of the unbalanced mass of the Soyuz, there were frequent correction from the attitude thrusters. It was a little like riding in a paint can that bangs against the ladder it's hooked on.

They docked at the aft ring of Belial with more effort than usual. Being nearly out of attitude propellant made it more than ordinarily difficult. "It is now time to fill the propellant tanks of the Soyuz." Kostolinkavitch had his weapon once again trained on Jack, as Vasily had his weapon on Katerina. "While the tanks are filling, your husband will unload our cargo."

"Anything that will speed you away from us is a welcome expense." Katerina took her time filling each of the thruster banks carefully. Jack was also leisurely in removing each of the three calves toward the can. Their eyes were rolling hysterically, and the bleating moans of the calves had little to do with the pastoral mooing of contented cows. As soon as he had put them into an elevator, tied down, so that they could not fall when they reached the bottom, he turned back to the docking ring under the twitching gun of the silent man who had accompanied Kostolinkavitch.

"Your little defection caused me to lose my regular income. As soon as the blastoff occurred, the market in secondhand weapons came under intense scrutiny and largely ended. I had a perfect situation going, reselling the same weapons over and over, and no one ever got hurt! Other than the criminals buying them of course!" Kostolinkavitch laughed again as if thoroughly amused by his own cleverness. "I found that I had to find employment after being in business for myself for all those years. It is difficult to find a position, which pays enough for one with my special talents. I did finally find a group, which allowed me a great deal of leeway in getting things done that they needed done, and we have had a very profitable relationship. This will probably be the final contract that I will accept from them, as the compensation was very adequate even for one such as myself with expensive tastes. Oh my, yes, very adequate indeed!" Kostolinkavitch seemed to salivate just thinking about his stowed away riches. Jack and the silent Vasily returned to the Nelleybell, and Jack entered the Soyuz a last time to remove whatever might remain. There was a metal suitcase secured against the bulkhead. "Yes, take that out as well. We will want to leave that behind." Kostolinkavitch again laughed. "I guess it is now time to meet the folks. Lets go, shall we?" Another gesture from the automatic pistol demonstrated that there was not really any choice in the issue, at least not for Jack and Katerina.

The strange party made its way toward the Can and the elevators that waited to take them to the inner surface of Belial. Jack and Katerina entered the car with the three calves followed by Kostolinkavitch and his partner. The hatch closed behind them. "I don't see why you keep things so dark here on your habitat. There would probably be a spectacular view on the elevator ride with just a little proper engineering. Oh don't worry, my friend here has starlight goggles on underneath his visor. He has no difficulty whatsoever with the dark." Kostolinkavitch again laughed. He was clearly enjoying himself.

The ten-minute elevator ride finally came to an end, and the hatch opened onto a beautiful ringset with the green arc of Belial meeting so far above their heads. The bodies of water scattered around the interior of Belial sparkled and flashed in the oblique light from the setting sunring no less bright than at any point in its course. Unlike a sunset, which was always red from the dust in the atmosphere, the sunring never varied in color, even in setting. The houses of the new settlement were just up the hill from where they stood. They had all the amenities as the homes of the crew and, in fact, were nearer to transportation. They were not constructed of the grand materials that the crew had used for theirs but were every bit as beautiful and practical. The structures themselves were constructed of a different Mokume-Gane, which used base metals like copper and stainless steel foams. The results were strikingly handsome, though not staggeringly beautiful as the homes of the crew were.

Jack untied the calves and turned them loose outside the elevator. Kostolinkavitch looked on with his scary smile and no comment. Jack returned to the elevator and picked up the metal suitcase. It was incredibly heavy. Jack no longer had any sort of doubt as to what it contained. Kostolinkavitch gestured with his gun. "Let's take a little walk to see the folks. There may be a few more things that I might want to take with me."

Jack carried the heavy suitcase with the fat Major and his friend puffing behind as they walked up the rather steep hill toward the little settlement. They walked slower than usual to allow the strangers with guns trained on them to keep up. Although the suitcase weighed at least a hundred and fifty pounds, Jack needed only his right hand to carry it, which drew somewhat quizzical glances from Kostolinkavitch. He had required assistance to carry it with both hands. Jack simply didn't look that big and strong.

They reached the structures that could be seen from the elevator hatch and found that the little village was deserted. From the sounds of laughter and the bright quick notes from Bob's Balalaika, it was clear that a celebration was underway at the homes of the crew. They were celebrating the saving of the Earth in spite of itself and the arrival of new friends. The party was very merry indeed.

"I don't want to spoil this grand party by not attending." The Major puffed between swift shallow breaths. "I hope that there are some good things to eat and drink!" Kostolinkavitch probably wouldn't care for the simple fare available to the inhabitants of Belial.

"Oh, Illya, I doubt that you would enjoy the tofu and leek stew or other items we currently have on hand, but there may be some more interesting items from the new arrivals." Katerina and Jack were looking more and more comfortable as time passed even though they, like their captors, were still wearing their vacuum suits. They had made a point of losing the helmets back in the docking ring so they were much cooler. Kostolinkavitch and his silent goon were wearing full excursion suits, which weighed at least a hundred and fifty pounds apiece. They were air-conditioned and supplied the wearer with a higher level of oxygen if required, but Kostolinkavitch had his visor up which compromised the airflow. His pig-like face was streaming with sweat, and his usually florid complexion was a dangerous color of red. He had not been ready for a steep climb in regular gravity. He looked like the shaking grip on the machine pistol could fail at any time. His aim at Jack and Katerina drooped from time to time, and the effort of raising it once again was clearly difficult. "Well step on along Illya, the company is waiting to greet you!" With that both Katerina and Jack broke into a sprint that quickly left the excursion suited Major and his goon behind. Jack carried the heavy suitcase as if it were a basket of sandwiches.

"I plan to send Illya and his goon back to Earth, but if he dies trying to keep up with me, I won't cry!" Katerina laughed over her shoulder as Kostolinkavitch tried to fire his pistol, which failed to work for some reason or other. By the time that Kostolinkavitch slowly walked into the little village, Jack and Katerina had had a quick shower and were dressed in their best party clothes. They had opened the suitcase and found that the nuclear weapon that it contained had not been armed. They had quickly disabled the device and placed it in a safe place.

Kostolinkavitch was practically on his hands and knees when he arrived with Vasily, who had finally removed his helmet and starlight goggles. They were still breathing hard. What little attention that they could give to their surroundings was focused on the platinum plates and diamond crystal in casual use at the outside party.

"Well Major, thank you very much for the cattle. It will be pleasant indeed to have milk and cheese again. I don't know what we will do with another thermonuclear device, but perhaps some constructive use can be found. Have some water. You look like you could use it!" Jake placed one of the larger diamond crystal tumblers in Kostolinkavitch's hand, frosty with the chill of the water inside. The Major almost choked himself trying to swallow all of it without breathing between gulps. Jake gave another tumbler to the silent man who just stared at the obvious wealth that gleamed around him.

"So, you intended to blow up Belial after it had missed Earth, is that right?" I guess you intended to kill all of us first so that we couldn't prevent the device going off or disposing of it before it did. Is that right?" Jack had stepped forward to take charge of the questioning.

"Yes, it was a simple plan that once you had taken us aboard your craft should have been unstoppable. I don't understand where we went wrong. Of course, I hadn't expected a full gravity or we wouldn't have been dressed this way." The Major's eyes roamed around everywhere searching for a way out of his predicament.

"Oh, your plan was doomed from the moment that you set your weapons down on the deck during the acceleration. Your weapons were colonized by nanomachines that started breaking them down as soon as they came in contact with fresh metal. Most of the finer metal parts were converted to dust by the time that you reached the inner surface of Belial. I recognized when you were beaten on the way down the elevator when it became possible to see through your hand gun." Jack reached into Kostolinkavitch's cargo pocket and removed the pistol, which he crushed in his hand. The tiny glittering shards and dust flew from between his fingers like the crust of stale bread. "Who are you working for, Major?"

The almost silent explosion of his personal weapon in the hand of his former helpless and cowardly prisoner had its expected effect on the near psychotic brain of Major Illya Kostolinkavitch. "I suspect it is a group of multinational corporations. I was contacted anonymously and the recompense deposited in a Swiss bank account. The rest consisted of title to a small island in the South Pacific and a large yacht with a helicopter on it to get back and forth. It would have been a great place to retire." The Major gaped at the empty tumbler in his hand. Jack took it away from him and handed him another filled with water, which the Major drank a little more slowly than the first.

During this time the party had ranged around the little group at its edge. The new arrivals to Belial had been overjoyed at their new homes, which resembled but were improved versions of their homes on Earth. There was some doubt that Honore' and Isolde had lived in a genuine chateau on Earth, but whatever exaggeration of their earthly holdings that the couple had practiced was looked upon as more humorous than it was considered theft. It simply wasn't much more difficult to make an absurdly big house than a smaller one. Everyone suspected that Honore' and Isolde would move eventually to a smaller more practical house with fewer echoing empty rooms.

Susan Schuyler had focused her considerable attention on Bob, who had never played the Balalaika with such fervor. Susan was a striking, tall young woman with raven black curls and piercing blue eyes. Jean, Lisa, Justin, Dianne, Stephen, and Patricia ran around spitting water on each other and shrieking.

The couples stood around and got to know one another and the crew. The cask of Scotch had been breached, and some of the tumblers contained a light amber liquid. Others not having Scotch were also trying the first vintages from the vineyards of Belial. This peaceful scene provided the backdrop for Jack and Jake and Katerina's questioning of the fat Major in the excursion suit. Major Kostolinkavitch was looking better now that he had caught his breath and had slaked his thirst. After he felt strong enough, he and his silent friend stood up. "What do you intend to do to us? We have done you no harm."

"That's true enough, although your intentions were otherwise. First of all you will not be allowed to stay on Belial, but will be sent back to the cesspool that you crawled out of. Second, it will be very clear that you failed in your assignment. As we speak, the eye of Belial is transmitting video of our little party, and your arrival was duly noted. Nina is keeping a running commentary on our conversation. It seems likely that you will not be allowed to keep your compensation. Additionally, the Soyuz, like your weapon, has been infected with nanomachines, and the controls that you used so amateurishly on your way up have been converted to vapor. It will not be possible to adjust the timing of your reentry in a way that you would prefer. Rather, I have determined to send you back to Mother Russia, where I believe you are wanted for murder and various other felonious pursuits. They will be very happy to see you." It was Katerina's turn to smile at Major Illya Kostolinkavitch.

Suddenly, the Major seized Patricia, who had run between the adults in their serious conversation in order to avoid Jean in hot pursuit with a mouthful of water. He reached into his cargo pocket and his hand now contained a hunting knife, which he held against the child's throat. "Perhaps we can renegotiate some of your terms, Major!" The knife in his hand cut just enough to cause a trickle of blood to run down the child's neck and begin to stain her white blouse slightly soaked with water. Patricia began to cry but not to struggle.

Faster than an unaugmented human eye could follow, Katerina reached out and took the knife away from the Major and in the process broke his hand in three places. She then, almost as quickly, kicked him in the side of the head. Before he could fall to the ground, Katerina removed his other hand from Patricia also breaking his wrist in the process and held Patricia close. The entire rescue had required less than a second and a half to complete. The only sounds made were a swish of air accompanied by some sharp cracks and the dull thud of the Major's fall to the ground. "I don't think so." Katerina pulled a scrap of cloth from her pocket and held it over the child's superficial cut.

Only the crew had actually seen what had just occurred. Madelyne immediately made her way over to take care of the child's wound. "I'll get around to you before your trip back to Earth, Major." Madelyne carried the crying child away toward her kitchen where she tended to the minor injuries.

Katerina held the knife in her hand and appreciated how close a thing it had been. She took the blade between her hands and broke it. It was still intact, as it had never come in contact with the metal of Belial. An eight of an inch of steel was all it would have taken to spoil her triumph.

Kostolinkavitch had begun to whimper and blubber as he lay on the ground before her. He had made the mistake of trying to raise himself using one of his broken limbs. His right hand was curled into a useless ball and his left wrist was buckled at an odd angle. Jack and his silent assistant helped him get to his feet and walk to the infirmary.

Jake, who had watched the entire exchange, raised his goblet of sparkling diamond. "My dear friends and colleagues, I give you Major Ekaterina Terescova Yerisivloskaya. Long may she bring her special light to our world!" The gathered company of escapees from Earth all raised their glasses and drank to Katerina, who blushed very prettily.

Epilogue

Major Kostolinkavitch had been fairly doped up when the modified Soyuz broke its contact with the docking port of the Nelleybell. It was a better craft in many essential ways and would safely carry the Major and Vasily back to their fates on earth. No active nanotechnology remained on the craft, but it was quicker, stronger, and entirely impossible for the people inside to control. They were as Chuck Yeager was shown to have said in *The Right Stuff* – "Spam in a Can". The Soyuz returned to Earth at the limits of its ability, even with its improvements. Belial had made almost two thirds of a complete orbit around Earth before breaking away to its rendezvous with the moon. The near miss of the moon had occurred almost three days after B Day, as July 23 was forever known - the day White Knights, Inc. saved the Earth. The new holiday was celebrated on Earth and Belial.

The near miss of the moon had gone exactly as planned and when the habitat came within sixty miles, it had completed almost half of an orbit. This further robbed it of relative velocity and curved its orbit even closer to the plane of the ecliptic. The resulting orbit was still eccentric and off of the plane of the ecliptic, but that suited the inhabitants of Belial just fine.

As the months passed, there were the usual frictions that arise among people of good will who strive together. After months of training and delicate negotiations between the crew, Honore' and Isolde left the habitat in a ship much like the Trigger but smaller, as there were only two aboard. Honore' had determined to bring in an asteroid of his own. Use of the ship and it's outfitting had cost Honore' a third part ownership in whatever he succeeded in bringing back to the Earth/Moon system. He was provided with nanotechnology to assist him in his mission, and his ship had a more efficient drive and reactor than the Trigger had had when it left the Earth. Ownership of the Lafayette remained in White Knights, Inc. Honore' had purchased a lease with a service agreement. A likely asteroid had been located at one of Jupiter's Trojan points. It was similar in composition to Belial. It would take longer to bring back because it wasn't already headed this way. That suited everyone. The mission would take at least eight years. That suited everyone as well.

The augmentation of humans was arrested after the crew received theirs accidentally. Tom had modified the little machines such that they were no longer airborne a year or so before B Day. Madelyne's argument was that the crew didn't know the long-term consequences of augmentation. Jake's argument was that he had to really know someone pretty well and like them a whole lot before he wanted them living a couple of hundred years with better than human abilities. Everyone else pretty much agreed with Jake. Honore' and Isolde didn't receive augmentation. Susan Schuyler did a year or so after she and Bob married. Augmentation came with a measurable percentage of stock in White Knights, Inc.

Two months or so after B Day, Madelyne, Margaret, and Katerina all noticed that they weren't menstruating anymore. Eight months later Michael, Gabriel, and Victoria were born to Madelyne, Margaret, and Katerina respectively. Interestingly enough, augmentation did turn out to be hereditary.

It was over three years after B day that the United Nations established its embassy on Belial. There were over forty embassies from other nations and multinational corporations by that time. The United Nations had come along after it had become entirely too clear that humanity's future was not on Earth alone. Most of the new growth would occur in the big empty.

White Knights Inc.

Nine years after B Day, Honore' and Isolde returned with New France. The new habitat had almost half again the inner surface area of Belial. Honore' made a large portion of it available to any of his countrymen who could make it there. Jack, who was the managing partner of White Knights, Inc. at the time, used his one-third control to insist on a screening process that rejected the uneducated, the unemployed, and criminals. Honore' and Isolde set themselves up as the Count and Countess of New France. That lasted about one year, and Honore' and Isolde returned abruptly to Belial to live in their chateau, which had been used as a guesthouse in their absence. They became innkeepers and valued members of the community. New France was brought under the control of White Knights, Inc. The primary industry was soon agriculture, and the wines of New France became the envy of the system. They also went into the business, under the crew's direction, of manufacturing ships to ferry new people from High Earth Orbit. Jack, Katerina, and Victoria had brought in another asteroid by this time that was converted into an elevator that ran from Ecuador to High Earth Orbit. The profits from the fares were used to buy most of Brazil and allow it to return to rain forest.

Tom established the first lunar colony as a retirement home. It unexpectedly became a major sports center after Jake built the first golf course on the moon.

It was only twenty years later that the first interplanetary war broke out.

Printed in the United States
137561LV00002B/2/P